SLATE RETRIBUTION

She's a monster, a murderer

EMERY HALE

SLATE RETRIBUTION

Copyright © 2021 by Emery Hale.

All rights reserved. No part of this publication may be reproduced, transmitted or stored in a retrieval system in any form or by any means without permission in writing from the copyright owner, nor otherwise circulated in any form of binding or cover other than that in which it is published and without similar condition being imposed on the subsequent purchaser.

This book is a work of fiction. All characters in this publication are fictitious, and any resemblance to real people, alive or dead, is purely coincidental.

Edited by Sam Boyce
Book Formatting by Derek Murphy @Creativindie
Author Photo by Justyna Makuch

For any information please contact:
emeryhale3@gmail.com

First Edition: August 2021
ISBN Paperback : 9798527878189

10 9 8 7 6 5 4 3 2 1

BOOK 1 IN THE *SLATE* SERIES

SLATE

RETRIBUTION

EMERY HALE

SLATE RETRIBUTION

For *wee* Mrs Lennox

To one of my many inspirational teachers, you can never know how much that second year writing class on a Friday afternoon meant to me. Even though the stories I came out with then were a little . . . dubious.

You are the reason I continued to pursue my career as a writer, and you gave me the confidence to do so. All I can say is thank you. Teachers are a huge part of any person's life because when you look back, anyone and everyone has a great story about a teacher.

P.s. The story about Mr Ferguson dressing up as Holly Willoughby and dancing to 'Let's Get Ready to Rumble' or the entire PE department dressing up like *Baywatch*.

Thank you.

CHAPTER 1

Drapetomania

The overwhelming urge to run away.

NAOMI JADE

18th June 2016, 17:04

Scotland, Edinburgh, The Reign Academy, Control Room.

That night defined chaos.

I remember shuddering as his brutal voice barked down the phone, the violent tremor in his hand returning. The forsaken woman stood stoic in the corner, biting her lip in agitation, any lingering hope in her eyes slowly burning out. The soldier gripped the table, her nails scratching into its surface as the sound of bullets cascaded from the speakers. The doctor paced back and forth in her blood-soaked scrubs, watching the entire spectacle on the large monitor ahead, observing and listening as the bullets echoed her own frantic heartbeat. The pariah never spoke a word.

I did nothing. What could I do? I wasn't trained, not like them.

She was my friend and I stood there, doing nothing.

Phones rang from all directions but no one answered, not now. No one could tear themselves away from the monitor as the spectacle unfolded. They'd all witnessed this countless times – in this job, who hadn't?

'She needs the evac team now!' the brutal voice roared, his dark hair masking his eyes.

I couldn't even bear to imagine the emotions that lurked there: rage, pain, betrayal?

His hand clenched into a fist and catapulted the phone down in a blind rage, cracking it off the hardwood desk. 'They won't get there for another half hour, she's too deep in.'

'Is there any way we can contact her?' the doctor demanded.

'No, the comms have been wiped out.'

'How did that happen?'

'Wait, give me a minute . . . Oh, that's right, I don't know because I'm not a fuckin mind reader!' Blind rage, blind panic, they felt like the same thing.

What could I do to help? She was out there alone, running for her life, and I'd promised I would never let that happen; not again.

Her ragged breaths scratched through the speakers, the little falters in her voice crystal clear, while the camera on her jacket provided the perfect view to the monitor. A perfect view of what exactly?

'You're really not helping!' the soldier exclaimed.

'Could you not tear each other's throats out for one minute?'

'She'll be OK – it's not like this hasn't happened before,' he muttered.

'Shut up!' the doctor yelled. 'She's trying to say something!'

'I need evac now, I can't shake this guy!'

The perfect view.

Then came the bang, the stumble, the fall, the thud – and then nothing.

My eyes felt like glass had pierced straight through,

embedding deep inside, slicing away at the images in front of me. I didn't want to watch, I couldn't, not when it was her.

'God, no,' the forsaken woman pleaded, hands falling limp at her side. 'God, please no.'

'Lilith, come in,' the soldier ordered, taking a step forward, the tips of her fingers pressed to the comm unit in her ear. 'Team Leader, come in.'

Then we waited, for a shred of evidence that would prove the inevitable.

All we could see from the angle of the camera was grass, raw thick blades that jutted and cut into the lens.

This happens, she'd told me. *This always happens, it only ends one way in this kind of work.*

Abruptly the camera jostled, bitter blades of grass crunching as it turned.

'Who is that?'

From what I could make out there was a figure, dark clothing – no! I couldn't watch this.

I hissed in a breath as a sharp pain sliced through my hand like a dagger, warm liquid flowing from my palm, my own clawing nails the culprit. I watched the first drop drip from my hand, gravity taking over as it plummeted to the floor.

BANG

Static, crackling, no movement and no background noise. Not one of us spoke a word.

Then even the static stopped as the monitor collapsed into darkness. It was as if someone had shut it off, like someone would turn off the blaring drone of a flatlining heart monitor.

The only light in the room came from the lamps on the desks: to me, they flickered under the crippling tension that bore down on my shoulders, crushing into the bone.

'Jess?' the soldier asked once more, but this time her eyes were filled with nothing but dread, as she used her Team Lead's actual name.

The soldier wouldn't believe this was real, not until she had seen proof – or was that me? I looked away. Was I a coward?

'Jess, can you hear me?'

Was I a coward? Yes, I was.

I turned on my feet as I tried to breathe, the blood in my palm turning cold. I closed my eyes, trying to think of anything else, anything but her. My hand pressed against the door.

She'd warned me, she told me to leave.

Now I was on my own, what the hell was I supposed to do? I couldn't do this alone.

'Agent down,' he said. 'Agent Jessica-Grace Winters inactive.'

Inactive. Down. Dead.

CHAPTER 2

Epoch

A period of time; a specific period of life.

NAOMI JADE

12th June 2015, 17:25

Scotland, Glasgow, Buchanan Street

I was caught amid the whirlwind of people commonly known as the Friday evening rush; everyone fighting against the tide.

Some marching towards the nearest bar while others headed deeper into the city for some well-deserved retail therapy. We were the latter – prom and exams were over, high school had finished and we'd decided we were in dire need of new clothes, shoes, and – of course – handbags. 'We' being the four of us: Katie, Jennifer, Allie and myself.

Unfortunately, now school was over I had to make my own

way in the world and face the crucial fact that I was skint. There was no way I could afford anything from today's shopping trip, considering these girls were only interested in brand names – a.k.a. the really expensive shit.

Katie loved clothes the most; it was all she ever talked about, and even more so since that lingerie shop opened in the city centre. I never knew anyone could get so excited over thongs and body glitter. Shoes were another subject: Katie's parents were loaded so she always had the newest pair of Gucci trainers or Chanel heels. Even though it gave her some class and taste, it sadly didn't negate the fact she was a two-faced bitch.

Now Naomi, why would you hang out with this girl? Well because I had to, since befriending the popular kids at school meant somewhat of an easy ride.

There was also Jennifer, who wasn't bad to talk to but did have a tendency to spill everyone's secrets the moment she had a chance to blame it on the alcohol.

Allie was the only nice person in the trio, but for some reason she was happy playing best friends forever. She was too nice, which was something I could never wrap my head around.

Perhaps she was in the same boat as me.

I didn't start hanging out with them until around a year and a half ago but since then, we've become really close friends.

'Hey!' Katie snapped angrily. 'Naomi, you're not even listening to me. God I've been trying to – you drive me crazy, you idiot. I don't even know why I invited you.'

OK, so when I said close . . . I swear she's nicer when you get to know her, she's just been in a bad mood recently.

'Sorry,' I said quickly, 'zoned out for a sec.'

'Just shut up, yeah? I *really* don't care.' Katie retorted, just as fast as I had spoken.

I glanced over to Allie and Jennifer but they were too busy mindlessly staring at their phones, before suddenly, like a pig on helium –

'Oh, that's too funny!' Allie laughed.

As we walked down the slope that was Buchanan Street I noticed Katie had started to push people out the way: she probably thought any surface gracing her presence was a catwalk.

'He was just –' Another fit of laughter from the pair, and this time it was so loud that people actually started to stare.

God this was embarrassing. Passers-by actually looked up from their own conversations when they heard my friends.

'And then he –' Jennifer clenched her Starbucks in hand before bursting out into her own pig squeal.

They were the definition of the basic popular girls at school and for some reason, in my off-trend style and beat-up Converse, I stood with them.

Why do you hang around with these people, Naomi? Oh yeah, cause you're rubbish at standing up for yourself and finding some decent friends. I didn't know how much more of their irritating voices I could take. Katie snapped constantly, Jennifer was like a walking talking venomous gossip machine and Allie was always busy on her phone.

I missed the good old days, when Jess and I would go into town and spend the entire day shopping and testing the chocolate cake in all the cafés. But then she got the scholarship of her dreams and all of that stopped. Occasionally we texted but not for long, she was always busy these days. I couldn't help but think I'd done something wrong; she was an entirely different person to the one I knew three years ago.

When I emerged from my train of thought I realised I'd followed the girls into a make-up shop. It was modern with black marble flooring and pure white walls, not a stain in sight. At one side, mirrors were built into the walls, as well as a vanity table with various brushes in cute little pots. The make-up itself started at foot level, stretching up to the ceiling where small circular lights shone brightly. The checkout counter sat at the back, with small clear bowls filled with mini-sized items and gift cards, chart music humming in the background.

Only one woman in her mid-twenties stood behind the counter, her sharp black hair falling by her shoulders and dagger-like eyeliner standing out from a mile away. She had piercings and wore a black t-shirt with the shop name Beauty Secrets printed in the centre, content in her own thoughts as she sorted through the till.

Katie didn't hesitate for a moment, marching straight over to the lipstick section. Given the amount of times she reapplies the stuff on a night out, I wouldn't be surprised if she bought it in bulk. Allie and Jennifer made a bee-line for the mirrors, snapping countless selfies, pouting their lips like there was no tomorrow.

Since the basic squad were busy with ... themselves, I headed through the shop and decided to look at the eyeliner, since I needed a new one anyway. I found a black one at the bottom of the shelf which was surprisingly cheap.

I stood up, pushing my messy dark hair from my face, trying to remember if the brand name was any good, when a shadow slipped to my side. I jumped back as soon as a cold, slender hand pressed on my shoulder.

'Do you need any help?' the jump-scare woman asked with a charming smile, casually returning her hand to her jeans pocket. 'Need any recommendations?'

'Oh, n-no thanks.' I stuttered, holding up the eyeliner like a prize. Yeah well done Naomi, you picked some makeup, not like it's hard.

'You know that's the sample, right?'

I glanced down to the eyeliner and saw the white label with the word SAMPLE written in big bold letters. For the love of – seriously? My thoughts must have been written clear as day because the next thing I knew, the woman's hand was on my arm, rubbing small circles into the skin which, weirdly enough, soothed me.

'Hey it's OK,' she said softly. 'We all have those days. Trust me, I've had my fair share. My name's Megan.'

She leaned down and grabbed another eyeliner for me, swapping it for the one in my hand.

'Come on, I'll put it through for you.' She indicated to the checkout behind us.

Megan withdrew her hand before heading behind the counter and scanning the liner. I noticed her painted ring-finger nail, a pastel shade with delicate yellow flowers. The only reason I took interest was because all her other nails were bare.

'I like your nail design,' I told her, she looked back to me with a small smile.

'Aw, thanks love, took so long to do, messed up who knows how many times. Anyway the eyeliner comes to –'

'Naomi, we're leaving,' Katie cut in pointedly from the front of the shop, cocking her hip.

Oh God, not this again.

She wasn't waiting, she was demanding I move. A few strangers browsing at the shelves threw their glances between us, like we were some sort of deranged tennis match. There weren't many people in the shop to begin with, but that didn't make the drop to complete silence any better.

'I'm just paying for this quickly,' I tried, but Katie wasn't amused.

'You don't need that. It's a cheap knock-off. Let's go.' Katie said, her voice filled with disgust as she looked around the shop one final time. 'Naomi. Now.'

I sighed, embarrassment flooding right back. It was like we were in high school all over again.

'Yeah, uh ... I'm just going to leave this, thanks,' I said, but my voice came out shrivelled and quiet, lips practically quivering.

Megan had opened her mouth in what I assumed was a protest but before she could speak, I was already walking away.

I shouldn't have let Katie order me around or make me feel so small and spineless. I did what she told me to and said what she dictated. Everyone in that shop must have thought I was one hell of a pushover.

Katie strutted out the shop flipping her hair over her

shoulder, Allie and Jennifer following close behind, their faces still shoved into their phones. While I tottered at the back, the runt of the litter.

Slowly but surely my arms wrapped around my torso. I felt as if I couldn't be any smaller.

I wanted to march over to Katie, scream and yell some sense into her, before going back and buying the damn eyeliner. I wanted to shout to the heavens about how miserable Katie and her merry band of bitches made my life!

Oh, if only I could.

Jessica would have, she'd happily smack Katie. She hated her – actually that's wrong, she despised her intensely.

A loud ping sounded from my phone, but when I looked down it was nothing but a news notification. There was no need to read it, the headline was clear enough.

YOUNG STUDENT KILLED IN HIT AND RUN

That was all the news was filled with these days: murders, missing people, new terrorism safety protocols and the odd piece about politics.

The sound of cars driving through puddles echoed around the streets, music blaring through an open window while the chatter of passers-by created a buzz in the air, but suddenly it grew heavy, weighing down on my shoulders. I took in a breath, trying to focus on Allie in front of me. As the people around started to close in, I felt like a sardine squished into a can.

I've always had a fear of getting lost in a crowd, a fear that I'd be pulled under by the ruthless current of people, unable to push my way to the surface.

Then through all the noise, I heard Katie gasp in shock.

'Allie, Jennifer!'

The two girls sped up the pace and in turn so did I – had a dog appeared or something? The three of them were frozen, observing the gasp-worthy sight ahead. Although when I stood beside Allie, I didn't see a dog or any form of adorable animal. I saw a group of girls sitting outside a small café. They were all dressed similarly: a slim-fit white shirt, plain deep navy skirt, sheer black tights, black stiletto heels and a fitted navy blazer with a crest I couldn't quite figure out.

I didn't take much notice of the other girls at the table, I only focused on one.

We had a tendency to spot each other in a crowd.

It had been nine months since I last saw her properly. Her fiery red hair ignited in the early evening sun but it exposed her porcelain skin, which seemed paler than before. Her cold blue eyes were cast down at the table, hands clasped neatly. She had long thin lips, her cheekbones naturally carved out. Her shoulders were broad but her figure was slimmer than I remembered. A sombre look pressed down on her like the weight of a hundred men – what had happened?

'The Reign girls have come down from their ivory towers to grace us with their presence,' Katie mocked, shaking her head.

She scanned the group up and down, her eyes green with envy, before she seemed to come to some conclusion. Even people walking past us stared at the group, like they were zoo animals. Who could blame them?

The Reign Academy had a reputation to envy; it was the most prestigious school in the entirety of Europe, offering any course you could dream of. If you were accepted you got a full scholarship and lived in the halls of residence, free of charge. No tuition fees, no living costs, nothing. From what Jessica told me when she started, things such as food and water got delivered to the individual houses each week, it sounded amazing!

The students who went there were apparently stuck-up and snobby, entitlement drilled into them from year one. I knew for a fact that wasn't true, since the girl with fire for hair had been my best friend growing up. Jessica.

We'd met in the sixth year of primary and been inseparable for a good portion of high school – but then Jess got the scholarship of her dreams.

Now, she sat with the Reign girls.

'That's like, the third time this week apparently,' Jennifer added, looking up to Katie for approval to continue. 'Josh saw them yesterday, then Mia the day before.'

'They must be getting bored,' Allie joked.

'I know, it must get terribly tiring going to your en suite bathroom and then taking a lift to all of your classes, while you get served breakfast by your very own butler,' Jennifer said, her voice getting irritably higher.

En suite bathrooms? Butlers? I knew the Academy was luxurious, but wasn't that taking it a bit too far?

'Where did you hear that?' I asked her, 'Cause I don't think that's right.'

Jennifer, for some reason, looked extremely offended at my challenge.

'My sources are never wrong, Naomi,' she told me. 'Never.'

'Yeah, but the thing is –'

'Yes. We all see Jessica over there,' Katie snapped, and once again I had to resist the urge to roll my eyes. 'We all see your precious friend. Who could never be stuck up or think she's above us. Can't believe she got a scholarship for jumping about a stage.'

I stayed silent after that since there was no use arguing with Katie. I'd learned that it's too much effort to fight back.

'She's not even that good of a singer,' Jennifer muttered.

'God, shut up Jen, neither are you,' Katie stated, before turning away from the group and strutting in the direction of the train station.

My eyes were drawn back to Jessica, who now talked quietly to the blonde girl beside her. Then she noticed me.

The sombre look was replaced with relief. As she stood up from her seat, the taller, slender, brown-haired girl across from her glared, but Jessica didn't seem to care.

It was amazing to see her again, and she wanted to talk to me! I needed to talk to her. Just as I was about to, a hand with a harsh grip grabbed my arm, yanking me back, Katie's disapproving stare glowering down at me. Oh great, here we go.

'What do you think you're doing?' she asked quietly, and I looked away for a second to get my bearings. 'Naomi?'

'I was going to talk to Jess,' I answered cautiously, looking up to her towering figure.

'Naomi, are we gonna have a problem?' Oh, now she was pissed.

'I'm allowed to talk to other people besides you, Katie.' As soon as the words tumbled out of my mouth, I realized what I'd done. 'No, Katie, I didn't mean it like that.'

She scoffed.

'Fine, go be with the prissy Academy freaks.' She took a

step towards me, then another and another until her body nearly pressed against mine. 'Just know that from now on you're on your own. Good luck,' she spat.

I shrunk back.

'High school is over, that doesn't matter anymore,' I tried, but my voice betrayed me, shaking like a frightened mouse.

How did she have this much power over me?

'Yeah, but Josh knows where you live. It would be a shame if there had to be a repeat of what happened at the party,' Katie warned, sending shivers down my spine.

My shoulders and head caved as Katie ran her fingers through strands of my hair. I tried not to think of the party, but she was doing the exact same thing he did. The horrid stench of alcohol was still fresh in my mind.

'Katie Danvers.' The smooth confident voice of Jessica spoke from behind, and relief flooded through me at her nicely-timed arrival. 'I wasn't aware you were still in the country. I thought you were supposed to be in Milan, but no ... you're here.'

Jessica casually moved to my side as Katie took a step

back, looking into my friend's eyes with uncertainty, arms crossed. Jess, however, didn't seem the least bit bothered by Katie, her eyes bright and ready for anything. Ready for what?

'I go next week.'

'Oh, really?' Jessica asked, feigning confusion. 'Cause I was under the impression you're still unemployed with barely any qualifications. Didn't you get bumped from the applicants for Milan because of – well, your face?'

Allie burst out into fits of laughter, struggling to cover her mouth, and Jennifer's jaw nearly hit the ground in disbelief. No one ever spoke to Katie like that; no one had the balls to.

Jessica slipped an arm round my shoulder, a smirk on her face. I'd forgotten how forward she was – it was shady, but still, how did she know?

'You can't just walk around the city like you own it. You think you're so great,' Katie countered, but it wasn't a strong argument.

I felt Jessica's arm slip down my back as she straightened it, her black heels smacking loudly as she stalked towards Katie. It mirrored our predicament a minute ago, but this time the pair stood toe to toe.

Katie crossed her arms.

'You're nothing but a prissy stuck-up little girl with no real meaning or purpose except to look pretty. You're never going anywhere in life. You're nothing, Jessica-Grace Winters, you hear me? Nothing.'

That's when Jessica's whole body language changed; hands propped on her hips and head lifted that inch higher. Then she stepped forward looking like she was going to push Katie but instead, lifted the back of her heel and spiked it down into the front of Katie's shoe!

Katie cried out in pain, her whole body jerking as she tried to get away from Jessica. Eventually she wormed her way free, but not until the heel had left its mark, blood visibly dampening the fabric.

What in the holy poop just happened?

Katie's eyes were fixed on Jessica's as she stumbled back to Allie, who took her arm in support. Jennifer had already left, dashing to the train station. Jessica, however, remained completely calm, stepping away.

Why did she do that? She used her heel like a frickin spear!

A couple of people threw looks our way but they kept their heads low, not wanting to get involved. Would anyone call the police?

'The thing is, Katie, I've been searching for many years, around the school, around this street and under my Louboutin heel, but I fail to find where I asked for your opinion.'

'Jess – Katie, are you alright?' My voice didn't sound like my own. 'Why did you do that?'

Jessica then turned, her hands falling with a prideful smirk.

'Come on. I'll get you a coffee,' she said to me.

Then she tossed her hair over her shoulder and walked away, swinging her hips, every step brimming with purpose. I, on the other hand, turned back to Allie but all she gave me was a shake of the head before she helped Katie limp away.

'You'll regret that, Winters!' Katie yelled back over her shoulder, but Allie hushed her until their conversation was out of earshot.

Jessica didn't retort, not like she needed to.

When I looked to the street behind me Katie and Allie were gone. I just caught a glimpse of Katie's purple jacket as it disappeared round the corner.

When I glanced to the group at the table, Jessica had her back to me, the girl with the brown hair glaring daggers at her, while the blonde simply looked down. The other girl whose black hair bathed in the dimming sun, looked confused at the sight of me. Her eyes scanned my entire body before she turned to Jessica, smiling proudly.

Well, this was just great.

SLATE RETRIBUTION

CHAPTER 3

Nepenthe

Something that makes you forget grief.

JESSICA-GRACE WINTERS

12 June 2015, 16:58

Scotland, Glasgow, Buchanan Street, Quick Brew Café

My arms rested on the cool steel table, the cup of hot camomile tea failing to bring me any warmth or comfort; in fact there was little comfort in any of this. The four of us had been sitting here for over an hour and a half but no one had broken breath.

What could we talk about that wasn't her? How could we not discuss the mission?

As Team Lead I should have been starting the meeting off,

seeing how the other team members were feeling and, more importantly, taking charge of the situation. That's what I'd been taught and now, due to the circumstances, I had to put those skills to use. However, one thought dragged any words back into the depths of my mind.

Willow Mae was dead.

It was meant to be a simple mission; a secluded area deep in the woods where an old, burned house sat proudly in its own ash and rubble. All my team had to do was get the information from the laptop stored in one of the vaults and get back out. None of us expected an ambush.

It shouldn't have been possible; it shouldn't have happened, but it did

anyway.

The persistent tapping of Grace's finger on the rim of her coffee cup made me look up from my bruised hands. The tapping mimicked the pounding in my head, the pressure slowly building under and behind my eyes, exhaustion riddling through me like a disease. The glaring sun sent sharp shooting pains through my head and I bowed to avoid its glares. I needed to breathe.

The growl of revving cars made my muscles go stiff.

I was ready to make a break for it. Ready to run.

The chatter of passers-by grew louder as they came close.

I was ready to hear any information they had.

The sobs of Quinn crying caused me to turn.

I was ready to let her cry on my shoulder.

But in reality I needed her to keep quiet.

'We shouldn't even be here.' Grace spoke quietly, breaking the agreed silence, a hard look set on her face as she tucked her long brown hair behind her ear. 'I don't understand the point he's trying to make.'

'Who understands that man, honestly?' Lily muttered, taking a sip of her drink before her eyes returned to the horizon. 'He's probably testing us, to see how we hold up under the pressure of . . . this place. It's the first death we've ever had.'

'It's to be expected,' I added coldly, looking away from Quinn who I knew wouldn't talk anytime soon.

I needed to be the Team Leader, I needed to state the hard and crucial facts, then we could figure out the next move. Only when we returned to the dorm house could we mourn in our own sanctuary, never in public.

'We should have been more prepared, I admit – we weren't counting on an ambush. He sent us here because he wants us to have time with one another. We're here because in this line of work you need to –'

'Move on like nothing happened?' Lily cut me off sharply, her glare slicing through my formal façade as anger boiled to the surface. 'You mean disregarding Willow like she didn't matter? Or are you talking about the fact that straight after it happened, you grabbed your laptop and wrote a report.'

I knew she wasn't mad at me; Lily was just looking for someone to blame.

'It's procedure,' I told her, trying to keep my voice calm as possible.

'You never mentioned her name, you used her ID number like that's all she was, some number.'

Lily was like a burning fire: stay back and she'll keep you warm but move too close, you'll get burnt.

'Lily.' Quinn spoke from beside me but her voice cracked, her eyes didn't look up from the blue polish on her nail.

She focused on it like it was the only thing left of Willow that she possessed. That wasn't true. Willow's room was still full of her belongings: her duvet, pillows, make-up, clothes and photographs. Everything sat waiting for her but she wouldn't come back for it, not this time. We would have to go through it, pick stuff that we wanted and then send the rest to storage. Her parents would get a couple of things but most of it would become classified.

Even though I'll be the one to deliver the news, her parents will never know the truth.

'No, come on.' Lily's voice rose in volume as she edged forward in her seat, her eyes void of any emotion apart from rage, her nostrils flaring. 'Come on, let's point out the obvious – Jess here thinks it's acceptable to do all this like she didn't live with Willow, like she didn't spend nearly every day with her. Jess wrote her report and then filed it away. You can't just file a person away.' There, right there, Lily's voice lost all power as she came to the inescapable conclusion.

If any one of us died on a mission, it would be written up then locked away in a drawer. To them, all we ever could be was a number.

'That's not what I'm doing,' I said, trying to keep it professional. 'It *is* protocol that after something like this happens it's written down. I didn't want to do it but I had to. I wanted to use her name but I couldn't because of confidentiality.'

I needed to shut Lily down before someone heard; this conversation shouldn't have been happening here.

'You lived with her for fuck's sake.' Gradually, as Lily spoke, her voice was overwhelmed with rage and heartbreak. A dangerous combination.

'Lily, if you want to be Team Lead, be my fucking guest,' I snapped. 'I spent the past three years with Willow, don't you think I'm hurting too? Or are you so focused on finding someone to blame? If you want to blame anyone, blame Harkness, he's the one who sent us there, not me.'

Hypocrisy, that's what was running through my mind, because in actual fact I didn't feel anything towards Willow. She was dead, that's it. Nothing more to say on the matter.

It was harsh but I wasn't going to take shit from anyone, it'd been too long a day.

I let out a sigh. trying to calm myself down; no one needed Lily and me to fight. Everyone needed time – it felt as if the smallest thing would set them off, snapping like a mousetrap. I needed to stay in control, of myself and this team.

Then, simultaneously, our phones let out a sharp ping, the notification we'd all been dreading. A sharp breath around the table sliced through the quiet as we read the headline.

YOUNG STUDENT KILLED IN HIT AND RUN

I quickly locked my phone knowing there was no need to look at it – the article was a piece of shit anyway, nothing in it was true. It was a cover story to give her parents closure. Fuck, what was I saying?

Would they want to know the truth?

I could tell them she felt no pain, that she looked peaceful.

I couldn't tell them that Willow was shot straight through her head, that a small trickle of blood dribbled down her small forehead. They didn't need to know that her body fell like a rag doll to the ground. I won't tell them that Willow died with fear in her eyes and a scream in her lungs.

Another ping sounded around the table but I had a feeling it wasn't my mother asking for the real story.

Harkness *Report back*

Outside duty was over; now we could go back to school with looks of shock on our faces, as if we'd only just heard the news. Pretend we weren't there, pretend that I didn't find Lily unconscious or discover Willow's body.

It was all a game and we needed to play along.

'We were out for the day when we saw the news, we headed straight back to school to see if it was true and were honestly shocked to find out that it was. It's a shame, I didn't really know her well, wish I could have.'

We saw Willow at her worst moments, we saw her at her best. We knew Willow Mae. She loved her camera and would go around taking random candid pictures of everyone. She'd been scared of the dark ever since our first mission years ago, so she bought a nightlight. Willow loved to dance around the kitchen to Amy Winehouse as she baked. She was the person everyone liked but, for some reason, she loathed me.

I saw out the corner of my eye that Quinn was blinking rapidly, trying to stop the tears. She was the closest to Willow, they spent every waking moment together, as the Technical Response and the Carrier worked closely. It didn't help that Willow was the youngest out of all of us.

'We should go back.' Grace spoke up, the pearls around her neck glinting in the sunlight as she slowly went to stand, but Quinn rapidly shook her head.

'No we can't, I can't go back there, not yet.' Her hands clenched and eyes shimmered like glass, while her lips trembled like flowers in a thunderstorm.

So many words going unsaid seemed to strike lighting within her, all the rain and torment of emotions caving in on the poor girl. Through all this, however, there was a blatant fact: Quinn wasn't scared of punishments, and she wasn't scared of Harkness. She wasn't afraid of what was there, she was petrified of what wasn't.

I didn't think the full weight of what happened had sunk in with the rest of the team, myself included. Maybe it would hit home the moment we got back. Willow wasn't sitting on the couch studying or writing a report, she wasn't curled up in bed and she wasn't dancing around the house.

Willow was in a morgue, in a freezer.

Even as the facts were in front of me, no tears sprung to my eyes. No emotions bubbled to the surface – what was wrong with me? Who doesn't cry at things like this? Maybe I was in some sort of denial?

'Grace is right, Quinn, we can't stay here. Besides, it won't make it any easier if we disobey.' Lily stood from her chair, the metal scraping against the hard ground. 'We need to get out of here, I can't stand all the noise.'

'I just want a minute,' Quinn begged, her eyes pleading to the girl in front of her.

The rest of the team had dealt with situations like this before, we all came from military or secret service families, somehow Quinn had managed to avoid it all.

'We need to go, I'm not being late cause of you,' Lily countered, shaking her head at the quivering girl beside me, who looked unmovable.

Lily grew tired of Quinn's antics and lunged over the table, grabbing her arm.

My hand shot out, clenching hers tightly and, just for the hell of it, twisting a little, so the small sensation of pain would make her stop and think.

'Lily. Don't you dare,' I said in a low voice. She of all people knew what small moves like that could do to a person.

Although it wasn't my voice that made her stop, it was the moment our eyes connected, and even if it was only for a second, it was enough for her to back down.

Lily snatched her wrist back from me, massaging it gently with her other hand as she sat down. Sloppily at first, but then she returned to the default position; legs tilted to one side and hands clasped.

When I turned to Quinn, however, irritation ran through me at her state.

'Well done Lils,' I snapped, my brows furrowing. 'We're supposed to keep a low profile so how we're going to get back without everyone staring at her shaking, I don't know.' She always had to cross the line, didn't she.

'People always stare,' said Lily.

'Lily, for once shut up,' Grace interrupted; she looked way past done with the situation and I doubted Lily was helping.

'Oh don't even start, Grace. They are staring right now. Three o'clock. Excessively skimpy shorts, strappy crop tops, hoop earrings and basic bitch coffee,' Lily listed, sitting forward in her chair.

'That's what you've been focusing on?' Grace shook her head in disappointment. 'You shouldn't be doing surveillance right now.'

'What, because this conversation is so riveting?' she asked, but there was no response, no one was in the mood for a petty reply. 'So what do we have? Tall blonde with hair extensions and the girl with dark hair . . . looks like her thong is on fire.'

I followed Lily's line of sight and suddenly, all the weight that had been pressing into my lungs simply lifted. All the tension and frustration disappeared as soon as I caught sight of her: the one person who didn't judge like Lily, worry like Quinn or lecture like Grace.

The one person who didn't know the real me. Naomi Jade.

She didn't and never would know about the Academy – as far as she was concerned, I got a scholarship and that was the end of it. Well ... it was supposed to be. When we joined the first thing we were supposed to do was cut ties with everybody that wasn't related to Government intelligence. I may or may not have completely ignored that rule.

'Jess,' Grace said, catching my attention, her hazel eyes filled with certainty, 'you can't, you know that.'

'I'm sorry, you actually know the all-star cast of *Mean Girls*?' Lily asked, looking back to the group who talked in a huddle.

I couldn't catch any glimpses of Naomi and that worried me a little. What were they talking about? Was she OK?

'That's Naomi, the one that doesn't want to be here,' Grace answered for me.

I needed to tell her about Willow, I needed to vent. Talk to someone who wasn't an agent, a Government official or a psychiatrist. I turned back to my group when I heard Lily let out a short laugh as she followed my gaze, shaking her head in amusement.

'Hold up – fire thong is Naomi, *the* Naomi?' Oh great, here we go. 'She's . . . well, for a start I thought she would be smaller.'

I etched my fingers into the table, biting my lip as I considered the three variables:

1. Risk a security breach so I could talk to my childhood friend who I've not seen in nine months.

2. Get the team and leave immediately, go back to the Academy and say no more about it.

3. Call her later and explain everything.

'Can we just go home?' Quinn asked, hiccupping a couple times before wiping away any stray tears.

If Quinn continued to cry we could pass it off as shock from the article, say they shared a class if anyone were to ask. Why was I like this? So cold . . . where were my emotions?

'Yeah, come on you guys. There's no point just sitting here,' Grace said, pushing her coffee cup away, tucking a piece of stray hair behind her ear. 'Not going to do us any good just –'

'What no way – the show's just getting started. My

money's on hair extensions with attitude.' Lily announced, taking a sip of tea which I swear she'd poured whisky into.

When I looked over to the group I didn't see a show, or any form of entertainment. All I saw was Katie Danvers' hand clamped around Naomi's arm, fear screaming from Naomi's body as she tried to get away from the bitch.

I pushed off the seat, ready to break this up before it turned into the Katie show, but a warm clammy hand latched onto mine. Quinn squeezed gently, shaking her head.

'You can't, Jess, it's protocol.'

Rules and regulations banged on in my head and I was already halfway back into my seat when Lily spoke.

'Oh my God.' Her voice was horrified.

I snapped my head back to see Katie run her hand through Naomi's hair, but it wasn't a gesture of endearment; they were dangerously close and Katie was in control. She was treating Naomi like a disobedient dog – what the fuck? Even strangers walking by stared in confusion, but no one moved to intervene.

Without even thinking I pushed the chair back, pulling my hand away from Quinn's.

'Jess, you can't!' Grace shouted after me.

My heels cracked on the concrete as I charged over – of course I still cared for Naomi, so any skank that thought they could treat my friend like property had another think coming.

'Katie Danvers,' I said with a smirk, stopping beside Naomi and slipping an arm around her shoulder, pulling her away from the Cara Delevingne wannabe.

I should really have walked away but there was part of me that wanted to punch that perfect little nose of hers so hard that it would reverse the nose job she got when she was sixteen.

'I wasn't aware you were still in the country. I thought you'd be walking a catwalk in Milan or something but no ... *you're here.*'

I kept a straight face as I spoke, having one solo thought in my mind: whatever this girl spits out of her Botox-filled lips, she had it coming.

* * *

I turned swiftly, flipping my hair, and strutted away from the cowering creature that was the pitiful Katie. Even though I shouldn't have wasted energy on the girl, it still felt amazing.

As I re-approached the coffee shop table however, I was met with three different expressions: from Lily there was a proud grin, from Quinn a look of sheer horror, while Grace gave a slow sarcastic clap, everyone's eyes flitting to the scene behind me.

'Well done. Great job there, subtle, real subtle.' Grace shook her head but Lily just laughed.

'I'm sorry but that was spectacular, did you actually stab your stiletto in her foot?' Lily asked, her voice filled with excitement as she edged closer to me. 'You did didn't you? Oh fuck me, you did.'

The gravity of what I'd just done crashed through me like a wave; if anyone had recorded that it would flag up at the Academy.

'I say Jess did the right thing.'

'No I didn't,' I said pinching the bridge of my nose.

'Jessica!' shouted Naomi from behind.

I turned and saw her running towards us, then the memory hit me – I'd said I would get her coffee. Bloody coffee! What was I thinking? Truthfully, I wasn't – one minute Katie was running her mouth then suddenly my heel was in her shoe.

'You invited her over?' Quinn asked shooting up and grabbing her bag.

'What the hell was that?' Naomi said, stopping beside me, her eyes wild. 'Katie's hurt and you just walked away!'

'Sup fire thong.' Lily said casually as she stared Naomi up and down with a satisfied smirk. 'You need to relax.'

'I'm sorry, what?'

'You need to relax, blondie was being dramatic, nothing more to it.'

'She stabbed Katie with her shoe!' Naomi said pointedly.

'A very expensive shoe. She should be honoured.'

Despite Lily's comments Naomi continued.

'You can't do that, Katie is the only thing that's . . .'

'The only thing that's what?' I turned to my friend, confused. When I left high school I made sure she had more friends than just me, what happened? It's not like – oh, you've got to be kidding me.

'The only thing you have left?' I prodded, but the girl in front of me looked down to the ground in shame, fiddling with her hands.

'Jessica,' Grace butted in, glaring me down. I tried to return it but it was no use, everything was piling on, weighing me down with each passing second.

My brother hadn't been in contact for weeks, I'd distanced myself from Chris, Willow died, I'd just technically assaulted someone and now I knew Naomi had been living under Katie's boot for a year. I thought this day couldn't get any worse but evidently, it just did.

'We need to go right now. It's getting dark, it's not safe,' Grace said.

I knew for a fact she wasn't talking about our safety in the city, she was talking about how it wasn't smart to be away from the Academy after we'd been ordered back. All our phones had trackers in them, they'd know we hadn't moved.

'Well it was nice to finally meet you, fire thong, heard a lot of great things, good stories,' Lily added, standing up.

Quinn didn't say anything but as her hand took mine for a moment, the grip alone made me want to leave.

As the girls left the table I paused – how could I leave Naomi like this? She stayed quiet, but once my team were out of earshot she turned her attention back to me.

'I can't believe you didn't tell me,' I said quietly, crossing my arms.

'Well, you were busy.'

'Naomi, I would have called you every day if I knew this was going on.' I quickly took a step towards her, but then she took a step back.

'But you didn't so you didn't call,' Naomi spat. 'You didn't text, you didn't do anything and I thought I had done something wrong.'

'What? No,' I said adamantly, 'you did nothing wrong.'

'Then why? Why did you just stop?'

'Jessica!' Grace yelled from behind, but I couldn't leave it there, not when Naomi was practically yelling at me for answers.

'I couldn't call you, I was –'

That's when I heard it, the revving of an engine and the car honk. A sleek black car pulled up at the corner kerb then sat there, waiting.

Fuck.

'Naomi, I need to go,' I tried.

This needed to stop now – they must have seen we hadn't left so sent the nearest car to collect us. Just as I was about to walk away, a firm hand grasped my arm. The instinct to retaliate kicked in, my own hand raising, but it soon fell as I reminded myself it was only Naomi.

'No,' Naomi said, but this time her voice was small as she let go. 'You don't get to just run out of my life.'

Another car honk.

'Jessica!'

'I'll call you tomorrow,' I lied, before spinning on my heels, running as fast as I could down the street.

We should have left, this could have all been avoided. What had I done?

'Jess!' Naomi yelled, but I didn't turn.

To a civilian, getting collected was a thing of luxury but to me, I would rather have walked the forty-eight miles back.

As my fingers pulled the car door open I hurriedly sat down in the far seat, the rich smell of leather bringing little comfort. I made sure to stay quiet in case the microphones situated around the car were recording; there was no need for the faculty to

SLATE RETRIBUTION

find out about Naomi.

Once we were all seated and the door closed, we were off into the darkening streets of the city. No one was allowed to see the driver; there was always a partition up and the front windows were blacked out. For all I knew, Harkness was driving.

Any relief Naomi had brought me slipped away as every muscle in my body tightened. What punishment would be waiting for us?

Ten minutes passed before I mustered up the courage to say anything.

'How late are we?'

'Twenty minutes, but with this traffic, thirty.'

'When we get out let me do all the talking,' I said to them, but Lily shook her head, as did Grace. 'It's my fault that we're late, OK just ... let me take it.' My hand went over Quinn's, which was no longer clammy but cold. 'You're gonna be OK. I'll do the talking and I'll explain what happened.'

'Do you think that he'll ... you know?'

'If he does there isn't much I can do. You three just go back to the house, OK.'

It wasn't a question and it wasn't intended to be – they shouldn't see what was about to happen.

'We can come with you, maybe he'll be more lenient,' Quinn tried, but I pulled my hand away.

'That's an order,' I said plainly. 'Go back to the house, not a word of what happened to anyone.'

Right then we should have been focused on Willow, we should have been mourning her death, but Naomi distracted me. Even though it wasn't for long, it was enough to take my mind back to high school. Away from all of this.

Why didn't I feel sad or upset about Willow? I should be crying but instead I was scared. I had no clue what to say to him. I knew one thing for certain though: I would never let Naomi find out about the real me, if it was the last thing I did.

SLATE RETRIBUTION

CHAPTER 4

Foresket

Enamoured at first meeting.

NAOMI JADE

Well, this was exactly how I wanted to spend my night.

'Carol, did you put my sleeping shorts in the washing?'

'Yes!'

'Why?'

'They were filthy!'

'I've only had them on twice!'

Here we see an old married couple in their natural habitat, squabbling over pointless questions such as: whose turn it was to take the bins out, who did the dishes last, and if the other had hidden their slippers. May I introduce my parents.

I plopped down on the couch in the living room next to my

dad, who was watching *Strictly Come Dancing*, as he did religiously, every Saturday night at seven o'clock. He watched with an idle smile, his hair greying and wrinkles crinkling as he laughed at the screen.

'They reeked, Charles!' my mother scolded from the kitchen.

At the shrill yelling of my mother, his happy manner turned to an irritated one.

'You need to get your nose checked!'

'You need to get your eyes checked!' my mother yelled in retort. 'Any man could see they were dirty, then again you couldn't, so what kind of a man does that make you?'

Someone save me. Anybody. These two were going to drive me to insanity. All they did was argue about who moved the washing powder and why my dad refused to iron the duvet covers.

The sound of the next dance routine played in the background while my parents continued their ridiculous argument. Meanwhile, I fiddled absent-mindedly with a thread coming loose from my yellow jumper.

Here I sat, single and ready to mingle with *no one*. Cause

all the guys I liked were either taken, fictional, a celebrity, or swung for the other team. Why was it so hard to find a decent guy? I'm a nice person! My mum said I was too anti-social, that I needed to go to more parties and make friends. Even though everyone was usually too drunk to remember me by the end of the night.

'Charles, turn that off and come and help me!'

My dad let out an exasperated sigh, pushing himself up from the plush grey couch, making his way through to the kitchen.

Our living room was of average size, a long couch and chair next to the window, a table at the other side of the room next to the French doors, with the TV in front of the couch. And to top it all off, my mum's amazing colour scheme: grey. Was every forty-something woman's favourite colour grey?

Wow, I needed to get out more, but given Jessica had stabbed my friend's foot, I reckoned I was pretty far down on the invite list. I still couldn't believe it – the average person didn't go around impaling others. To be fair though, we do live in Scotland.

'Look!'

'I am! You know you should get tested because with your

hearing, sight and absurd sense of smell, you may as well be something off the TV!'

'Right! That's it, they're going in the bin!'

'Carol!'

I knew Jessica and Katie didn't get on, but that never meant one of them would end up in A&E. I heard a rumour that Katie slapped her once – school gossip would be the death of students. It was all about the popularity competition that the faculty swore wasn't a thing.

'Naomi, will you tell your father!'

'Naomi, will you tell your mother!'

There was something about Jessica that I didn't understand. All she could give me were half-hearted promises. Like the one where she was meant to call and explain whatever that was the other day but didn't bother her ass.

I let out a breath, spinning in my seat so my back rested on one of the many cushions, pulling the blanket over my black pyjama bottoms.

I watched how the pair on TV twisted and turned around the dance-floor. Apparently it was musicals week so I didn't recognise too many of the songs, not really my area. Although I vaguely remembered the one they were dancing to, it was one that Jess sang in high school. Even though she loved musicals I couldn't stand them half the time: everyone's either dead happy, dead sad or dead.

'Oh for crying out loud, I've worn it twice!' Dad was still fighting the losing battle with my mother. 'I'll wear it tomorrow night.'

'You are not wearing it to the MacKinnon's house-warming party.'

'Why not?'

'It's filthy!'

'We must have different eyes, Carol, there is no stain there!'

'You'll wear the yellow shirt I got you –'

'I hate yellow!'

'You'll wear it.'

'Naomi!'

Then, as though sent from the angels above, there was a loud, brash knock at the door.

'I'll get it!' I shouted, bolting up from the couch and running to the door.

I didn't even think twice before opening it, a smile of relief plastered on my face as my parents' yelling ceased. Since the door was open they'd resume the 'we're not a crazy, overbearing or deranged family' act until it closed again.

Yet stood before me wasn't someone handing out charity bags or the man who checked the meter, it was a complete stranger. He was around my age with a broad face, sharp cheekbones and a jawline that would give anyone a paper cut, his teardrop-curved eyes drawing me in. Despite the charming smile he wore, his outfit spoke volumes. All his clothes were dark: a thick black leather jacket, a navy shirt that fit tightly around his waist emphasising his muscular body . . . going down he wore black jeans and big black combat boots.

Well, he had all the makings of a bad boy – presumably a really bad boy with a motorcycle and a really big –

'Excuse me.' His heavy baritone voice cut me from my thoughts.

Then I realised I must have been staring at him for a solid

five seconds, in pure silence. What must he think? I probably looked like a total creep.

'I think this is yours,' he said, and my eyes filled with confusion as he held out my phone, the purple case battered and torn.

What the – how on earth did he find my phone? Sure, I wasn't attached to it like Allie, but I'd been sure it was in my bag when I got off the train. How hadn't I noticed?

If mum knew I'd lost it, *she* would lose it.

'I found it on the platform at the train station,' he explained as I took the phone from him, quickly sliding it into my pocket. 'One of the girls on the lock screen is a friend of mine and she told me where you lived – don't worry, I'm not a stalker.' He let out a nervous laugh, sticking his thumbs into his jeans pockets, then stared at me, his eyes tracing me up and down.

He sounded and looked fucking gorgeous. Woah, OK calm down.

I could just make out his warm hazel eyes and olive skin in the low light, as he took a small step towards the door. Then suddenly it occurred to me that through all this, I still hadn't said anything back.

'Thank you,' I blurted, grasping the phone in my pocket. 'I didn't even realise it was gone. Thank you so much, I honestly don't know what I would have done if I'd looked later and it wasn't there.'

'It's no trouble,' he said. 'My name's Kayson, Kayson Ashford.'

Oh my fucking God.

Kayson flashed a charming smile and it felt like my heart melted into a mushy red puddle. He could take my hand right now and I would willingly go with him. Jesus! No I wouldn't, who was I, Bella Swan?

'I know how attached to the phone some people can be, so I thought I should bring it back asap.'

I nodded along with whatever Kayson was saying but everything, including the dog walkers and the buzz of the streetlights, faded into the background. I couldn't tear my eyes away from his. There was something about him that piqued my curiosity – perhaps it was the way he held himself or the way the wind rustled his jet black hair.

'W-Well thanks,' I managed, but my voice came out stuttered and quiet as I tried to compose myself.

For goodness sake! Pull yourself together Naomi!

I should clarify, I wasn't the kind of girl that guys hung around with outside of school, I was always the friend they could rely on for homework if they needed it. So when a random stranger rocked up at the door with decency and manners, it meant something.

'Are you alright? You look a bit shaken up,' Kayson asked.

'Yeah, course.' I nodded.

Unfortunately, my rapid head-bobbing didn't seem to convince him – by the look on his face he was even more concerned than before. I probably looked like a Duracell bunny on steroids.

'I know it's late on a Saturday and everything.' Kayson cast his eyes down for a moment, embarrassment evident on his face.

'Oh no, it's fine. More than fine, actually,' I answered.

I briefly glanced at the lock screen photo and saw it was of

Jessica and myself ... what the hell? How did she know everybody?

That meant he was one of them, a student at the Reign Academy.

I mean, just because he went there didn't mean he was a right ass who ditches his old friends for new ones, skips coffee dates or cancels for no reason at all. I may have had some pent-up anger against Jess.

'How do you know Jess?' I asked, taking a small step forward – although when I mentioned her name, Kayson coughed nervously and rubbed the back of his neck – did they not get along?

'She's in my year. Share a couple classes, nothing too exciting.'

So, they were acquaintances then. Interesting.

'You're Naomi, right?' he asked and I almost let out an audible groan of frustration. I really needed to catch up, I hadn't even told him my name for crying out loud!

'Sorry, yeah, my name's Naomi Jade.' A blush burned through my cheeks.

'Yeah, I gathered,' Kayson said, shaking his head with a smirk. 'I mean I thought I should know your name before I came sauntering to your door. Right, well, I'm happy you got your phone back.'

Then suddenly he turned and started to walk away.

Wait, what now? No, he was not walking away from me! I mean not that he couldn't, it's just I thought I should do something to say thank you first.

'Wait!' I blurted, going down a step.

Kayson whipped around, his eyebrows rising, waiting for me to say something. Crap, what was I supposed to say? I had not thought this through. *Come on Naomi, you got an A in Higher English, you can string a few sentences together.*

'Uh . . . sorry you brought my phone back.'

'It was no trouble,' Kayson said dismissively.

'Yeah, but still do you wanna, I don't know, come in for something to eat?' I asked crossing my arms over my chest in the bitter wind.

Come in for something to eat? What kind of an invitation was that? Kayson seemed sceptical, beginning to shake his head in protest but I quickly added 'It's dark, I mean you could come in for some food and then I could drive you home?' I tried to gauge his reaction.

For a moment he looked like he could be warming to the idea, when the shrill tones of my mother called from inside.

'Naomi Jade! I know it's June but there's a chill in the air, whoever it is they either come in or shut the door!'

Mum should be on one of those talent shows: she had incredible sight and smell, and apparently amazing timing to ruin any chance I had with this guy! Not that I had any sort of chance with him to begin with, but maybe he could be one of those friends she's always on about.

'You know, I'll just leave it,' Kayson said, and I felt myself physically deflate.

'Right.' I trudged back towards the door, glancing him over one last time while I still had the chance.

I wanted to remember every feature of the boy before he disappeared. His chiselled jaw, tanned skin and inviting hazel eyes. Well this was it, dream boy was going, never to be seen again. I placed my hand on the door handle ready to walk inside when, abruptly, he spoke again.

'Although if you want, you could take me for a drink.' Kayson took out his own phone and clicked a few buttons before showing me his number.

Oh my God! Oh my God! It was happening, the James Dean of Scotland was giving me his number. This was actually happening! OK calm down, it's just a drink.

'Drinks.' I nodded, with a hopeful smile instead of the crazy excited one I wanted to pull.

I took out my own phone and punched his number into my contacts, this was one I wouldn't lose.

'Great.' Kayson's smile widened as he tucked his phone away. 'Well then, call me some time. We can go for a drink and you can thank me, again.' Then he flashed another charming smile but this time, there was something devilish about it.

That's when he turned and strode up the street, the wind now whipping through his hair.

I felt utterly smitten.

Of course, I knew it was just drinks, but the way he spoke to me made me believe it was something more. Maybe I was overthinking this? So without another thought I walked inside, shutting the door.

Had Jessica maybe mentioned something when they talked? Maybe she thought we could be friends?

The contact in my phone seemed to glow as I stared at his name.

Kayson Ashford

He'd asked me out for drinks! Did he ask me out on a date? I mean, that's impossible since we've only just met, but I mean ... no, this was just a friend thing, he seemed like a nice person to hang out with. Kayson could have walked away, but instead he'd stayed and given me his number. *He gave me his number!*

Giddy, I took in a breath as I walked into the living room and sat down on the couch, practically bouncing. This was crushing on someone, right? Not just some celebrity, since Kayson actually knew I existed, unlike Jamie Dornan.

'Naomi, who was that at the door?' asked my mother from the kitchen, over the sound of the washing machine clattering.

'No one. Just a friend.'

As soon as my dad walked back into the living room, an instant cover story rambled its way through my brain but it didn't seem I had time for one, as he sported a disappointed frown. Oh crap! He knew I was lying, he overheard I'd lost my phone. Well, that was the end of this story since I would be grounded forever.

Then again, I'm eighteen so technically they can't ground me, that's a thing, right?

'Dad –' I started, ready to blurt out an apology when he cut me off.

'I can't believe I somehow married your mother.'

Oh, I couldn't have been happier! I'd gotten away with it! Mum and Dad were none the wiser about my lost phone and new friend.

For once in my life I wanted someone to look at me instead of Jessica. I wanted someone who would like me for me.

I think I'm falling for him.

Calm down, you've only known the guy five minutes!

I pulled out my phone, nodding along with whatever my dad was grumbling about this time, as he turned his attention back to the television. As his voice faded I pulled out my phone, punching a couple of buttons before typing a quick message.

Naomi Jade *Seriously thank you for bringing my phone back, means a lot. Let me know if you're free and we could go for those drinks?*

EMERY HALE

CHAPTER 5

Lyssophobia

The irrational fear of going insane.

JESSICA-GRACE WINTERS

I couldn't decide if the staff were in a bad mood or just taking the piss.

Amongst the dark abyss that claimed the sky, thunder snapped like a bone and thick clouds swarmed over the beach, ready to wipe us out. The shadows so damning, it was like a black and white film.

My threadbare grey top was like a second skin on my arms as the torrential rain pounded the fabric, my leggings resembled a wetsuit, covered in clumps of grey sand, while my bare feet were ice-cold. We weren't allowed to stop, not until either Harkness or Duke gave us permission. I wasn't a rule-breaker, and after I got off lightly last time, I didn't intend to be.

The purpose of this training exercise was to build up stamina in tough terrain and conditions (it certainly was a shitstorm out here). Various stations were set up around the beach; some filled with circuit training from hell, while others meant carrying a partner over your shoulder as you ran, or submerging yourself neck-deep in the ocean, the current determined to pull you under, as you held a weighted bag over your head.

I was powering through one of the circuits, my arms beginning to shake under my own weight as I held myself millimetres above the sand before pushing myself back up.

Up and down, up and down.

My teeth clenched as the pain in my torso begged me to stop but I couldn't, not until they told us to. My nails clawed into the sand, fingers clenching for any grip, but all they did was sink. There was no relief, not even from nature.

Through my exhaustion, I couldn't tell my own tears from the rain.

There were only thirty people on this beach, but from the pounding of our steps and cries of exhaustion it sounded like ninety, our heavy sighs and pained breaths drowned by claps of thunder. The salt air nipped at my nose and dried my already cracked lips.

I wanted to give up – we'd been doing this for nearly four hours, two in the dry and two in the storm. Not even the rain could keep me cool; my cheeks were burning to cinders.

'Stop!' Harkness yelled, his rigid voice finally bringing relief rather than pain.

My head thumped against the ground as my entire body caved. I brought my knees to my chest, trying to even my laboured breathing, but each one was filled with a powerful ache, my throat raw.

It's over, it's over for now, I thought.

A polished black shoe smacked down in front of me, and with great effort I lifted my shaking head. Duke towered over my limp figure, his clothes bone dry as his slender fingers held a large black umbrella over his head, his dark hair seemingly unaffected by the high-speed winds battering against my back. His harsh glare penetrated my last shreds of composure.

'Get up, Winters,' he ordered. 'Follow.'

With quaking arms I pushed myself up, holding my head as high as I could, putting my best foot forward. I couldn't show any sign that I was ready to give up; in the field that choice didn't exist.

When I went to Harkness' office he sent me away with no punishment. He didn't even look in my direction, just dismissed me with the flick of his hand. Disobedience was usually followed with something but for once, there was nothing.

I trudged forward, my head bobbing up and down from the weight of the pummelling rain, Duke keeping just enough distance so I wasn't shielded by his umbrella. Dick. He didn't speak or look at me again, the umbrella blocking out most of his face, as if I wasn't meant to be looking at him. That's when I knew he was taking me to Harkness, and instantly my heels dug into the sand.

Harkness hadn't forgiven my disobedience, he was waiting to make an example of me, in front of everyone else.

Even though my mind protested, my body was on autopilot, following orders even when I wanted to run in the opposite direction. Doing what I was told without question. Why didn't I question it?

Harkness stood up ahead, his head held proudly as he observed the other students who wheezed in pain as the storm battered them down. Of course he was shielded from the rain by his own umbrella, but I had no problem spotting every single one of his features; his dark brown hair, angled eyebrows and the two scars running diagonally from the base of his forehead to his chin.

As I clambered over he turned to me, and that was what shot the fear of God through my body. His eyes were cold and calculating, but there was something ferocious about the way he analysed me; something almost wicked.

A wicked man with murderous rage and barbaric tendencies.

I could barely hold eye contact with him as I came to a stop at the end of the beach, the rain filtering into the background as I focused on the man who had yet to speak. All Harkness seemed to do was stare at my heaving chest and aching torso before his eyes finally came back to mine.

No matter how much I tried to hide my exhaustion I simply couldn't. Painting a different emotion on your face was one thing, extending it to your entire body was a different matter.

I opened my mouth, but he cut me off before I could utter

a syllable.

'Pull yourself together before you even think about talking.'

I tried to compose myself, but everything loaded on my spine like a ton of bricks: my throbbing thighs, the spiking pain that shot through my chest every time I took in a breath, my hands shivering from the bitter temperatures, the icy winds finally settling deep inside my bones. I wrapped my arms around my body, trying to conserve some heat, my teeth clattering together as my body felt the extremes of what fighting in a storm would be like.

When I met Harkness' eyes again, I knew I'd just made the worst decision, his piercing grey eyes closing in on me. In this light, they looked black. I should have stood tall and proud like him, an unbreakable force against the elements. I should have presented a blank canvas, clay ready to be moulded. I shouldn't have curled into myself like a child waiting to be rescued.

He looked away from me after that, handing his umbrella to Duke, the rain rapidly drenching him. I didn't even register the shove until my feet stumbled back, my arms flailing as I tried to catch my balance.

'Move!' Harkness yelled, his voice scorching with a rage I had never heard before. 'Fucking move! Get in the water!'

The maddened man's fist crushed my wrist as he dragged me towards the icy water. I struggled against him, placing all my weight into my heels, which dragged through the sand like it was cement. Despite my attempts Harkness' strength outweighed mine, and no matter how much I writhed and thrashed his efforts continued.

'Let go of me!' I cried.

Harkness seized both my wrists, hauling me into the shallows, my toes curling as bitter pins shot through my skin. My knees bent as I tried to run but the water chilled my body, every muscle spasming at once.

'Winters!' Harkness yelled through the storm's frenzy, his eyes alight with a fury that could rival a god's.

As he dragged me deeper and the water reached my hip, the students abandoned the bags over their heads and sprinted from their positions as if their lives depended on it. The only sign that they'd been there, a murky trail in the black water.

'You are one thing and one thing only!' He hauled me round to face him, his hands coiling around my wrists. 'You are a soldier. You will take my orders and you will obey them!'

My palms opened and shut but before I knew it, I had lost all sensation.

'Please don't do this,' I panted, trying to free my wrists.

I tried to wriggle my way out, tried to loosen Harkness' grip but he only used the momentum to bring me closer, so close that the droplets on his face splashed onto mine. I could feel the heat of his breath, the power of his eyes stripping everything away.

Then, I looked over to the people I knew wouldn't judge me, the four of them standing in a huddle watching us, watching him. As I locked gazes with them the wind relented, its merciless lashings reduced to tender brushes of the skin. As the black waves rolled, one after the other, each ripple and wake carried the crippling weight of an eternity, foam clinging to memories, only to be swept away by the tide.

Grace's chest heaved, hair matted to the side of her face, her arms wrapped around Quinn. After the dismissal the other night, the look on her face told me she was waiting; waiting in *anticipation.*

Quinn's arm was hooked around Grace's back while she held Lily's hand in the other, shaking all over as adrenaline left her body. Her eyes shot rapidly between Harkness and myself with a look mimicking Grace's. *Anticipation.*

Lily stood tall since she was the fittest of the four of us – she had already done most of this training on her own time. Then wiped the mix of sweat and rain from her brow, as another boom of thunder cracked across the sky. There was a look on her face I recognised, as she cast her gaze to the sand. *Acceptance.*

The boy I thought I knew stood with his own team but his eyes were solely on mine, his dark ragged hair slicked back, his lips pressed into a thin line which then opened to yell, and only then did time speed up.

SMACK

A solid unyielding right hook battered my cheek, sending me crashing down into the choppy waters. As my head thumped off the sand and salt water blasted up my nose, my head and throat burned. Ignoring my body's protests I shoved myself out of the water, coughing and sputtering.

BAM

Harkness' unforgiving kick tossed me onto my back, icy black water obscuring my vision, disorientating me as salt stung my eyes. I heard different voices yell, some closer than others, but they were just that, voices.

His nostrils flared as he hauled me out of the water, his knuckles white.

I tried to stand but my mind was still spinning, everything growing dark as I struggled to tell the sky from the ocean.

Now all I saw was Harkness, his wicked eyes brimming with rage and iron fist clenching harder as he peered down at me, inching closer. I tried to move but he held my body, he pulled the strings.

'You're a pathetic little girl who doesn't know when to shut her fucking mouth,' he spat, the immaculate scowl steadfast. 'You are flesh and bone, and I will break you, Winters. I will tear you and your world apart until you beg.'

Why did I deserve this? I didn't understand. We were late back to school . . . this wasn't a school.

'Disobeying orders gets soldiers killed. We need soldiers. What part of that don't you get?'

We needed an army or our vital assets died in a war that we'd begun to lose.

I didn't dare answer as my breathing finally slowed, time now moving at a great speed. I could hear Grace's shouts, Quinn's screams and the pounding of footsteps splashing into the water.

The waves crashed into my legs as the sky above spiralled relentlessly.

'I thought you were one of them.'

I didn't even try to move when his fist reeled back. His knuckles cracked against my cheekbone, the pain jolting through me, but I never felt the crash of water as I drifted down through the waves.

* * *

Click. Click. Click.

'No, I don't . . . that doesn't help us, Ashford . . . come down here yourself . . . even if she is I'm not letting her.'

The clacking of a keyboard and hushed motherly tones

were what I woke up to. My eyes heavy and cheekbone searing hot, a dull throbbing hiding underneath.

'Ask him about –'

'I know, Quinn, just focus on writing that up - yes, I'm still here.'

My lips parted as I tried to take in a deep breath of clean air but it caught in my throat; it felt raw, like I'd been screaming for hours. The breath escaped me as ragged coughs wracked through my body. I tried to roll onto my side but pain shot through me like a bullet.

'Shit,' Grace muttered.

I heard the clatter of the phone before warm hands rubbed my back – at first I could only make out a figure, but soon Grace came into focus. Worry written all over her face.

'What happened?' I asked, but the words were stolen.

'Don't try to talk, get your breath back,' Grace instructed as she grabbed me, straightening my body out.

Oh here comes Dr Aspin everyone, here to save the day.

Every muscle in my body ached; I wanted nothing more than to curl into a ball, shut out the world and sleep for an eternity.

It would be better than remembering what had just happened.

Why did I let him do that to me? Of course it happened – most punishments entailed some kind of physical altercation – but rarely in public. I thought he knew we all appreciated the fact that happened in private.

All the bruises, scars and burns stayed *private* – but now Harkness had made the message clear. He wasn't going to take any more rebellion.

As my senses returned the coughing came to an end, and I realised we were the only students in the medical wing. You could tell from the absence of shuffling feet and laughter, something priceless in this place. I managed to spot Dr Williams typing away on the computer at the nurses' station but he didn't meet my gaze.

I returned to what was right in front of me. Quinn, who sat at the side of the hospital bed working away on her laptop. Her eyes flitted up to meet mine a couple of times but she didn't say a word.

'What are you doing?' I asked as Grace did the usual check over, lifting my damp top to look at the new bruises I certainly felt. 'Quinn?'

'It doesn't matter,' Grace answered, her golden cross swinging freely from her blue top. 'Just keep still, I don't think you fractured anything.'

Shouldn't she have said 'I don't think *he* fractured anything'?

Quinn finally closed her laptop, the slow hum and bright light snapping off. She gave me a look so full of emotion, I couldn't figure out what she was about to say.

'Homework,' she said, but it was blatantly a lie. 'How are you feeling? Grace said that Dr McKay doesn't think there's anything serious, just a few bruises –'

'Why didn't you stop him?' I blurted.

There were two people in the water, which left twenty-nine students and one teacher on the beach – did none of them think to intervene? I thought at least my own team would try to stop him – I knew I deserved discipline, but what happened was on a completely different level. Harkness had held me like a puppet. I could have stood up but I let him grind me down until I was nothing but a small grain of sand.

I let him do it because we needed soldiers, ones that were

willing to go through a little pain. Did that include this? Should I have let him? How could I? These thoughts belonged to a madwoman.

Both girls remained quiet. Quinn opened her mouth to speak but Grace shook her head and the girl curled back in the large leather chair. She suddenly looked so small in her pink jumper, her pleated white skirt exposing her legs as they anxiously rubbed together. Quinn was one of the most intelligent girls I'd ever met but she knew fuck-all when it came to lying.

The damp material of my shirt sent a small shiver through me as Grace pulled it back down, then lay a thin cotton blanket over my body. I stared at Quinn, wanting answers even if they'd make me pissed. I needed to know why no one even tried to stop him.

But after a few seconds I'd already answered my own question: it was the same answer I'd given when Harkness poured water down Lily's throat. Fear.

'Ashford was on the phone.' Grace said, drawing my gaze back.

'So?'

'Whatever you two talked about last night, he told me to tell you he'll take the case.'

I turned to Grace as she made her way around the wooden bedside table and lifted up my burner phone, showing me the message.

Ronan *I went to her house. She doesn't suspect a thing.*
I'll keep Jade safe like you asked.

A sigh of relief ran through my body – well, at least she was taken care of.

Grace didn't put the phone down, re-reading the message herself. I didn't say anything since I knew she would catch on to who 'Jade' was any sec –

'You've utterly lost it, did Harkness knock a few brains cells out? Never mind protocol or exposure because that never applies to you. This is illegal, it's called stalking you know?'

'It is not stalking.' I retorted. 'I wouldn't send Ashford to stalk Naomi.'

'I know we're agents, but come on!'

Quinn hushed Grace, motioning to Dr Williams, who had perked up, interested by our conversation. Although the training doctor was anything but pleased as Grace jammed the phone into Quinn's chest, who read the message over for herself.

'You sent Kayson to her house?'

'Yes, yes, OK fine.' I pushed myself up in bed, my arms shaking a little.

The ward spun, but stopped after a couple seconds, so there was that problem solved – just don't move anywhere too quickly. Grace's arms shot out to grab mine but I pushed her away; there was no need for her to mollycoddle me. I'd gotten knocked out, not hit by a car.

Then she took her motherly stance, crossing her arms. 'Naomi is eighteen, I'm sure she's developed social skills. She's a big girl and doesn't need you watching over her. Honestly, you were meant to cut ties with her in first year and now you've sent Ashford of all people to . . . '

Grace's dulcet tones drifted off into the background as I focused on getting my head in order, it was no use scrambled.

After the incident at the beach, it was entirely possible that from here on out the punishments would get worse. If I wasn't careful I'd be spending a lot more time cooped up in here.

Punishments were normal and I knew how to avoid them: by following orders to the letter.

They needed soldiers and I couldn't be trained unless I stopped caving.

I no longer had to worry about Naomi – now she had Ashford to look after her, Katie wouldn't get close. So I could focus on the performance next week. There was an information pass with vital data that the Government needed to take down Trojan, the relentless terrorist organisation that plagued our country.

I needed to stand tall, become a force to be reckoned with.

SLATE RETRIBUTION

CHAPTER 6

Irascible

Having a hot temper; easily angered.

JESSICA-GRACE WINTERS

It had been nearly a week since the incident at the beach, and the aches and pains had subsided – though they were the least of my worries. Tonight were the crucial package drops – they were supposed to have happened yesterday, but got pushed back because of another attack. A Trojan terrorist attack.

Two days ago there was a small explosion at the Hatchet Bank in the city centre – thankfully it was contained but it took three lives, enough to catch the Academy's attention. Ever since the destruction of the Twin Towers on September 11th, the Government knew they had to come up with something to combat any future attacks, and somehow they came up with us.

The news had covered the bombing as a one-off, nothing to worry about, some alcoholic who'd gotten hold of TNT. Terrorist attacks had become a common occurrence in the past decade: protocols and evacuation plans were sent out every week, and a bomb exploding wasn't anything new.

Since the seniors of the school were shipped out to deal with any leads concerning Trojan, we were low on numbers. My team, along with one other, had been brought in to oversee the drops. I wouldn't be controlling the situation from backstage this evening: for once I was the decoy.

THE HALLWELL THEATRE

PROUDLY PRESENTS

CHICAGO THE MUSICAL!

Even the theatre was under the Academy's management: it was why the package drops were made here, so that the environment could be monitored by them. The whole reason they offered a musical scholarship was for this exact purpose. Everyone would be too busy watching the stage to see what was happening a couple of seats over.

'Jess.' Lily's smoky voice drew me from my thoughts.

As I sat at my dressing table, make-up brush in hand, I realised I was the only performer left in here. Lily was dressed all in black, a gun holstered to her thigh, her hair pulled back from her face. Since we were down a Carrier after Willow's death our roles had to shift slightly: tonight Grace would take over as a Runner and Lily would switch to the Carrier, collecting all three of the packages from their secondary pickup points.

'You're meant to be on stage in five.'

'I heard the call, I'll be ready,' I told her, with another swipe of the brush across my lips.

I was already in my sheer black costume, microphone tucked into my hair and secured with tape. My role was in the ensemble so if I needed to slip away to help Lily during a number, it wouldn't be too noticeable. The downside though, was constantly having to wear a comm unit – it was difficult to sing while everyone else was having a conversation in your ear.

'What have you eaten today?' she asked and I let out an

annoyed groan, glancing down at my dressing table.

It was covered in various things: spare sheet music, pens, make-up, brushes, and a plate with food on it and a drink. Most of it was just for show in case a civilian came back here.

'I'm eating it,' I said, motioning to the half-eaten food in front of me.

'That's a sausage roll and a can of cider,' Lily stated.

'Uh huh.'

'You're drinking?'

'Don't start, Lily.' I said tiredly, dropping the lip brush back into the pot. She was starting to sound like Grace. 'It's one can, it doesn't do anything.'

'Your nutrition is shit.'

'Well so is your singing, high kicks and banter, but you don't hear me complaining.'

I set out my powder and brush to the right, along with some lipstick, since I'd only have time to grab things. I didn't hear any more from Lily so I'd assumed she'd left, but when I looked up she still stood there, arms crossed.

'Even though I'm the Carrier, I'm still your Runner. Due

to the complexity of the drop-offs I want to take you to the stage myself.' Her voice was firm.

'The complexity?' I asked.

'We have a separate agent dropping off each of the three packages. First one will be with the band, second one will be in the audience,' she said, but then stopped, holding her breath for a moment. 'The third agent we don't know – whoever it was went quiet two days ago. We don't know the drop-off point.'

That was when I spun around in the chair to face her.

'You're worried whoever the agent is got caught?'

'Yeah, after the bank . . . so can I take you to the stage or are you going to make this more difficult?'

I stood up, taking my friend's hand with a sigh. Lily cared about her job, but first and foremost she cared about this team.

'Well, I guess having an escort would be nice.' I smirked playfully, squeezing Lily's hand and slyly moving it down my thigh. 'Did you do this with the whole cast?' In shock, Lily ripped her hand from mine, and I burst out laughing at her disgusted face.

'Not that kind of escort!'

I feigned hurt, a hand over my heart.

'Well you need to be more specific, don't get my hopes up like that.'

'Even though I find this little black number insanely attractive Jess, doesn't mean –'

'Come on. You told me I was your type, and frankly, you're mine.'

'Unfortunately, *you're* taken.'

'Shame that. You know I'm only teasing,' I said, pulling away.

BANG. BANG. SMACK. CRACK.

Both our heads whipped towards the open door before we bolted out in the direction of the sudden gunfire.

The last time I checked, the walls were cream but as we made our way down the corridor, dark red blood was slathered all over them. Directly opposite on the floor lay a limp body, legs contorted like a dead spider.

'Someone!' a panicked voice called.

I ran as fast as I could to the open door, but as soon as I set foot in the dressing room one leg nearly went from under me as I slipped on a red smear, my hand sliding down the wall, now coated in warm, thick, sticky blood. The place was a riot: chairs knocked over, mirrors shattered – but then I realised there wasn't just one dead body, there were two. A tall man dressed in an usher's uniform lay face down on the floor, a bullet through the back of his head, gooey brain matter clumping in his hair, while an unnecessary anatomy lesson decorated the white walls.

When I glanced at the first body, anxiety thumped in my heart – she was one of the lead actresses, who was meant to be on stage in the next couple of minutes. Shit.

Three girls dressed similarly to me stood shaking in the corner, one with a gun in her hand as she stared at the dead man.

'Eve?' I asked the girl with the gun; she was a couple years below us.

Lily leaned down to feel for a pulse, then she looked back to me, shaking her head. Oh, this was just great.

'Eve, what happened?'

I tried to stay calm, but nerves plucked away in my chest as the seconds ticked by. The reason? Because the opening number had started to play through the speakers and none of us were where we were supposed to be.

'I-I don't know,' Eve stuttered. 'He came in waving a gun and this.' She held up something small and compact, but with an antenna sticking out the top.

Lily barged past me and took the thing. Even though her back was turned, I knew it wasn't good news.

'It's a bomb detonator.' She knelt down next to the man's body, searching his pockets, but came up empty.

'A bomb?' Eve asked. 'There's a bomb here?'

'Obviously here to deliver this – there must be a second one.'

'Trojan's here?' Eve asked, becoming more hysterical by the second.

'Yeah, and they want us to know about it.'

Hold up, let me get this straight: the show had already started, four of us were meant to be on stage, one of the lead actresses along with a possible terrorist were dead in the dressing room and now there was a bomb in the theatre . . . *you've got to be fucking kidding me.*

'All of you get on stage,' I ordered. 'Go!'

Without having to be told again, the three of them ran from

the room. But when I turned to Lily, I was greeted with a face full of uncertainty.

'Trojan were only ten feet away, he must have snuck in after I passed,' she said, glancing over the two bodies – but as I grabbed another dress from the rail, Lily paused. 'What are you doing?'

'I'm gonna have to go on for her. Get Quinn, tell her what's happened.' I tore off my dress, shimmying into the new one before stepping around the pool of blood to get to the door. 'I need to get to the other side of the stage. Harkness is with Quinn, get him to stop the show.'

'He's not going to do that!'

'Two people are dead, convince him!'

I barrelled down the corridor as fast as I could, down the stairs to stage right before sprinting to the lift at the back. The echoes from the pit reverberated through backstage but for once they didn't bring me joy, only dread. Harkness had to stop the show, it wasn't meant to go down like this. No one was supposed to die.

Wind swept from behind as Lily rushed past me to the

other side of the stage, but even after a few seconds, the band didn't stop. What was he thinking? The package drops could happen another night, there were too many innocent lives at risk!

Another set of footsteps came from behind, but this time they were lighter than Lily's.

'Jessica.' The small voice of Grace whispered in my ear, dressed all in black, earpiece in hand.

I took it from her, quickly placing it in my ear.

'The pit are extending the music and it's been relayed to the dancers. Sorry about your friend.'

'Didn't know her . . . Christ, I've got her blood all over me.' I frantically rubbed my hands together but the blood smeared into a sweaty goop.

'Fits the character though, right?' Grace asked as I wiped the blood on my tights.

OK, I didn't know the woman but she only died a minute ago.

'Too soon?'

'Yeah,' I said, as if it was obvious. 'If Quinn's with the stage manager tell her my mic is number nine, she'll need to turn it up.'

'OK, we'll keep you updated.'

'Quietly though, I can't concentrate when you yell at each other,' I said to Grace, and she nodded before running out of sight.

As the instrumental of the opening number climaxed I let out a shaky breath, pulling myself together. I'd always wanted to play this role, but not like this.

Even though I couldn't see much, I caught sight of Quinn talking into her headset, then to someone beside her, presumably Harkness. He controlled this whole operation, he had to stop the show. Of course we needed the package drops but surely there was a safer way to go about it?

'Lilith.' Quinn said, using my codename. 'Your microphone is set and the volume's up.'

I was about to reply when the pit roared to life and the lift started to move. I positioned my hands and cocked my hip as the blinding spotlights hit my face – here we fucking go.

* * *

As I walked downstage and let the first notes out of my mouth I knew one thing: this was already going horribly.

'Alpha team report.'

'We have control of the first package, we also have control of the auditorium.'

'Nightingale and Blackbird, do you have eyes on the bomber?'

'Negative.'

The usual chatter started in my ear so I turned my attention to singing. If I ever left this line of work, I was going to put 'multi-tasking under intense situations' on my CV.

With my sultry cover in mind, I gazed out to the first couple of rows, hoping to gain some insight into where the package drops were happening. I wasn't used to being kept in the dark.

The Alpha team was here, which consisted of five guys in our year including Luca and Kayson – they didn't choose the team name but if anything, it matched their egos. We rarely worked with this team because if they didn't get their way, they mimicked a five-year-old throwing a temper tantrum.

I knew Kayson had to be near the front since he'd be helping Lily with the package hand-offs.

But when I saw him sitting two rows back, I also saw the familiar dark hair and bright eyes of Naomi. What the hell was she doing here? She hates the theatre! Sure, I'd asked Kayson to keep her safe, but that didn't include bringing her into the middle of a fuckin op! He knew bombs didn't mean an explosion of flowers, right?

'We have movement from the second row, Ronan is in position to collect the second package,' Luca said. He must have been somewhere in the audience.

Oh yeah, Kayson was going to receive a package alright, a kick up the ass.

Through it all, however, I continued to sing, containing my emotions whilst restraining myself from yelling *Bomb!* and undermining this whole operation.

Then Lily's voice sounded in my ear.

'Station One, we have eyes on the suspected target.'

'Do you have control?'

'Stand by,' Lily responded.

At that I turned, making my way to the back of the stage, forcing myself not to make eye contact with anyone. There was tension around me that wasn't usually there – the dancers constantly asking the silent question *What's going on?*

They didn't know there was a bomber in the theatre, they didn't know there was a dead man in the dressing room, and the fact I was on the stage instead of the leading lady didn't help matters.

'Station One, the bomb is strapped to the target, male, dark hair, dressed in an usher's uniform. Heading towards the back stairs,' Grace said.

'Charlie Nine Nine, secure the perimeter,' Harkness radioed to the agents in cars outside before he spoke to the ones on bikes. 'Bravo Five, cover the back entrances. No one leaves the building.'

'Roger that,' someone replied.

Well, at least this suicide bomber wouldn't be able to escape – but that also meant he was stuck here.

As I spun back around, two people were leaving the auditorium – must have been Luca and another member of their team. Come on, Harkness, stop the show.

'If this goes clean, Executive Action stand by, repeat stand by,' Quinn's voice fluttered through.

Suddenly a line prompt broke me from my autopilot, and I remembered what I was meant to be doing – ya know, acting. I replied with a smirk and a hair toss before pushing forward.

My eyes hardened as they landed on Kayson, who squirmed under my glare. Well, at least he was getting the message. Who the hell did he think he was, bringing a civilian to an op? As the thoughts swarmed my brain, I sucked in a breath – if I kept getting lost in my thoughts, I would miss every cue. Get it together.

Everyone huddled around me, striking all kinds of poses while I sang.

'Blackbird and Nightingale are in pursuit,' Lily said. 'Target is heading for the lighting rig.'

'Is there any way to divert him?' Quinn asked.

'Negative, we'll get him on the rig.'

I didn't have to be next to Harkness to know he wasn't happy; his disapproving glower was almost audible.

'Multiple threats over the west corridor.' Luca's panicked voice rang through, but I didn't let my composure fall – no one could know what was going on behind the scenes. 'Alpha team has control, but we won't reach Nightingale or Blackbird in time.'

'Nightingale, get around to the other side of the lighting rig,' Quinn said, 'with one at either side you'll be able to cut him off. Are you both armed?'

'Affirmative,' said Lily.

'Omega team, finish him,' Harkness snapped.

'Roger that.'

I didn't even have to look to know more of us in the audience were leaving to help control the area, but what surprised me was Kayson darting from his seat. Oh great, bring her into this mess and then just ditch her. I didn't get a chance to see him go before I was being picked up and carried across the stage – *seriously Jess, you have your own job to do!*

'Executive Action, hard stop. I repeat hard stop.'

Hard stop? Did they seriously think arresting the guy was gonna to do anything? Sure, he might have intel but the target worked for Trojan, probably had a cyanide pill under a fake tooth.

As I rolled gracefully back down to the ground, I gazed out at the audience with the same seductive smirk I'd practiced in the mirror a hundred times – and then, I heard it.

CLANG

I opened my mouth wider, trying to sing as loud as I could to cover up the noise, but judging by a few faces in the audience, they heard it as well. A scraping sound slid past my ear and I turned just quick enough to see a gun skidding into the wings. Fuck, that better have been the bomber's gun.

'Report,' Harkness demanded, but only silence answered him.

Thankfully, at that moment I had to spin onto my back, so I'd be able to get a good look at what was going on up there. What I saw, however, was not fully under control – and when I say fully, I mean at all.

The fake usher had Lily in a tight headlock, one of her legs dangling from the silver rig, her face red as she struggled to breathe. Opposite stood Grace, gun raised, but her hands were shaking. My eyes must have been bulging because when the two lads pulled me up from the floor, their expressions shot straight to worry. As I made my way down the stage everyone in the cast started to exchange looks. Great.

Fortunately, the stage was set up so you couldn't see the rig from the audience, but that wouldn't matter if Lily plummeted down and cracked her skull open.

'Ronan, what's your position?' Quinn asked.

'I'm on my way to the lighting rig,' Kayson replied, his voice breathless, his pounding footsteps mimicking my own heart. 'ETA one minute.'

If Grace didn't take the shot and the bomber pressed the detonator we would all go up in smoke; if she took it she could hit Lily. I hated being the decoy – how the hell did Willow do this?

Once again we all huddled together, everyone on edge because now we were stuck as spectators.

'Nightingale, if you can shoot the target, do it.'

'I can't,' Grace muttered quietly. As soon as she started talking the ensemble and I cranked up the volume – if she needed to speak we were going to do our best to accommodate. 'I can't.'

'Take the shot.'

'I can't, if I shoot him they'll both go down.'

'I'm ordering you, take the damn shot.'

'They'll hear.'

'If you don't take the shot they'll hear a bomb go off and then be incinerated,' Harkness said, almost barking at her.

'Nightingale.' The smooth voice of Quinn spoke. 'There's a part in the song with gunshots. You can shoot then.'

'I'm almost there,' Kayson told her, but Grace didn't respond.

That's when it came, the drum ready to smack down.

'Now,' Quinn said hurriedly.

BANG

All of us onstage mimicked the bullet hitting us, as choreographed, but at the same time we all looked up to see what was going on. The man stumbled back, his shoulder falling.

BANG

He fell to his knees and Lily elbowed him in the chest before lunging forward, keeping low.

BANG.

Head shot. The man landed face first in the middle of the lighting rig.

I think I speak for all of us that night in saying everyone one on that stage let out a sigh of relief. Then, just like that, we continued singing the final chorus, which took us to the end of the song.

'Threat neutralised,' Grace said softly.

'Executive Action stand down,' Quinn said. 'Wait for further instructions. Bomb Squad rendezvous with Bravo Five, we need you at Station One.'

'Roger,' a man said – and just like that, it was over.

Now I felt like I could go on with the rest of the show without stress, even though there would be questions – especially in the reviews, but we could deal with that later. Right now, I just needed to get to the end of this bloody number.

With a deep breath I belted my last three notes, enjoying it while I could before the song snapped to a close.

* * *

When the band stopped and the lights went down, I practically ran off stage and into the wings. I wanted to talk to Quinn, get some insight into how my team were going to carry a dead body from the lighting rig, but she was too busy directing someone through her mic. My attempt at leadership was short-lived as Eve and the majority of the ensemble surrounded me, whispering their desperate questions in my ear. I pushed them away, heading to the back corridor, and motioned for them to follow.

Once we were all crammed into the slim space and the door closed behind us, the hallway erupted into chatter.

'What happened?'

'Why the hell was there a body found?'

'Is she alright?'

I lifted my hand and banged against a door to my right twice to get their attention, then twenty beady eyes centred on me.

'As the show started a Trojan operative delivered one of the bomb detonators to a dressing room. The operative was taken down but she . . .' God, I didn't even know her name. 'Our fellow agent was fatally wounded.'

Chatter, rumours and gossip fell deathly quiet. Some of the agents in front of me were filled with shock, others with disbelief. Emotions flooded through me, everything I'd seen hitting me like a train. Lily could have fallen from the rig, Grace could have been hurt, we all could have been blown to ashes. My breathing hitched a little as I pushed the thoughts from my mind. The threat had been dealt with, time to move on.

SLATE RETRIBUTION

'Dead?' a younger girl asked – I didn't recognised her, but Eve took her hand in comfort.

'Yes,' I replied, there was no use in sugar-coating it. Tonight, I wasn't the Team Lead, but someone had to take charge of this situation. 'No one anticipated this but the building is secure, as you've heard, and the threat has been dealt with.'

My own voice drifted past my ears: this was almost the exact same speech I had given my team after Willow's death. Was that what my job was? To reiterate the same platitude over and over again but with a different name? A different number? It didn't seem right.

The sound of the door to the stage opening made me fall quiet in words and thought, as Harkness stood there.

'Shouldn't you all be getting ready to go on?' he asked, his voice even colder than before.

Harkness stood tall, but his head leaned forward expectantly, at me. Even though no one here was due on anytime soon they filed out of the corridor, one after the other. Then he let the door go and, as it swung shut, made his way towards me.

Every ounce of leadership and composure left me as he

marched over, grabbed my shoulders and threw me back against the wall.

'You do not undermine my authority.' I wished he'd yelled but he didn't; his voice was something feral, primal. 'You do not tell me what to do. I am your superior officer, Winters.'

'One of our agents was murdered and there was a bomb – the safest solution was to stop the show. Claim there was a technical fault,' I tried, but it was pitiful.

He was right. I shouldn't be questioning orders when it came to things like this; he had more experience than I ever could.

'That threat was neutralised within the first song. Plans change. The package drops tonight are more important than you, Winters. We need this information. You should learn that agents are easily replaced.'

'The package drops still could have been made.'

'We will not show Trojan we are inferior. If they saw that, they would send more suicide bombers. We need to show them that we do not surrender. By stopping the show we would have done just that.'

'Someone is dead!' I shouted back.

SLATE RETRIBUTION

Without a moment's hesitation Harkness grabbed me by the chin, but then his hand lowered, crunching my throat like a boa constrictor. I sucked in as much air as I could, my hands grabbing his. I knew how to stop Harkness, I had to disorientate him – shove my thumbs in his eyes, knee him in the crotch and then deliver a swift right hook – but did I do any of those things? No.

'I will not have you undermining me.' Harkness pushed harder against my throat and suddenly my airway got smaller, only slivers of air getting through. 'We need soldiers, I told you this. I let it slide the first time. I won't do so again.'

I tried to speak but Harkness' grip was like iron, and the only noise that came out was dry gasps for air.

Then the swing of the door sounded. I craned my neck to see Quinn standing there: her face was one of concern, but soon after she bowed her head, avoiding the sight in front of her. Abruptly, Harkness let me go and I fell forward, hands on my knees. I didn't even watch where he went as he headed past me down the corridor. I waited until he was gone before I let coughs splutter out, the scratchiness in my throat returning.

'Jessica.' Quinn said, now finding the courage to move, her voice full of worry as she ran over to me, pressing her hands to mine. 'Nightingale, we need a medic.'

'No, it's fine,' I told her. A couple more coughs left my throat before I straightened myself back up. 'It's fine, doesn't matter.'

'Doesn't matter?'

My hand shot forward and covered her mouth – Harkness was on the same frequency as us, he would hear it. I couldn't imagine what he would do to me if he came back.

'Repeat, do you need a medic?' Grace asked, her voice a lot clearer than before.

'No,' I said, keeping my voice as level as possible, swallowing down another cough. 'No, we don't need a medic.'

'Alright.' And with that, Grace's voice was gone.

I dropped my hand, but Quinn's eyes pleaded with me to reconsider. She didn't say anything but her mouth opened and closed like she wanted to, her mind scouring for the questions she wanted to ask.

I could never understand why – why Harkness would do

that. It was like all his rage was focused on me, like I could ruin his reputation. Did I have that much power? Did he believe it was the only way to get me to listen?

After everything I knew, I should have kept my mouth shut, I shouldn't have undermined his authority, but Naomi was here and she shouldn't have been. Kayson was meant to keep her safe!

Without another thought I stood up tall, my head held high, and walked back through the doors to the wings, trying to shake all the tension from my body. I grabbed the water bottle from the side, downing a gulp before setting it back.

I needed to get it into my head that tonight, I didn't call the shots.

I needed to stand there and look pretty.

EMERY HALE

CHAPTER 7

Dimensional

Undeniably believable.

NAOMI JADE

After nearly a week of intense online shopping and breaking in shoes I bought two years ago, I was ready for my first date with Kayson! Well, I actually couldn't tell if it was a date or not, maybe he meant for us to be friends? I could get behind that – by *that* I didn't mean him!

He did seem like a good guy, a gentleman. He went to the trouble of picking up my phone, calling Jessica and then bringing it back. Who does that? Especially around this area. It had to be a good sign.

There I went with the overthinking again! Ever since I'd met Kayson all I worried about was screwing everything up – he went to Reign for crying out loud, he probably had exceptionally high standards. Perhaps he was rich, maybe his family were politicians or lawyers. Shoot, he'd be able to see right through my glib small talk. If he saw through that *and* my terrible pickup lines, this whole thing could go up in smoke.

OK stop! Come on, Naomi, you can do this.

'How many times do I have to tell you?' The shrill tones of my mother called from the bottom of the stairs. 'If you're going to eat in your room, bring down the plate and cup afterwards. Not to mention the *three* you've already got in there!'

Everything came back to cups and plates with this woman, she needed to get her priorities straight. She had me drying the sink yesterday – who goes about their day drying sinks? Not any sane person.

I rolled my eyes before shouting down.

'I was gonna bring them down once I finished getting ready!'

'That's all I hear from you these days, "I was gonna". Honestly.' With that, my mother's high heels clacked away to the kitchen.

SLATE RETRIBUTION

She'd just come home from work and gone on a cleaning spree – ever since that small explosion at the bank she'd been antsy.

The news reported it as a suicide bomber, some drunk who'd gotten a hold of TNT. I remember the Chief of Police saying that the man was no longer a threat and had no links to any known terrorist organisations. I found it a bit odd, but hey, who was I to question the man in charge? My mum worked as a journalist for the *Scottish Times* and something had convinced her there was more to the story, whatever that meant.

Late that afternoon, I stood in front of my full length mirror, proudly smiling at my reflection: the pink and white skater dress hugging my waist, stopping halfway down my thigh, the cropped denim jacket matching my low cut Converse. The one thing I will never do is wear heels to impress a guy – besides, Kayson didn't wear them (I presumed), so it wasn't as if he would ever out-heel me.

During the entire process of getting ready, my room had become something similar to a bomb-site: towels from my shower lay on the bed, unwanted clothes strewn at all corners of the room, make-up scattered everywhere and a glass of rosé sat on the floor next to me. Cause, you know, pre-drinking before a date was a solid move.

Ignoring the state of my room, I grabbed my bag, closed the door behind me and headed down the grey-walled and grey-carpeted staircase. Just as my foot hit the bottom step and my hand reached for the door, I heard my dad.

'Where are you going?'

Yeah, I hadn't told them about Kayson yet.

'Out . . . with Katie and the girls,' I lied.

'I thought you said you were done with that group,' my dad said, pointedly crossing his arms.

'We made up,' I lied, again.

'You women, I'll never understand you. One day you hate each other, the next you're best friends again.'

Not knowing how to respond to that, I said the first thing that came to my head.

'We're a complicated species, Dad.'

'Tell me about it, you know your mother asked me to hoover under the couch today. Under the couch! No one even looks there – I don't even look there!'

'You know how Mum is.'

From the front door I had the perfect view through to the kitchen and out the open back door, where my mum was occupied hanging up the second washing of the night. My fist almost punched the air – no interrogation today!

'Right, I'll be back later,' I blurted to my dad before practically yanking the door open and running out.

'Naomi!' Dad shouted after me.

I looked back for a moment.

'I'm late for my train!' I shouted. 'Don't wait up!'

* * *

The train ride to Queen Street dragged on, every stop lasting for an eternity. For me, the moments leading up to any event took forever, either because of nerves or fear. This one seemed more like a nerves thing. Everyone got nervous going on 'kind of but probably not' dates, right? I still didn't know much about Kayson. Sure, he had all the makings of a bad boy: a charming smile, glorious hair and pearly white teeth, but there had to be more to him. He went to the Academy so there had to be something credible in his family – it was the kind of place you needed to know someone to get in.

I'd thought about sending in an application once, but in the end I didn't, since I wouldn't have gotten in anyway.

With a shaky sigh I ran my palms down the floral dress a couple of times, trying to collect my thoughts. I needed to get it together.

An agonising half-hour passed before the train pulled into the station, the platform bustling with the evening crowds. The carriage where I sat was densely packed, and when everyone stood up we were like a tin of sardines, all mushed together. I kept my head down and shuffled towards the doors as best I could, trying not to bump into anyone. One man dressed like a waiter, or maybe an usher, shot up from his seat and barged into my shoulder, sending me stumbling forward. I was about to call out to the man but he disappeared before I could say anything. Must have been late to his shift or something.

After that, the stream of people in the carriage lessened so I quickly moved onto the platform. I was always scared of losing my mum down here when I was younger; you could lose sight of anyone. I pulled my jacket a little closer as I walked up the stairs, taking them quickly and darting around anyone who was too slow.

One of my strengths was speed – I was always picked first for sports teams in school because I was a good runner, and I played a mean game of badminton too.

I made it through the ticket turnstile and headed out of the station, the streetlights popping to life as I walked onto the street and stood at the edge of the pavement. The buzz of chatter was quieter than usual, everyone keen to keep to themselves, though there was blaring music from the bar opposite and the occasional drunken yell. It was nearly seven so everyone was either dressed for a night out or still in their work clothes.

Wait, could I be overdressed? Should I have gone for the jeans?

'Hey gorgeous,' the heavy baritone voice called.

My head whipped around to see Kayson sauntering over, and a blush rose to my cheeks. No one had ever spoken to me like that before. He wore a tight-fitting black T-shirt, black jeans, combat boots and a plaid shirt tied around his waist. Once again he wore a couple of rings on his fingers and had a silver chain around his neck, but it was tucked under his shirt, so what lay underneath was a mystery. How he could go without a jacket was beyond me since I was practically shivering.

'You coming?' he asked, holding out a hand for me to take.

A giddy feeling rose in my chest as the butterflies fluttered intensely in my stomach. In return for accepting his hand, he squeezed it, his hand rough but his touch gentle as he tugged me down the street.

Kayson let out a rich laugh before he spoke again.

'So ... have you lost your phone again since I last saw you?'

'No,' I said, dipping my head. 'No, I've kept a firm grip on it.'

'I'm glad. I don't think your parents would appreciate a stranger turning up every couple of days with your phone. Might look a bit weird.'

'You probably wouldn't be a stranger by then.'

'Guess not.'

We headed down the pavement away from the station,

SLATE RETRIBUTION

keeping to the main crowds near George Square, when the question popped out of my mouth.

'You said we were heading to a bar for a drink?'

Kayson and I had talked all last week, about random stuff like movies and our favourite places to eat, after which he suggested that we make good on our plan to go for a drink. Now I wasn't the biggest drinker in the world, but I could do two shots of vodka and not feel anything! So it was safe to say I could hold my own for a couple hours, but from the stature of this guy, he would drink me under the table.

'Yeah well, actually,' he started, and I glanced up to him confused.

He himself looked unsure of what he was about to say ... oh shit. I knew I shouldn't have said yes to this sorta date! I barely knew the guy! Why did I agree to this – next thing I know my organs would be on the black market and I'd never see my family again! Or even worse, I'd be involved in his parents' political scandals! Was his mother on the Shadow Cabinet?

'I got us two tickets to see that musical at the Hallwell Theatre.'

Wait, what now?

At my unenthusiastic expression, Kayson groaned. 'I knew I should have asked you first, wanted it to be a surprise, you know?'

It took me a moment, but I managed to blurt out a response, shaking my head vigorously.

'Oh no, no it's not that. I just – I'm just shocked is all,' I babbled. 'You know, I've never seen a musical.'

'You hate them don't you?' he asked, cutting me off, and continued before I could answer. 'This is why I'm terrible at surprises.'

'It's not a terrible surprise.'

'It's not a good one either.'

The bad boy image I'd built up in my head melted away. Embarrassment was written all over his face, his eyes moving rapidly around the street, looking anywhere except mine.

'Hey,' I said, squeezing his hand, which grabbed his attention, 'I'd love to go to the theatre. Who wants to go sit in a pub with loads of drunk old men yelling about football anyway?'

Kayson had gone to the trouble of buying tickets which

probably weren't cheap, to surprise me. It was a sweet gesture and I certainly wasn't going to ruin it. Sure, I wasn't the biggest fan of musicals, but I wasn't complaining. No boy I'd ever gone on a date with had gone to so much effort.

My words seemed to relax Kayson a little as he ran a nervous hand through his hair, before I pulled him to the side of the pavement. Countless people passed us but I didn't pay them any attention.

'You planned a surprise and I was surprised, end of story,' I said to him.

I knew I needed to look confident.

Part of me wondered if I had always been this confident, especially around guys, but the other part of me knew it was always there. Sometimes it just took the right person to bring it out.

With that I took my hand out of his and walked a couple of steps backwards with a stupid grin on my face. I crossed my arms over my chest, looking the boy up and down, and he finally relaxed, his arms hanging limply at his sides, but there was something in his eyes that contradicted that. It was almost like the cogs in his mind were on overdrive, working at a million miles an hour – was he an overthinker like me? I hoped not, we'd both be screwed.

'So, are we going to this thing?' I asked, tilting my head a little. 'Or are we going to stand out here in the freezing cold?'

Kayson let out a laugh, rolling his eyes.

'Yeah, I guess so.'

'Oh, don't pretend to be cool now,' I said, walking backwards as Kayson came towards me, his strides a lot bigger than mine.

'I'm not pretending, sweetheart.'

'Oh, really?' I asked, shaking off the fact he called me sweetheart, 'Cause you looked pretty shaken for a second there.'

'You think so?'

'Oh yeah.' I held my hand out for him to take. 'I'll let you lead, pick up your confidence somewhere along the way.'

Kayson scoffed, his eyes wide with disbelief – I could barely believe what I was saying.

'You have a cheek.'

'What do you mean?'

'Oh, so you don't remember when I came to your door? You stared at me for a solid minute before you actually said anything.'

To that I paused and cringed. Thinking back, maybe he did have a point.

'Wanna call it a draw?'

* * *

By the time we got the theatre it was already packed, people pouring in the doors from all directions. It was like being back on the train but this time the feeling was multiplied by a thousand, everyone pushing and shoving to get past.

Kayson and I were next in line to get our tickets checked when I saw someone strange out of the corner of my eye: the Head of Scotland Yard at the other side of the lobby, in a heated discussion with an usher. I was sure his name was Edward, he'd been in the news a few times this past week explaining the new anti-terrorist protocols. What the hell was he doing here? Had something happened?

Before I could question anything, I felt Kayson's hand press against the small of my back, nudging me forward. The corners of my lips shot up automatically, and I had to resist the urge to bite my lip. When I looked back, the Head of Scotland Yard and the usher were already walking away down a corridor.

'Luca, how you holding up?' Kayson asked the usher checking our tickets. He was a little smaller than Kayson, had dark skin with brown eyes and a brilliant smile.

'Good, man, you know me, hanging in there.' Luca had a kind voice but as soon as he saw me, that tone fade along with his smile. 'Who's this?'

'Naomi, she's my date for tonight.'

Date? Oh so this was a date, it was a date! Although Luca didn't seem too enamoured by what his friend had to say.

'But she's not part of –'

'Yeah, I'm aware,' Kayson snapped sharply. Luca scoffed as he checked the tickets before handing them back.

'You're the second row. I'm guessing you can count your way to your seats.'

Did I miss something? Kayson and Luca must have been friends, given how they spoke to one another, but it didn't look like this usher approved of me being there.

SLATE RETRIBUTION

As we walked past Luca and through the double doors to the auditorium I turned to look back at him. My instincts told me there was something I missed and they were right. Luca pressed his fingertips to his ear before he spoke – it was quiet, but I was close enough to hear.

'I need Blackbird to front of house.'

Blackbird? Was that theatre code for something?

Even though I tried to slow down and hear more, Kayson was already pulling me down the aisle to our seats. My gut was telling me there was more; something about this theatre was off. Maybe I was just paranoid, but little things were starting to stack up in my head.

As Kayson and I made it to our seats near the front, the chatter in the auditorium grew while the whistles of the orchestra warming up flowed through the air. The ceilings stretched to the heavens, the wallpaper a rich red encasing the entire place, while the lights varied from small chandeliers to built-in circular ones in the ceiling. There were two floors above us for seating and from what I could see, they were completely full.

There he was again! Edward, the head of the police

standing at the front of the first floor, watching like a hawk. What was he doing here? I doubted it was to watch the show.

'So you've never been to see a show before?' Kayson asked, popping into my line of sight. I darted around, but once again the hawk-like man had disappeared. Who was he, Jason Bourne?

I shook my head, turning my attention back to Kayson.

'Never. I mean, Jess made me watch the movie *Hairspray* one time, but that was about it.'

He seemed surprised at this.

'Seriously? Jessica dragged a bunch of us to see one.'

At that, I paused: Kayson told me they were acquaintances. If Jessica dragged him and a group of friends to a show, didn't that make them more than just two people who shared a couple of classes?

'I thought you barely knew each other?' I asked.

Kayson's mouth popped open, ready to blurt out an explanation, but then all of a sudden it seemed he decided not to. Just like earlier, I could practically see the cogs turning behind his eyes. What wasn't he telling me?

'Well, that was at the start of the year when we all met.' His expression had morphed into something completely unreadable. 'They had a mixer for all the scholarships.'

A mixer? Uh huh . . .

'So where you from?' I asked changing the subject completely, since I knew he wasn't going to give me a straight answer.

Kayson blew out a breath. 'Well I was born in Seoul, in South Korea, but my dad and I moved here when I was two.'

'Is your mum still in Seoul?' I asked, but he only nodded in return. 'Have you ever been back?'

'Can we talk about something else?' he asked, running a hand through his hair.

'Yeah, sure.' Parents must be a touchy subject. 'What did you get into the Academy for?'

At this he burst out laughing.

'You'll never believe me.'

'What? Are you a mechanic or an athletics scholar?'

'Mathematics,' he said simply.

I'm going to frank, the guy sitting beside me did not make

any sense. One minute he was a confident bad boy, then a mathematics scholar. Not that they couldn't be smart, it was just really uncommon, especially in my high school.

'What? Is it really that bad?' Kayson asked, knocking me from my thoughts.

'No!' I exclaimed, throwing my hands out, but soon become very aware that we were sitting in a row full of people, amongst a crowd of other people who probably thought I was crazy.

Kayson chuckled, but didn't say anything in return, and suddenly I felt the stares of at least ten people on the back of my head. I almost caved in on myself, but then another stare met my eyes and this one, I didn't object to.

'You know, I've never had a girl yell at me that maths isn't lame.' His arm now lying loosely on the back of my seat.

'Sorry,' I said, in a voice like a mouse. 'I didn't mean to yell, it's just you don't seem –'

'What?' he asked, a charming smile replacing his grin.

'The kind of guy who would like maths.'

'Oh sweetheart, I do a lot of things that would surprise

you.'

I was about to ask what he meant when the gentleman next to him started up a conversation. It seemed like a polite and harmless exchange so I looked away, fiddling with my nails. They needed a serious re-painting, the purple polish was a month old at least.

As I left Kayson to his conversation with the stranger I couldn't help but wonder about earlier: what business did Scotland Yard have here? They don't turn up for the fun of it. Were they putting in new terrorism procedures? If they were I was writing to my MP! There was no need for more, we already had to take a test every month.

Then there was Kayson's friend Luca, he said I wasn't a part of something, maybe he meant the Academy. Then he asked for someone called Blackbird – I'd never heard of it before but it didn't sound like a common term.

Suddenly Kayson shoved a programme in my lap. 'The guy said you could have it if you want, it has all the actors inside.'

I looked past him to the man in question, but his back was turned. Huh, that was nice of him.

Kayson fiddled with his ear for a second but I'd already started to flick through pages. Halfway through, I stopped. There was a head shot of Jessica, she was in the ensemble – but the name underneath was the reason I stopped to check because it wasn't hers, it was someone called Jemma Robertson.

'That can't be right.'

'What?' Kayson leaned in closer to my side, and my shoulders caved in on themselves as he moved in, the feeling in my stomach rising again.

'Jessica's in the show but she's under the wrong name.'

'Must be a typo or something,' he said dismissively.

'She didn't even say she was doing this.'

'Maybe she didn't think you'd be interested.'

Was that what was happening? Did Jessica think because of our distance that I wasn't interested in her life anymore? I knew friendship was a two-way street, had I not met her halfway? Maybe the other week she needed space. Jessica looked stressed, and then I went barging in – was I too overbearing?

Before I could dwell on the thought any longer the lights dimmed and the stage lit up with a single spotlight. As the show started and someone walked out I felt Kayson inch closer, his arm still resting behind me but shyly, and slowly I leaned into it.

I'd always pictured something like this happening, except at the cinema, but I didn't care! Any doubts fell from my mind as I felt Kayson's arm around me. He was wearing some kind of cologne, something spicy that wasn't familiar. Something new.

Dancers flooded onto the stage as the music picked up. I glanced over at Kayson – the lights reflected on his face, but the shadows from behind carved out his cheekbones and jawline, his features sharply defined. It was only then that I caught sight of three almost scratch like scars on his temple, as if from a knife. However I pushed the thought away quickly, probably an accident when he was younger or something. As I stared at him I realised just how close we were, my face inches away from his. For a first date it was a little fast-paced, but I didn't mind, his embrace was warm and inviting. Perhaps I was following my gut wrong, maybe my gut was telling me there was so much more about Kayson I needed to uncover.

I was so distracted by the man beside me I didn't even see that Jessica had taken centre stage. Now I wasn't savvy when it came to the theatre, but I didn't know that ensemble members didn't take the spotlight, singing on their own while everyone danced about them.

Kayson also picked this up.

'I thought you said she was in the ensemble?' he whispered softly in my ear.

'That's what it said.'

Kayson turned away, confused for a moment, before the look left his face and he relaxed again.

As soon as Jessica started to sing I knew she'd spotted me because she threw a glance my way – but then I realised, the frosty glare wasn't meant for me, it was for Kayson. He shifted uncomfortably, fiddling with the crease in his jeans. Maybe they were more than acquaintances.

As I watched Jessica perform it felt as if we were back in my bedroom, the same spark alight in her eyes as she sang. She always had the confidence I lacked and the beauty I . . .

Suddenly the warmth disappeared from my back and Kayson leaned closer to whisper in my ear.

'I'll be back in a minute.' He stood up and strolled out of

the row and then up the aisle out of view. Must have needed the bathroom or something.

My attention was drawn right back to Jessica. She commanded the stage, her entire presence captivating the audience, and I had no doubt she would kill it. It was in her nature.

Kayson retuned about ten minutes later which left me questioning where he went in the first place, although the whole audience was silent and I didn't want to have another random outburst.

For the rest of the performance I didn't ask him any questions, even in the intermission or after it had finished. I stayed quiet because as the lights came up in the auditorium for the second time I was waiting for him to explain why he was wearing an earpiece covered in blood.

Perhaps being so close to someone on a first date wasn't the brightest idea.

* * *

As we walked out of the auditorium I kept to myself – I didn't know what to say. Kayson was wearing an earpiece! What was he a part of? Was that why Scotland Yard were here? Was Kayson involved in something illegal?

Kayson took my hand and my whole body went rigid. Now I knew he was lying about something. He cast me a confused look, but I didn't dare return anything, especially when I didn't know where the blood came from.

'Everything OK?' he asked, his voice breaking a little.

'Yeah, fine,' I answered.

We managed to make it to the lobby before Kayson pulled me down one of the corridors, the endless chatter that surrounded us now fading.

'OK, what is it?'

'Nothing, I said I was fine.'

'Yeah,' Kayson said with a knowing look, before letting his hand drop from mine. 'Isn't it a rule that when the girl in front of you goes rigid like a board, then proceeds to tell you she's fine, that it's safe to assume she in fact isn't?'

What was I supposed to say to that? This was Kayson Ashford, a bad boy on the outside and a genius within. Was *any* of that true? Maybe I was overreacting, but you don't just get an earpiece because the magical fairies gave you one. The blood was another thing – whose was it?

The fear I felt suddenly dissolved and curiosity rose in its place. There were so many questions I needed the answer to, but not here. Especially since the noise was beginning to die down. On the outside Kayson looked like a regular guy but now I knew, that was only the first layer to the man in front of me.

'Did I say something?'

Abruptly a loud voice echoed down the corridor.

'I don't fucking care!' I knew right away the voice belonged to Jess. 'Get it sorted.'

She stood at the other end of the corridor, still in the same flapper dress I'd seen her in moments ago – she looked incredible, but no amount of make-up could hide the harsh glare storming her face.

Kayson let out a breath, rolling his eyes as he called out to her.

'Oi! Winters, your friend is here to see you!'

At that Jessica turned to face us, the glare on her face fading as she looked at me in what I can only describe as relief.

She full on sprinted towards us, pushing past Kayson and pulled me into a crushing hug.

'You're OK ... ' Jessica trailed off, her voice soft and weak. Now I was beyond confused, what the hell was going on? Of course I was OK. 'Did you enjoy the show?'

'Uh yeah, you were great,' I mustered, trying to put the pieces together in my head.

'What? Was I pitchy?' she asked. 'Oh, I bet I was.'

'Oh, no – it's just in the programme your name was Jemma, and –'

'Oh yeah that, that's a misprint, they'll get it sorted.'

'But your name wasn't in it at all Jess, if it was a misprint wouldn't it be somewhere else?'

Jessica dismissed the idea pretty easily.

'You know how these things happen – besides, anyone who comes to see the show will know it's me.'

'Oh, is your mum coming?' Silence. 'She's not coming?'

'You know, work and all that,' she said, smiling softly.

I truly didn't understand anyone in front of me right now – Jessica was talking to me as if nothing had changed. Ever since she'd moved to that godforsaken school she'd given me the cold shoulder, what happened?

'I need help with clean-up back here!' an unfamiliar voice shouted from down the corridor. Both Kayson and Jessica turned, sharing a look before my friend sighed.

'I'll try to call you tonight,' Jessica said, taking my hand and squeezing it softly before running back down the corridor.

Well, better clear my schedule for the call that will never happen.

'Come on, let's get out of here,' Kayson said, but he didn't try to take my hand again.

Instead he walked ahead through the lobby and out the doors, where he stopped, waiting for me, but I couldn't stop staring at the blood spatter on the back of Jessica's tights as she turned the corner. I tried to convince myself that it was fake but in the end the blood was splattered too randomly and frankly looked too convincing. That meant both Jessica and Kayson knew about the blood, but neither of them said anything. Even the look they shared told me they were hiding something.

The rest of the night was spent at a bar nearby; we talked

for an hour or so before I decided to go home. I had the feeling Kayson picked up on my sudden distance, and I noted that he'd ditched the earpiece. I didn't mention what I saw, not when it could be passed off as trivial or my imagination.

Kayson walked me back to the train station, making me promise to text him when I got home, which I did. After which, he sent another text to apologise for whatever he'd done but I didn't reply.

When I stepped back into the house it was quiet, only two lights were on.

After slipping off my shoes and hanging my coat I walked into the living room, but the sight there wasn't a common one. My mum was staring at her laptop, a hand over her mouth, and her expression was one of sheer horror.

'Mum?'

She whipped around, sliding the laptop screen out of view.

'Yes?' she said, her whole face like a deer caught in the headlights.

'What were you watching?' Hurrying over to the table, I made a grab for the laptop, but my mum pushed the lid down.

'Mum?'

'It's nothing, work stuff.'

I was already being lied to by two people; I didn't need another. My mum was a journalist and that came with its own horror stories, but I'd never seen her react like this. Ever. I pulled back, crossing my arms over my chest and standing as tall as I could. I wasn't moving.

The pair of us stared each other down for five minutes, it seemed, before mum broke with a sigh, pushing away straggles of hair from her face.

'What I'm about to show you, you cannot tell anyone.'

'Of course.' That was how it rolled with her job.

'I'm serious. You can't tell your father, your friends, no one. You understand?'

From my mum's grave tone I didn't know what this could possibly be. Was it a terrorist making threats? Those were usually published on the news first, not my mum's laptop. Could it be something to do with the explosion at the bank?

I nodded slowly – if there was one thing I was good at, it was keeping secrets. Mum pulled the laptop back around so I could see.

From the look of it, the video was alright quality, a bit blurry but good enough to make out the two figures. The Head of Scotland Yard pinning Jessica against the wall by her neck, strangling her. Even though I didn't want to look, I couldn't pull myself away.

'That's –'

'Edward MacDonald, The Head of Scotland Yard strangling a student.' My mum cut me off. 'Yes, it is. I always knew there was something off about him.'

'Mum how did you even find this? That was tonight, it has to be. I saw Jessica, she was wearing that on stage.'

'How exactly did you see Jess? Weren't you out with Katie?'

'Yeah, about that . . . I lied.'

'Excuse me?'

Not bothering to answer my mother since it would result in a lecture rather than a congratulations on achieving a social life, I listened more closely to the computer's audio, hearing the faint sound of music playing in the background.

SLATE RETRIBUTION

'Can you turn it up?'

Mum clicked a button and the volume boomed. I recognised the song, but I didn't know the title – it had been on after the first one Jessica performed in. That's when it must have happened. Why he was strangling Jess was beyond understanding. He surely couldn't just be there to do that, that's not what the police do.

'Mum, seriously, where did this come from?'

'I got the clip in an email, I recorded it just in case it was something. This is something,' she said, shaking her head in disgust.

Just then a ping sounded, making the pair of us jump. My mum clicked out of the video back onto her emails, where a new one sat waiting to be opened. There was no subject and the email account was just a bunch of random letters and numbers. From my mother's rapid clicking to open the thing, I could tell this was probably from the same person who sent the video, but this time, instead of a video clip there was a link.

A new page opened. The film was the same quality as before but this time it was dark, and extremely blurry at the beginning, like the camera was being moved around.

'This is live,' Mum said.

Soon the view cleared and light flooded the image. The camera was pointed down a large corridor, the walls a stony grey, the floor concrete, the light coming from above. As some of the answers I craved earlier appeared in front of me, I no longer wanted to know them.

Three people stood in a line facing the wall and all of them I knew. Jessica was first, and then her two friends from the coffee shop, but now I could see Jessica had bruising around her neck. What the hell was happening?

'Aspin and Winters, get on your fucking knees!' a brutal voice barked as a man came into view. It was Edward MacDonald, the same man who was at the theatre, the same man who assaulted Jess.

The pair of them knelt down leaving the girl with raven hair standing in the middle, hands clasped in front and head held high.

'Chan, care to explain what the fuck happened?' the man asked. 'You were a Carrier tonight and somehow a fucking terrorist managed to get past you, in your fucking area.'

As he spoke I felt like I couldn't breathe – was that what happened backstage while the performance was going on? Terrorism?

'I don't know, I didn't see him.'

'You should have fucking seen him!' the man yelled; he was so close his spit landed on her face.

The girl didn't flinch, she didn't move at all. I couldn't believe my eyes. What I didn't understand was how this man's job included yelling at a bunch of students from a private school. Even so, they all seemed to know what he was talking about. Was that why Jessica looked so relieved to see me?

The man sighed tiredly and swatted his hand in the air.

'Take off your clothes.'

'What?' the girl asked, horrified. 'You're joking, no, I'm not –'

'Chan, take off your clothes.'

'Sir, with all respect –' Jessica tried, but the man cut her off.

'What did I say about questioning my authority?' Then he

knelt in front of Jessica, who flinched as he took her jaw, gripping it tightly before he slapped her across the face. 'What did I say?'

'Not to.' Jessica said shakily, although there was a fear alive in her face that I had never seen before; that I had never seen on another human being.

Her entire body shook for a couple of seconds but she didn't look away from the man, even as he stood up and walked out of frame.

'Get her fucking clothes off,' he said.

Two new figures came into view, both male, but their faces were turned away from the camera as one pinned the girl to the ground while the other ripped off her clothes. We watched her writhe and scream as her top was removed, then her leggings, then her shoes and socks. Her screams of protest echoed through the speakers, but neither my mum nor I moved to turn it down.

'I want you to feel vulnerable, Chan, like we were tonight because of you. Your actions meant there was a suicide bomber in the theatre. Now that wasn't very smart, was it?'

'Leave her with a bra for Christ's sake!' I heard Jessica yell, but it wasn't met with a response.

The girl whose second name was Chan now lay on the floor completely naked. Shivering.

'I asked you to take your clothes off Chan, no one was going to do anything to you. Why can't you do as you're fucking told?' the man asked. 'You do your job right or you don't have a place at the Academy, do you hear me?'

Silence. The girl quivered and shook from the cold; she shifted to a kneeling position but didn't answer as she glared at the man. Her absent reply only provoked him further.

'Find Eve Smith, she was in the ensemble tonight.' The man addressed someone behind him. 'Shoot her.'

'No!'

'Then answer the question, do you understand?' the man barked. 'Because believe me, your smart mouth is going to cost someone's life.'

'Yes! Yes I fucking understand, just don't hurt her!' the girl shouted.

Suddenly the video cut out and it took us back to my mum's inbox, the email still sitting there at the top.

I didn't know what to say, what could I? Mum sat back in

her chair rubbing her slender fingers over her face. From those videos it was clear that the Academy wasn't some prestigious school. It dealt with terrorists.

'Mum –'

'Don't,' she cut me off sharply. 'There is a reason someone would send that live link.'

'Yeah, cause it's insane.'

'Did Jessica tell you what was going on? Did she tell you this happened?'

'No.'

'Then it was because she couldn't. These girls must have been subjected to God knows what to keep them quiet about this. She didn't tell you because if she did . . . I think what we watched was just the tip of the iceberg.'

That was when I blurted everything out about what happened this evening: the earpiece, Kayson's friend, the blood on Jessica's tights, anything I could think of. She would know what to do, this was what she did for a living. Surprisingly, my mum didn't seem shocked when I told her.

With a solemn sigh she spoke.

'There have been rumours about the Reign Academy ever since it was set up fourteen years ago,' she said. 'Rumours of misconduct and abuse from the faculty. It was never proven and any allegations were soon withdrawn, or something happened to them. It was one of the reasons I didn't want you applying to that school.'

Young Student Killed in a Hit and Run.

'You knew this was happening?' I asked. 'So when I told you Jessica was going, you didn't think to say anything?'

'I didn't think there was any truth to the rumours – the allegations were withdrawn, they claimed it was all a prank. If it's Scotland Yard running the show then it would be easy to bury small leaks like that.'

'Do you recognise anyone else in the video?'

'No. Only him. I suspect Edward McDonald is a fake name he uses. Then there's Jessica and I'm assuming those are her friends.'

'Yeah, they were at the café when I bumped into them,' I told her.

I couldn't wrap my head around this – it didn't seem

logical or even possible. I thought the police were meant to be on our side.

Then a thought came to me – a really stupid, really crazy idea.

'Kayson goes to the Academy.'

'The secret date guy who you lied to me about?'

'Yeah him, he knows all about this. If I show him that video then . . . '

'Then what?'

'I can blackmail him.'

'To do what?'

'To get me inside the Academy.'

SLATE RETRIBUTION

CHAPTER 8

Esoteric

Private; secrete; confidential; belonging to a select few.

NAOMI JADE

I didn't want to believe what I'd seen the night before. Part of me wanted to forget everything, but I knew deep down I couldn't ignore it. Those videos explained everything: why Jess had been so cold, why she never returned any of my calls, why there was blood on the back of her tights. The Reign Academy was an institution that dealt with terrorist threats. The abuse was another matter entirely.

The way Jessica knelt down without question, the way she didn't react when he slapped her, told me this wasn't a new thing. Was that how so-called Edward stopped them from talking? The man mentioned that they didn't have a place at the Academy if

SLATE RETRIBUTION

they didn't comply – would the Chan girl end up in the news as just another hit and run? Today, I'd get those answers.

After a lot of consideration and staring at the blank ceiling for a couple of hours last night, I'd come to the conclusion that this was an incredibly stupid idea. My mum didn't fully agree with the plan and tried to turn me away from it but she soon gave up. I was eighteen, an adult in grand scheme of things. Although we both agreed that if we were to take this further, we needed someone on the inside. That someone being me.

Much to my mother's protest, this morning I was kitted out with a microphone taped under my shirt that would record any audio, a set of instructions in case of an emergency and my mum's old video phone from the early 2000s. If I saw anything that could be used as evidence, I had to film it. That was the bit that set my set my teeth on edge – how exactly would I do that without being obvious?

So as I sat in the noisy local pub, constantly checking my phone for any texts, my mind wandered to Kayson. He was my way into the Academy, it was the reason I'd asked to meet him again. Would he show up with bruises or fresh wounds?

The pub itself was busy since it was a Saturday afternoon – there weren't any tables left and most people were crowded around the bar. I'd picked a table near the back next to the window: there were a few chairs around me, but everyone else was either too drunk or too busy in their own conversations to pay me any attention. I needed to be forgettable, my mum told me. She said to pick an area that's filled with people – that way when I pulled out the video no one would hear.

I didn't even know what I should start with, I couldn't just come out with *'Hey Kayson, I know you're going to a school that deals with terrorists but also threatens to beat and shoot you.'*

Yeah, that would go down well.

When I brought it up I had to appear professional and factual because this wasn't a date – to be truthful I don't think I'd ever want to go out with this guy, considering what he's involved in. Could he be like that man on the video? Like those men who stripped a girl of her clothes just to humiliate her? Were they the end result for students of Reign? Was that what Kayson would become?

The clinking of glasses and clattering of plates put my

mind at ease; this was just a regular pub with no connection to terrorism or Reign. I was safe here. The occasional shouts from the bartenders and idle football chatter gave me something to focus on, as my knees bounced up and down. I needed to focus on something otherwise I'd never be able to do this.

For Reign to go untouched for so long they must have people in higher places than Scotland Yard; it must go way beyond that. What was I getting myself into? Were these two videos enough to cause a stir in the public eye?

I didn't have time to think anymore as I saw Kayson heading my way with a charming smile, which had to be his signature look. He wore a similar outfit to last night, but as he got closer, there was no sign of an earpiece or blood spatter.

'Bit random, gorgeous,' he said, leaning back in his chair. 'You know if you didn't like last night, you didn't need to bring me out for an apology drink.'

'It's not that.'

'Then what? Cause if this was meant to be a second date then you could have given me some warning, maybe let me take a shower after class.'

The guy in front of me had a glow about him but nothing to suggest he needed a shower as his spicy scent floated over. Kayson was looking me up and down, like he was analysing me, but I had to hold off as long as I could. Despite everything, he seemed like a genuine guy and I couldn't shake that feeling.

'You made it sound like an emergency on the phone.'

'It is,' I blurted, and at that Kayson leaned forward, full of concern.

'What? Did something happen at home?'

At that I didn't respond. Now I had to tell him – tell him I knew about the Academy. Sure I didn't know everything, but I knew enough and I had proof. With one final glance to Kayson and a shaky sigh I opened my phone, pulled up the video and turned it around so he could see.

As soon as Kayson saw the clip, all emotion dropped from his face. His eyes cast down to the table while his fingers drummed against it gently.

'Naomi,' he said, but this time the rich tone had vanished, replaced with something gritty and cold.

Everything I thought I knew about this guy changed like

the flip of a switch – he held himself higher, and flashes of the man from last night flickered over his face. His lips pressed into a thin line as his calculating eyes darted from me to the video. Suddenly his physique seemed larger, bearing down on me. What I theorised must be true: the man on the other side of the table wasn't the charming one that walked in moments ago. It's funny how certain words can shatter an entire persona.

I knew I couldn't trust anything he told me. I'd been so desperate to find the man of my dreams and then he just turned up out of the blue – of course it was too good to be true. Now Kayson sat there staring at me like a piece of meat, something to be toyed with, something *he* could control.

The sinking feeling of embarrassment and shame settled deep inside my stomach as I pulled back the phone and swiped to the next video. I had to keep my mind focused, the guy in front of me was a walking lie and I held the high ground. Hopefully.

'I know about the Academy. I know that it deals with terrorists and I know that last night . . . there was a bomb in the theatre.'

Suddenly Kayson grabbed my wrist with a bone-crunching

force. I let out a cry, trying to pull away, but he wouldn't let go.

'You have no idea what you're talking about.' Kayson's voice grew low as his stare burned through mine. 'You don't know what you're getting yourself into.'

No one around us took notice of what was happening, too absorbed in their own conversations.

'Let me go or those videos will be the least of your worries,' I told him adamantly.

I knew I had to stand my ground. I motioned around us to the poor unsuspecting bystanders, and his eyes followed. He hesitated for a second before the clamp of his hand released my wrist. I snatched it back and shoved the phone in my bag. His intense glare didn't stop – in fact he moved closer, his head jutting forward.

'The videos that you have in your possession aren't –'

'Are real,' I corrected him. 'Don't try to spin some story about how it's the drama department having a laugh. If I saw Jessica today, I know for a fact she'd have bruises on her neck.'

That's when he said something that sent a chill through my body.

'You're never going to see her again.'

'What?'

'You watched what happened – you seriously believe Jessica is going to come anywhere near you after last night?'

All the small insignificances of the Academy finally came together to create a perfect picture: the small intake of students, the Ivy League status and the secrecy of it all. Everything Jessica had done now made sense – she pushed me away because she didn't have a choice. I had to throw a spanner in the works. I needed answers.

'About that, are you and Jess part of a little murder club?'

'If this is about when I left, I told you I went to the bathroom.'

'So you both just happened to have blood on you?' I said, courage finding me for a moment as *I* leaned forward.

Kayson let out a bitter laugh, shaking his head.

'You saw that, did you? Well, you're not a complete idiot.'

'You're unbelievable,' I scoffed.

'Come on,' Kayson said, his face now home to a winning grin. 'You actually went on a date not knowing me at all, practically fell into my lap when I brought up the theatre, loved the fact that I'm into maths. You were like a lost puppy.'

At that I paused. Of course I knew things about him, we talked for almost a week before the date. His favourite movie was *Die Hard*, I knew that! Was that all a lie?

'Why?' I asked, the embarrassment flushing through me once more. It was true, I had followed him blindly. I'd assumed so much: his parents, his personality.

Kayson sighed.

'Well, Jess told me you liked guys who wore leather, who were spontaneous.' He laughed. 'Honestly, I wasn't a fan of black jeans or combat boots before I started this, but now I've tried it I might stick to it.'

I felt utterly mortified. Jess had told him what kind of guy I liked then, he became that guy – of course she was right, but this! This was insane.

'She –'

'Jess asked me to look out for you, after that whole incident with your school friends,' he admitted. His intense glare started to fall but it didn't help me gauge him at all, as underneath,

SLATE RETRIBUTION

his face was completely unreadable. 'She was worried about you, and with everything going on, she didn't have time to babysit you.'

'So she sent a random guy to date me?' I exclaimed, horrified. Kayson tried to shush me, take my hand, but I pulled away. 'No, no – don't do that. You dressed up and took me on a date because Jessica felt sorry for me?'

'I wouldn't say sorry, more concerned.'

'So through all that concern you thought it was a great idea to take me to a theatre where there was a bomb?'

'She was right, you are sensitive.'

At that I shook my head. He'd called me sensitive, and basically stupid. I knew that I wasn't the smartest in the country but I wasn't stupid. Was I? No, no, I wasn't. Just because Kayson and Katie told me I was didn't mean it was true, but given the situation, did everyone think that?

No! I held the cards, I held the evidence in my own frickin hand and I could discredit the Head of Scotland Yard. I wasn't the brightest, but now this story was in my clutches, I wasn't letting it go. Sure, I couldn't figure out quadratic equations or chemistry, but I could chase a lead. I'd been chasing Jessica for the last couple years – I didn't see why I should stop now.

'Get me into Reign,' I blurted.

'What, are you crazy as well as stupid?'

I pushed past his insults, knowing the charm he gave off last night didn't count for anything. Now he was a stranger and his opinion of me didn't matter.

'If these videos go online, you seriously think they won't go viral?'

'What, with the amazing friends you already have, you counting on them to share it? Those videos will be taken down and there's nothing you can do about it.'

Then finally I let out smile, because I knew something he didn't.

'Oh, so you don't know that my mother is a journalist for one of Scotland's biggest newspapers?' I planted my feet firmly on the ridges of the bar stool, crossing my arms. 'Or that she has a blog with over three thousand followers? So sure, if you want to take the chance of the whole city reading about this, be my guest – but part of me thinks that you, along with your fucked-up teachers, wouldn't like that.'

I'd said my piece and now I had to deal with the man in front of me. Kayson himself looked stunned but he didn't say anything. If he thought I was stupid he could think again, asshole!

'Why are you defending them?' I asked, now I had the upper hand and could pose any question I wanted. 'What, do they beat you?'

'Just shut up.'

'Oh come on, no one can hear us,' I shook my head. 'Besides, we're going to be seeing each other a lot more now.'

'You're not going near Reign.'

'Yes I am. Otherwise, those videos go live and in print in tomorrow's papers.'

'I can take your phone – by the time you get home the videos will be found and deleted, all recordings, the lot,' Kayson tried, but I only felt the smirk grow on my face.

'You know if I don't text my mum by . . . ' I checked my watch, two-thirty, 'three o'clock, then everything will be released to the public.'

As Kayson's frustration rose I knew I had won this battle.

He didn't look like he knew what to say or, frankly, what to do. I bet this had never happened before.

'So I'll ask – no, I'll tell you. Get me into the Reign Academy.'

* * *

Kayson gave me a lengthy lecture before we even took a step out the pub because he felt the need to lay down the rules: keep my head down, don't speak even if spoken to, and if anyone asked I was overseeing an issue on behalf of Thames House.

I'm sure impersonating a government official was illegal but since I was breaking into a secret institute I pushed that though to the back of my mind. That and I didn't want to ask any more questions right now. Kayson was angry – he barely looked me in the eye as we left, concentrating on the small pay-as-you-go phone in his hand. That's the explanation for all the 'new phone number' texts from Jessica over the years then. What would the faculty do to him if they found out he'd helped me break in?

He told me he didn't have his own car, because anything involving the outside world, the Academy drove them to. Apparently Kayson did have his licence and, I quote, 'would put

SLATE RETRIBUTION

Ethan Hunt to shame'.

While we waited for the car to arrive I texted my mum to let her know everything was going to plan. She didn't respond, so I assumed she was busy with work. Bet her boss wouldn't be a fan of sending me undercover to sniff out a story.

The wind became harsh and bitter as Kayson and I stood on the street but as I wrapped my arms around my torso, I felt the wire shift underneath my shirt. I was worried that anything recorded would be muffled, but I didn't try to shift it – if Kayson saw I was wearing a wire there was no way he'd take me in.

'You're sure about this?' he asked me, jamming his fingers into his pocket.

'Of course I am. No one deserves what they do to you,' I said. 'No matter how much of an ass you are.' I glanced his way but he didn't return it.

He remained silent as a long, sleek black car pulled up, exactly like the one I'd seen before. But now it was up close, I could see the front and back windows were tinted so even the driver remained a mystery. Kayson opened the door and got in without so much as a word to me, before I climbed in after him.

Just as I did, I noticed that passers-by had started to stare, some muttering under their breaths. I wanted to tell them to piss off, since none of them knew the first thing that was going on. How getting collected was probably the opposite of luxury.

The interior, however, screamed luxury: plush leather seats with a silver R etched into them, little compartments along one side, presumably filled with various things, and the other side stocked with water bottles and power outlets. You could legit straighten your hair in here. There was a partition separating us from the driver, so hopefully he couldn't hear what we were saying. This school must have funding in the millions to afford all of this.

'Could you look any more surprised?' Kayson asked condescendingly as he sat back, not bothering to put his seat belt on, tucking something from his pocket under the seat. He reached into the compartment beside him, pulling out sunglasses and tossing them to me. 'Put those on.'

They were simple and black, nothing special at all, but as I gazed over to the compartment he pulled them from, more than five pairs were stashed in there.

'Why?' I asked, but didn't get an answer.

Kayson reached into another compartment and pulled out what looked like an ID badge with a silver clip. He contemplated it for a moment before chucking it in my lap without a second glance.

'If anyone asks to see your ID you're going by the name of Marsha Evans – you're here from Thames House and have been instructed to speak to no one.' As he spoke the car started moving, and that's when the unreadable face became extremely readable: nerves and anxiety shooting from every crack and crevice of his body.

'Why do you keep fake IDs in here?'

'Emergencies.'

His palms rubbed together as he shifted in his seat, looking anywhere but me, his eyes cast firmly out the window. I was right, this whole operation went above Scotland Yard – and, it seemed, the British Government. Maybe this was something behind the Government? Or worse, something ran through them. No it couldn't be, they were on our side, the whole reason we had a Government in the first place was to voice the concerns of the people, and they sure as hell wouldn't approve of this.

'You want me to pretend to be this Marsha person?' I asked.

'Yes, if you want to keep your head bullet-free,' he snapped. 'Do you even know what you've gotten yourself into? I'll answer that – no. Your friend asked me to protect you, to keep you safe, and now you're blackmailing me.'

Keep your head bullet-free. I knew these people were abusers, but would they shoot me on the spot? I had my theories – did they warrant my murder? I had a feeling I was about to step into a different world, where people were replaceable and murder took the moral high ground.

At that I paused and thought carefully before I spoke.

'If the videos went live what would happen?'

'Well, you –'

'Not me,' I interrupted, 'you, what would happen to you?'

Kayson finally looked my way, uncertainty clear on his face, then took in a breath, regaining composure and that unreadable expression.

'Why don't we just focus on keeping you alive?' he asked.

SLATE RETRIBUTION

Alive, was that was this was? I felt like I didn't know the meaning of the word. My life was mundane: I went to school, got good grades, planned to find a job that I liked and stay there. Was that living? Going from one thing to the next, A to B then C to D. Surely there had to be more – Jessica and Kayson were proof of that.

EMERY HALE

CHAPTER 9

Defiance

Open resistance; bold disobedience.

NAOMI JADE

The car ride took a little over an hour since there wasn't much traffic. Kayson remained quiet, constantly checking his phone, but for what reason he wouldn't say. I'd pinned the ID to my jacket and was repeating the fake name over in my head so I wouldn't forget it. The badge was a peculiar one: no photo, only a name, security number and a barcode at the bottom. I wondered if Marsha existed at all.

As the car slowed I turned my attention to window. Despite danger and uncertainty pressing down on me, I couldn't help but spectate in awe as we drove past the tall, black, pointed iron gates. The stretch of drive was lined on both sides with a cathedral of trees, the leaves draping over one another. Each side looked well-tended: the grass lush, the trees a rich green with vibrant flowers planted below, and there was a subtle crunch of gravel as we drove over it. If only this wasn't a cover.

I wanted to reach for the video phone, but since this was what you saw in the pictures online, I decided the audio would work best for now.

When we reached the end of the gravel drive the car turned to the right, giving me the perfect view to the Academy. It wasn't modern: the entire building was made of stone, mimicking the structure of a fortress, with a large looming tower to the left, complete with stained glass windows. The front of the building was prominent and dark, with monstrous mahogany doors. Below, a set of wide stone steps led down to the head of the drive, but the car didn't stop there.

I turned around in my seat to look out the back and saw another, separate building, a stark contrast to Dracula's castle. It was completely modern, with a full glass front and a thick grey roof. From what I could tell, it was filled with gym equipment. This place had its own gym? What next, a vineyard?

Suddenly, Kayson knelt down on the floor, sifting frantically through various compartments.

'What are you doing?' I asked.

I couldn't see what he was doing, but the way he stuffed tissues into his jeans pocket made my face screw up, what the hell? Was he a hoarder as well? I bet he was the person who nicked all the shampoo and towels from hotels.

'Seriously, what are you doing?'

Kayson shuffled further over and pulled open a drawer, taking out an ice pack, which he threw on the seat beside me.

'Put that in your bag.'

'Why?'

'Just do it.'

I rolled my eyes, shoving the stupid thing in my bag before zipping it shut. God he was an asshole. Do this, do that – how did anyone put up with him? Even his name, Kayson Ashford, sounded like a right bampot.

The car came to a halt and Kayson got out quickly, slamming the door behind him. Guess it was time to get out, then.

Once I stepped out the car I slid the sunglasses on, but

Kayson grabbed me roughly by the elbow, leading me down a small concrete path and around a corner until we stood at the tail end of what I assumed were the dorm houses. They too were made of stone, ivy weaving throughout, while windows lined the entire block, multiple houses joined together sharing nothing but the path in front.

'If I'm Marsha Evans I don't think you should be dragging me,' I said to Kayson, taking my elbow back.

This was it: I was going to see Jessica, and then get her the hell out of here. She would probably jump at the chance to escape.

'Well walk faster – the security cameras can't be allowed to pick you up,' he snapped, and that's when I clocked a camera to my left, mounted on a nearby tree.

I didn't have time to look for any others as Kayson grabbed my hand and dragged me to one of the doors, near the back. There was grass at the side of the door, almost like a small garden. A fairly new tree stood tall, but what caught my eye was the small red birdhouse lodged on one of the branches.

Kayson's pounding on the door turned my attention straight ahead: this was it. I was about to witness something no one on the outside had even glimpsed.

The door was mahogany like the main building, but it slipped open with ease. One of the girls from the café stood behind it; she was around five foot four with thin, dirty blonde hair, dull blue eyes, fair skin, a round face, and long lashes which honestly looked like they could lift her fragile figure off the ground.

'Quinn, let us in,' he said.

The girl didn't even look surprised when she spotted me hiding behind Kayson – in fact she opened the door wide, a smile brimming on her face.

'Quickly,' she said, moving aside.

Kayson charged ahead while I shuffled behind slowly, gripping my bag tightly as the door closed behind me.

'Hi.' Her voice was small and timid as I slid the glasses off my face. I glanced back to the closed door: now I was in the lion's den.

As the three of us stood in the hallway, I realised this place was better than my house: the wallpaper looked expensive, solid dark navy with gold accents, the ceilings pure white. To my left there were two rooms but both doors were closed, and to my right another two rooms – the one closest to me looked like a living room while the other was a kitchen. From what I could see the expensive taste continued throughout the house. Straight ahead was a set of stairs with a dark brown banister and carpet leading to a small landing, then continuing to the left with another set of stairs, but I couldn't see where those led.

'You brought Naomi?' Quinn asked, crossing her arms over her chest.

'Yeah, cause she fucking blackmailed me,' Kayson spat. 'Fucking bitch.'

I felt my nostrils flare and my eyes bulge at the remark – he did not just say that! Who the hell gave him the right?

'I'm sorry?' I asked.

'Hey!' a brash, thick voice called from the kitchen, followed by a patter of footsteps.

The girl I knew as Chan from the live video walked through, but this time I got a better view of her. She was much taller than I'd first thought, probably about five-eleven, with thick raven hair, brown eyes and warm tawny skin. She had a muscular build despite her narrow face, and her eyebrows were arched and pointed. A cheeky grin rested in her carved lips as she tugged down her red bralette.

'What have we told you about using big grown up words?' she asked, like she was talking to a child.

'Lily, piss off,' he sneered. 'Where's Jess?'

'Where do you think? After last night's fiasco she's been called in for rehearsals.'

Lily didn't see me for a couple of seconds but when she did, her grin fell and her stance became rigid. She took a couple of steps back but that didn't stop me from seeing every fine detail on her face: the major dark circles under her eyes, greasy hair, and the flaky dryness around her lips. She looked like she hadn't taken care of herself for weeks.

'You're fucking joking, get her out of here!' she yelled, startling me.

'What, you think I brought her here willingly? I'm not an idiot.'

'You know what they'll do – *your* team will be the one that goes down for this, not us!' she shouted.

It frightened me how quickly Lily changed, just like Kayson.

'Please, calm down,' Quinn tried, holding out her hands, but her friend didn't listen.

'Calm down? Calm down? I'm not going to fucking calm down! There is a civilian here in broad daylight!' Any courage that had grown within me was quickly squashed.

I'd only been here a minute or so but it was clear I was in a place I didn't belong. There was something in Lily's eyes that scared me though, something frantic, like she would shove me out into the cold without another thought.

Just then, one of the doors to the left was flung open and another girl walked out, dressed in jeans, a white top and long white sheer shirt with some fancy brand logo on the breast pocket, that complemented her olive skin. In contrast to Lily's worn boots, she sported insanely high sapphire-coloured heels which clicked on the floor as she clipped on a pair of pearl earrings.

'You know it's hard to prep for an interview when everyone is yelling,' she said, pulling out a gold cross necklace from her pocket – but she didn't get a chance to put it on as her eyes met mine. Strands of her immaculate rich brown hair falling in front of her face. What stood out though was the copper ring on her finger, the blue intricate detailing of a human heart engraved into it's centre.

'Grace, don't be mad.' Quinn took a step towards her friend but Grace only raised a finger, a testing look in her eyes.

'Since when was this part of the plan?' she asked, turning to Kayson. 'This wasn't part of the plan.'

It seemed like everyone was well aware of what Jessica had asked Kayson to do, which made my shoulders cave: more than two people were in on this. It was humiliating. Jessica thought I needed babysitting and told everyone here about it.

Grace wasn't shouting which surprised me considering these past few minutes had been nothing but a screaming match. Her tone was calmer but there was something underlying that told me she meant business.

'Oh, I know it fucking wasn't!' Kayson shouted. 'Why don't you ask Little Miss Perfect over there why we're here in the first place.'

Four heads turned my way and suddenly I felt incredibly

small; the walls moving towards me and the ceiling bearing down. Perhaps this wasn't a good idea, maybe I shouldn't have volunteered. I had no experience in the field, certainly not as a journalist. I hadn't thought this through at all – I knew I would get into Reign, but after that I had no plan except to grab Jess and run.

Stares burned into my head but I didn't dare look anyone in the eye.

SCRATCH

A sharp sting shot through my palm as my nail dug deeper, the pain distracting me. I needed to think – needed to come up with some sort of plan that wasn't just a grab and run.

'Well?' Grace asked, clearly irritated. 'What are you doing here?'

The last time I saw Grace she'd seemed like the one in charge, the one that had to stick to a schedule, the one that liked to plan. Even now that hadn't changed as she searched my eyes for an answer. I guess what Edward did last night had set everyone on edge.

'I have –'

That's when thundering footsteps barrelled down the

stairs, and Jessica appeared.

She looked tired, her hair tied back – and then I saw the purple blotches on her neck, clear as day. Along with the dull brown bruise marking her cheek. Oh my God.

'Can you all resolve this scream-fest by the time I get back?'

But when she saw me it was like her brain stopped, unable to process what was in front of her. 'What in the holy fuck are you doing here?'

Quinn was overwrought with panic as she turned between us all.

'I thought you'd already left.'

Jessica ignored her.

'How did you get in?'

'I brought her,' Kayson admitted.

'What?'

'In a pickup car.'

'In a – Kayson, you've fucking lost it!'

'It's her fault!'

As the yelling went on I glanced at Lily and Grace: they

were throwing dagger-like glares at Kayson, but part of me feared they'd do the same to me. Judging from the last couple of minutes, none of them wanted me here.

'There are microphones in the car! They could have been recording!'

'They weren't, I made sure of it!'

'Oh and how did you do that?' Jessica asked. 'You can't even change a lightbulb.'

Suddenly, everyone joined in: Lily started screaming profanities at Kayson while Grace yelled at Jess. What I didn't expect was Quinn – the quietest and most timid-looking of all – to yell, her face all scrunched up.

'It was me!' her voice squeaked. 'I'm the reason she's here.'

The screaming match came to a halt at Quinn's confession and, everyone, including me, looked at her in confusion. What was she talking about?

'Yeah, alright Quinn,' Jessica said dismissively, but Quinn protested.

'I sent her mum the videos!' This time her voice echoed

with power.

Then she shifted, mirroring my own position: hands wrapped tightly around her torso, head bowed and leg bouncing from nerves.

Jessica's face contorted into something I didn't recognise – a look of sheer authority.

'Videos?' Jessica stared down at the girls below, hands gripping the banister, her knuckles pure white.

Now she'd admitted the truth Quinn looked a little scared, and swallowed hard before she spoke again.

'Yes, two of them. One recorded and one t-that was live,' she stuttered.

Jessica blew out a breath, stress evident. As she turned her face to the ceiling, she looked like she was praying for strength.

'Quinn, get in the kitchen.'

'But –'

'Quinn, Ashford, get in the kitchen,' she ordered. 'Lily and Grace, keep Naomi away from the windows, we don't need any of the juniors grassing on us.' With that, Jessica barged past Quinn, nearly knocking her over. 'Now!' she yelled.

Suddenly everyone burst into action. Quinn walked hurriedly into the kitchen, Kayson marching after her. Grace headed to the room she had come out of and held the door open as Lily ushered me through, her hand gripping my shoulder.

The room was small, but it had a TV, and couch covered in flash cards and highlighters. Guess she really was prepping for an interview.

Grace closed the door behind us and stood by it, examining me up and down just like Kayson had done earlier, and shook her head.

'Quinn is almost as bad as you.'

As she spoke, Lily started to pace.

'Did you have any idea what you were doing when you came here?' she asked, but there wasn't anger in her voice anymore, it was fear. 'Any idea of what this might mean for us?'

I swallowed.

'I saw what they did to you last night, I'm sorry.'

'Sorry for what?' Lily asked sceptically. 'Sorry for seeing it, or sorry for coming here?'

'Sorry that no one stopped them.' At that she paused and I

took cautious steps towards her. 'This is abuse.'

'Oh look at Sherlock Holmes over here,' she scoffed defensively.

I understood why no one spoke out – I mean, it was basic psychology – but now I had an out, for all of them maybe.

'My mum is a journalist with the *Scottish Times*, and she also has an online following. When the videos are released and people see what's going on in this place, the Government will shut it down.'

'Harkness has been getting away with this for years.' That must be the man from the video's real name. Lily seemed to contemplate what I'd said, running a hand through her hair, but then I realised she was no longer looking at me but Grace.

'I assume you care about your mother?' Grace sked, her face stern.

'Yes.'

'I assume you know, or have theories about what will happen to you and your mother, and to us?'

Why was she asking me all these questions? Sure I had my theories – it was hard not to speculate given what I'd seen. Last night my mind had spiralled to a dark place, and I'd thought the unthinkable, but a small part of me knew I didn't go deep enough. I was scared to think what I might discover here, but I had to know the truth.

'Yes,' I answered.

'Then you know that by coming here you put your life at risk and your mother's. At her work there's a man called Richard Douglas. He's the boss.'

My eyes widened, how did Grace know that? I only knew of him as Richard – apparently he was charismatic, charming and thoughtful. That's what my mum said, anyway. Did he work for the Academy? No, he couldn't, that wasn't possible.

Grace pursed her lips. 'His real name is Craig Thompson,' she said. 'He's a teacher here.'

Grace was close now, so close that I felt the warmth of her breath hit my face as her fingertips brushed mine. How could the Academy have people in so many different places? It didn't make sense: they had Scotland Yard and the newspaper, how had this never come up? Had no one ever dared to look this far into the Academy? How many palms had they greased?

'Any story put forward has to be approved by him and, considering the content I assume is on those videos, they'll mysteriously disappear never to be seen again. You've had a wasted trip,' Grace told me knowingly, but I shook my head.

'My mum has copies, she isn't going to let this go,' I told her adamantly. 'What they do to you isn't right.'

'They nearly put a bullet in someone's head last night. Do you seriously think that if your mother gets too loud, she won't end up the same way?'

I froze. They wouldn't do that – they couldn't. I wouldn't let them.

'A bullet in her head,' she continued, 'a car crash, or maybe one day she just goes for a drive and never comes back.'

Anger clenched my jaw as I inched closer, shaking my head.

'They won't get near her.'

I didn't even notice Lily push me back until my heel caught on the rug. She stood between us, her hands up so we couldn't get any closer.

'Alright fire thong, simmer down.' She glanced to me,

then back at Grace. 'Maybe we should wait until Jess is done before we start dishing out the impending doom and gloom?' Just like that, Lily's whole attitude had changed. Maybe what I'd said interested her.

'I have evidence that the school is corrupt – if everyone here testifies in court then there's no way they could dismiss it,' I tried.

Grace just laughed in my face. 'Yeah, if we all come together nothing can stop us,' she mocked. 'Naomi, this isn't a movie, we are all replaceable. You know how many people apply each year. If four of us are dismissed, they'll just bring in another four and the process will start all over again.'

I shook my head. 'No they won't, I'll make sure we get in front of a judge that isn't part of this.'

'You have the Academy's lawyers, which means whatever lawyer you choose to represent our case will be corrupt.'

'How do you know that?' I bit back.

'Because that's the way it always is!' she shouted, exasperated, a twang coming through her voice. 'When are you going to get it? The Government won't do anything because they endorse this place. The Academy *is* the Government!'

That was when Lily piped up. 'What about the Queen?'

'What?' Grace asked, as though the idea was ludicrous. 'The Queen?'

'Yeah, I mean if Naomi gets those videos to the Queen and she sees them, then something has to happen.'

Grace stuttered.

'An audience with the – no, no, Lily, this isn't happening. No one is seeing the Queen because nothing is changing.'

'Oh come on, Grace, your parents could swing something – they have high up connections with Italy.'

'That's because they're Italian,' she replied flatly.

'Exactly, nudge a few people and we can see Queenie.'

'You seriously did not just call the Queen of the United Kingdom and Northern Ireland and Head of the Commonwealth Queenie.'

'Well, I wouldn't say it to her face, I'd want to get to know her first.'

I stood there bewildered as the pair talked. I'd never thought I'd meet the Queen in my life but from the way Lily spoke, it was like we'd just pop down on a Friday afternoon for tea and a biscuit.

Then door to the room opened and Quinn peeped in, her eyes bloodshot.

'You've to come through to the kitchen,' she sniffled, tugging at the collar of her shirt. 'All of you.'

Had Quinn been crying? What had Kayson and Jessica said that we couldn't hear? Grace didn't seem to think too much of it – she grabbed a tissue from a box on the side, handed it to her, then walked out.

'Are you OK?' I asked, reaching for her arm. 'What did they say?'

Quinn sniffled, shaking her head. A couple tears fell but she wiped them away with the tissue, then pulled back motioning behind her.

'We better, uh ... Jess wants us in the kitchen.' Quinn practically power walked across the hall. I turned to Lily, confused as hell.

'What was that about?'

Lily shrugged her shoulders and sighed. 'Quinn just

doesn't like arguments, long story.'

I took in a breath – I'd get back to the subject of Quinn once this so-called meeting was over. Right now I needed to focus on getting my point across: I had evidence, and no matter where the Academy had people, I would get this place shut down. Maybe not today – there had to be planning, and a trial could go on for months – but now was the time to start. The fact that they'd all gone along with this for so long baffled me; even at the beginning, couldn't anyone see the red flags? I had to make sure these videos went viral or God knows what would happen next.

***

With caution and trepidation I entered the kitchen. It was long and narrow, the walls painted a pale green, the floors tiled black and white. It was colder than the other room, and not just in temperature. Jessica stood at the far end, arms crossed and face furious. Quinn leaned against the counter, her head bowed as she held the tissue to her mouth, muffling her sobs. What the hell had they said to her? Surely Jessica couldn't have been that mad? There was a table to my right where Kayson had positioned himself, Grace sitting opposite, typing away at a laptop. But what

I took notice of was the blotchy redness around Kayson's nose and the dripping blood below.

He held one of the crinkled tissues he'd shoved in his pocket against it tightly.

'Give me the ice pack,' he demanded.

I reached into my bag, grabbed the now-soaked ice pack and threw it on the table. I wasn't going to hand it to him, he couldn't have cared less when I was in the car, why should I wait on him hand and foot? Probably because he was bleeding. Kayson didn't seem to notice my grievances as he picked it up and rested it against his nose. I didn't know for certain who'd punched him, but I had a pretty good guess. My eyes flitted over to Jessica for a moment; I glanced at her knuckles and noticed they were now stained red. Well, that's that solved. Considering the abuse from the teachers I'd have thought there wouldn't be fights between the students, but I guess not. Why had she punched him?

When I opened my mouth to repeat my rehearsed statement, Jessica spoke.

'What you did today was reckless, unwarranted and dangerous. You put your parents' lives at risk, your own life and ours.'

'Jessica, I –'

'Shut up,' she growled. 'You have no idea what you've done.'

'Yes I do.' I didn't realise my voice was raised until Jessica's eyebrows shot up.

'No, you don't. You don't have the first fucking clue. If anyone saw you come in here – which undoubtedly they did – you, along with your videos, will never see the light of day again.'

I didn't want to believe her, but given what I'd seen so far, it wasn't exactly outside the realms of the possible. Was my mum in danger? Should I call her? Had we really not thought this through? Mum and I should have worked out a proper plan first. We were both so excited, so riled up with the thrill of the chase, that we just jumped in head first.

'Naomi, what part of *you could die* aren't you getting?'

I guess the thought hadn't vividly crossed my mind; I was so wrapped up in everything else that it hadn't occurred to me. I could die, she was right. I imagined it a little – I guessed they would probably make me kneel then put a bullet through my head.

I didn't understand why, but right now I was more concerned about what Jessica had planned for me instead of that supposed bullet.

As I grew closer to Jessica, the purple bruising around her neck became prominent; there was no way it could be fake.

'I'm sorry about what happened to you last night.'

Grace let out a laugh, looking up to me from her laptop.

'All this girl says is sorry.'

'I don't need your apology,' Jessica said, 'I need you to leave.'

This was insanity: Jessica expected me to leave without her? When I glanced back at Quinn, a notion pulled at my heart as she cried silently in the corner, her thin hair shuddering along with her. If she couldn't be strong then I would be. If Quinn was the one who sent the videos, then she had hope that they could change things.

'Well, I'm not going anywhere.' I brought my bag to my chest and started rifling through it for my phone, ready to call my mum so maybe she could try and reason with them, but suddenly Jessica had me pinned against the fridge, a hand down my bra.

'What the hell?'

I stumbled forward the moment she let go, but my whole body went still when I saw she held the black wire in her hand. Oh crap.

'You're wearing a wire.' Jessica stated, before she turned to Kayson. 'You didn't think to check her?'

'How the hell was I supposed to know?'

'Because she told you her mum was a journalist, did it not cross your mind? Oh wait, no, it didn't.' She threw the thing at my chest before she walked back to the other side of the kitchen, running a tired hand over her face 'Carol sent you to get intel on us.'

I couldn't hold it in any longer – all of them were just standing there when I was offering a chance to escape.

'We have footage that can get you out!' I exclaimed. 'I have a way out for all of you and you won't take it? If Quinn sent those videos then there had to be some hope that this could work!'

That was when Jessica stalked towards me, eyes sharp like an eagle's.

'You can either leave or Kayson will take you to the car.'

At that Kayson laughed.

'Oh yeah, Jess, like that's gonna happen.'

'Naomi, your life is in the balance right now and you want to endanger that?'

I sucked in a breath, standing toe to toe with Jess, and looked her dead in the eye.

'Yes.'

I understood my own life was at risk, as was my mum's, but we were willing to fight. I was going to do everything I could to stop this because Jessica was my friend. I was not going to stand by and watch this happen.

All of them may have been willing to, but I wasn't.

SLATE RETRIBUTION

CHAPTER 10

Oblivion

The state of being unaware or unconscious of what is happening.

JESSICA-GRACE WINTERS

The girl standing in front of me was *an utter lunatic*. Despite everything she knew, Naomi persisted, and I couldn't understand why. Christ, she didn't even know how this place worked but she'd created an escape plan anyway (and a stupid one at that). Sure she had video evidence, but that didn't mean anything when it came to the Academy.

They had the best lawyers, judges, police officers and politicians in their clutches, so making something like this disappear wouldn't be difficult.

Although what would be was getting Naomi out of here.

I couldn't believe Kayson had brought her straight here, no

SLATE RETRIBUTION

phone call to ask for assistance or even a thought to check if she was wearing a wire. The guy was the ultimate pavement artist, but shove my best friend his way and all that training got thrown out the bloody window.

The situation in front of me was one I had actively tried to avoid but, as always, it was *inevitable*. I wanted to put Naomi in the nearest taxi and hope that nothing would come of it but that wasn't going to happen. The badge pinned to her jacket almost made me smile – at least Kayson had thought to give her a cover story. Now my main concern was getting this Marsha Evans to rediscover her sanity, but from the way Naomi held herself so tall and stubborn, I doubted the realisation would hit her any time soon.

I couldn't wrap my head around why we kept meeting. I'd tried to cut ties with her but every week there was a new text or missed phone call. Ever since I started at the Reign Academy three years ago, Naomi had been nothing but persistent. I couldn't blame her though; I would have done the same thing.

Even as I glared and everyone fixated on the back of her head, Naomi showed no signs of moving on the matter, she was so fucking stubborn.

If Quinn planned this whole thing she must have heard me mention that Carol was a journalist, broken out the camera, and sent it through a fake email account. That was the part that didn't make sense, since all contact with the outside world was monitored. How had she managed to get past the Academy's security?

Before I spoke, my arms fell at my side and I took on a softer tone. I couldn't bring myself to shout at Quinn anymore. There was no need to and besides, she looked like a kicked kitten.

'Quinn, how did you send the email? All communications are monitored.'

She threw her head up in surprise, wiped her nose and sniffled. I knew arguing like we had, especially around Kayson, wasn't good for Quinn but I was so frustrated. What Naomi had done amounted to high treason.

'Well, you know we all register our laptops and phones to the main server when we arrive?' She asked, popping the tissue in the bin. 'When we went into town a couple of months back and I said I needed to go get something from the pharmacy.'

'Oh yeah, I remember that.' Lily said. 'I thought you were getting a pregnancy test.'

Quinn choked in surprise, her cheeks and ears flushing red as she spluttered a response.

'What? I'm a – no, I couldn't be getting a pregnancy test – Lily!'

'Quinn love, we all know you're a virgin and that your adorable tutoring sessions with the totally cute but sexy junior were completely platonic.' Lily said flatly.

'Lily!' Quinn exclaimed turning her back on the girl.

I rolled my eyes, biting back a yell.

'Anyway,' I butted in, trying to draw the conversation back. Poor Naomi didn't know where to look as she fiddled with her fingers.

But Lily thought this was the perfect time to give Quinn a pep talk.

'Love, I know you're eighteen but being a virgin isn't a bad thing.'

'Why – why are we talking about this?' Kayson asked, his voice muffled from the ice pack. 'How did we go from Naomi blackmailing me to Quinn's sex life?'

'I don't have a sex life!' she squealed.

'That's the whole concept of being a virgin,' he said bluntly.

'And it's not anything to be ashamed about,' Lily said, taking her friend's hand, but Quinn looked ready to run out the front door.

OK, that was it.

'Guys!' I shouted grabbing the attention back. 'We can all have a good chat about everyone's sex life later.'

'I won't be included in that,' Kayson said.

I turned to him, lips pressed into a thin line, eyes brimming with impatience – why was he adding to this? We weren't continuing this conversation! If his nose wasn't bleeding already. . .

'Right now, we need to worry about keeping Naomi hidden until we can securely get her out. I need to know what time the highest number of cars leaves: with that pass she could hop into one of the –'

'Jessica, I'm not leaving,' Naomi interrupted, and I sighed.

SLATE RETRIBUTION

This day wasn't going to get any easier was it? 'I'm staying.'

That was when Grace spoke up, her eyes as cold as ice.

'Oh yeah, that's fine, Naomi. It's not like you're implicating us or anything, putting *our* lives at risk.'

Naomi spun around to face her, exasperated.

'I'm trying to help you! If I stay here and gather more intel then at least my trip can be worthwhile.'

Students had spoken out before and gotten nowhere. All of us knew what the faculty were doing, it wasn't like we went into this blind, but we were given a promise: *The work you do will change the world for the better.* I had to believe that. Did I agree with the way the faculty went about it? No. Did I agree that every single aspect of our life had to be monitored? No. Did I think it was necessary to dismantle the organisations that threatened to destroy us? Yes. Now, anyone can say this was bullshit but it's what I believed. It's all I'd ever known. My mum was one of the donors for the Academy, it's not like I had a choice to think anything else.

'Quinn, circling back to the computer.' I quickly held up a hand. 'Not how you got it, since I assume you just bought it, the part where you got around the Academy server.'

She nodded.

'Well, you know my step-dad is part of the management team at the Hatched Bank? When I was passing it on outside duty, I hopped onto the Wi-Fi and piggybacked their server,' she said. 'It doesn't stretch back here so I just snuck in one day and took one of their mobile servers. You know, the black box things. Then I could use it here. I made an algorithm to hide it from the Academy's scanners.'

'Oh, so the asshole has his uses.' Lily muttered. 'Glad you finally found one.'

Quinn stayed quiet but I offered a sympathetic smile. Even though she'd done this without our knowledge, I knew she'd done it for a good reason. Quinn's mum was in a witness protection programme so my best guess was that she used it to speak to her. I knew I could get away with a text to Naomi here and there without pulling up any red flags but the loving relationship between Quinn and her mum needed more than a simple text.

'So you can call, email and text people through this private server of yours?' I asked.

Quinn shrugged. 'Yes, but I still keep the calls to once every three weeks, just to be safe. You never can tell with the new tech Thompson is developing.'

That was when Naomi perked up. 'You can upload videos through the server to the internet, right?"

Something changed on Quinn's face, hope glimmering through her.

'Yes, the Academy would still be able to find them but they wouldn't be able to pinpoint where they came from. When I sent it to your mum I sent it through the server not the internet, the only people that would be able to see it are me and maybe my dad if he ever learned how to fix his hard drive.'

That didn't give me much reassurance – given who was in the videos it wouldn't take a genius to figure out who posted them. I didn't know the ins and outs of the Reign Academy's tech department since that was Quinn's area, but I presumed the videos would raise some red flags the moment they went live. Besides, how many people would actually see them?

'That could work,' Lily said. 'If we used that fancy server thing we could get a good head start.'

Grace's face was stricken with anxiety, shaking her head rapidly.

'Are we seriously discussing this?' she asked. 'Two videos aren't going to do anything.'

'I agree.' Nodding in her direction. 'You would have to have way more evidence: videos, audio. Something irrefutable.'

Instead of hindering Naomi, this sparked a lightbulb behind her eyes. 'Well, that's all the more reason for me to stay, I should be able to gather loads of information –'

'Woah, hold up,' I cut her off sharply. 'It's bad enough I'm even considering letting you stay here more than ten minutes.'

Grace's chair scraped angrily against the tiled floor, like nails grinding against a chalkboard.

'Jessica, you can't seriously let her stay. Get her in a car and get her the hell out of here.'

I knew where Grace was coming from because I shared her concerns. If anyone found out a civilian had infiltrated one of the Government's best-kept secrets, I feared to imagine what would happen to her, to us. Had anything like this happened before?

Harkness had threatened to shoot Eve last night; if he

found Naomi here she'd see the same fate. As Team Lead I had to ensure the safety of my team but as a friend, was I glad to see her.

Naomi wanted to help us, she wanted to put her neck on the line. Even after all this time, she still cared. Not that it mattered cause I wasn't going to let her stay. The Academy can't just be dismantled. It's been going on since 2001, they've probably got protocols for rebels. The most prominent one being a bullet to the head.

But the alternative could set us free – God I was dramatic, but it was true. If these videos got out then there would be a trial at least, and if we were able to get a lawyer we could convince them to get us out of here.

'You're not actually considering this?' Grace asked.

Despite what I believed I knew this could be an out for all of us. If the videos were released, would this wretched dictatorship fall? Could it be that simple? Doubt riddled through my mind but there was something there, a soft spot of hope, that maybe this could work.

Then it hit me – we were monitored twenty-four seven. By the cameras Naomi just walked past.

'Did the cameras catch Naomi on the way in?' I asked urgently, and I kept my eyes firmly on Quinn as she darted over to the table and sat down next to Grace.

If anyone could tell me the answer it would be her.

She gently took the laptop and started to type: it was a good thing we still had a techie in our team. If someone had seen Naomi come in here then we had limited time to get her out. Marsha Evans didn't exist after all, and certainly didn't work at Thames House – the name was just in case they bumped into faculty and an idea that's been passed down through the students ever since we started. None of that mattered though if the cameras caught her.

The tapping of keys filled the silence for a few moments before Quinn, thankfully, shook her head.

'As far as I can tell there have been no motions made or flags raised,' she said, but she continued to type, briefly exchanging glances with Naomi. 'Your profile hasn't brought any questions up either; I don't think that the technicians have noticed anything.'

At that I let out a sigh of relief, my head falling back. Well there was one less thing to worry about – no one would crash through the front door any time soon.

Naomi walked over to the table and glanced at the screen, but her face screwed in confusion.

'How can you tell that?' she asked. 'It's just code.'

'Well yeah, it's the *tech department*,' Quinn told her. 'Basically, it just means you're in under the radar.'

Naomi smiled, but before I could say anything Grace stepped in front, blocking my view. She was the rational one in the group, but it sometimes led her to overthink everything. No one heard what she said as she leaned forward and whispered into Naomi's ear. It only lasted a brief moment, before Grace knocked into her shoulder and left the kitchen in a hurry. She'd never liked the idea that I kept in contact with Naomi, and now it was starting to show.

Last night she'd made me and Lily sit down and gave us both a full medical examination, given the relentless punishments over the past couple of weeks. I knew she cared, but sometimes her mother-hen tendencies clouded her judgement. In fact, she managed to squeeze supportive, judgmental and condescending into one facial expression. I'd never have admitted it but it scared me a little.

Naomi seemed visibly shaken, her eyes wide, head bowed and feet turning in on one another. What the hell had Grace said to her?

'Naomi?' I asked.

But unfortunately that had to wait as the familiar ringtone echoed through the kitchen. My eyes darted to Quinn as she scrambled for her phone, a wave of worry rippling through her. She answered it hurriedly.

'*Mamo, co się stało? Jesteś . . . Czekaj zwolnij nie rozumie cię . . .*' Quinn could switch between Polish and English like it was nothing – fortunately, it was one of the languages my brother had forced me to learn and one most of my team were fluent in. '*Ciemny cień?*' Quinn seemed puzzled.

A dark shadow? Oh this wasn't good.

Before I could give the order Lily darted over to the cabinet under the sink, rummaging around, pulling out a folded piece of paper. I knew Quinn's mum had been given code words to say if she thought she wasn't safe but I hadn't memorised them all so I certainly didn't know what this one meant.

Darting back, Lily slid into the seat beside Quinn, unfolding the piece of paper, while I walked past Naomi and over to the two girls to get a better look at the situation. Lily scanned the piece of paper for a moment before she spoke up.

'*Ciemny cień?*' she repeated and Quinn nodded.

Kayson and Naomi shot me expectant looks but I didn't explain because I knew the two of them would ask way too many questions and use up the time we don't have.

'A dark shadow means Quinn's mum thinks there's a man following her, could it be him?' Lily said looking up from the paper.

'No.' Quinn said firmly switching back to English. 'I checked – he's not left the country.' You could read Quinn like a children's book, her worries clear as day. '*Dlaczego nie ma ciebie w mieszkaniu? Mamo – w porządku, wróć do mieszkania jak najszybciej.*'

'Pull up the program, we need to trace this call,' I said to Lily. She quickly grabbed the laptop and started a program Quinn had developed.

Luckily it seemed to already be connected to Quinn's phone as it worked its magic. Then on the screen, the dot landed in the middle of Morocco, which was a good sign since that was where Quinn's mum was staying, but there was no live feed. We couldn't see the city, never mind the street.

'Załatwię to dobrze, ja z dziewczynami sprawdzimy czy nie jesteś śledzona... jeśli coś znajdziemy zadzwonię do ciebie przez zwykłe kanały... tez cię kocham.'

As soon as Quinn hung up she looked at the laptop but then shook her head, looking to me.

'I need satellite but only the control rooms –'

I cut her off before she continued.

'We're going now, there aren't any ops scheduled, grab the laptop and let's go.' She'd already lost a dad, I wasn't going to let her lose a mother too.

Everyone moved in unison: Quinn grabbed the laptop and ran like a bat out of hell to the hall, and I could hear the scuffle as she tried to put her shoes on. Lily grabbed her own phone then spoke to Kayson.

'You have connections in Morocco, right?' she asked.

'Your dad used to work there?'

I watched Kayson carefully as he dropped the ice pack and nodded, pulling out his own phone.

'Possibly. I might still have someone I can call.'

'We can use Quinn's server.'

'She doesn't know if it's secure enough,' Kayson said.

'Well then, we'll use the Academy's phones. It's not like they look at the bill every month,' Lily muttered. She stood up and Kayson followed, shoving Naomi out of his way.

God he could be such an dick.

He lingered at the door waiting for me. I needed to talk to him later about this, it was ridiculous. I shot an apologetic look towards Naomi, this was the last place I wanted to leave her, but she couldn't exactly come with us.

'What's happening?' Naomi asked, startled. She tried to follow but I held a hand up and she stopped dead.

Before I could speak however, Kayson spoke for me.

'Naomi, for once can you shut up and stop asking obvious questions. I would try to explain but I don't think you'd understand it,' he snapped. 'Now we need to go, so stop with the pestering.'

As Kayson took a couple of steps towards us, Naomi shrank back, the spark of curiosity diminished. I whipped around to face the man behind me, my patience breaking with every syllable he uttered.

'Apologise,' I demanded, crossing my arms.

'I'm not apologising, she doesn't know the first thing that's going on.'

I stood straighter, ready to actually break his nose this time, when Lily shouted through.

'We're going to need to move this to the control room now, the tracking is beginning to lag!'

'Kayson?' I didn't move, but neither did that prideful dick. How did I ever date the guy?

'You're not my Team Lead, I don't need to do anything,' he replied, an egotistical grin creeping its way up his face.

'Jessica, we need to go if we're to stay on top of this!' Grace shouted from the hall, as that sorry excuse for a man still didn't budge.

I glanced back at Naomi with a small smile; she didn't

need to be on the receiving end of my hatred of him.

'Stay away from the windows – my room is the last one on the right, have a look around,' I told her quickly.

Then I barged into Kayson's shoulder as I walked out of the kitchen, smiling a little as I heard his feet stumble back. He was twice my size but that didn't mean I couldn't take down his lanky ass.

Leaving Naomi here was not something I planned to do, but plans can change. Maybe if she had some alone time here she might find something useful. Right now I had to focus on Quinn and my team, they needed me. Apologies would have to wait – first, we needed to focus on getting Quinn's mum out of a hostile situation, and Naomi had to make sure she didn't get herself into one.

EMERY HALE

CHAPTER 11

Plexure

The act or process of weaving together.

NAOMI JADE

As the last sound of footsteps disappeared a shrill gust of wind blew through, the chill tickling my bones. As the dark, foreboding door swung shut and warm sunlight waned I was locked within the cold empty house.

Of course the door wasn't locked, I could walk right out – but I was curious, not stupid. They'd all made it very clear what could happen; what *would* happen. I had to face the facts: if anyone saw me and reported it to the faculty my death would end up in the news as a hit and run. That seemed their preferred method for disposing of people.

I had no idea what was going on with Quinn and I wanted

to help, but Kayson had made it very clear it wasn't my place. Well you know what was? Finding enough evidence to get this institution shut down. With that thought in mind I hurled myself up the stairs to the next floor.

I was right, the expensive taste did continue throughout the house. The wallpaper was the same navy blue with gold accents, three mirrors placed exactly along the wall, opposite a random painting with a white cabinet below. The cabinet was messy, covered with magazines, unopened letters and papers with large red stamps plastered all over them. When I took a closer look I realised they were delivery slips, listing food, water, toiletries and medical supplies, but most of the items were scored out in red, leaving only the bare essentials.

This couldn't be enough for everyone here – even toilet paper was marked off. I had no idea the Academy had this much control – so much that they could deny supply deliveries.

I took out the camera phone, snapping a couple of pictures of the sheer insanity printed in black and white – this must be Jessica's normal. If the Academy was cutting supplies maybe it was because money was tight? Or was it for some more deranged and twisted reason?

With a sigh, I gathered everything I knew about the Academy in my head. It was run by the Government; they had 'agents', so to speak, embedded throughout society; they abused their students into obedience through physical violence and controlled vital supplies. I had to go deeper because, like my mum said, this was just the tip of the iceberg.

With that in mind I followed Jessica's directions.

The corridor was in the shape of an L, with three doors to the right and two to the left. I walked around the corner to see a tall brown door ahead of me. As I gripped the handle, a sense of paranoia washed over me. What was behind this door? Would there be blood all over the walls? Would it be stripped bare of everything but a bed? Would there even be a window? Theories ran through my head one after the other, like a carousel at warp speed.

If your bedroom is supposed to mirror your personality, then why did I have a feeling Jessica's would be similar to a prison cell?

With a swift push I went inside. In front of me wasn't a

cell, or anything that resembled a prison – in fact it looked like an ordinary bedroom. Compact but not crowded, one wall painted black while the others were a cold cream, a white ash wooden floor and a simple grey desk and chair. Sheet music piled neatly to one side in a container; black and white pictures of New York on the wall. A double bed with duvet covers, pillows and blanket all in the same shade of grey, along with wardrobes built tightly into the wall.

Apparently Jessica and my mother shared the same love of grey – they did know there were other colours out there, right?

What I noticed was missing, however, was any sort of laptop. I'd assumed Jess would have one but apparently she didn't. Another thing she didn't have was an en suite bathroom or a private lift – if only I could tell Jennifer.

As I stepped further into the room I saw a black duffle bag shoved under the desk. It was large and bulky but I presumed it was just washing, since a couple of shirtsleeves were poking out the top. Without another glance I ignored it and sat down on the bed with a sigh.

What was I really doing here? I wasn't a detective! I didn't have any training or experience so I had no idea what to look for. Sure, there was that delivery slip but anyone with eyes could have spotted that. Kayson was right, I had no idea what I was doing. Grace also had a good point, my being here it put them all in danger. Right now it felt like I was doing more damage than – wait, what was that?

Something sharp dug into my butt. I shot off the bed but didn't see the outline of anything – was I imagining things now?

I knelt in front of the bed, gently pushing back the covers to reveal a laptop hidden under the bottom sheet. Now, I don't speak for everyone but I was sure hiding a laptop under your bedsheets wasn't the norm.

Carefully I lifted the sheet and pulled out the laptop: it was brand-new, unmarked, apart from a few rock band stickers. As I held it in my hand I felt something scratch against my palm. I turned it over, thinking I'd ripped off one of the stickers, but when I smoothed it out again I saw it was a label with a name printed on it – one I could scarcely believe.

JAMES WINTERS

Jess had told me her brother died in a skiing accident years ago.

This was a new laptop and if his name was on it, then maybe he wasn't as dead as I thought. But why would she tell me her brother died if he was, in fact, alive? Had there even been an accident at all?

If she'd lied about that there must have been a reason – which got me thinking. What else had Jessica told me about her family that was a lie? At the theatre she said her mum was busy with work – what was her job exactly? Did she know what was going on here? If I could somehow get a hold of her, she could help. I had only seen Jess's mum a couple of times and let me tell you she was one of the scariest people I'd ever met. Her face sculpted and eyes piercing like silver daggers.

I didn't get time to dwell on the thought before I heard the slam of a door; the front door. It couldn't have been Jessica, it was too soon – then the sound of a woman humming floated up to me, and it wasn't a voice I recognised.

Without a second thought I tucked the laptop under my arm and ran frantically towards the wardrobe hoping to hide inside, but when I got closer I realised they were far too slender.

SLATE RETRIBUTION

My luck dwindled as the thumping of feet started to make its way up the stairs. Oh poop. I bolted as fast as I could out of the room and into the one opposite, where I hoped there was a place to hide.

This room was a stark contrast to Jessica's – it had pink walls, but interior design wasn't my main concern. I spotted a large wooden wardrobe at the other side of the room and knew it was my best shot.

I grabbed the handle and yanked it open before throwing myself inside, closing the door and pushing myself through the clothes until my shoulders hit the wooden panels at the back. If there was anything I learned from the nature channel at two in the morning, it was that just because you couldn't see the predator didn't mean it couldn't see you. Hiding in here was the best option rather than under the bed – but now I thought about it, wasn't the wardrobe one of the first places a killer in a slasher movie would look? Well . . . guess this was it then, goodbye cruel world!

I stayed as silent as I could, one hand over my mouth to quieten my rapid breathing, while the other pushed clothes in front of my face to muffle it further. My legs trembled as the threat of a bullet rang through my ears. Suddenly this had all got very real. I didn't want to die, and yet here I was.

Then I heard the room door open and a tightness gripped my throat – had she seen me?

Her footsteps were quick and light, but she must have some heel on her shoes as they clicked across the floor – then abruptly stopped. Then I heard something like material being moved or shuffled. Was she checking the bed for something?

Was this someone the Academy sent to go through everyone's stuff? This place just got stranger.

A ringtone blared through the room, and my eyes bulged as I scrambled to find my phone. Then I stopped. That wasn't my phone. It must have been hers. Lowering my bag back down carefully, I listened intently as she spoke.

'I'm in but there's nothing here, everything looks the same as it did this morning. You've got the wrong person. I don't think Quinn is the one you're looking for.'

So this was Quinn's room.

What was this woman looking for? Did she know about Quinn's private server? Did someone pick up on the email she sent my mum? It sounded like the woman had tried this more than once; maybe Quinn wasn't as secretive as she thought.

'I know that . . . wait, let me try her computer.'

There was more shuffling across the room before I heard the clacking of keys, but the sound grew heavier. Whatever this woman wanted, she wasn't getting it. I hadn't known Quinn long but she seemed like the kind of girl who would have more security on her tech than a flimsy password.

'I can't get in, you'll need to send Thompson over to crack into this thing . . . send him over right now, the entire household is out.'

If Thompson, who apparently was my mum's boss, came over then I'd have double the chance of getting caught. These people were trained.

'What do you mean?' the woman asked. 'No, how on earth would she know about Black Scorpion? Like I said, get Thompson over here, we can get a look at this – I'm sorry?'

Who was on the other end of the phone? Was it Harkness? Black Scorpion must have been some sort of mission but why would Quinn have anything to do with it? The loose wire that Jess had thrown back at me was halfway down my shirt and dangling out my jeans so there was no way it could hear any of this audio. I wanted to reach for the video phone but by now it was at the bottom of my bag – if I went rummaging around she'd hear me! I pressed record on my own phone which was luckily in reach, my hand trying to avoid rustling the bag.

'Yes, I understand. Fine,' she said sharply, before I heard the click of the phone.

Then, just like that, the sound of her shoes clacked all the way back across the room and the door slammed shut. Was that it? Did she leave? I didn't care, I was not leaving this wardrobe until I heard Jessica or the other girls.

So many nerves rattled through me that I didn't think my legs would move, even if I wanted them to. I could hear the woman walk about the corridor, opening another door, but as each minute passed the sound of her faded until the bang of the front door closing echoed through the house.

I hadn't realised I'd stopped breathing until the wrenching tightness of my throat reminded my brain I needed air. I sucked in an abundance of it, let myself pant for a few seconds before coming back to the situation. Just then the weight of the laptop made itself felt: it was time to see what was on this thing.

Lifting the laptop from my arm I slid down to the bottom of the wardrobe, moving a few rogue shoes out the way. I propped the laptop on my bent legs and opened the lid. I was glad for the rack of clothes in front of me as the laptop fans kicked in. Even though I'd heard the woman leave, paranoia lingered. What if she came back?

As soon as the blue screen popped up it asked me for a password – oh, great. How was I supposed to guess this guy's password? I'd only met James twice.

I flipped the laptop round and picked a name from one of the rock band stickers.

ACCESS DENIED

OK, maybe someone who was dead but apparently not anymore was smart enough not to use something so blatantly obvious.

Come on, think! Maybe he put his password as Jessica? Yeah no, he wouldn't do that. It was hopeless. Jessica never told me much about James at all apart from a couple things, like the time he swapped sugar for salt and how he always forgot her birthday ... Hold on. When I want to remember something important I just repeat it over and over again. What if he used Jessica's birthday as a password?

31-10-1997

ACCESS GRANTED

Oh you beauty! Yes! In your face, Ashford!

As the screen changed to the desktop it was the same blue, like no one had switched it from the factory settings. The small icons down the side, however, were definitely not part of the everyday run of the mill laptop.

RECORDS AND OPERATIONS

FIELD OPERATIONS

CHARLOTTE

JESSICA

CHARLIE

SECURITY FEED

If Jessica had this hidden in her room it had to be important.

I guessed that records and operations were things to do with espionage – that's what this whole thing was, right?

Charlotte was Jessica's mother's name; Charlie I didn't recognise. Then my eyes landed on the security feed folder – what could be on here?

When I clicked on it there were different sub files, but their names were too simple to give much away. Entrance 1A, Corridor 2C, Passage 5G, the list went on. What I didn't expect to see when I clicked on a random file was a live feed inside the Academy. It was from the other side of those big mahogany doors at the entrance to the school. Probably a reception area: I couldn't see too much since the camera was pointed at the door, but I could see students walking past, some in uniform and some not.

I hit the right arrow and the feed changed to a completely different point in the building. The walls were made of bricks, but it was too grainy to make out the finer details. If I had to guess I'd have said this place was underground, going by the dim lighting and low ceilings.

The Academy couldn't have known about this laptop; it was a major security breach. If Quinn was so worried about the top-grade firewalls, wouldn't they have picked up on this? Was this why Jessica was hiding it?

When I moved to the next feed, it was from a spacious office. Only two people were inside, and one I recognised: Harkness. The other woman was in her late forties, very sophisticatedly dressed. I spotted a little mic button at the bottom of the screen and clicked on it and, just like that, sound tore through the speakers.

'What is it you wanted to show me, Lennox?' Harkness asked, his voice coming through with gritty static. 'I asked for an idea, not a PowerPoint presentation.'

I watched as Lennox closed the laptop, leaning against the desk, arms crossed. I didn't need HD to see she was not amused.

'Well if you're going to be an ass, you can wait until I announce it later.'

The microphone quality, though littered with static, was actually quite good – I could even hear Harkness' sigh of annoyance and the strut of Lennox's feet. Now I was in the clear I made a grab for the camera phone, opened it up and pressed record. If I was going to see this I'd be damned if I wasn't going to record it. Anything these maniacs said could be evidence.

'Lennox, just tell me.'

'A new drug has just reached the market.'

'I don't need to know what you get up to on your Friday nights.'

Lennox rolled her eyes.

'One that can alter a person's perception, make them more likely to be susceptible. Give them this drug and whatever you say will stick in their heads. You wanted obedience – you have it, all in a little pill.'

'I thought we were already using that,' Harkness said, unimpressed at her proposal.

'Not like this – they don't take it themselves, not like the other ones – this drug is put through the water system.'

What? The Academy forced their students to take drugs and now planned to give them further doses without their knowledge? Jessica couldn't have known about this, she was bad enough trying to swallow a paracetamol never mind whatever this was!

'It's distributed evenly throughout?'

'You always said you wanted the younger years to learn compliance and obedience earlier, here's how.'

'But what's it going to cost?'

Knowing the phone was recording I let myself fall back against the wardrobe's side. This Lennox woman introduced the idea of drugging students into obedience, and Harkness' only concern was how much it would cost? I didn't care what Jessica said anymore, this was fucked up. How on earth did this place even open if this was what they did?

One thought struck hard in my heart: if they're going so far as to drug the students into compliance then what were they going to force them to do? Shoot someone? Kill someone? Wipe towns off the map?

I couldn't speak for the rest, but Jessica had changed. Before she came here there was more of a spark about her, but now it was like it had never existed. Was it part of the faculty's plan to rid someone of that spark? The true light that made a person unique? The way she controlled a room, the confidence in her walk, the purpose and look of intent in her face. If they took that away and replaced it with teams, drugs, minimal food, little water, no sanitary or basic supplies, then what was that person clinging onto? How long did it take to break someone?

SLATE RETRIBUTION

Jessica must have been holding onto something, like everyone else on her 'team' – they all seemed relatively normal compared to the faculty. What was so powerful, so innately impenetrable, that held her back from becoming just like them?

CHAPTER 12

Ignivomous

Vomiting fire.

JESSICA-GRACE WINTERS

For the first time in months we were able to get Quinn's mum back to the safe house by ourselves. Kayson called his dad and he was able to call in a favour from another agent, who escorted her mum back home. It honestly saved the whole operation; I guess it really did pay off to have allies in this industry.

Of course Kayson was taking all the credit since it was his contact, but I knew we would have thought of another solution, so while he boasted about his miraculous save, I focused on blocking out his boisterous gloating.

As I started to shut down the Command Room, Quinn was already deleting the log history and looping the cameras so if anyone were to look back, they wouldn't see anyone rushing in here like a wild pack of headless chickens.

Of course we were panicking: even though an operation like this was something we'd trained for, it always sent my heart racing. Most of our ops were field work, Quinn the only one used to staying behind. I had no idea of the nerve and strength it took to stand there and watch the monitor, and it was then I found a new respect for Quinn. When the last op went south, all she could do was stand here and watch, observe through my camera as I came across the bloody crime scene.

Flicking the monitor off and putting a couple of phones back on the hook, I looked over to Quinn who was shutting down the computer we'd used. Of course there was no need to remove our fingerprints, but there was a shred of doubt hanging in the air – what if someone saw us come in? No, I couldn't work on what if's.

The op was finished so now we could get back to sorting out the mess that was a civilian in our dorm house.

But as we all headed to the door Grace stood still, her arms crossed, brows furrowed and lips tight.

'Keep the door locked, we need to talk,' she said,

motioning to Lily whose hand slowly fell from the handle. 'About Naomi.'

I exchanged a glance with Lily but there was a knowing look on her face.

'I think you already know what I'm doing to say,' I told Grace, sighing. 'If Naomi's willing then this could work in our favour. Why are you so against it?'

Of course I understood her concern, but I knew what was best. If Naomi was handing us an out then we were going to take it.

Grace scoffed in my face. 'How about the fact that this could affect us all? If she's caught there's no telling what they'll do to us.'

I held back the urge to roll my eyes – what would she know about punishments? Grace was the golden child, followed all the rules, never got in trouble, she didn't even speak up last night. Who was she to give us a lecture on this?

'I'm Team Lead, Grace. If I think it's best for my team then it's what we'll do.'

Grace was my second but it was my decision that counted,

and she couldn't exactly stop me. But as she spoke, her words were laced with venom and disgust.

'Exactly who made you Team Lead? It certainly wasn't us.' Grace's face hardened as she edged towards me. 'We didn't choose you – wait that's right, everyone already knows who chose you.'

She had to be fucking kidding. Was this what it boiled down to, jealousy?

At her words the whole atmosphere in the room shifted: Quinn froze rigid, Lily's mouth dropped open, even Kayson stopped.

'Excuse me?' I asked.

'You know what I'm talking about,' she said, but I just laughed. The tight-assed golden child was jealous, someone get it on video.

'It was Harkness that decided,' I told her.

'Oh, we all know who influenced him.'

Lily stood by me, a warning look on her face. She was usually the one instigating fights – I'd never seen her play mediator before. 'Grace, this isn't the time for your shitstorm of emotions, OK? Let's just get out of here and we can talk about it later,' she said.

'Later? Is that before or after Naomi leaves?'

'Why are you so against her?' Lily asked.

'Why couldn't Jessica have just cut ties with her when she was supposed to?' she said.

Here we go, back to square one! I knew Grace didn't like her, but Naomi had been my friend for years – didn't she have someone like that on the outside world?

'Why can't you learn to follow my orders?' I snapped harshly. I had to shut this down, she was my second but she had no right to question me like this. In front of my team, no less. This was big, I got that, but she should know me well enough to trust my judgment.

After everything that's happened I didn't need Grace's emotions smothering me, couldn't she have waited at least an hour or two before bringing this up? Why did it matter who made me Team Lead? I was the best for the job and everyone knew it.

That was when Grace started to yell.

'Look at you, just like Harkness! Follow my orders – no

sense of democracy!'

'Oh, it's democracy you want?' I asked. 'Well, maybe you should have said something to me instead of taking it out on Naomi!'

'She is the problem! Can't you see that?' You're meant to care about us, your so-called team, and yet all you want to do is bring her into the equation!'

'I'm not the one who brought her here!'

Kayson's eyebrows shot up.

'Hey, she blackmailed me! If I hadn't, the videos would have been released!' With that Kayson turned, unlocked the door and marched out, like a child having a temper tantrum.

'It wouldn't have gone anywhere if they'd been released, we've discussed that already!' Then she turned to us. 'We would get the backlash, we would get punished because of it –'

That was it.

'Punished? You don't even know what that means. You haven't exactly been on the receiving end of any of them.' I crossed my arms, stalking towards her.

Maybe I was like Harkness. I needed them to take my

orders because without that we'd fall into chaos.

Lily placed a hand on my arm and for a moment I thought she was going to pull me back but instead she slipped past me, her other hand curled into a fist.

'I don't think you've ever gotten so much as a bruise on yourself,' Lily said. 'You are so concerned about getting Naomi out of here so *you* don't get marked up.'

Grace's mouth fell open, utterly offended but she stayed quiet, she wasn't even going to fucking deny it. The tight-ass bitch. It was one thing to tell me I wasn't prioritising my team but it was another when she prioritised herself. Who the fuck did she think she was?

'I have shifts on the ward, you seriously think I can go in there all beat up?' she asked. 'Never mind that, I'm not putting my neck on the line for someone I don't know!'

'Well maybe you should actually get to know her or see what she has to offer before deeming her useless,' I said.

'You know what?' Grace asked the group before turning to me. 'Considering that Willow died on the last op, Naomi's not the only one that's been utterly useless.'

SLATE RETRIBUTION

SLAP

My hand sliced across Grace's cheekbone before I could blink; she fucking deserved that. She stumbled back holding her cheek, but all she had in return was a bitter smile.

'Are you shitting me, Grace?' Lily asked, but her voice was different. It was like Grace's words were a physical blow to her ribs, her voice weaker than before. 'You're blaming Jess for that?'

Grace never spoke, she just looked me in the eye, sporting that know-it-all glare like she always did. Was I meant to feel bad for hitting her?

'If you look at it from the perspective of Harkness, what's the reason our food supplies keep getting cut?' she asked. 'It's cause Winters over here won't do as she's told. If you want an answer as to why we don't have enough food to last the week, look no further than the famous Jessica-Grace Winters.'

My main concern was getting Grace to shut her mouth. All she ever did was take the high ground, never admitting when she was wrong or apologising for it. She called me a hypocrite. *Who else could you blame, Grace? Oh right yeah, everyone but yourself.*

'Why haven't you said anything before?' I asked. 'If you're so jealous of me.'

'Jealous?' Grace said, like the idea was ludicrous. 'I'm not jealous.'

'Doesn't seem like it, sweetheart.' I replied bitterly, then I walked away.

Lily shouted some profanities at Grace but I wasn't listening.

I didn't need to follow protocol; I was going to do the best for my team and having Naomi here was a benefit. It wasn't my fault Grace couldn't see that.

But at the sight of the door I halted, and any arguments from behind faded to nothing, the weight of the room collapsing from the ceiling. Duke stood there, hands pressed against the open door. He stared at each of us individually, assessing us. How much had he heard?

Duke didn't break the silence, it was Quinn's shaky breathing that did, and his eyes quickly fixated on her.

'What are you doing in here?' Duke asked bluntly.

'We needed to have a team meeting.' I answered quickly, but I felt Lily shift from behind me. OK, maybe that wasn't the most believable lie.

'And you couldn't have done that somewhere else?'

'No.'

Duke slowly waded his way over to me, his eyes scanning my face and then my body. It was like he was trying to detect the lie, even though it was clearly right in front of him. We had no reason whatsoever to be in here, so why hadn't he started yelling? Why hadn't he dragged us all to Harkness' office?

If Duke was truly Harkness' right hand man, then maybe he couldn't dish out punishments without his say-so. Did he have to wait for permission?

At my silence Duke slipped a black phone from his pocket and punched in a couple buttons, before taking it to his ear.

'I need security footage of Command Room 3B sent to me,' he said to the other person on the line.

Well, fuck.

Quinn had looped the cameras which would now show an empty corridor. Shit. Would they check the phone log? We'd called at least four people in the last ten minutes.

It would take around three minutes for the files to be sent over so I had to come up with something, but I was drawing a blank.

Grace spoke up. 'Sir, we need to get going, I have a ward shift and Jessica has rehearsals.'

Duke didn't look interested in what her royal highness had to say, not that anyone else in the room did either. She painted herself as such a saint, studying medicine, pulling shifts at the hospital, bandaging the team up after an op, but she was just in it for herself.

Duke slipped the phone back in his pocket.

'Winters, tell me, why has Harkness taken such an interest in you?' Of all the questions I thought this man would ask, that wasn't one of them. 'I assumed such punishments were kept for the seniors, but Harkness has taken a liking to you and your team.' His beady eyes flitted behind me.

Hold up, liking? I'd hate to see what he'd do to people he loved.

'No,' I replied simply.

SLATE RETRIBUTION

In my head I could almost predict what Grace was thinking, I could practically feel the snide smirk burrowing into my head. Her sickly sweet tone plaguing my mind.

She thought that Harkness had taken an interest in me because of my mother. Grace assumed that because he and my mother worked together I'd gotten ahead without trying. If that were the reason, I had no idea about it. I believed that I was the most suitable person for the job, proving it every day in training, fighting and standing up when no one else would. If Grace was after my job, she'd have a fight on her hands.

'Interesting,' Duke mused, before fixing on Lily. 'You get in the gym, can't very well be a Runner if you're lounging about. I want fifty lines then three miles. Get it done in twenty-five minutes or you can forget the next supply delivery.'

You know, the start of that could be passed off as a coach talking to his star athlete, but then came the last bit, which in simple terms meant *get your shit together or you'll eat scraps for another week.*

Then Duke nodded and left.

If I was brutally honest, we couldn't keep living like this.

Three weeks in a row our food had been cut back, how long could we go on?

'Swap with me,' I said, throwing off my hoodie and trainers, tossing them at Lily's feet.

She smiled gratefully, taking off her boots. It was a good thing we were the same size.

'What if Ames gives me something else to do?' Lily asked. 'What if I don't make it in time?' Her voice was drowning in worry.

I could take the hate and glares for the lack of food and so could Lily, but after last night, I feared her nerves might not be as resilient.

'You will make it,' I told her. 'You have to.'

SLATE RETRIBUTION

CHAPTER 13

Unconditional

Without judgement despite any and or all flaws.

NAOMI JADE

Surprisingly, sitting in the wardrobe for over an hour wasn't the worst way to spend my time: I rearranged Quinn's shoes into different categories, made friends with a tiny spider and waded through more of the security footage. At one point there was a classroom filled with students which looked pretty normal, but once I turned the volume up and learned that this 'teacher' was talking about emotional manipulation, that thought soon left me.

For some reason Kayson and his stupid egotistical voice kept butting into my mind; the entire night I spent with him was an act. The guy I encountered today was a different person, a dickhead to be blunt. Jessica sent him after me, like I needed babysitting. I'd have to bring that up at some point.

I clicked out of the security footage folder and shut the laptop. I could look at everything else later, right now I needed to get out of the wardrobe because I'd lost all sensation in my butt. Fear made me pause – what if someone was out there waiting for me? Sure, I hadn't heard anything, but there was a pesky itch of worry. I had images of that woman standing there with a gun – or worse, Harkness.

BANG

The sound of a gun fired through my head, but then I realised it was actually the slam of the front door. Had they come for me?

'I don't care if she's bloody royalty, she can shove her tiara right up her fucking ass. You know, I fear for her patients, she might murder them if she gets a tad jealous!'

Well, Jess was back.

Since that woman seemed keen to conduct whatever investigation under the radar, I assumed the coast was clear and crawled out of the wardrobe. I was a bit stiff from being stuck in the one position, but with some shimmying and destroying the better part of a shoe box, I tumbled into the empty room. Even though the door was closed and I was a floor up, Jessica's brash voice continued to boom.

'Does she not think I blame myself? I know this is my fault, but I don't see her stepping up!'

What was she on about? I assumed it wasn't about Quinn's mum.

'Naomi!'

Oh! That's me.

'Yeah! Still here, I'll be down in a minute!'

As a pair of quick footsteps sounded from outside I left the room, but in doing so barged into Jessica and Quinn, who jumped back.

'Are you OK?'

'Uh yeah just ... been stuck in your wardrobe for an hour.' I said with a tired smile.

'The wardrobe?' she asked, confusion written all over. 'What were you doing in there?'

'There was this woman who came in, looking for something and I couldn't hide in Jessica's room so I hid in yours.'

Instead of singing my praises for outsmarting this woman, Quinn whipped out her phone, charging into her room while Jessica grabbed my shoulders and forced me in behind.

'What are you doing?' I asked.

Quinn darted to the other side of the room where her computer was and grabbed a cable, hooking it up to the monitor. Jessica ran to the window and pulled the curtains over.

'The woman, what did she look like?' Jessica asked.

'I can't see through wood,' I said, but Jessica gave me a pointed look.

'She had a pair of heels on, sounded on the older side.'

Jessica thought it over for a moment. 'Helen,' she said. 'She manages the accommodation.'

Whoever she was, I'd managed to outsmart her. OK, she wasn't looking for me but still, brownie points and all that.

As I glanced over to Quinn I saw that her monitor took up the majority of the wall, with two small screens either side and a rose gold keyboard beneath. An image popped up on the screen like some sort of group chat but when I took a closer look, it was actually a log.

FRONT DOOR OPENED AT 16:15

JGW DOOR OPENED AT 16:17

FRONT DOOR OPENED AT 16:21

QE DOOR OPENED AT 16:21

QE DOOR OPENED AT 16:22

WM DOOR OPENED AT 16:25

FRONT DOOR OPENED AT 16:30

FRONT DOOR OPENED AT 17:22

They had logs for when certain doors were opened? Well that was top notch security. Quinn studied them for a moment before pointing to the top of the screen.

'The first one, that's when we all left and the last one was us again, so we can cross those out,' she told us. 'Then Jessica's room was probably Naomi?' Quinn looked back to me and I nodded. She highlighted those three entries in blue, moving onto the next. 'Then the third, that must be when Helen came in.' Quinn highlighted that in yellow.

'The Academy gives you access to these?' I asked.

'Security purposes if there's a break-in.' Jessica said. 'So Naomi, you ran the moment the door opened, and then what?'

I felt like I was in a movie, the team coming together, figuring out a plan, taking down the bad guys.

'I ran in here and hid in the wardrobe,' I told her, trying to hide my excitement.

Quinn nodded but she pulled a face as her eyes ran over the remaining time stamps.

'Helen was in here for three minutes, what was she doing?' Jess asked me.

'She was looking for files I think, on Quinn's computer, but she was also on the phone with someone. She thought that you'd done something,' I said, looking in the small blonde's direction.

Jessica pinched the bridge of her nose. 'Quinn, tell me you were careful and didn't leave any trace of the server for them to find?'

'No, of course not,' she said, then pulled out a little black box – I presumed the one she'd spoken about earlier – from her bra. 'I keep it on me when I leave, just in case.'

When Jessica looked back to the monitor for a brief moment, I saw the sharp edge of sadness cut through her face like a knife. 'Helen stayed in Willow's room for a further five minutes before she left, why?'

Willow? Could that be the girl from the hit and run? I had a theory that Jess knew her, but I never imagined she lived with her.

'Willow?' I asked. 'She was the girl in the news, she was killed in a hit and run.'

'She's more than that,' Quinn said sharply, her nails etching into the white wooden desk. 'She's not just some girl.'

I sighed. OK, maybe jumping on the bandwagon so fast was a bit insensitive.

'You're right, I'm sorry.'

Willow was more than just a mere acquaintance then? I guessed she'd been as close as the rest of the girls were on this team. Now I thought about it, half of the team was gone. Did something happen at the Academy? From the way Jessica came in shouting the place down, it must have.

'I know you were close with her, Quinn, but Helen thought

you were a hell of a lot closer,' Jessica said. She didn't seem bothered or affected by what I said, that small glimpse was all I got in terms of emotion. 'They must have thought that you two were up to something. Was she helping you develop the server's algorithm?'

Quinn shook her head, protesting. 'No, Willow was hopeless with coding.'

'The Carrier and the Technical Support, would have been a scandal,' Jessica laughed.

'What?' I asked, confused.

'Nothing, just positions in the team,' she told me, before she turned back to Quinn. I would ask more about those so-called 'positions' later.

'Dig into Willow's past, I'll get into her bedroom see what I can find.'

Then, just like that, Jessica was off, heading for the door. As I glanced back at Quinn it wasn't just a glimpse, there was a tidal wave of grief plummeting through her body. Her eyelashes fluttered, knuckles turning white, her whole body rigid – with one touch I knew she'd collapse. Quinn was a lot more than a mere acquaintance to Willow, a hell of a lot more. Maybe the pair could have been like sisters? Even that conclusion didn't fit the profile. Oh God, were they more than just friends?

I thought Jessica had left the room but when I turned, she still stood there, leaning against the doorway, sympathy in her smile.

'You can go through her room if you want,' she said softly. 'Willow would have wanted you to do it. Besides, you know where all the secret compartments are.'

Quinn stood up a little straighter, bit her lip and nodded quickly.

'Thank you,' she said, before running into the hallway out of sight.

Jessica closed her eyes for a brief moment, taking in a breath before she shut the door.

'You know, seeing you here, it's – I only ever imagined something like this would happen.' Her voice was different now, soft and void of anger. 'You're actually standing here.'

I tried to understand where she was coming from, I suspected moments like this were extremely rare. With the security and staff, I imagined any contact from the outside world was scarce. This place was starting to look like a cult.

'Yeah,' I replied, 'and I'm not leaving you, not again.'

I dropped the laptop on Quinn's bed, slowly edging my way towards her. I'd read somewhere that after trauma fast movements were a no-go so I stuck to slow and steady, since it always won the race.

As I got closer I smelled that same perfume from her room, something refreshing but brittle with salt. When I took her hand I felt the small thin scars on her palm; her whole body told me a different story to the one that'd come from her mouth. I hated myself for not seeing the signs until now; she'd been at the mercy of Harkness all this time.

Everyone on the outside had been too caught up in the rumours and conspiracy theories about this place that they'd never really looked at the people who lived inside it. No one ever saw that the students endured so much.

'I'm going to be with you through all of this, I won't leave you again.' I promised.

With those words, Jessica did something I didn't expect –

she pulled me into a tight hug, burying her face in the crook of my neck. I hid the shock as she squeezed me even tighter. Two hours ago she'd been yelling at me to leave, but now it seemed she needed me to stay.

Jessica wanted me to carry out this investigation and I knew it was because she trusted me. The past didn't matter because I understood why she did it. Everyone was always driven by a motive, and now I knew Jessica's was fear.

I'd expected tears but when she pulled back there were none. I guessed she wasn't fully ready to let me in and that was OK, I'd get there eventually. She crossed her arms and leaned back against the shut door, but her glacial look didn't return; all I saw was warmth.

'If I can keep you here under the radar then I need you to collect as much data on this place as you can,' Jessica told me. 'Enough to take us to trial.'

I nodded quickly, a victorious smile crawling up my face.

'I promise, Jess, I'll do everything I can.'

Jessica didn't share my enthusiasm, in fact she seemed sceptical. I knew I didn't have the ins and outs of the place yet,

SLATE RETRIBUTION

but I must be on the right track?

With a heavy sigh she took my hand and led us to sit on the bed.

'Naomi, when it comes to building a case against these people, others are going to come up against you.'

'I know that.'

'People like Katie,' she said, and I took a sharp breath in.

I highly doubted Katie would take an interest in this, but there were people like her all around the world. If anyone got wind that my mum was working on a huge story they'd bang down the door and bribe her to get it.

I hadn't considered the implications of this fully yet – it was all well and good standing up to Jessica, but it was another thing to stand up to strangers; people that don't know, trust or accept you. They would judge on facts, rumours and speculation. If this all went public was I ready to be in the spotlight? I had to be, not just for me, for Jessica too.

'I'll be ready when the time comes, they won't get anything from me.'

'Naomi, you might think you're uncrackable like ... a

Rubik's Cube but you're not. They'll make you talk.'

'Did you just call me a Rubik's Cube?'

'Naomi,' Jessica groaned, 'this is serious.'

'So is calling me a cube!' I exclaimed, trying to lighten the mood.

Jessica laughed, her head falling, but as she glanced up it was like she was searching for something – maybe it was sanity, since I'd clearly lost mine.

Suddenly Kayson butted into my mind, his smile, his charm, his jawline – Christ! I had to remember he only acted like that to get close to me, but there was this feeling that inched its way through my gut, convincing me it wasn't all fake. It couldn't be. You can't fake the connection we had, that I felt, could you?

'Why did you send Kayson to babysit me?' I asked her. She seemed surprised at first but then sighed, like she knew this would come around eventually.

'After the whole thing with Katie, I had to do something.'

'She wasn't doing anything to me,' I said quickly, and subconsciously I felt my hand pull back and rest in my lap, my head dropping a little.

Jessica scoffed. 'She treated you like a pet, Naomi. I mean look at you.'

I knew what she said was true, honestly, I didn't know why I continued to defend Katie. We were friends, so to speak, but on a different level, a totally different level.

Then I felt a warm arm wrap around my shoulders. 'If you won't leave me, then I am never letting that idiot near you,' she told me. 'All she did was manipulate, and I know the same could be said for me.'

'Well, you did tell Kayson what I liked in a guy, then sent him to my door,' I said bluntly.

'I'm sorry, I shouldn't have done that. I was just worried.'

I took in a deep breath. 'Well then, worry like my mum does – just ask a million questions every time I walk by or even better, go off on one when I don't do the dishes.'

She let out a chuckle.

'Well you know what, I will,' she told me. 'You're on clean-up duty while we're in classes.'

'Isn't that Helen's job?'

'Nah, she just manages us, comes in every once and a

while to make sure we're not dead.' I laughed at the comment but Jessica didn't, was she not joking? Dear God!

I had so many questions for Jessica; her apparently not-so-dead-anymore brother, the true story behind Willow's death and what the hell 'outside duty' was, but for now I silenced the need to know, pulling out of the warm embrace and grabbing the laptop from the bed.

As soon as the warmth disappeared I craved it, this was the first time in years we'd just sat and talked, I didn't want it to end.

But if I didn't show her what I found then Jessica might disappear – not physically, mentally. If she became like Harkness then she would just be a shell of the girl I once knew.

A look of recognition sparked on her face as I lifted the laptop into my lap. When I opened the lid and explained what I found she told me it was her brother's; he'd left it purposely a couple of weeks ago when he was at the Academy on business. James had given it to Jess so she would have access to any reports he made, but also so she could spy on the Academy.

I moved on quickly to my phone, showing Jessica the video with Harkness and Lennox. I don't think I could have prepared myself for the expression of pure shock. Well it's official, we were in crazy town now, people!

'They're going to – shit.' Jessica's hand went to her hair and pulled on it, the emotions clear as day on her face: worry, anxiety, stress.

'Are you on any medication right now?' I asked.

Jessica walked over to the small organiser beside the computer and pulled out one of the drawers, then took out three different silver foil pill packets, holding them up. Dread dripping from her mouth.

I looked at her expectantly. 'You all take those?'

She nodded. 'Every day.'

Without missing a beat I picked up the video phone and walked over, taking the foil packets to examine. There weren't any words on them, but I noticed on one there was a red dot, on the other a pink one, and on the last a blue. I snapped a couple of shots before looking up to Jess.

'What do they do?' I asked.

Jessica picked up the one with the pink dot. 'This is just for the girls, stops our periods.' She let that one drop onto the desk before picking up the blue-dotted one. 'This one is apparently a multivitamin.' Then she stopped and just looked at the red-dotted silver packet. 'That one . . . I don't know.'

'You don't know?' I asked, my eyes bulging and mouth gaping. 'Jess, if you don't know what that is, why the hell would you take it?'

As soon as the words came out of my mouth, I knew they were stupid and pointless. Jessica's head dropped, her arms wrapping around her torso, a look of shame rising within her.

'When we get to the Academy we all go through a medical, then leave with this cocktail of pills. We're told that we've to take these, once a day for the entirety of our stay here. If we don't . . . we get taken to the medical wing and the stuff is injected into us.'

Piss off, injected?

'So you can't refuse? It's your body, even in hospitals they can't force you to take anything without your consent,' I told her, but Jessica only shook her head.

'You think I let him pin me against a wall?' she asked. 'You think any of us would be here if we had a choice?'

Choice, something that was in short supply at the Reign Academy. Basic rights completely disregarded.

Just as I was about to ask another question Jessica continued, like everything she had kept pent up for years was tumbling out of her mouth. 'My mother sent me here because she has shares in the Academy. Quinn's mum is in a witness protection programme that's controlled by the Academy, Lily's sister is a lawyer in a firm governed by Duke, and Grace's father works in a pharmacy, also run by guess who?' Jessica asked. 'We can't say no to this.'

Their families were intertwined with all of this. I didn't even think that was possible, I just assumed none of them knew about it. This must have been done under the table, behind closed doors. If they had Scotland Yard, then they had control of the police. They had control over witness protection schemes, lawyers in the courts, chemists in pharmacies and journalists in the media. The Academy's reach was much wider and more powerful than I'd ever anticipated.

It horrified me that Jessica's mother had shares in this place, but what chilled me to the core was that her mother knew what they did and invested anyway.

'So your mum knows what goes on here?'

Jessica scoffed. 'Knows? The woman practically wrote the how-to guide. She invested her hard-earned cash into this place, to develop assassins for the war.'

'What war? What are you talking about?'

'The war against Trojan,' she started, but I remained oblivious as ever. Sure there had been attacks, but those were the norm around here, I never thought we could be in the middle of a full-blown war. 'It's a terrorist network, they were responsible for the bomb at the bank and at the theatre.'

That's who was responsible, Trojan? All these attacks that we had been told were completely random came from the same organisation?

'Trojan was one of the reasons the Academy was created,' Jessica said. 'Amongst others of course.'

I could barely string two words together – trying to wrap my head around all this felt like I was running up a foggy mountain, out of breath, with no sense of direction. The Academy had so much control, held power in every sense of the word, but its methods were barbaric. I assumed they got results, but surely there were easier ways?

'So this school trains spies?' I asked.

She shook her head. 'This institution trains the next generation of killers, faster and stronger than the last. Agents send their kids here thinking they'll receive the same training as they did, but it's a lie. You don't just become a killer, you become a weapon.'

The question popped into my head but I only just managed to get it out through gritted teeth.

'Have you killed anyone?'

When Jessica shook her head relief ran through me, but it didn't last.

'Grace has, shot a man in the head, at the theatre,' she said. 'It changes you. Ever since the whole thing she's been different. It was only a matter of time.'

Only a matter of time? Jesus, the way Jessica spoke, it was as if tomorrow when she walked down the street it might happen. Even so, I wouldn't leave Jessica, not when I could change something for the better, help more than one person. They endured so much but it wasn't right. None of them should have to kill, take unknown pills, be subjected to abuse and have their right to choose taken away.

'Naomi,' Jessica said, catching my attention. 'You know how dangerous this is going to be? You know this is going to implicate you for the rest of your life? With the info you already have, if they find you out, you'll have a bounty over your head until you're in the ground.' A bounty? Oh great, that's not concerning at all.

But if I didn't risk my life, no one else would.

I wouldn't stand by and watch Jessica become the next Harkness – she wouldn't be dancing around my room to ABBA, she'd be planning her next hit. What kind of life was that to lead?

Then I cracked a smile. I knew what I was getting into now, so I might as well enjoy it while I could.

'Is that supposed to be a warning?' I asked. 'Some kind of threat?'

Jessica returned my look, excitement alight in her eyes.

'Naomi darling, it was an invitation. Welcome to the Reign Academy.'

– SLATE RETRIBUTION

EMERY HALE

CHAPTER 14

Affrap

To strike down.

JESSICA-GRACE WINTERS

I would never have left Naomi's side if it could be helped, but I still had a show to do. Despite everything, we needed to carry on as normal.

While on that stage that night, I was comforted by the knowledge that Naomi was safe, tucked away in Quinn's room.

There was only one package drop happening, so there was just a basic surveillance team in the wings, nothing like before. I didn't know any of them but frankly, I was enjoying myself too much to listen in to the comm chatter.

Theatre was a way for me to escape, to lose myself in the ecstasy of movement and sound, rhythm dictating my body. I could forget the life I led for a brief three hours, but when I walked out the stage door, a cold wind set the pole of lead straight in my spine.

Maybe this new drug wouldn't be so horrible. Flashes of Willow's face would no longer haunt every absent second. Wouldn't it take the pain away? Make everything just stand still?

It was the back of ten o'clock before we all managed to sit down together.

Part of me was grateful for the time apart to gather my thoughts, collate some kind of answer for my team. At the end of the day I only had to convince one person: my second, Grace.

The only good thing about this meeting was that Kayson wouldn't be in attendance, so there wouldn't be the use of the bitch word. Well, that was unless Grace decided to act up and in that case, I took no responsibility for my actions. I still didn't regret slapping her.

Everyone on my team except one wanted Naomi here. Grace was outvoted, there's her fucking democracy.

Lily, Quinn, and Naomi all huddled together on one couch in the living room, while Grace sat sourly in the lone chair. My intention had been to mediate any arguments, but since I was the one involved in the outbursts, no mediating took place.

'You all can't keep fighting against one another,' Naomi said. 'If you wanna beat the bosses we all have to work together.'

'Aw come on, what Lifetime movie did you grab that from?' Grace scoffed, leaning back. 'What chance have we even got at getting this to court?'

Being outvoted didn't seem to lift her dour mood, in fact it made it worse.

'Well, since we don't know what pills we take and now they're going to start drugging us through the water system, I'd say a good one,' Lily said. 'It's wrong, we didn't agree to drugs and physical abuse.

'Our world will become a better place if we stick to the rules,' Grace said adamantly. 'The country is at war and if we don't keep to the training then there won't be any country left.'

When Grace whipped her head around to face me, I forced myself to look away because she was right. Trojan were winning the war and if the Academy planned to drug us then they must need graduates fast. It was the only theory that made sense;

something had scared them. Whatever it was, the world in the next year was gonna be a fucking mess.

'Trojan have a hold in Eastern Europe but they're also advancing from the north, that's the latest I heard from my brother.' I knew I had to say something, and that was all I could muster. 'The Academy must think they're advancing towards the UK.'

'So your brother isn't dead?' Naomi asked.

'No.'

The voice in my head started to nag away. Grace was right, if we didn't stick to the programme everything would fall into chaos. It wasn't just about saving lives, it was about preventing attacks in the first place. If we rebelled, who would stop the bombings or shootings? There were other agencies, but they weren't trained like us. The Academy conditioned students specifically to take down Trojan agents; we had access to info that no other agency knew about.

'I don't want to be a mindless drone, Grace.' Quinn said, her voice louder than usual.

'I second that,' Lily said. 'If they're going to use drugs in the first place, they'll order us to do something awful, like murder innocents.'

'They won't need to because if we do this, every innocent will either be dead or taken hostage,' Grace said condescendingly.

'They are going to do it regardless!'

'No they won't, it's just an idea, it's not like they're going to go ahead with it.'

'For the record,' Naomi said, the camera phone now recording as it sat on the brown coffee table.

Well, here goes the bloody interviews. It's not that I disliked them, I just wished we had planned out when we were going to do them. It would have given me more time to prepare answers.

'Trojan are advancing; isn't there someone else who could deal with this? I think you're overreacting, surely someone else could help?'

Those certainly weren't the words I expected to hear – she thought we were blowing this out of proportion?

'Elaborate?' I asked, crossing my arms.

'Like you said, the Academy trained you to do this, but

couldn't you ask for help? Collaborate with other secret service agents?'

There was the reporter in her, of course she would take after her mother. I knew then her questions weren't personal, they were just there to rule out any possibilities

'No,' Quinn answered firmly, beating me to it.

'We tried to reach out to Gabriel Hale once,' Lily added. 'He worked with Jessica's mum when she was younger.'

'Yeah, and we all know what happened there,' I muttered.

'Source B,' Naomi said pointedly to Quinn. 'Can you elaborate?'

'The sole purpose of this ... institution is to make the choices that no one else will.'

'What do you mean?'

'We are trained to make choices like a computer, without emotion. What the Government wants rather than what is right. What's morally acceptable.'

'Morally acceptable?'

Quinn fell silent and my eyebrows furrowed. Where was she going with this?

'Well, I don't think the army would murder one of their recruits because he posed a security threat.' Quinn's voice was shaky, like there was a chill in the air that made her teeth chatter together. 'I used to study with this guy called Rhys, we were both in technological engineering. He spoke about what was happening here, after – I told him not to, but he told the police. Two days later he disappeared, then the next day he was found dead.'

'In the city?'

I took in a breath, closing my eyes as images flew across my vision. Now I knew exactly what she was talking about.

'No.'

'Then where?'

Quinn stood up slowly and walked over to the window, pulling back the curtains a little, pointing straight ahead.

'You saw the tree, with the birdhouse in it?'

'Yes.'

'There.'

Naomi's gasp filled the room as the rest of us looked away. I wondered if the Academy was any better than Trojan. Were we the good guys?

'For the record, the tree is a couple of metres away from the subject's front door,' Naomi said. She looked ready to throw up, hands clasping at her throat. 'The subject known from now on as source A will answer the next question.'

At that I turned; Naomi was looking directly at me. Her whole body screamed that she wanted out of this place and I didn't blame her.

'If I was found here, would the same thing happen to you?'

For once, I didn't know the answer. I presumed it would be yes, but I'd been taught never to presume. The likelihood was that the whole team would face the consequences: would they kill us all and make an example of us to the rest of the students? Even though I had screamed at Kayson earlier that they would, I doubted it. Apparently Harkness had taken an interest in me; maybe that was something I could use.

'Yes,' Grace answered. 'They would string us all up for this.'

Naomi's gaze didn't deter from mine; she didn't even seem to register Grace's answer.

'Source A?' she asked.

Would they? Would they really kill us all? How far would they go to keep their secret? I had to understand that I wasn't invincible. Just because my mother had a reputation didn't mean I was safe.

'Yes,' I answered. 'If he found out that the whole team were in on this, then the consequences would be filtered through us all.'

'He?'

I paused – was it right to say his name on record? That would expose him. Maybe Harkness was just following orders himself. Before I could even string a few words together, Lily spoke.

'Edward McDonald, but his real name is Daniel Harkness.' She sat forward in her seat. 'He controls Scotland Yard.'

Naomi nodded.

'OK . . . Trojan, do you know their motives?'

'These people murder to make a point,' I snapped, and Naomi shrank back.

Did they even have motives or did they just want to reduce the world to ash and cinder because they could?

The murders so far were mercy killings; unlike the rest, they decided to make their deaths quick. The unlucky ones were kept alive, their organs strung from their bodies. I had seen the footage – the sick bastards filmed themselves as they stripped a man's kidney, liver and one of his lungs. In another they tortured an MI5 agent to death. They started off slow, only plying a toenail from its bed, but she only had so many toes, so they moved on to fingers, and then her eyes.

'We all know how bad things are getting. Attacks are becoming monthly and Thompson can only tell the public they're unrelated for so long. As much as we hate to admit it, people aren't that stupid,' I said. 'The bank and then the theatre only a couple of days later, they're planning something big.'

'What are you saying?' Lily asked me.

'That until we have more information on how bad the situation is getting, we comply with the rules.'

At that there was an outcry, but I held a hand up. My throat was almost eroded, I couldn't shout anymore. 'However, so will Naomi. The longer she stays here, the more evidence we get, and that will lead to a bigger case.'

'What about the water?' Quinn asked. 'We all drink it and I don't think my filter jug will get rid of whatever they're putting in.'

'What drug is it?' said Lily. 'I mean you'll see what it is in the pharmacy.' She looked to Grace, who only replied with a blunt stare.

'I'm studying to be a doctor, go ask a chemist. I'm still learning.'

'Learning? What does that mean? We're safer giving Quinn a scalpel?'

'Computers and human bodies are different things, Lily,' Quinn said.

'Not for much longer,' she muttered.

I shook my head. We'd have to come up with a solution to the water problem later, right now I needed to get them on board with the plan.

'With the restrictions and tight security, we're going to have to be smart about this,' I started. 'What I want to do is gather as much intel on this place as possible. That includes interviews with Naomi, and we're also going to need lapel cameras.'

'Lapel cameras?' Grace asked.

'Well I wasn't under the impression we could shoot this professionally, but give me a couple days and I'll assemble a full crew. Make sure to get the lighting just right so everyone can see you getting punched in the face,' I said sarcastically.

Grace's face dripped like sour milk, but it made me smirk. She was going to comply. Even if she hated the idea. Another small victory.

'How are we going to get the cameras to see the abuse?' Lily asked. 'We can't just wait around for it to happen.'

I sighed, here goes nothing.

'Because we're going to instigate it.'

'Excuse me?' Grace asked horrified. 'No, no way.'

Naomi sat up a little straighter. 'I can't ask you to do that.'

'Well it's a good thing I'm not asking,' I retorted.

Glancing over to Lily I saw the glint of an ember sparking in her eyes as she grinned. This wasn't an order for her, it was an invitation to raise hell.

'What were you thinking?' she asked. 'I'm guessing it's not covering Harkness' office in toilet paper, I was going to go for the more violent approach. We do have access to knives.'

'We're not stabbing anyone!' Quinn exclaimed, her hands flying out.

Lily seemed to reconsider. Nodding her head, she reached over, pulling Quinn into a hug, then placed both of her hands over the girl's ears and whispered.

'Minus Quinn, we're going to fuck some people up.'

I let out a laugh, the rigid pole in my back easing for a moment, God I loved her sometimes. Lily was the person I could always rely on to have a laugh and make dark situations just that little bit brighter.

Naomi chuckled. 'We probably don't want to hear you planning murders on the record. Don't need to incriminate yourself.'

'It'd be worth it,' Lily muttered as she pulled away from Quinn.

Quinn had a confused look on her face and it hit me that she really hadn't heard what Lily said. Oh, the wee lamb.

Then Grace chimed in. 'Do you have a plan?' she asked condescendingly, 'or are we just going to run around with cameras and voice recorders?'

No, I didn't have a plan but I had an idea – did a horrible idea count as a course of action? Probably not.

'Sometimes all you need is patience,' I told them. 'We get the cameras, every evening Naomi will interview us and we'll give an account of our day. Lily's sister is a lawyer, she can represent us in court.'

'Her firm is run by the Academy, her clients have to be approved. I bet they won't agree to this.'

'We can worry about that when we actually get there, right now we need to gather as much intel as possible. Instigate a couple of fights with the faculty, find out what buttons to push,' I said. 'Each of us will take a member of staff. Grace, you'll take both Dr Williams and McKay since you already work with them.'

'You want me to start a fight in the medical wing?' she asked sceptically.

'As much as I would love to sit and watch that with popcorn, no,' I told her. 'First I need you to get friendly, find out what they know about this new drug.'

I caught sight of a small smile from Naomi – at least she

wasn't completely terrified yet.

'Lily, I need you to get closer to Duke, Quinn you handle Thompson considering you're close.'

'We're not . . . close.'

'You have tea together.'

'If you expect me to code without my green tea, you are asking too much of me.' Aw, the wee lamb had to have her tea in order to function.

This plan wasn't a plan, it was based on a what if. What if we instigated a fight? What if we asked too many questions? What if we stepped out of line?

'What are you going to do?' Quinn asked, although it looked as if she already knew my answer.

'I'm going to get close to Harkness.'

What if I disobeyed orders to the point of sheer lunacy and in defiance of all expectation? I had no clue – let's find out.

* * *

Rather than putting Naomi in Willow's room, Quinn had given up her bed and since Lily's room was bigger, she would move in there for the time being. Lily wasn't the happiest about it but she couldn't exactly complain.

My plan was crazy, and if things got out of hand we would have to lie low for a while. Sure, they could continue to cut our supplies, but if the worst came to the worst I could get in contact with my brother. He didn't fully understand what was happening, but he trusted me to take care of myself. I hadn't exactly been doing that, but he didn't have to know. Besides, it's not like he could talk; the guy faked his own death.

The clock had just struck midnight and the girls were trickling up the stairs. I lingered just to make sure everyone got up alright. Besides, I had to do all the checks on the house: make sure all the doors were locked, the windows shut tight, the security code set, the motion sensors on and the door logs activated.

Naomi had headed up with Quinn to get the room sorted out. I still couldn't believe she was here. Of course it was something I'd fantasized about, but fantasies rarely came true. Why had this one? Of all the things I'd dreamed about, the one the world delivered was Naomi. Was she my guardian angel? My saving grace? I didn't follow any religion but I've prayed, I don't know who to, but I've prayed that someone would get me out of this mess. Could it be her?

I grabbed the black duffle bag from where I'd tossed it at the bottom of the stairs then headed up to my room. I need to stretch off before I went to bed or I'd regret it in the morning. Just then I realised I hadn't had dinner. I'd forgotten to grab food on the way home, shite. The last time I checked there was barely anything in the fridge.

As I opened the door to my room, I nearly jumped in surprise. Naomi sat on my bed, the laptop resting on her legs.

'Sorry, didn't mean to scare you,' she said sheepishly. 'I just wanted to ask you a couple more questions before we all went to bed.'

'Course,' I said, chucking the bag under my desk and flopping onto my back beside her.

'When we talked earlier you mentioned that the Technical Support and the Carrier would be a scandal. What's the whole thing with the teams?'

Every time I thought about the team it became clear just

how much of a mess it was, we were down a Carrier with no one to replace her, not that I had had given any thought to it. My second was constantly against me, my Runner was ready to break out the murder weapons while my Techie just wanted to see her mum. Then there was me, where to even begin?

'Teams in the Academy usually consist of five people. Both genders can mix.'

Naomi whipped out the phone, pressing record.

'Team Lead is the highest position, they make the decisions and have the final say. They're also responsible for the actions of the entire team, and any consequences fall on their head first.' Like an axe, I wanted to add.

'The second in command is debated, it's usually an academic scholar rather than a physical or creative. Their job is to question everything, and if the Team Lead isn't present, they make decisions on their behalf.'

'If she's meant to be your second, why is she so against the idea of this?' Naomi asked, quickly catching on.

'I know her like she knows me,' I admitted. 'Admittedly, I can get careless. The second in command is there to make sure the

Team Lead doesn't screw up.'

'But also tries to take your place.'

I laughed. 'Seems it. Our second in command is also the Medical Response, so we got lucky with her. Next is the Runner. Their job is pretty self-explanatory – they give a target the run-around or tail them.'

Naomi nodded but the look of curiosity never left her face, it was like she was on the hunt. Ready to see around every inch of this story, and by God was I going to tell it.

'The Technical Support is in charge of any command rooms we use whilst in the field, monitors, comms and maps. They work closely with the Carrier, more personally.'

'Personally?'

'The Carrier has one job – get any packages from the target or as a pass-off from us, then get the hell out. They are the Technical Support's first priority.'

'You mentioned outside duty?'

'That's nothing: every team or a couple take it in turns to go into town, either here or in Glasgow. Just to establish our presence, but also for any agents passing by to pass info if they're out of options.'

With that Naomi stopped the recording, her lips pressed into a thin smile. She looked satisfied at what she'd heard, and I hoped it had cleared up any burning questions she had. However, as she slid the laptop off her lap and onto my bed I sat up.

'Anything else?' I expected her to ask about James, Harkness or the Academy, but the next question caught me off guard.

'Were Willow and Quinn dating?'

What? Dating? Of course the pair were close, but I'd never considered it. Willow was something of a free spirit, she didn't care for labels, and before the Academy had dated everyone from here to Aberdeen. Quinn I thought was as straight as an HB pencil, but if Naomi suspected it then maybe it was a lot more personal than I believed. Of course they spent a lot of time together, their roles on the team demanded it.

'Dating?' I asked. 'No. Not that I know about, you'd have to ask Quinn.'

She nodded, deflated at my answer. She must have seen something I hadn't to spark that question. Abruptly, Naomi pulled me into a hug, her shoulders squeezing mine before pulling away.

'I'm going to get you out of here,' she said, 'whatever it takes.'

'Thank you.'

Naomi seemed to be waiting for me to say something else but I couldn't find the words – in truth all I wanted to do was take off my make-up, change, then sleep and block out the world. Tonight, I could sleep with the knowledge that Naomi was across the hall, my guardian angel.

Then, with a wave and a small-voiced goodnight, she left.

As I got ready for bed I put on some background noise to distract myself, some rock band but I didn't really pay attention, I was focused on the beat as it hammered out the voices of guilt. Tomorrow was a new day and I had to be ready, but for now I let the beat take me.

Thump, thump, thump.

I stared in the mirror. The fresh bruises had now mutated to yellow ones, similar to those on my cheekbone and lower back. If I kept this up I was going need more concealer.

Shut the fuck up! I didn't deserve this.

I wouldn't let him control me like that ever again. I would comply with the rules but I wouldn't let him lay another hand on me. Harkness had power, but not anymore, and I'd make sure he knew about it. He'd hurt me before but he wouldn't do it again.

The music raged on and I let every riff wash over me.

Things were going to change, and this time I'd be in control.

SLATE RETRIBUTION

CHAPTER 15

Heterize

To transform.

NAOMI JADE

Despite being in a strange and worryingly dangerous place I slept quite well, only waking up when I heard what I assumed were pots banging from downstairs. I had thought that my regularly scheduled hot guys on jet skis dream would be consumed with torturous nightmares, but thankfully that wasn't the case. It was only a matter of time though – how long before the horrors of your waking day slipped into the unconscious movies in your head? I wished I'd taken that psychology class, might have helped, although you'd probably need someone with a PhD to sort out all this whackadoo.

When I opened my eyes, soft pink walls greeted me, it felt

like waking up in a modern-day princess room. Instead of curtains there were sheer white drapes and the bed covers were pastel pink with a soft, tan-coloured blanket on top (the fluffiest thing ever!).

Finally found a good thing about this place! If you put up with all the shitty trauma, you get the room of your dreams ... yay.

Quinn told me last night that she'd tidied the place up before I came in, which told me she was a complete neat freak, since it looked exactly the same when I came back. What was with everyone? I felt quite ashamed because my room looked like a bomb-site while all of theirs were military-grade clean.

I didn't want to leave the bed since I had worked the covers and blanket into a luxuriously warm cocoon, but I knew I had to make a start, strip this house from floor to ceiling. I had to treat this like a crime scene, anything could be evidence.

With a groan and pulling a lot of unflattering faces I shimmied out of the bed. It took me a moment to realise I'd taken the duvet and blanket with me though, so when I went to take a step forward, my foot caught and I landed flat on my ass. Let's pretend that didn't happen.

At least it couldn't get worse from here – what's worse than landing on your butt first thing in the morning?

Then I felt it, wet, warm and dribbling. Oh no. I shot up, dropping the covers and looked down to the grey pyjama bottoms with adorable little smiling avocado cartoons on it, to see red seeping through the crotch. Oh come on! Now? Would they even have any pads or tampons? They all took that pill – wow, this was embarrassing. I didn't even know where the bathroom was but I needed toilet paper fast.

I threw open the door and ran, but didn't see a sign for the bathroom anywhere: every door in the hallway was closed and completely identical. The sticky warmth started running down my thigh faster so I lunged for the closest door and barged in. Sadly, it wasn't the bathroom.

Lily sat on her bed throwing a basketball into the air. She looked up a little startled, and her eyes quickly travelled down to my crotch.

'Oh, honey,' she said with a knowing smirk.

'Where's the bathroom?' I pleaded.

She shook her head. 'OK, first calm down, we have stuff

to get the blood out and I'm sure Quinn won't kill you for wrecking her fave pyjamas,' she said, standing up from her bed and dashing out.

Oh crap, these were her favourite? Why the hell did she give them to me?

I followed Lily two doors down into the bathroom. For a communal place it was quite big: three bathroom stalls, a large mirror opposite that took up a big portion of the wall, with three sinks underneath. Lily slid open the tall cabinet beside the door, rummaging through it.

'Now, are you a tampon or pad girl?' she asked.

'Pad.' This felt a little intimate.

Lily handed me a pad and a fresh pair of pants, along with some scrunched up loo roll, which I stuffed into my pants for the time being, 'Sometimes we miss the pills by mistake and end up with that lovely wake-up call,' she said. 'Believe me, you don't have to be embarrassed. We're ladies after all.'

'Thank you,' I said quietly.

'Don't sweat it. Just throw your undies in the washing basket, then grab some shorts from my room.'

As she turned to leave I asked, 'Lily, what about your parents? Do they know what's going on?'

The girl stopped dead, her hand hovering over the doorhandle, then slowly turned around. She took in a breath, almost like she was forcing herself to talk.

'My parents think I'm attending a posh boarding school. They live in Osaka, when my sister became a lawyer they couldn't ship me off fast enough.'

'Osaka, that's in Japan, right?' I'd heard of the place before but only seen it in pictures.

'Yeah,' she said with a melancholy smile. 'You know I hated it there, but I'd give anything to see it again . . . now you get changed, don't need a crime scene in the bathroom.' With a two-fingered mock salute Lily left, closing the door behind her.

I thought Lily would have been harsher, or wouldn't care as much but she was the opposite. She reminded me of a tomboy or like someone who'd rather have a group of guy friends than girls. Even the way she dressed, black jeans, baggy top, plaid shirt tied around her waist, tall combat boots and part of her eyebrow shaved off. If I saw her in school she'd be one of the girls I'd try and avoid – they always looked at me like a speck of dirt, like I wasn't tough enough to join their group.

Maybe I'd been getting this all wrong, turning away from people like her because of a couple of glances. To me, Quinn was approachable since our style and personality were similar. I'd have to get comfortable with everyone in this house, even though they were all so different.

I quickly changed my pants, sticking the pad to the fresh pair before grabbing some wipes from the sink, cleaning myself up. I pushed back the flood of embarrassment as I peeped my head out of the bathroom and darted to Lily's room for the shorts. What was I doing? They were all girls for crying out loud! Besides, I could create life in my uterus, that was something to be proud of. Although just as the thoughts of how great my reproductive system was ran through my head, sharp twisting cramps crunched through my lower stomach.

OK, I needed to find pain killers.

Just as my uterus recreated the *Battle of the Bastards*, I made it into Lily's room. Heading straight for the brown chest of drawers opposite, filtering through tops and questionable red thongs, I found a black pair of shorts. As I slipped them on I noted how Lily's room was red and grey with a couple of classic film posters on the walls. She had a large glass of red wine on a small black desk but the rest of the room was mostly taken up by the pull-up bar and weights station, along with a lot of clothes and more questionable lingerie all over the floor. Maybe it was just Quinn and Jess who were neat freaks?

With that in mind I left the room and plodded down the stairs. What I was honestly expecting was to see everyone walking about with guns and grenades, but that wasn't the case at all. Jessica and Lily were in workout gear, Grace in scrubs, while Quinn was still in her pyjamas, nibbling on a single piece of toast as she watched something on her laptop.

'We have half a loaf of bread, about a slather of butter, two oranges, one avocado, and two bottles of water.' Lily announced proudly but there was a smirk on her face. 'Since now we've basically been told we're getting diddly-squat for another week, I say we call your brother.'

Jessica turned around, mixing what looked like a protein shake.

'Yeah, I'll drop him a message today, see when he can get here.'

'Do you think Christopher will come this time?' Quinn asked innocently, and Lily's eyes lit up, while Grace, standing beside Jess, looked completely bored by the subject.

'Oh yes,' Lily started. 'I wonder if good old, handsome yet daring Chris will grace us with his presence – but then again, none of us get any sleep when he does.'

'Bite me,' Jessica snarked.

'I'll leave that to Chris,' Lily teased.

Who the hell was Christopher? Was he a student here too? I really needed to get up to speed with everyone, there would be no use in writing this story if I didn't know who half the people were. Just then, Jessica caught my eye and she smiled.

'Morning. How'd you sleep?'

'Oh! Auntie Flow came to visit,' Lily announced.

My cheeks flushed red as my eyes darted over to her – why did she have to tell everyone? What happened to privacy? Or, I don't know, the girl code.

'We can give you stuff to stop that,' Grace suggested.

'The plan is to get us out, not her in,' said Jessica.

'Just saying.' Grace raised her hands in surrender as she went to pop the kettle on. 'Thank God for coffee.'

'Yeah Grace, can you pray that the coffee doesn't run out?' Lily asked. 'Or we'll all have to resort to green tea, and then the world really will be ending.'

Grace rolled her eyes, holding up a hand to tell her to shut up. Lily didn't comment further but she had a smirk on her face. How did she have so much energy?

'So, briefing,' Jessica said, taking a quick shot of her protein drink. 'Today is simple, we go about our business. Lily and I have training with Duke and Ames for a couple of hours, so we'll deal with that. However, if Ames starts banging out the suicide drills we'll hold back on the questions. After last night I don't think I can run another five miles.'

'Mr Tommy Ames, now he would know his way around a woman,' Lily muttered, and Jessica gave her a disgusted look. 'What? I may be gay but I know a hot guy when I see one.'

'Stop with the comments, it's too early in the morning. And I said get close with the staff, not sleep with them.'

Once again, I was out of the loop. I barely knew who they were talking about so stood at the door in silence, arms wrapped around my torso. I didn't belong here at all. I wasn't trained from a young age like them, I didn't know what all the code words meant or who all these people were.

I felt like I was right back at the start. Not two minutes before, I'd told myself I had to pose questions, be the first one to speak, but now all I seemed to do was stand around. Was it my place to ask questions?

'So define close – am I supposed to snog Dr McKay on my ward shift?' Grace asked as she poured her coffee. 'Cause I don't think his wife would be too happy about that.'

Jessica sighed, exasperated. 'No, all I'm saying is get more friendly than hostile, maybe they'll answer more of our questions.'

'Your type of friendly or our type of friendly?'

Jessica pointed to the door. 'Just grab a mic and get out.'

'All I'm saying is that last time you were friendly with someone Chris ended up in your bed.' My mouth dropped open. Hold up, what now?

'Mics are by the door!' Jessica exclaimed, her eyes cast down to the floor.

Grace let out a scoff, and as she grabbed her coffee cup on the way out she patted my shoulder. 'Good luck, you're gonna need it,' she laughed, before leaving.

I turned to watch her go and saw her pick up a black microphone from the table and attach it to herself as she went out the door. This was it then, we were really doing this.

Although, corrupt governments could wait, I wanted to know who Chris was.

'So, Christopher?' I asked, crossing my arms over my chest. Sure I didn't know much about the spy world but I could talk boys. 'He's what? Your boyfriend?'

Jessica groaned. 'Naomi, don't,' she said coldly, sliding into a seat at the table.

As I walked further into the kitchen I realised Lily and Quinn wore smug grins – oh, so this *was* her boyfriend? I tried to get any information from Lily, but she pulled two fingers over her lips like a zip. Well if I wasn't getting anything from her then there's no chance –

'He works with her brother!' Quinn exclaimed.

'Your brother's best friend?' I asked, surprised. 'You slept with your brother's best friend? When did this happen?'

'We did not sleep together,' Jessica said, and Lily let out a laugh.

'Yeah Jess, and I'm a unicorn,' she said, grabbing one of the water bottles from the fridge. 'Naomi, don't worry, we'll supply you with earplugs or a good playlist.'

I couldn't believe what I was hearing. I guess it couldn't always be doom and gloom around here. If anything, I was proud of her for getting some action.

A playfulness rose through my cheeks as I saw a small tint of blush on Jessica's. 'Oh come on Jess,' I said. 'You and I used to talk boys all the time.'

Suddenly, Jessica flipped, her chair screeching back as she stood, fury raging through her shaking body. What the hell had I said?

'We don't have time for this, we have a job to complete. The team has bigger issues than idle gossip. You have a job of your own, Naomi, get to it,' she snapped, before turning to Quinn.

'I also said I needed those reports by nine, Quinn, look at the clock once in a while.' Then she snapped her fingers at Lily. 'You, outside in three minutes or I will leave without you.' Jessica marched out of the kitchen, and the door slammed shut.

My whole body went rigid – what the hell was that all about? I hadn't said anything out of turn. What was it with everyone around here? One second it was all happy town and the next they were jumping down my throat.

'Did I say something?' I dared to ask, and Quinn shook her head, but without the sympathetic smile I expected. She looked worried.

Lily still stood at the fridge, watching the empty space where Jessica had sat, biting her lip in agitation. Then she locked eyes with Quinn. They shared some sort of mental conversation before Quinn spoke.

'Grace and Jessica have been acting out lately, more aggressively,' Quinn started. She sounded horrified. 'We think it's the red pill, whatever's in it. Lily and I wanted to test the theory so we stopped taking them for a couple of days, but ever since everything went pear-shaped those two have been taking them like their lives depended on it.'

'Christ, we're going to need to take them before the Friday check-up,' Lily groaned.

From their reaction I knew that this behaviour had become common. But the pills had to do more than just make them snap.

Yesterday was full of emotion: she'd hugged me, let me catch a glimpse into her life, but now I was shut out, like a stranger. I had to break back in.

'Grace said she's going to check at the pharmacy, see what those pills really are.'

At that I paused. 'Wait, does Grace actually work at the hospital?'

'Kinda,' Quinn said. 'We have a medical wing in the Academy, she works there mostly, but any time they need an agent at the hospital to protect someone or transport them, Grace goes. She's still studying medicine, though.'

'That's what I don't get,' I said. 'Why go to the trouble of a scholarship? Surely there's enough going on in your lives without having to study for a degree too?'

Lily shrugged. 'Lennox – she's the resident psychologist –

said it would be healthy to have something else to focus on. It makes us flexible in different situations. Instead of relying on the doctors here, our team rely on Grace for anything medical. For all technical needs we go to Quinn, anything involving sports I'm your gal, then anything to do with theatre Jessica steps in.'

'So it's all about purpose?' I asked. 'You all have different skills –'

'– so shove us in a team together, we just about cover everything.' Lily cut me off, although she seemed to muse for a moment. 'Maybe that's why Harkness takes such an interest in our team.'

Quinn shrugged. 'Could be, not every team is like ours. Kayson's team doesn't have a Techie or Medic, it's made up of Runners.'

Interesting – not every team was constructed like this one. I wondered what that was about. Not everyone could specialise in certain things, but I'd thought there would have been some structure to it. If they didn't choose their own teams, then the staff must have put them in certain ones for a reason. If Kayson's team was filled with Runners then maybe that's what they needed? It couldn't be random – the Academy calculated every move meticulously.

If the Runners were like Lily and Kayson, then I assumed they were all muscly and extremely fit – maybe the Academy wanted a team that specialised in fighting? So if they needed a strike team, they'd send Kayson's? Could that be how it worked? They created teams for specific purposes then developed them through different kinds of training? It was a lot to assume, but after catching sight of what this place really was, it wasn't entirely out of the question.

'I better get going,' Lily said, but before she moved she looked to me. 'We were only able to get wires for today so you'll have to deal with just audio until Quinn can snatch us some cameras.'

'Temporarily misplace,' Quinn added quickly, and I let out a small laugh. I had a feeling that even though the girl was sweet she could make your life a living hell with a couple of taps of her keyboard.

Lily snorted and headed out of the house, but she called back, 'We're training at the back of the school, use your fancy laptop, get a good look at the first years when they arrive!' Then the door swung shut.

Oh yeah, that's right, even if we didn't have the lapel cameras we had James' laptop. We'd only get stationary access but I wanted up and personal. Then, just like that, I was hit with another insane idea.

'First years?' I asked.

'Yeah, they're doing an orientation day, they get to put on the uniform for the first time, get a black card ... why are you looking at me like that?' she asked, her face crinkling at the growing smirk on my face. 'I don't like that look.'

'How hard do you think it would be to put a new first year student on the system?' I asked. Quinn's eyes widened as she caught on to my utterly amazing yet completely flawed plan.

'No – No!'

'Oh come on, you want to help your friends, I'll borrow someone's uniform then I'll be able to walk around the school without being noticed.'

'Without being – Naomi! They only take thirty students in every year, you seriously think people won't notice?'

'Not if you put me in as a first year, they'll be too busy to count us all'

Quinn groaned, her head falling into her hands. But what gave me hope was seeing the gears turn in her mind. Was she actually going to let me do this? Sure, it was crazy, but that way I would get to see for myself what kind of place this was. Besides, I wanted into the Academy, not the dorms.

'There's an intense screening process – I can't just drop you in without being noticed. I'd have to do it from the main computer lab, and even then you'd need a fake name, background story – you can't memorise all of that.'

'Jessica used to run lines with me – I know the entirety of *Legally Blonde* inside out and that was over one day. I'm sure I could get this in an hour.'

'Jessica is never going to agree to this. She's Team Lead – anything we do has to be sanctioned by her.'

'I'm not on her team, Quinn.'

Quinn opened her mouth but she looked like she was running out of ideas to deter me.

'Thompson, has he ever seen you?' she asked. 'It's an

orientation, you go around every department.'

Shit, mum keeps a picture with me on her desk, and as her screensaver – would he recognise me? If I was caught there was no doubt I would be taken out, to put it politely.

'There's a chance.'

Quinn mulled over the thought but then she looked up, hope glinting on her face.

'What am I saying? In espionage, looks are never an issue.'

* * *

One hour and thirty minutes, that's how long it took Quinn to transform me from average to – well, less average. In the movies all the glow ups had amazing results, but according to Quinn no one ever looked better in a disguise. She said the idea was to attract next to no attention, and frankly I was grateful because blending in was a strength of mine.

I was kitted out in a dark blonde wig, a small prosthetic nose, brown contact lenses, fake freckles, fake eyebrows, fake teeth, a pair of glasses and, to top it all off, the Reign Academy uniform. As I caught myself in the mirror's reflection I hardly recognised myself. I'd been too busy learning my backstory and fake name to watch what Quinn was doing.

'What do you think?' she asked, jumping up and down giddily.

'How are you so good at this?' I turned from side to side in the mirror: she had contoured my cheekbones, turning my round faced into a carved one.

'My mum worked as a make-up artist before she went into witness protection – that and I took disguise in year two,' Quinn replied proudly.

I could tell she had a good connection with her mother, there was something about her that simply lit up. Even as she was putting the make-up on, Quinn told me stories about her, the movie nights and small tea parties. She was such an empathetic person, I wondered how she'd ended up in a place like this.

'Now,' she started, before reaching into one of her drawers and pulling out a flesh coloured earpiece, 'you wear this at all times, I need to be able to talk to you. I'll guide you to different parts of the school, all you need to worry about is not being seen.'

Now it was my turn to get excited as I fiddled with the

small contraption. This was it! I was going in undercover for real, this was actually happening! I wasn't just a little girl playing pretend in her bedroom, this was the real world. I slipped the device into my ear before turning back to Quinn, who typed away at the computer.

The screen was black except for a grey tab down the left side but as I took in a breath I realised that what I assumed were soundwaves moved slightly. Then a beating heart icon continually spiked up and down – were these my vitals?

'I don't have a visual, but that's fine – all I need is audio. We have the laptop, so I can monitor you through there. If a teacher starts asking too many questions, curl your hand into a fist,' she told me. 'That's the signal, I'll get one of the girls to get you out.'

'What if they're busy?'

'I don't have a reason to be in the building, so once I'm hidden I can't move. If anything happens you're on your own.'

'Splendid.' I said sarcastically.

Quinn squeezed my shoulders, resting her chin on them and, armed with a mic and camera phone, I was ready.

SLATE RETRIBUTION

Quinn would take me to the crowd of first years that were gathering outside of the accommodation, claiming I'd gotten lost, then she would head to the Academy to input my details in the system. Since this had never been done before, we were just kind of presuming there weren't too many measures in place that would screw this plan up.

Once I was on the orientation trip I would slip away from the main group, be guided by Quinn to Jessica and Lily's class, then to the hospital wing. There had to be something going on that I could use as evidence.

However, fear kept finding its way to my heart. It pounded in my chest, the echoes ringing through my ears. This was the stupidest idea I'd ever had.

Well, I never said I made good decisions.

EMERY HALE

CHAPTER 16

Masquerade

A false show or pretence.

NAOMI JADE

Well this was terrifying, scary and utterly insane! After Quinn ushered me out the door and took me to the growing crowd I immediately wanted to do a one-eighty and run back inside. This was the stupidest plan I'd ever come up with, and I had done a lot of stupid things in my short lifetime. Jessica's plan was to keep me hidden from the Academy and here I was skipping into the joint.

As I slowly edged my way towards the group flashing a smile, some of the girls turned in my direction, then so did the guys. Their eyes scanned me up and down before a couple turned, whispering to their friends. Was something out of place? Had a contact gone squinty? Did I have toilet paper on my shoe or something in my teeth? Were they talking about me? I felt like I was right back in high school – everyone had already sorted out their groups and here I was, Maggie no pals.

I was so caught up in my own thoughts, I didn't hear the familiar click of heels walking towards us. A tall, slender woman appeared with worrisome pale skin and thin, straw-like hair, dressed formally with a key hanging from her belt. Was that some sort of master key? I thought it would all be plastic cards like you see in the spy movies: I sincerely hoped they didn't have a dungeon here.

'Welcome to the Reign Academy, you may address me as Ms Helen. Nothing more, nothing less. Anything other will result in disciplinary action.'

It was her – that was the same voice I'd heard in Quinn's room. My mouth clamped shut, my lips pressing into a fine line. There was no way she could tell it was me, she didn't even know I was in the room when she came in. Despite the blatant facts I couldn't put aside the anxiety crawling up my throat. If we'd get disciplinary action for calling her a different name, it was no wonder everyone hated the staff here.

'Follow me,' she said.

I did as I was told.

I followed at the back of the group, slowly at first, staying behind people instead of beside them. If I did that then maybe it would be easier to slip away. I wasn't trained like Jess or Lily, and I certainly wasn't a master at surveillance. I was only guessing at what I had to do. Quinn said she would head straight to one of the command rooms, set up a small station and then connect to my earpiece. She better do it soon.

We left the accommodation scheme through a path to the right – it was long and lined with smaller, growing trees, and through the bobbing heads in front of me I could see it opened up to the main building. Well if this wasn't a crazy school, I'd say that it would be great that classes were only a two-minute walk away. But it was a crazy school.

As soon as I caught sight of the tall mahogany doors fear chilled through me. This was it, once I was in there was no turning back. I would be on at least one security camera so better make this quick.

'Hey,' a small voice whispered. I darted to the sound, thinking I was rumbled. 'You know it's just scare tactics, right?'

The girl was a little younger than me, sixteen perhaps. She had platinum blonde hair and honestly resembled a younger Anne Hathaway.

'We're not actually going to get a warning or detention because we didn't say her name properly.'

Detention – I wanted to laugh in her face. Oh no, you wouldn't get a detention. You'd probably get slapped or, better yet, not eat properly a week.

'My name's Jackie,' she said, and I gave her the biggest smile I could muster, which was probably smaller than I imagined. 'Guessing you're one of the civilians they recruited?'

'Civilian?' I asked, a little confused.

'Yeah, you don't have any military parents or background with the secret service?'

'Oh, no just your, uh . . . regular girl.' Wow, I was horrible at this.

'Where's the others?' she asked. 'They take in five a year, I'm sure.'

SLATE RETRIBUTION

I didn't answer her as we walked up the stone steps and the grand doors swung open. My dad would be livid if he found out his taxes paid for this huge marble floor. This place was bigger than the security cameras made it out to be: the ceiling resembled that of a church, immensely tall, decorated with gold, and what looked like renaissance paintings. What struck me as odd though was the bleach smell that burned my nose hairs, like the chemicals themselves floated in the air around me. Older students steered clear of us – I tried to make eye contact with one guy who was around my age but he didn't even glance in my direction. There was barely any chatter from the other students, it mostly came from our group. Ahead sat a large security desk, two burly, armed men at either side, but the chair behind was empty. Men with guns, I'm sure there's a joke about that somewhere.

'This is the main reception. Formal and informal visitors must come through here before they are granted access to the rest of the building. This is where I am stationed throughout the day, if you need anything I am the first port of call. Now if you *all* could scan your passes, then we can get started with the tour.'

Poop. I didn't have a pass – did they mail it out to you if

you got accepted? Quinn never said anything about a pass. I was rumbled. Done for. Now those two men were going to escort me out of here like a common criminal. Oh well, this was it then, this was how I died.

As the group filed forward to scan their passes I stayed completely still, trying to keep my breathing as even as possible. Our plan had failed at the first hurdle. Just then, Jackie gripped my shoulders, squeezing them, a bright smile on her face.

'You'll get used to it, everything is done with security passes around here.'

Yeah but Jackie, I don't have one because I'm impersonating a first year student so I can expose this school for what it really is! I wanted to shout in her face. We didn't have a backup plan! Why didn't we have a backup plan?

Suddenly I felt someone barge into me, nearly knocking me off of my feet. Luckily Jackie threw out her arms and caught me.

'Watch where you're going!' she called behind her, but I didn't hear a response. She quickly helped me up, kindness swimming in her eyes. 'You OK?'

SLATE RETRIBUTION

Even though I had known Jackie a whole two minutes I was ready to word-vomit, beg her to help and hope she didn't rat me out. Just as I was about to tell her everything I realised there was a white plastic card in my hand, with the name of my cover alias *Ellie Smyth* printed on it. I shot onto my tippy-toes, and just made out the back of Quinn's pink blouse as she disappeared into the crowd.

Oh I liked Quinn.

'Yeah,' I replied. 'Great actually, just clumsy.'

'Older students, think they're everything, honestly,' Jackie said, shaking her head.

As we shuffled down the makeshift queue towards the scanner I let out a sigh of relief as the card rested in my hand. Well, first hurdle dealt with, let's worry about the others when we got there.

Soon enough I was at the front and placed my card on the thin black scanner. The little red light flashed green and without another thought I left, walking as calmly as I could to the rest of the crowd. I had to act like I belonged. One of the rules when undercover was that you don't run, don't attract attention, you walk around like you're supposed to be there. That's what Quinn told me.

I had to act like I belonged; something I've struggled with for years.

Well, I had motivation – it was either this or a bullet in my head. I avoided the gaze of the armed guards and tried to focus on whatever Jackie was saying, but something claimed my attention. Harkness, walking down the marble steps to my right. He was so close, I could punch him in the face, stick a foot in between the banisters and trip him up – maybe he would fall and break his neck. Not that I'd actually do that, of course. That would be wrong, no matter what he'd done.

Harkness wore a permanent scowl, like the world was just a place of misery for him. He was dressed formally like Helen: white shirt, black trousers, and by the looks of it, fancy Italian shoes. Five hours of shoe shopping with Katie had apparently stuck with me. Without even a hint that he saw the large group, he walked past us. I guess he wasn't the kind of person to say hello, but Jackie stared after the man in awe.

'Do you know who that is?' Jackie asked. *An abusive*

corrupt asshole. 'That's Daniel Harkness, he's got one of the highest kill counts. I heard that here he's like a God.'

'Really?' I asked, feigning confusion.

'But I also heard he's into dodgy stuff, I don't know the details but whatever you do, stay on his good side.'

'Why?'

'I don't know.' *Oh, someone's parents didn't teach them how to lie.*

If Harkness had this reputation, how were parents comfortable sending their kids here? Maybe they didn't have parents or any guardians but still, common sense? Did that exist in this place?

Once everyone was done Helen led us through the wide corridors. She didn't tell us to follow, we just did. I expected the boys to be making one hell of a noise, or throwing comments to the girls who passed, but they stayed quiet. This wasn't like high school at all. Sure, there were small murmurs amongst the group, but nothing obnoxiously loud. Weird.

In the corridors there were cabinets filled with trophies from sporting events and a couple of stone statues that belonged in a pantheon. I didn't expect there to be windows, but it was like they couldn't get enough of them: there were five on this corridor alone. Was this school so untouchable that the people inside could be seen clear as day and no one would do anything about it?

We turned a corner and headed down a set of stairs. Suddenly the luxurious walls turned to pure concrete, followed by a set of black doors. When they opened and we stepped through, a thin carpet met my feet. This room was bigger than any lecture hall or classroom. A monitor took up most of the wall ahead and six rows of desks worked their way back, all busy with students, some of them occupied on laptops while others were talking on phones. On the monitor there was a picture of someone walking through Glasgow Queen Street low level – was there an op going on right now?

The room was lit with a dim blue light, most of the light coming from lamps on the desks. But as I looked above I saw an entirely separate floor with a front wall of glass. It looked like an office, but too big of an office for just one person.

'I'm in position,' I heard the small voice say in my ear – the thing was so lightweight I'd forgotten it was there. 'Presently your position is in the main command room.' I whipped my head around, trying to find Quinn amongst this chaos. 'Stop, don't look for me. You can't attract any more attention.'

I ran a hand over my face trying to regain some composure. Now I had Quinn by my side, she'd know what to do and how to do it properly. I just had to follow her.

'You can't slip away now, it's too difficult. You'll have to do it when you're going to the next place,' she said.

My attention was diverted as I heard the cool tapping of a man walking down the black steel stairs at the other side of the room. He barely acknowledged us, but I knew exactly who he was. Come on disguise, don't fail me now. The man was scrawny – might have given you a papercut if you touched him. He was tall with dark hair and age spots littered his face. Despite the dim lighting I could see there were bags under his eyes. I knew teachers got stressed over schoolwork, but this wasn't a normal school – what had he been up to?

'This is Thompson,' Quinn told me. 'Don't engage, he's hopeless in combat but smart as hell.'

I wanted to laugh. Don't engage, what was this, *CSI*? No,

it was an institute for mindless assassins Naomi, get with the programme.

'Thompson,' Helen said, and the man nodded politely. He didn't give a smile, he just glanced the group up and down, then turned back to Helen.

'I thought you weren't bringing the students until later, I'm busy.'

Since Helen ran the accommodation, I guessed she didn't have much of a rank when it came to the teachers, but I didn't like to assume.

'Well, it's orientation, we have a lot of technical support students here.'

'I don't care if they're the next SAS, they're cluttering up my control room. Get out.'

What a charmer.

I know what I said before, but Thompson must act differently at work because if he ever spoke to my mother like that, she wouldn't be working there anymore. Helen rolled her eyes before she took off to the door, leading us away. I did another once-over of the place, but couldn't spot Quinn – she must have been tucked away in another room.

Jackie took my hand and I looked at her in surprise, but she didn't return it. Well, it was going to be hard to slip away when someone was holding my hand.

'Naomi, you're not meant to make friends, who is that girl?' Did Quinn remember I couldn't respond? 'Wait I've got her, Jacqueline Buchanan – woah, she is rich as hell. Her parents bought their way in, that's – that's seven figures.'

Hold the bloody number two bus, someone invested over a million pounds in this place? Where did people get that kind of money? I had a feeling I wouldn't want to know the answer to that.

That was when Jackie whispered. 'You're nervous, it's fine, I heard Thompson's not a people person.'

'It's just a bit much. Not what I expected.'

'They're still expanding – don't know what though, my dad won't tell me.'

Expanding? Is there going to be a jacuzzi? I still didn't understand what there was to invest in – surely this place was bad enough already? The money could be paying for the new drugs they want. You probably couldn't grab the blue ones from a pharmacy.

As soon as we left we turned down another corridor, then another. This place was constructed like a maze, I had no clue how to get back to reception. The corridors were so long with so many different doors and alcoves.

As we walked I asked, 'Your dad works for Reign?'

'Oh no,' she replied. 'He's Head of Security in the House of Commons, but I'll be real with you, he also works with the Americans.'

The Americans? Were they in on this too? Maybe the better question was who wasn't involved with this whackadoo? That list would be significantly smaller.

What I didn't expect was Quinn to start shouting in my ear.

'You're heading straight for the back end of the school! Jessica and Lily are – wait, that's weird.'

Oh shit. I was nervous for this bit – would they recognise me? I wanted to ask what was weird but I couldn't exactly speak to thin air, not with Jackie next to me. Maybe Jess's class would

SLATE RETRIBUTION

be too busy taking lumps out of each other to recognise me. If I stayed at the back of the group I should be fine – *please let that be true.*

'Can you slip away yet? There's a turn up ahead and you could get into one of the classrooms. There's one on your right that should be empty.'

Jackie had a firm grip on my hand, how could I slip away?

'I have to go to the bathroom, I'll catch up,' I said, quickly pulling my hand back.

'Really? You sure it isn't just nerves?' she asked.

'Yeah, one hundred percent,' I said to her, before pointing a finger behind me. 'I saw a sign back there, don't wait.' With a forced smile and eyes pleading for her to leave, I turned my back and started heading the way we came.

I thanked my shorter stature because it meant Helen was less likely to see me pull away from the crowd. I took a couple of paces before I looked. Thankfully, Jackie had caught up with the rest of the first years and was whispering something to the other girls. Was she talking about me? Telling them how weird I was? *Aw who cares Naomi!* You're probably never going to see them again.

Once I knew Jackie was preoccupied I spun around and marched into the classroom on the right. I didn't even look to see if it was empty, I just shut the door behind me, thanking my lucky stars for some respite.

'You're safe,' Quinn said. I was never going to get used to having a voice in my ear; it was like she was inside my head.

The classroom I had ended up in actually looked like a regular science lab. It had high white desks, stools and a couple of Bunsen burners connected to gas taps. On the board was some fancy chemistry equation – yeah, I sucked at sciences.

'OK, so you should wait another couple of minutes before getting out of there. A class is going to start in fifteen minutes so you don't want to hang around too long.'

Fifteen minutes? I could ransack this place for a little while before anyone would notice. I ran over to the filing cabinet and starting flicking through the different folders trying to find something. I mean, it was a science lab – they could be building bombs in here for crying out loud.

'Uh, what are you doing?' Quinn asked.

'There might be something in here.'

'These are the second-year labs, there won't be anything.'

THUD

I pulled back, thinking I'd dropped something out of one of the folders, but when I looked there was nothing. Slowly I knocked my knuckle against the bottom of the drawer and it sounded again. A hollow sound. As I took a closer look I noticed a faint square shape with a small strap at the side. This drawer had a false bottom – it was just like the movies!

'Now Quinn, I'm not an expert, but people with nothing to hide don't usually have a secret compartment,' I said, trying to keep the excitement out of my voice.

'Over comms you call me Pilot, we don't use our actual names,' Quinn scolded.

OK miss fussy pants.

I lifted the latch, pulling up the lid of the drawer. Inside was ... a camera? Oh god a camera! I dropped the files and shoved the drawer shut with a clang. Was that live? Was that a camera placed by the Academy?

'What? What happened? Was there a spider?'

'A camera.'

'What? What's a camera doing in there?'

'Quinn – Pilot – how the hell am I supposed to know?'

There was silence for a couple of seconds before Quinn let out a sigh of relief. 'There's not a live feed signal coming from it, it's just an ordinary camera.'

Why was a camera stashed there? Did it belong to the science teacher? Did this place even *have* proper science teachers? They were probably just insane scientists with a degree in how to blow things up. I didn't get a chance to ponder on the thought any longer because the door opened and Kayson walked in.

'Oh crap, cause the camera's looped I didn't – sorry, I didn't know he was coming,' Quinn said, but I didn't answer.

The guy looked at me almost analytically, but what surprised me was the blotchy bruising on his face. Not him too . . .

'You lost or something?' he asked.

Part of me wanted to answer, but the other instinctive part knew I should stay quiet. He could recognise my voice and put the pieces together, so I just nodded.

Kayson groaned.

'First years, always getting lost.' He held the door open pointing out it. 'Well go on then, what you waiting for?'

He didn't recognise me, should I be offended? Of course I didn't want him to know it was me because that would blow this whole thing open, but still!

I ducked my head and quickly walked past him out into the corridor that was slowly building up with students. Most of them weren't in uniform, they were in workout gear or comfy clothes. I didn't see the first years ahead of me, which was a good sign – now I could go wherever I wanted.

'OK that was close, I don't trust Kayson as far as I can throw him and believe me, I'm not athletic in the slightest. Since you're closer to the medical wing you can go there first, so after the next couple doors, go left.'

I could get used to this – Quinn was like an on-the-go satnav. I had a quick glance around to see Kayson staring directly at me. I whipped my head back around and continued down the hall. I didn't need him breaking my cover, even if I secretly wished he'd recognised me.

If Quinn didn't trust him then that was good enough for

me. What did I ever see in that guy? Of course, none of what happened between us could have been genuine, but there were facts, and then there were feelings. There was a connection between us, I felt it. Did he?

'OK, now there's a lift at the end of the corridor, take it to floor four, that's where the medical wing is. I've got you covered with cameras, don't worry you can move freely.'

Four floors? Was that just above ground or did they have more?

I followed the directions and pressed the button for the lift, fiddling with a loose thread on my skirt while I waited. My knee started to bounce as paranoia crept up on me. How did the girls do this? It was worse than going through airport security, even though the worst thing I've ever done is stolen my granny's bag of Murray Mints. When the lift doors opened I stepped inside, looking at all the buttons.

 F 4

 F 3

 F 2

 F 1

SLATE RETRIBUTION

G

B -1

B -2

This school covered seven levels? No wonder they needed all the money. Jackie had said they were expanding – what for?

You know that little voice in your head – the one that tells you to jump from really high places or smash something? My gut was telling me there was something going on in the basement, so without another thought, I pressed B -2 and with that the lift doors closed.

Here goes nothing.

'What in the holy cow are you doing?' Quinn squealed. 'No one goes to that level, I don't even know what's down there!'

'I have a feeling,' I said aloud, knowing that this was one of the only times I could talk. 'Ya know, a gut feeling.'

'Well me and your gut are going to have words when you get back here,' Quinn muttered. 'You can't just – right, just stay low, I guess. Oh . . . '

'Oh?' I asked. 'What do you mean, oh?'

'There aren't any cameras down there, not on this laptop

anyway. Whatever happens down there, you're on your own.'

Those were the words I didn't want to hear today. I couldn't be on my own – what was I supposed to do? Stay low? There better be a good wall for me to hide behind somewhere.

That was when the lift doors opened and I was greeted with pure silence. There was a smell of damp coming from somewhere but there was light, dimmer than the command room upstairs for sure. There were small bulbs every five metres but I still couldn't make much out.

I pressed my hand against the wall: bricks. Was the camera that I saw on the laptop, the one that looked to be underground, on the floor above? Course I had to go and pick the one where there weren't any cameras. I made my way along the dingy corridor, walking on my toes so the shoes didn't smack. No use in hiding if the enemy can hear you coming. Was that what the Academy was now, my enemy?

'Can you use the camera phone?' Luckily Quinn's voice sounded in my ear. 'To film it.'

I reached a hand into my pocket to pull out the camera phone, would this even register a picture? It was ancient. I pressed myself against the brick wall, loading the phone up and pressed it to my chest to hide its glow.

The next thing that happened made me want to run away – a blood-curdling scream tore through the corridor, crashing off the walls. The air chilled around me as I clamped a hand over my mouth and a weight sat dead in my chest. My gut was right, why did it have to be right? I didn't recognise the scream but Quinn did.

'T-that's Lily.' Her voice shook.

As another scream crashed through me I realised that the most fucked-up thing in the whole situation was that Quinn knew it was Lily. How many times had she heard this? What the hell was I doing here? I couldn't fix this.

'You need to see what's happening,' she said.

'I can't,' I whispered, as quietly as I could. 'What if someone's torturing her?'

'Then . . . you need to video it. That sounded horrible, I didn't mean it like that.'

I knew she was right – if someone was torturing students then it would be damning evidence – but was it right to stand there and watch? Shouldn't I try to *do* something, rather than become a bystander to someone else's trauma? I sucked in a breath, pushing myself off the wall and towards the screams.

'When I checked the cameras at the back of the school Jess and Lily weren't there; the class wasn't either. Why would he do this down here?'

I knew she was thinking aloud and didn't answer. As I turned the corridor at the end of the hall it opened up, and the top half of the brick wall was now glass. I pushed into the corner to keep myself hidden, but there were rough voices coming from inside. From what I could see through the glass the room was pure white, the bright lights blinding me for a moment. Then I saw the walls were padded. What the hell?

'What's going on?' Quinn asked. 'I can't hear anything. Record what you can see, and if it's too risky get back to the lift.'

My whole body shook in that moment – I didn't even think I could hold the camera straight never mind film something.

'Now you're going to answer me, or the next thing that will go down your throat is water.' The low growl of Harkness gritted its way through the glass.

Water?

'It was there from my last op, I forgot to take it off,' I heard Lily say, but it was soon followed by gargling and choking sounds.

I pushed the phone from my chest, clicked record, then got on my hands and knees. Crawling forward using the brick as cover, I slowly pointed the edge of the camera at the glass. What I saw through the lens made me want to scream. Harkness had Lily strapped to a chair with a cloth over her face, while he poured a large bottle of water over her mouth. He was waterboarding her. This wasn't a class, it was an interrogation. Behind them stood Jessica, hands clasped behind her back, watching, her face dripping blood. I couldn't make out details because of the crappy camera quality but what I could see was red.

Harkness tossed the bottle to the man beside him; he was a little taller, with a beard. As soon as he caught the water he stepped back, remaining as silent as the students. Harkness took the cloth off Lily's face before he gripped her throat.

'Answer me. Why do you have a wire on?'

Shit. He saw the wire? This was my fault?

Lily got a few words out as she coughed and spluttered.

'I-I had it on f-from the last op. I-I swear.'

As I watched through the screen I couldn't believe what I was seeing, or what I heard next.

'Ames, get me the scalpel.'

The man with brown hair, Ames, was shocked at the request. 'Lily said she forgot to take it off, you know how kids are.'

'But she's not a kid, she's an agent. She will tell me or she won't walk for the next fortnight.'

'Their medic will be stretched as it is with the next op, she doesn't need to be caring for two others.'

'Agents, Ames. Besides they should have thought about that before lying to me.'

A scalpel – why did I have to watch this? It was inhuman. I couldn't sit here and do nothing, I couldn't be a bystander – but what was I supposed to do? If I charged in there no one would be better off.

'Please,' Lily begged. 'I just forgot it was there.'

That was when I heard a phone ring. I yanked mine down,

but all I saw was the camera menu – oh thank God it wasn't me. Luck must be on my side today. I would touch wood but, ya know, there's none down here. I slowly moved the phone back up and watched him answer the phone.

'Ames?'

I heard Lily let out a few coughs, her head turning to the side, and I also noticed it wasn't just Jessica there, it was the whole class. What? There was what twenty of them, thirty? Couldn't they overpower the two men? It was two against a whole group, why weren't they fighting back?

'What?' Ames asked, alarmed. 'I'll send her up.' Then he hung up.

'Is Helen making a fuss again?' Harkness asked, condescendingly.

'No, it's James Winters,' Ames said, and my eyes widened. I even saw Jessica turn. 'He's at reception, he wants to see his sister and wouldn't take no for an answer.'

James was here?

'You've got to get out of there,' Quinn said urgently. 'Now.'

I didn't need to be told twice. I tucked the phone back into my pocket and power walked down the corridor towards the lift, as soon as I pressed the button the door open and I threw myself inside and a cry slipped from my mouth. I couldn't hold it in any longer.

'Are you alright?' Quinn asked. 'Come in.'

'He was torturing Lily, waterboarding and a scalpel,' I managed to get out. 'Those weren't scare tactics. He was torturing her because of me.' Guilt flooded over me: if I hadn't pushed things so quickly we wouldn't be in this situation. Lily wouldn't be drowning and Jess wouldn't be covered in her own blood. This was all my fault. I caused this.

'No, it's not.'

'It is,' I cried, shaking my head.

'Get back to the house as soon as you can. Don't run but hurry.'

When I reached the first floor the doors opened, and I ducked my head, keeping low, no one needed to see how much of a mess I was. Quinn directed me to the main doors and thankfully no one asked me any questions. Not that I would have answered, my thoughts consumed me so much I wanted to give myself up. Anything to stop what they were doing to Lily. All she had been was kind and now she was strapped to a chair because of me.

Me.

*　*　*

An hour later, I'd told Quinn everything as she took off all the make-up. Then I showed her the video. Her lips trembled the entire time. Did she blame me for this? Because I did.

Now I sat in her room on the bed, my back against the wall, as Quinn uploaded the footage to her computer. She was telling me she would encrypt it so it would take Thompson a couple of hours if he tried to break in. But that didn't matter now; all I could hear were Lily's screams and all I could see was Jessica's face.

What would her brother say when he saw her? Could he help us? I didn't even think to look for him when I left, I couldn't bear being in that place for one more minute.

I didn't know what to do, how could I stop this? Was this place too far gone? Was this fortress really unbreakable? I didn't want answers, not anymore. I just wanted it all to stop.

I couldn't keep doing this.

SLATE RETRIBUTION

CHAPTER 17

Coronach

A funeral song.

JESSICA-GRACE WINTERS

'What?' Ames asked. Then, 'I'll send her up.'

'Is Helen making a fuss again?'

'No, it's James Winters. He's at reception, he wants to see his sister and wouldn't take no for an answer.'

'James knows the protocols, he can't just –'

'Well, Daniel, he has, so what the hell are we going to do?' Ames asked. 'Considering she looks like that!'

Nothing, absolutely nothing. I didn't know anything, I only knew what I was told by my superiors. How could I know anything? Everything from intel to possible operations were always on a need-to-know-basis and I didn't need to know. My position was Team Lead; my role was to deliver results without fuss, complaint, or defiance. My priority was my team; anything else was either a privilege or an honour. I should be thankful of my place here because without it I had no purpose, no motivation and no use. Without the Academy I would be out on the street; my brother couldn't take care of me. James . . .

'What are you staring at?' Harkness barked, and it took me a couple seconds to realise he was talking to me. I hadn't even registered turning my head. 'Don't just stand there, go and get cleaned up.'

I nodded. If my brother saw me like this he would ask too many questions – after all, he was trained, but not here. Some other institution. I didn't know how bad it was, but every so often I felt blood thicken my lashes then drip down my cheek.

I took a step forward but a sharp pain lashed through my knee, singeing like lighting.

'What the fuck did you do to her while I wasn't here?' Ames asked.

I grabbed my leggings and pulled them up past my knees,

and saw the vicious slice marks going back and forth, some deeper than others. He'd twisted the knife in; he was the one that did this. How could I forget that? I glanced over to the scalpel on the metal tray and saw that it was doused in blood; my blood.

'Winters, get up,' Harkness said to me and I nodded straight away, using my stronger leg to stand to attention.

I needed to be strong, an unbreakable force like him. I wasn't any use otherwise.

I put most of my weight on one leg, the other hovering. I had to walk out of here so I needed to accept the discomfort – after all, suffering was good for the soul, that's what my mother told me.

'Go get sorted by the medics, don't make me do this again. I don't want to but you're leaving me with no choice.'

Yes, I had been disobedient. I had worn a wire when I wasn't supposed to, and for a rebellious cause. I'd wanted to act out but I knew the consequences. I deserved this.

I limped as little as I could towards the door, my hand reaching out for the handle, when I felt it again, that lightning bolt of pain. I whimpered, falling against the door, as my other hand trailed down the glass leaving a smear of blood above. How bad did I look?

'Oh Christ,' Ames cursed.

It was at that moment I remembered Lily was behind me, why was she strapped to a chair? Oh yes, she'd had a wire taped to her like me. Why was she all wet? Her hands were curled into fists, her whole body tense and back arched, what was she feeling, pain? No, can't be. Her pupils were slitted, her eyes shrinking back as she stared at me, was she scared of Harkness?

'If he tells Charlotte, we're done for.'

'She'll thank us.'

Lily's mouth opened like she was going to say something, it was funny, she looked like she was choking. My eyes flitted behind to the rest of the class, I'd forgotten their names but it didn't matter, they all looked like statues now.

'What are you still doing here?' Harkness asked me.

'Daniel, give her a minute.'

I didn't answer him but I pulled open the door slowly, I couldn't lose my footing now, if I fell I'd be disciplined. My pace was apparently too slow, as the harsh grip from Harkness lifted me off my feet and thrust me out into the corridor. That wasn't the end – he shoved me down the corridor, his brutal grip not easing up as we marched forward. I kept tripping over my feet, the speed was too much, but Harkness was relentless. Once we made it to the lift he threw me against the doors, but this time I refused to cry out. I had to be strong – and besides, the coolness of the metal doors brought me some comfort.

'Get sorted. If James sees or hears of this, believe me, Lily will take a trip down the wrong alley at a bad time of night,' Harkness muttered into my ear.

My eyes were closed, focused on the cooling metal as I rested my cheek on the door. This was it now. This was what my life would be. I had to do this for Lily.

James was an interrogator for a living so I needed to do a good job.

If the Academy needed soldiers for the war then I would give them one. I wasn't going to disobey anymore; Lily didn't need to get hurt, and James didn't need to know the real reasons for these wounds.

I didn't remember getting in the lift, pressing the button or leaving. The first thing I registered was standing in the middle of the medical ward. It was quiet, only a few seniors lying in the beds, X-rays on the pillars. The steady beeping of a ventilator sounded, who was that? Someone should pull the plug, they'd be better off dead.

'Are you OK?' I heard a voice ask, male, early thirties. I hobbled around slowly to face him. Oh, it was Dr Williams. He wasn't in scrubs which was unusual – wasn't he a doctor here?

'David!'

Why was he yelling? I didn't feel ill, in fact I felt numb. The pain in my leg had disappeared and now everything was light, like I was walking through clouds, my throat closing as the air slowly dwindled.

Dr Williams rushed towards me but then everything became blurry, what was happening? I saw a figure in blue behind the doctor, but that was it. Was I becoming smaller or was he becoming taller.

Then I realised, I was falling.

***

Why was my bed so uncomfortable? I had just washed these

sheets. The duvet was thinner than it was last night, had I kicked it off in my sleep? Why were my pillows rock hard? Why was there someone holding my hand?

I yanked away as my eyes opened – fuck that was bright, I could have sworn I shut the curtains.

'Jess you're fine, you're safe,' a voice said, but I didn't pay it much attention as I felt a weight on my face. 'Hey, hey, look at me babygirl, you're OK.'

I stopped as I felt warm hands taking mine and finally realised that I was in the hospital wing. How did I end up here? Why was I in a bed? Why was my knee throbbing?

None of that mattered when I saw the man sitting at my bedside. Jamie. Why was he here? He was dressed too formally for a visit, black suit with a navy tie, he was even clean shaven and looked like he'd got a haircut to fix that usually fluffy sandy brown hair of his. Even wore that stupid sweet-smelling aftershave.

What was he doing here? He wasn't allowed, how could he have gotten past security?

BEEP ... BEEP ... BEEP ... BEEP

'Jess I need you to breathe OK, breathe with me,' he said, and I realised that sound was my own heart. I tried sucking in breaths as slowly as I could, watching Jamie's chest go in and out – the oxygen mask was helping at least. 'There ya go sweetheart, just keep breathing.'

'What are you doing here?' I asked, pushing myself to sit up in the bed. 'You can't be here.'

James stopped, his eyes fixating on me like he was reading my mind. Shit, I wasn't supposed to say that. Now he knew something was up. What kind of an agent was I? When Harkness found out he would take me back down to the basement. James was an interrogator, I'd have to be careful.

'I go where I like.' James said pointedly. 'Speaking of which, after coming into this fine establishment next thing I know, I'm being rushed here because apparently my little sister collapsed.'

'I'm fine, and I'm not little,' I protested.

James scoffed. 'Fine? I swear to God, Jess have you taken a look at yourself recently?'

'No, I've been busy training.'

'Oh, is that what you're calling it?'

What did he know exactly? I knew James had an understanding that the school used a few unsanctioned methods of discipline, but that was it. Had he found out? Had he looked through the cameras and seen something before he dropped the laptop off at my dorm?

'James you can't just come here unannounced, the dorm is a mess and I was busy.'

That was when my brother stood up and started to pace at the side of my bed, his expression unreadable – oh here we bloody go.

It was only then I realised I was in a small private room. Why had they put me in here? James took off his suit jacket and threw it on the chair beside me, running his hands over his face numerous times. What was James on? Nothing out of the ordinary had happened, he needed to calm down. Who cares if I got a little bloody.

'I asked to look at your records.' James told me. 'According to those you were only in here last week, but I could have told you that myself, considering the bruising on your neck.'

'I was training.'

'Tell me, how is getting strangled and beaten part of your training? How is getting a scalpel driven into your knee or cutting your face up part of this outstanding curriculum?' he asked, exasperated.

Fuck shit fuck. Why did they give him access to my records? I thought they were private. Harkness told me I had to keep him off the scent, but it was pretty hard to do that now he was screaming this in my face. Of course he knew it was a scalpel, James does this for a living, the bruises on my body were hard to lie my way out of, especially to him. Wait, when had I been injured with a scalpel?

'Give me a mirror,' I said, not bothering to answer his question.

'A fucking mirror? You're going to tell me what happened!'

'Well I can't remember, so a mirror might jog my memory,' I snapped right back.

James cursed under his breath, then walked over to other side of the room, returning with a small hand mirror. He tossed it into my lap before resuming his annoying coping mechanism, pacing.

As soon as I saw myself in the mirror I wished it would shatter. The bruising around my neck had gotten worse, it was darker but showed clear finger marks; the bruising on my cheek was yellow and my lips chapped and cracking. That was when I noticed the slashes and cuts – mostly near the hairline, but a couple sliced down my chin. There was one at the left side of my forehead that was deeper than the others.

'Why are you wearing a wire?'

'Stop, please!'

'Hold her down.'

'No!'

I took a breath, my hand shaking like a leaf as I dropped the mirror. How did I forget that? How could I forget he pinned my head down to that godforsaken chair while he cut into me with a scalpel?

'Jess you're safe, calm down,' I heard James say, but I shook my head as tears rose to my eyes.

'You need to leave, you need to leave. You can't be here,'

SLATE RETRIBUTION

I told him frantically.

James came back to my bedside holding my hands tightly even though I tried to pull away, his blank glare replaced with a soft and gentle one. When he took my hands, it wasn't with a harsh grip or to show he had power over me; the way he held me said that he cared. How could I forget that? He practically raised me.

'Don't worry about that, OK, you just focus on healing.'

'No – if they find out you're here they'll –'

'Jess, sweetheart, remember our sorry excuse of a mother has shares in this place – they won't kick me out. I'm here to see you and if they want to get rid of me they'll have to shoot me.'

That could be arranged, I wanted to tell him. Harkness would have no bother doing such a thing, it was in his *nature*, and it was in mine.

That was when the door opened and Dr Williams walked in, he gave a quick nod of respect to James before moving to the foot of my bed, pulling out a folder from the bottom.

'How are you feeling?' he asked.

'Fine.'

'The alarm was raised twice since you woke up, don't give me that nonsense.'

Oh great, Dr Williams and James were on the same side then. Hold on, how was that supposed to work? I didn't ponder on the thought much longer as I caught sight of the IV next to my bed. The fluids were clear but I felt my heart quicken – was that more of the drugs? I wasn't due in until Friday for a check-up and I'd been taking the pills. There had to be some in my system to prove it, they didn't need to give me any more, I was playing by the rules.

The beeping on the monitor quickened and the doctor sighed.

'See what I mean?' he asked. 'Don't worry, those are just fluids, we wanted to get as much of the drugs out of your system as possible before you woke up.'

Dr Williams moved swiftly, pointing a small flashlight in my eyes. I tried to pull away but he had a firm grip on my shoulder. Wait, get the drugs out of me? What was the man on about? I thought the whole idea was to get the pills *in* our system. Never mind that Jamie was sitting right there!

'Drugs?' I asked, feigning confusion.

'I know everything,' Jamie said, shaking his head. 'I have Dr Williams here on speed dial.'

'Everything?'

'Everything. I just wanted to see if you would admit it yourself, which you didn't.'

How could I deny this? If he already knew then why was he just sitting there? Jamie was the kind of guy to punch first and ask questions later, why was he so calm? Did Harkness or Duke know? If they knew I was done for.

'We had to do the same to Grace earlier,' Dr Williams told me, and that was when I gave him a look of genuine confusion. 'She was acting out, yelling at Dr McKay and myself, but then it was like she wasn't there at all. It was like she was an empty shell of a person.'

'Which is exactly what you were when I saw you,' Jamie said, clenching my hands just that little bit tighter. 'You weren't there, sweetheart, sure your eyes were open but they were empty.'

Empty, was that what I was now? That was what the drugs had done; made me a shell ready to be filled. What had happened today? The last thing I remembered was going to bed last night, I don't even remember walking down the stairs or having breakfast. Naomi had to be safe since I'd appointed Quinn her guardian while I was gone, Grace was working here all day and Lily was . . . with me.

'Lily?' I asked. 'Where is she?'

I threw the covers off and tried to get out of the bed but James grabbed my shoulders, pushing my back down.

'Woah, take it easy.'

I kept fighting, trying to grab his wrists and push – I kicked my leg out, bending it, trying to get some grip, but then a sharp shooting pain jolted in my knee and I cried out as it fell limp on the bed. That was when James let go and I looked down to see my knee was heavily bandaged. When had that happened?

'Jessica, do you remember how you got that injury?' Dr Williams asked.

I tried, I really did, but there was just nothing, my mind drawing a complete blank. I couldn't remember what kind of injury it was. All I could see right now was Harkness' face looming over mine as he cut into my head.

'No,' I said slowly, taking the oxygen mask off my head, 'I don't remember anything.'

Dr Williams stared at me and then back down at the notes in the folder but I wasn't focusing on that, all I could feel was the warmth of my brother's hand on mine. The comfort and security of his touch, telling me everything was going to be OK.

Ever since I could remember he'd been there. He was the one who taught me to read and write, made sure I ate properly. Every memory I had of him was a good one, despite our arguments.

But I do remember one day distinctly, when James told me to go to my room and lock the door of whatever safe house we were staying in. Then there was a screaming match between him and our mother that went on for hours. I never understood what it was about when I was younger, but now I did: James needed a life of his own. He didn't want to take the role of two parents.

He was one of the best people I'd ever met and that was exactly why I kept pushing him away. I was ready to lie my way out of this to keep him safe, I don't know what I'd do if I lost him. Who I would become.

'This is getting out of control,' Dr Williams said. 'How can they expect our medical students to work efficiently if they lack compassion? Then there's you, a solider, but surely empathy would come into it?'

'Do you know they're going to put a new drug through the water system?' I asked bluntly.

Dr Williams reeled back, as if I'd struck him.

'What? Who signed off on that?'

'Lennox,' I said.

'Who's that?' Jamie asked.

'The resident psychologist,' Dr Williams answered. 'You know she came in here the other day saying something about a new drug. Told us we were to administer it, we refused, and then she went off on one.' He shook his head. 'After seeing the effects of the ones you've been on, I don't see why they need another.'

'But you have seniors, surely they've displayed similar symptoms?' Jamie let go of my hands, taking out his phone.

'What year are you, Jessica?'

'Third.'

'Ah, yes the newer batches get tested on the third years

then filtered down. Fourth and fifth are still on the old ones.'

This was ridiculous – the medics refused to administer them so the next best thing was to shove them through the water system. Even in a diluted form this new drug could do anything and we would be none the wiser.

'What are they doing this all for?' my brother asked, looking up from the phone that he appeared to be taking notes on.

Before Dr Williams could respond I answered, 'Compliance. They want soldiers for the war, ones that won't object to any task, no matter how cruel. No one would have to worry about corruption.'

I hated that I'd been a part of this. I had sworn I'd be strong and fight against anything or anyone, but I was controlled by Harkness like a marionette. I didn't want to be, but wouldn't it be better for everyone? Grace was right, what use was rebelling if there was no world to rebel against? Maybe if I couldn't remember carrying out missions then I could go on as normal. If I couldn't remember it, then it didn't happen.

'James, if you don't leave I will call for you to be removed,' I stated coldly.

'Excuse me?'

'You can't be here, the visit wasn't scheduled, you know the rules as well as I do.'

I couldn't afford to lose him, of course I wanted him to stay. I wanted Jamie to stay by my side, but if Harkness had his way I would never see him again. My brother was all I had left and I'd be damned if I played a part in his death.

James stopped cold before he spoke. 'Yes, and I know as well as you do that if they ask you to sleep with a man to get information you will do so without question. I know that if you took those pills and Harkness asked you to shoot Lily or Grace you would. I *know* that if you continue down this path you will no longer be my sister, just an empty shell of the woman you could have been.'

'James,' I tried, but he spoke again before I could say anything.

'No, don't sit there and pretend you're in control of this situation, because you're not. I know what they're planning, and if you follow their orders you will not survive.'

'My purpose isn't to survive, it's to get the job done!'

SLATE RETRIBUTION

Dr Williams coughed awkwardly and I tried to calm my shaking limbs: James had no right barging in and telling me what to do. This was my life, my decision, I chose to do this. Ever since I was young all I'd ever wanted was to be on the stage, but I had duties and expectations, no matter the cost to myself. If I could save innocents then any suffering I endured would be worth it.

As I thought over my brother's words, one thing stuck out to me the most. I couldn't remember most of the day. Sure I was lifeless without that spark, but part of me already knew it died out a long time ago. Wasn't I too far gone by now? Wasn't it too late to stop this?

I expected Jamie to leave: he never liked it when we fought, so naturally he would storm out, cool off and then go back to work after a quick apology and an espresso. I turned away from him and looked out of the window: there were thin blinds but I could tell the back of the school grounds from a mile away. It looked like a group was heading out there now.

If they were filtering the drugs down through the years would that mean that the girls like Eve and the rest of them who were what – Sixteen, fifteen? – would just disappear. Would their days soon blend together until it was nothing but a big messed-up jumble in their heads? Because that's what mine was becoming.

I heard the swing of the door and without turning I knew Jamie had left; everyone does in the end. I hadn't managed to push Naomi away, but she was different. Family had never been one of my strong suits: my dad left for some unknown reason, and my mother was consumed by work after the death of my older brother Charlie. Grandparents were never in the picture – after dad left I guess they never really wanted to get to know me, and our mother was too busy moving us around to ever see them. Probably wouldn't want to get to know them anyway.

Naomi and my girls were now all I had left; I wasn't going to lose them. Now I had to play by the rules, no matter what it took.

What I didn't expect though, was the warmth of my brother's hand – this time clenched in desperation. It was Dr Williams who had left the room, not him.

'I'm begging you, let me help.'

It was then I knew it wasn't just me that was scared of losing him. James was terrified of losing me.

SLATE RETRIBUTION

EMERY HALE

CHAPTER 18

Delassation

Weariness; fatigue.

NAOMI JADE

'Something's wrong.'

For someone who was blatantly innocent, sweet and kind, Quinn had a great talent for pessimism. I couldn't exactly blame her; after what I'd witnessed there were countless scenarios running through my head. Maybe Harkness had killed them, maybe they were still being tortured, or he could have taken them out for a public execution. Would they come back at all? Well of course they might come back, but not them, not truly. The Jessica I knew would fight Harkness and Ames off with her bare hands to stop them from hurting her friend. The girl I knew had disappeared.

The toughest spirits can be broken, even the most fucking stubborn ones.

I'd thought Quinn would have been a little more optimistic, but she'd cleaned the bathroom twice since I got back and looked like she might go for round three any minute.

'They should have been back by now, something must have happened.'

'Yeah, Lily was waterboarded and Jessica looked like an extra in a horror film, of course something happened to them.' I said bluntly.

I wasn't in the mood for playing detective anymore, I just wanted to go home and forget this had ever happened. As soon as I got out I wanted to call my mum and tell her to drop the story, publish the videos online and see if it did anything. I wanted out of this mess. My mum was all I wanted right now but I couldn't call her because of this stupid, fucked-up Academy monitoring every call sent out of the building and I wasn't about to abuse the server in case we needed an emergency call out of here.

'We need more evidence,' Quinn said, biting her lip as she

grabbed the bleach from her desk again. 'We have the video you took today, no doubt we'll get the audios from the microphones if they get back –'

I stood bolt upright, grabbed the bottle of bleach from Quinn's hand and threw it on the floor. I was done with all of this. Every single thing I had seen in this fucked-up place was, well, fucked-up. Maybe if my mum released the videos they'd gain traction and someone would do something. Not me though, there was nothing I could do here.

'Open your eyes, Quinn!' I exclaimed. 'You know as well as I do that the Academy has people in every inch of society. Their lawyers will shut us down the moment I try to take this to court. I'm sorry.'

I was tired, I didn't know what to say to her. What could I do?

'You're giving up?' she asked timidly.

Once my mum uploaded the videos then someone else would take the case. I was eighteen, I couldn't be caught up in some media frenzy. I needed safety and security but none of that would happen if I continued to support these girls. I didn't want to be tortured or abused. Someone else would come along to help them.

'No, of course not.'

'That's what it sounds like,' Quinn, said crossing her arms over her chest. 'I came to you for help, you can't just give up.'

'I'm not.'

'Yes you are.'

'Someone else will come along.'

'Who?' she asked. 'I sent those videos to your mum because I knew she was a journalist. At ten o'clock sharp, because that was when your mum would go through her emails.'

'What?'

'I'm good with tech,' she sassed. 'I know your mum's routine because I've been checking in. I thought she could help.'

'Well, you thought wrong. If Harkness finds out we're involved there's no telling what he'd do to her, to me. Grace said it herself, I'm not putting my family on the line for some wannabe spies!'

It was then I knew I'd said something I could never take back; the look on Quinn's face was like I had pulled her heart fresh out and held it in front of her.

'Is that what you think this is?' she asked, her voice just above a whisper. 'That we're just running around playing pretend?'

'That's not what I meant.'

'You were our last shot,' Quinn told me.

She moved to sit at her desk, resting her head in her hands for a moment before she looked back up, but not at me, out the window to the little birdhouse that sat in the tree just outside. Jesus, I didn't even think. She'd lost her friend, what did she say he was, sixteen? Did she mention his age? There was something in her eyes that was unfamiliar to me, something that I didn't quite understand. It wasn't dread or shock, it wasn't worry. It was hopelessness. What? I thought Quinn never gave up – surely me passing the torch on to someone else would have given her boost rather than a sedative.

'We didn't choose this, none of us did. We chose to be trained in combat, weaponry and technology, but not this. Drugs, abuse, starvation. Naomi, we are losing our footing here. Jessica and Grace aren't themselves. Lily and I can only stop taking the pills for so long. You were our last chance.'

'I'm sorry.' I didn't know what else to say.

'The bystander, you help in the beginning but when it gets too tough you decide it's not for you anymore.'

'Hey, that's not fair.'

'Not fair?' she scoffed. 'I want to see my mother, I want to live a life where I can leave this compound without worrying if I'll end up dead in an alleyway because I spoke to the wrong person. I want to be able to love who I want without having disciplinary action. I don't want to take drugs, I don't want to be tortured. I just want my friends back.'

How was it selfish of me to want a good future for myself? How was it selfish of me to want my mum to live a long life without fear that the police will break down the door?

'You can go back to your life, get a job doing whatever, live to your nineties – but here's the thing, sweetheart, you wouldn't be here without us. You went to the theatre: without this team you yourself would be dead. We saved your life, and today I helped guide you through the school so you could get evidence. Now you want to quit? How about the consequences for me if you do that? I stuck my neck on the line for you because you said you would help us.'

'I want to,' I tried, 'I really do.'

'I get that you're scared but if you wanted to help us you'd stay.'

'I can't.'

'Then don't come crying to me when your best friend is six feet in the ground, because I will not help you. I will not comfort you, I will bring your memory back to this very moment; the moment you decided to walk away.'

Christ what had I done? I just wanted my family to be safe. When I got involved sure, I knew the risks, but now I'd seen the truth of the Academy. I wasn't any use here and clearly didn't belong. All I felt right now was guilt. Quinn had stuck her neck on the line for me, and so had the rest of the team. Lily and Jess were tortured because of the wires; they wouldn't have had them on if it weren't for me.

It seems a lot of things wouldn't have happened if it weren't for me. Grace wouldn't resent Jessica and Harkness wouldn't be cutting their supplies. All I had done was cause more harm.

God, if I said the words *I* or *me* one more time I was going to smack myself. If I walked away I'd live a reasonable life, but none of these girls would. Jessica could be in a grave within the next year as could Lily or Grace – dammit, even Quinn. All these girls wanted was the basic right of choice, but all I seemed to care about were my own priorities. Before I left my mother told me to damn the consequences. It had nothing to do with her selflessness or honour, it was simply the right thing to do.

Quinn let out a pained sigh, leaning back in her chair, eyes fixed on that birdhouse. It was like she herself was a little bird trapped inside the wooden box. What could Quinn's life have been like if she hadn't attended Reign? She was incredibly smart and frankly scary. Never judge a girl by her cover, never judge a Technical Support by her hardware.

'I'm sorry,' I said again.

'If you're going to go, just do it,' she told me. 'I'll tell the girls if they come back.'

If. There was always that threat for Quinn. I think that's what her biggest fear was, being alone. The Technical Support was the one in the van or the one in the command room. There was always the chance that she would be the survivor of this team and that day could be today. Even though she looked to be the youngest in the group her eyes were like an eighty year old's: worn, tired and fraught with knowledge.

Knowing so much but being able to do so little must have driven her to insanity – so much so that she reached out to someone she'd never met in the hope of changing her life. I thought she was always the one brimming with hope, but now I knew she wasn't, she was running on fumes. There's a tell, when you give up hope. Quite a few, actually.

Quinn had chosen my mother and me to help her with this case and a couple of minutes ago I turned her away. Now what was she left with? It certainly wasn't hope; I feared it was acceptance.

When I watched all those old documentaries in school about oppression and segregation I wondered why no one ever stood up. It was only now I realised why. I was the person on the screen who I proclaimed I would never be.

What Quinn said rang with truth – if I didn't step up who

would? I knew the answer, no one.

'I won't leave.'

'Don't patronise me.'

'I'm not. You're right. You're right, Quinn.'

She turned, throwing a hard stare, like she was trying to anticipate my next move. I knew now that there was no way I'd be walking out that door. I certainly wasn't going to attend any of my friends' funerals, because there wouldn't be any. Of course I wasn't trained or smart like Quinn, but I was a fast learner.

The idea that I could live a secure life was an utter joke. The Academy could access anything and everything, they were probably monitoring the entire nation. Maybe I didn't have security but what I did have was choice. I could choose to walk out the door or I could grow a pair and stay.

'What in the holy ghost?' Those were not the next words I expected out of Quinn's mouth.

'I don't think I'm holy but thanks,' I said, trying to take it as a compliment.

'No, not you.' Quinn stood up from her chair and walked over to the window, pulling back the sheer curtains. 'It's James and Jessica.'

I joined her by the window and looked down to see the pair, their arms linked as they walked, and soon saw the heavy limp that Jess tried to hide. Her face was covered in cuts and slashes but at least she wasn't bleeding. I only had one thought about her brother: he looked different from the last time I'd seen him. He was a lot older than Jess but they shared a resemblance. He was tall but well built, his hair gelled back while his shirt sleeves were rolled up to his elbows. His eyes flickered between the path ahead and his sister. There was this kind of aura around the guy, something superior.

'I thought we'd already established he isn't dead.'

'Yeah but I've never actually seen him in person before,' Quinn told me. 'I've only read his record, it's weird. He's classified as dead to most parts of the intelligence agency except some of the highest offices in MI6. He's a hero, for the most part.'

'The most part?'

Unfortunately, Quinn didn't answer my question – instead she let go of the curtain and ran out of the room. I heard her hurtling down the stairs. Was this like meeting a celebrity? If

James was here before his sister called then something must have happened, or he could have overheard something through the grapevine, was that how secret service agencies worked?

I ran after the girl as fast as I could but stayed on the first landing, just in case there was a camera outside pointing through the door. I heard it close but no voices, so peeked out from the side to see that Quinn had Jess locked in a hug, her head buried in the crook of her neck.

'Quinn, I'm fine.'

'Jess, if you say that one more time I will hit you with my shoe,' James said, and I cracked a smile. 'Now come on, you need to sit down so we can sort this out.'

Sort what out? Was there a plan I wasn't aware of? I didn't get time to ask because the man caught my eye and suddenly his guard went up.

'Who are you?' he asked coldly – it reminded me of the way Jessica spoke.

'Naomi.'

With that, James paused, a hand propping on his hip.

'Hold up, your childhood friend gets to hang out here

undercover, but if I come to visit you threaten to call security on me?' he asked, offended.

'Don't start,' Jess groaned.

'Quinn, help my idiotic sister to the living room please,' James said and the girl obliged with a kind smile. She took Jessica's arms and, despite her protests, led her into the living room.

That was when James turned to me and I inched my way down the stairs. His face was set firm as cement, lips pressed into a thin line while he stuck his hands in his suit pockets.

'Nice to finally meet the real you,' I said to him. 'I thought you were dead.'

'Most people do.'

Awkward silence, what the hell were you supposed to say to that?

'So, tell me your story,' James said.

'My story?' I asked.

'Well, you didn't just walk through the front doors now did you?'

'I mean technically . . . '

It took a little to explain but James got the idea of my role here pretty quickly, but he was not a fan of me getting dressed up and walking into the main building. Something about being an untrained civilian. I tried to fight my corner but he did that thing with his eyes that I thought only a mother could do, ya know, the look.

I had told James that the videos, if he wanted to review them, were on Quinn's computer. He quickly agreed, but said he wanted to sit down and discuss the next move before going any further. That was the reason all four of us were now sitting in the living room – well, Jess was lying down on doctors' orders, and because James had threatened to sit on her.

'Trojan is getting more aggressive, that information is correct. In fact there's been some speculation that they're going to hit a small town up north in the coming week.' James told us.

'Hit?' I asked.

'Explode,' he answered bluntly.

Say what now?

'Of course the Academy wants to strike back with equal, if not better force, however their methods are ... barbaric, in a word,' James said as he begun to pace at the front of the room.

'You don't have to say that again,' I muttered.

'What I want your team to do, is stop it.'

Say fucking what now?

Jessica sat up a little on the couch.

'You're giving us an op?'

James nodded, shrugging his shoulders.

'I don't see why not, I'm an officer in MI6, I've commanded many a team. I'm sure I can delegate this op.'

Jessica laughed.

'Harkness would never allow it.'

'Well it's a good thing I'm not going to ask his permission. If my superior wants specific agents out on loan, Harkness can't refuse.'

'And how are you going to convince your boss?' Quinn asked.

'Well I shag her quite a lot and take her on romantic dates, so I hope she'll do it as a small favour,' James replied smugly.

Everyone's mouth dropped open at the comment. I certainly knew Jess didn't expect that as she sat up on her elbows and gave him a pointed look.

'You landed Nicola?' she asked. 'You are punching there, did you blackmail her to go on a date with you?'

That was when James stopped pacing, walked over to the couch, ushered me and Quinn out of the way and sat on his sister's stomach.

'James!' she groaned, hitting his side, but her brother didn't flinch. 'James, get off of me!'

'What happens if you're sarcastic when we're trying to have a grown-up conversation?' he asked.

'You're the one who said you're shagging your boss!'

'Quite vigorously, I might add.'

'Make it stop!'

Quinn and I couldn't help ourselves from laughing, I mean it was one way to pull in a favour.

Then the front door opened and we all fell silent. Was it Harkness? James stood up and moved in front of Jessica, blocking her from view; Quinn pushed me behind her and I took that as a cue to hide. I crouched down next to the sofa, holding my breath as two sets of footsteps approached, one heavier than the other.

'Lily?' I heard Quinn ask.

I shot up from behind her and saw Lily and Grace hovering at the door, both looking the worse for wear. Lily's entire figure shook, her eyes bloodshot and face rash-red. Her top and hair were still damp, but thankfully I couldn't see any blood. Grace was ash-white, still in her scrubs but she seemed a little more stable than her friend. What had happened to her? Had Harkness let her go?

'Waterboarding, not fun,' Lily croaked, letting go of Grace's arm and flopping onto the couch. 'I will overlook it now he's here, what food did you bring?' she asked James, but he shook his head.

'Why would I bring food?'

'Because they cut our supplies again this week,' Lily said, as if it were obvious.

'They did what?'

As their conversation filtered into the background I focused on Grace. She looked like she'd seen all the horrors of a lifetime, even glimpsed the other side. Her figure was slender and carved but not in a healthy way, in a sickly way. Then, just like that, my stomach rumbled and I remembered I hadn't eaten anything since yesterday afternoon. Then I realised none of the girls in this room had eaten anything proper apart from Quinn. How were they still functioning?

I glanced over to Jessica who lay back down on the couch, her eyes closed as she breathed what I could only guess was a sigh of relief. Now I saw her for what she truly was – broken. Physically and mentally. Covered with bruises, aching with fatigue and hunger – how could I have not seen this coming? I think she just hit her breaking point.

I placed a soft hand on her shoulder. Jessica's eyes snapped open but soon relaxed, her own hand squeezing mine. How could I have ever thought of leaving?

'I want a report,' I heard James say, and I turned my attention back to him. 'Now, from everyone. Vitals, health, personal emotions.'

'Personal?' Quinn asked.

'Well, not your sex life, sweetheart.'

'I don't have a sex life!' she shouted.

I burst out laughing, my head falling back. It was a hearty

laugh, one I enjoyed. Jess joined in from below and before I knew it, the entire room was laughing – even Grace cracked a smile.

'OK ... ' James trailed off, like he wasn't entirely sure what he just witnessed. 'Jess, you first.'

She groaned.

'Health is fine, no sign of the cold, physical wounds extend from the face to the knee meaning I won't be able to walk without a significant limp for about a week. Bruising is healing nicely apparently, doesn't feel it. Haven't eaten properly in two weeks and personal emotions – well, while we're on the subject I haven't had sex in a while, so feeling a little down.'

'Jess I don't need to know that!' James exclaimed. 'But on the other hand good work, keep your panties on.'

Jessica was smirking, enjoying tormenting her brother. He looked to Grace, who already appeared to hate the idea of this talking circle.

'Fatigued and starving with no physical wounds,' she answered. 'I could murder a piece of chicken right now.'

'Great,' James muttered. 'Quinn?'

'I mean I'm a little hungry but generally OK.'

'You sure?' he asked, prodding a little. I followed his gaze to Quinn who looked more self-conscious and nervous as James walked towards her.

'What's the op?' she asked in return.

I saw Jess glance to her friend with a look of sympathy before she turned back to her brother, shaking her head, telling him not to push the issue.

Wait, was this the part where I left the room? If this op wasn't controlled by the Academy then it didn't have much to do with me. They were trained in dealing with terrorists, I was trained in dealing with spiders, and Jenny-long-legs to a certain extent.

'Well, the town up north is called Brora,' James started. 'There has been intel that in the next week Trojan are going to wipe it off the map. We don't know why but we can assume there's vital information there. What I want this team to do is to find the information and get out. Simple as. My own team will handle the evacuation.'

'Brora but that's where – we're not a full team,' Jessica groaned, her eyes screwing shut.

'I'll just call in another agent, then.'

'Like anyone would even take a look in our direction.'

'Well then, Naomi can step in as a Carrier.'

I can do what now?

'I – Uh, what?'

'You can't just replace Willow,' Quinn shot out. 'She's not even been buried yet and you want to replace her?'

Jessica winced as she pushed herself around to sit, shaking her head vigorously.

'No, no way, she is not getting involved.'

'I'm sorry, can you not *see* her standing right there?' James pointed to me. 'She's already involved.'

'Yes but not as a Carrier, she's not trained in the slightest,' Jessica told him. 'She's never been inside the Academy, never mind in the field.'

'Actually,' I butted in awkwardly, 'that might not necessarily be true – a couple of hours ago I went into the Academy in disguise.'

'You did what?' she asked.

'I may have helped,' Quinn said.

'See, sorted.' James shrugged.

For the first time in her life Jessica was utterly speechless, her mouth gaping. I gave her a small smile but that didn't seem to help as she groaned, pinching the bridge of her nose.

I couldn't get over the fact that I had been sworn in as the Carrier, it didn't make any sense. I had been in the Academy once but that didn't mean I was ready to take on the world! It must involve a lot more than following directions from Quinn – these students trained for years. How could I learn the ropes in just one week?

I expected to hear something from Grace, as she'd been quite verbal about my presence, but there were no snide remarks. On the couch across from me she simply looked done, her eyes dull and body limp. Had everyone lost hope?

Jessica had left high school just before her sixteenth birthday, now she was eighteen turning nineteen in October – you needed years to break people.

But when I looked over to Lily, she was smiling at me. Even though she looked ready to keel over, her smile only grew. I knew she always supported me but even after what happened she still believed. What would Lily think if she knew ten minutes ago I'd been ready to give up on the whole thing?

'I think she'd be a great addition to the team. We have what? A week to train her?' Lily asked, her voice still soft. 'I can cover the hand to hand combat stuff, Quinn can work with her on anything to do with the Carrier. She doesn't need to be an expert.'

'Yes she does,' Jessica stated. 'The reason we train for years is so that we don't fuck up.'

'Well our last Carrier died because she fucked up, Jess, we can't dance around the fact forever. Willow is dead and like you said earlier in class, we need to defend ourselves against Trojan. This is the way to do it.'

Silence. How could I replace someone like Willow, who the girls had known for so many years?

'No one else will touch Trojan because of their power over the British Security Service – there's intel that they're inside Thames House and Downing Street. They're corrupting us from the inside,' James admitted, sitting on the arm of the couch.

'The Academy is flawed,' Grace said, finally speaking up. 'But the teams we're put into work. We've had countless successful ops and if we can train Naomi there's a possibility that it won't be a complete disaster.'

'Hold up – you don't want to chuck her out the front door anymore?' Lily asked, and Grace shook her head.

I felt like a tiny fly on the wall. I'd love to be a part of a cool spy mission, who wouldn't? I was getting excited at every little thing and of course it was warranted, but I'd also seen the horrors of this school. Did I really want to be a part of this team?

'No,' Jessica said. 'It's not happening. James, I'm the Team Lead, I approve all members of this group.'

'And technically I'd be your superior officer, so I decide,' James said, crossing his arms. 'If Naomi agrees to sign on unofficially as your Carrier for this op, it's up to her, not you.'

All the heads in the room snapped to me, but all I was capable of doing was staring at the trodden-down carpet, nerves seeping through. Was that what I wanted? Willow was apparently an expert Carrier and she still got killed – my chances of getting shot were growing higher by the second. This wasn't what I was here to do. I was here to get information, not join the bloody team.

'You're pulling rank on me?' Jessica spat.

'If it gets you to take the silver spoon out of your ass, then yes.'

Jessica shook her head, looking down to her lap and muttering to herself, fiery hair falling past her cheek. From this angle the bruises were covered, and she looked normal, like she was just tired from performing the night before. I wished that were true.

'It's not fair,' Quinn snapped harshly, before she marched out of the room slamming the door behind her.

I wanted to go after her, but I had a feeling I was the last person she'd want to see right now – after all, I was replacing Willow. I hated that word, replace, you can't just replace a person. Though apparently in this place you could. I understood both sides of the argument but I sympathised with Quinn the most – she was in a relationship with the girl, after all.

'I'll head out and bring back food,' James said. 'You decide what you want to do, Naomi, and if you give me the green light we'll start going through the motions.'

James gave one last look at Jessica but she didn't return it, then he left quickly through the back door. Grace followed soon after but she headed up the stairs, probably to Quinn's room. Just as I was about to speak to Jess, Lily motioned me over.

I darted up, seeing her reaching out her hand for mine and pulled Lily to her feet. She pointed to the stairs and I nodded, leading the way. Maybe some time apart would be good. I threw a glance round my shoulder to Jessica. She lifted her head slowly, meeting my gaze, and all I saw was dread. I didn't get to look for long as Lily tugged me away.

As we started to climb the stairs she spoke. 'She'll get over it. Quinn, I mean.'

'Oh no, I totally understand.'

Lily gripped the banister, knuckles turning white, but she continued nevertheless. It was obvious she was in pain but from the stern look on her face, she wasn't giving in.

'You know, I think you'd be great. Mix the team up a bit. We all come from military families or spies, be nice to have a civilian on the team.'

'Yeah.' Then I remembered what Jackie had said earlier. 'You take in five a year.'

'That's just so we can be seen to the outside world as

prestigious. I think they're experimenting with compliance. Who's more willing to do the crazy shit? You or the ones born into the industry?'

'Uh –'

'You don't need to answer that, it's just a theory.'

'Right.'

The ascent was a long one but I didn't mind, it wasn't exactly like I had anywhere else to be. It did get me thinking though – how many times had they come home like this and Grace had taken care of them? Who cared for the team when she was out of action?

'Stop looking at me like that,' Lily said, breaking me from my thoughts.

'Like what?'

'Like you're a puppy and you just got punched in the face. Shit happens, alright. It's fucked-up but there's nothing we can do to change it. Willow's dead and in the next couple of weeks Harkness would have refilled her position with a newbie.'

'It doesn't feel right.'

'None of this feels right, especially my ribs,' Lily groaned.

'After Grace has eaten something I'm going to get her to take a look, see if I can't get myself excused from training for a week.'

'You can do that?' I asked.

'Well, no, but Ames has a soft spot for me.'

I didn't think that could happen here – then again, he was the empathetic one in the room when Harkness was torturing her. Maybe a couple of the teachers weren't truly horrible.

'Jess is going to kick and scream through this whole ordeal because you being involved is her worst fucking nightmare.'

* * *

James came back a couple hours later with a boot-load of food, using the excuse that he was Charlotte's son and if standards weren't upheld he would call her. He left out the part that they'd not spoken in nearly two years, but that didn't matter according to him. Even though I was starving I let the rest of the girls go first, and as soon as it was ready they were grabbing different things from all kinds of pots and pans – I think there was even a wok in there at some point.

'James, you should become a chef,' Lily said as she tucked into the beef on her plate.

SLATE RETRIBUTION

We were all crowded round the table in the kitchen. The blinds were rolled down and the curtains pulled over, the only light coming from the lamp above us. Jessica had called in sick to the show so someone could take her place, and so had the rest of the team.

Quinn was slow to come down, but the smell of her favourite comfort food, sweet and sour chicken, brought her down like a shot. James even had whisky, but I think that was for him rather than us.

'Maybe when I retire,' he considered.

'See, he can do this,' Jess started, 'but ask him to make toast and he burns it.'

'At least I didn't put a fork in the microwave,' he countered and Jess laughed.

Their earlier fight didn't seem to have affected the pair as James slung an arm around his sister's shoulder.

'No more of those pills OK?' he said to Jess.

'OK.'

Then he turned to the rest of us. 'Or for any of you. Dr Williams is prepared to edit the test results and pill prescriptions for the next couple of weeks. After that we'll figure something out.'

This was amazing – James had sorted things out and he'd only been here half a day. Well, he hadn't sorted everything out, but he'd made the next few weeks more bearable.

I picked at the remains of my chicken, I was too busy watching them all. The rest of the group, minus James, had scoffed their first helpings of food and were on seconds.

'Helen may come in and check the place,' Quinn said. 'What are we gonna do when she sees all the food?'

'I'll pull the mother card,' James said. 'Everyone's terrified of her when she's cross, and Helen's a housekeeper, not much of a standing here anyway.'

'We need to get Naomi out of here for this op, how are we going to smuggle her past the cameras?' Grace asked.

'Leave that to me,' Quinn said. 'I'll deal with the cameras and her disguise.'

She'd perked up a bit, after everything in the living room. I still hadn't said yes to the job but wondered if she would hold it against me if I took the spot on the team – unofficially, of course.

I could never be an assassin – geez, I'd be terrible. You'd know I was coming from a mile away because you'd hear the clattering of every object I bumped into. Just because I was fast didn't mean I was agile.

'So do I get an answer?' James asked. Everyone went quiet again, and I realised he was talking to me.

'Oh uh . . .' I trailed off, not knowing where to look.

Jessica pulled away from her brother and Quinn's eyes immediately fell to her plate. Should I accept? Would they hate me for it? Lily said that if I joined the team it would be Jess's worst nightmare and I knew why. If I joined this team then I was involved with everything and my chances of staying alive would run thin. This didn't deter me, though – in fact it excited me.

I didn't want Quinn to feel like I was replacing Willow, though. If they hadn't even buried the poor girl, was it the right thing to do?

'Stop thinking about everyone else,' James snapped and I jumped, my fork clattering onto the plate. 'If you're gonna make a decision don't let it be because of what you think Jess and Quinn want.' Was this dude a mind reader?

Shouldn't I consider the girls' feelings? If I was going to be on this team then I needed to know that no one would resent me for it. Jessica was staring straight at me, nodding encouragingly, but her eyes begged me to stay quiet.

'Naomi, I need a decision,' James said. 'Now – so that if you say no I can start making phone calls for another Carrier.'

'I'll do it,' I blurted out, without another thought.

When the words tumbled out of my mouth Jessica's face dropped, but her eyes never left mine. What had I done? I had just agreed to be trained and then go on an op to stop known terrorists! Had I been taking the pills without noticing? What the hell had I just signed up to?

'It's what you want?' Jess asked. 'Truly, you're not just doing this out of obligation?'

'No. I'm in too deep.' I looked to Quinn and offered a small smile. 'No going back now.'

The rest of the dinner passed with idle conversation and some chatter about the new binge-worthy TV series that James said he'd done in one sitting. Despite feeling guilty about replacing Willow I couldn't help the rush of adrenaline – I was going to be trained as a Carrier! I wouldn't feel useless anymore because now I was going to be a part of this team (temporarily).

As the dishes were cleared away, everyone headed upstairs to get ready for bed and I planned to follow soon after, I was knackered.

'You can crash in my room,' Jess said to James as she stacked the dishwasher. 'We'll both fit.'

'Great. Be like old times, just don't steal all the covers,' he warned, before heading outside. He had his phone out so he was probably going to make that call to his boss or girlfriend, whichever it was.

Jessica and I walked around each other in uncomfortable silence. It had never happened before, but things were different. Of course they were.

Just as Jessica closed the dishwasher and started it up I opened my mouth to speak, but for a moment no words came out. Nowadays it seemed like they either fell out or not at all. Jess noticed, and held up a hand.

'Don't. It's fine, it's one op. You'll be trained, and besides there's not much I can do about the decision. It was yours.'

'I just don't want you to think I'm replacing Willow.'

'You're not replacing her,' Jessica said. 'This is a one-time thing. It will never happen again.'

'Yeah, right – yeah, course,' I said, nodding quickly, biting my lip a little. 'Lily said that this is your worst nightmare, me joining you on an mission.'

'On the scale of where I'd rather have you, the field on a mission involving terrorists is the last place.'

I knew it, of course Jess was protective – and even though I wouldn't admit it out loud, I kinda liked it.

Jessica turned to leave the kitchen when I grabbed her hand.

'Hey,' I said. 'I intend to keep my promise. I'll get you out of here.'

'If you live long enough,' Jessica said as she pulled away.

There's Jess for you, miss rainbow sunshine with unicorn stickers on the side.

SLATE RETRIBUTION

CHAPTER 19

Psychodysleptic

Hallucinogenic.

QUINN EATON

The next day I was out the door before the rest of the house woke up. I just needed my own space for a little while and there was only so much of Lily's snoring I could take. I got dressed quietly in the bathroom, grabbed my stuff and headed out.

I really missed the Sunday dinners mum used to make. I hated that she had to live in witness protection for the rest of her life, and what made it worse was that the entire thing was set up by the Academy. It happened when I came here as a first year and I thought the idea was great, but as time went on I saw it as quite the opposite. Now, I was lucky to see her twice a year.

The clock had just struck five and thankfully it was still

dark outside. I assumed that everyone in the accommodation was still asleep since even the Runners don't get up this early to train, and I was glad I wouldn't have to talk to anyone. Not that I'm unsociable – I just liked to think of the early morning as me time. I'd go to the main command room with my mug of green tea, laptop and fluffy blanket and sit at my desk near the back. I did most of my work there undisturbed until Mr Thompson came in at half past eight. My work varied: sometimes it was for my so-called degree, and other days it was strictly mission prep. On the odd occasion, it was the time Willow and I would spend together.

Looking back, I guess that was how we grew so close to one another, spending our mornings going over strategies and blueprints. Then one day she brought breakfast, then the next and the next. Before I knew it there were croissants and white chocolate-covered strawberries. It wasn't till I was going through her room the other day that I found out Willow had made the pastry from scratch. I never realised how much effort she put into everything she did, not until it was too late.

The Academy was extremely quiet and another reason I came so early was because I liked to listen to the sound of my kitten heels clicking over the marble floor.

You're vintage, retro and classy, I heard her say. *How could I ever look at anyone else?*

Even though Willow was gone, when I was alone her voice floated around me, like she was some kind of angel. Screw that, like they would ever let her into heaven. Willow would be too busy twerking in hell or purgatory. Whatever was waiting for her in the afterlife, I knew she'd greet it with a Sex on the Beach and a bottle of tequila.

My heels seemed to click louder as I made my way to the main command room, my hand running across the wall as it changed to concrete, although it was strange that the door was left wide open. You always had to have a security pass to get in here . . .

Had someone broken in? Oh Mary and the wee baby! What do I do? Should I call for Helen? I couldn't exactly call the police.

See, this is what I got for being a productive early bird, a break in! Oh why couldn't I be Lily, she'd kick these attackers into next week, well maybe not next week since she was feeling like crap, more likely this coming Thursday. I searched for a place to put my things down since my hands were full but there was nowhere, this place really needed some shelves! It had everything else but did they think of shelves? No!

Mid freak-out I realised that Mr Thompson's bag was tucked under one of the desks straight ahead of me – wait, so this wasn't a break in? Then I heard a cough and some more shuffling from inside – OK, maybe no one broke in.

I walked in as quietly as I could, popping my head around the door to see Mr Thompson sitting at one of the back desks. My desk to be exact, but I wasn't going to fuss – well, I might actually, he could mess up my station and I'd just got the succulents in good condition.

As I took a proper look at him I realised just how ragged he was, his shirt wrinkled, hair greasy and now that the floodlights were up, the bags under his eyes were as heavy as designer ones.

'Is this a bad time?' I asked, stepping into the room.

Mr Thompson flew out of his seat, his arms flailing in fright, but when he saw it was only me he groaned, a palm slapped to his forehead. Should a spy be so jumpy? I mean, what if I'd been trying to break in?

'Christ, Quinn, do you know how late it is?' he asked.

'Do you know how early it is?' I asked in return.

The man blinked slowly, his mind taking a while to catch up, before he gazed at the big digital clock on the wall.

'Oh . . .'

I didn't bother asking him if he'd been here all night since it was obvious he had – why, though? There was no need for him to, classes weren't until this afternoon. I knew an op happened yesterday but there wouldn't have been much clean-up.

I dropped my stuff on another desk, pulled up a chair and sat down.

'Is everything OK?' I asked.

Thompson was a cold man but there was part of him that had thawed, I put it down to all the green tea I'd been giving him.

'Shouldn't I be asking you that?' Thompson answered, and I felt my face fall.

I'd forgotten he knew. I mean, it was hard to hide, especially when he walked in an hour earlier for work one day.

'I'd rather we didn't talk about her, at least until after the funeral.'

'Closed casket,' Mr Thompson muttered under his breath. 'Parents haven't set a date yet, Lennox is arranging the whole thing.'

What? How could anyone let her plan such an important event? That should be left up to Willow's parents, not Lennox of all people. Hell, I'd be a better choice and they didn't even know about me!

I didn't realise Mr Thompson was staring until his shoe began to tap against the hollow floor. A lump of metal slid down my throat as I met his gaze. I wasn't ready to talk about Willow yet. That was allowed, right?

Maybe I should go speak to Lennox, she was a psychologist after all, it's what she's here for.

'What have you been doing all night?' I asked, trying to change the subject.

Mr Thompson let out another annoyed groan before frowning at the computer – was he not a fan of the inspirational stickers I put on there? That was when my eyes trailed down to the half empty bottle of whisky.

Step in the right direction if you ask me I heard Willow say, but I shook my head, trying to silence her voice.

I knew this wasn't healthy but if she disappeared for good then what would I be left with? Then she really would be gone.

'You've been drinking?' I asked, even though it was blatantly obvious.

'Eh,' he mused, 'passes the time.'

Oh OK, should I offer to get him help? I knew he drank a lot, but even by Scottish standards this was a bit excessive. And the empty bottle of vodka in the bin next to him didn't help his case.

I knew he wasn't going to answer me so I shot off the chair, gently pushing in front of him to look at the computer. I noticed pretty quickly that he didn't try to stop me and I soon saw why, there was no way – cells?

There were blueprints on the screen marked '-3B' but it wasn't just another floor, it was a prison. Cells were clearly marked out, a walkway above to observe everything. Then open on the next window was a mock-up of what they looked like: solitude cells, the entire room padded, with no windows. You wouldn't even be able to tell who was in there unless you opened the door.

'Confinement, solitude. Seems nice, don't you think?' said Thompson, and I shook my head, nearly leaping back from the computer. 'Any troublesome agents will be dealt with, throw them in there for a couple of days. I just signed off on it.'

'You what?' I exclaimed, my throat becoming dry and itchy as I tried to calm my breathing.

A prison, that's what they were building. Who needed punishments when you could just throw us in a cell. If we were injured would we be seen to first? What if it was severe?

'What can I do?' he asked. 'I'm just a teacher, I sign off on plans, I sign off on the budget sheet. It's just my job.'

'You could have said no!' I practically yelled in his face.

I presumed it was because his veins contained more alcohol than blood, but Mr Thompson didn't even seem to care.

'What would have been the point?'

I stopped: the point? Did I have to spell it out for him? This was meant to be an institution of learning but now it was one of torture, and fast becoming a living hell. I knew Willow wouldn't want to be here; maybe she was in a better place after all.

Were we better off mindless or dead?

Darling, I'm meant to be the dramatic one here, Willow whispered in my ear.

'Shut up!' I yelled, my fingers clawing at my head.

A cold wet hand pressed on my shoulder and I slowly looked up to see Mr Thompson's stoic expression. Then he picked up the half-empty bottle, handing it to me.

'No shame in it, I hear voices too. After Duke shot my wife.'

My nails clenched the bottle tighter as I spoke. 'You told me she died in a car accident.'

'Do you think he would let me live if I told anyone otherwise?'

The cool glass of the bottle slipped through my fingers, clattering to the floor. None of this made sense.

If I ever left the Academy they would throw my mother out onto the streets without protection. I thought it was the staff who blackmailed us, but apparently they did it to one another.

SLATE RETRIBUTION

Then on top there was Harkness, superior and untouchable.

Is that why none of them left? Is that why some were kinder than the rest? Were they prisoners here just like us?

EMERY HALE

CHAPTER 20

Repentance

Remorse about one's sin.

GRACE ASPIN

I woke up around seven. I say that, I didn't leave the bed until half past. It was just one of those things.

The day before, I'd felt as if the sacred soul deep inside had left my body. I may have taken one too many pills and let me just say I felt their effects – maybe not straight away, but as soon as I stepped foot on the ward it was like I was floating above my own body, an observer to my own life. Then, nothing.

David – I mean Dr McKay, told me that Jess experienced some memory loss as well, so whatever was in this drug made sure we would forget. I prayed that it would all come to an end soon – how far could they realistically go with this? Not much further by my calculations. With Naomi here, maybe those limitations could be pushed – this had never happened before, so the outcome was impossible to predict, but possible to hypothesize.

I sat down at my dressing table grabbing a brush from the drawer, I really ought to get a new hairbrush since this one was made in the dark ages. It's been passed through the Aspin line and I was not going to throw it away, well I was actually, it wasn't like my grandmother would ever find out.

Quinn had said something about borrowing it because it matched her aesthetic – I swear if she wasn't in the Academy she would be an influencer of some sort.

I'd slept with my hair up so it was more knotted than usual; I hadn't bothered with my usual routine. After we'd eaten all I could think about was sleep – maybe it was the drugs or a food coma, I didn't know and didn't care, because my thoughts were elsewhere.

You can't tell anyone about this. His voice rang clear, as I relived yesterday morning. I stared in the mirror, my fingers tracing the boundaries of my lips, then I inched them deeper towards the centre. I couldn't remember much of yesterday but I did remember that the time was nine thirty-five, the curtains were drawn, patient files sat neatly at the side of the desk and Dr Williams was doing his wards round. If I were to be exact, I specifically remember Dr McKay's hand up my scrub top and his lips crashing against mine, filled with lust and passion. Ten minutes later he was in next to nothing while I quickly slid my bra back on.

I won't if you don't. I'd said in return.

A married man had experience, nothing wrong with that.

Of course there was the issue of his wife but she was a cunt, she had the audacity to accuse him of cheating when it was her who had done the deed in the first place! He was just getting even and I understood that, this wasn't anything more than sex.

Now, my mother would smack me around the head if she ever found out, and I couldn't even imagine the lecture from my dad or the amount of praying he'd force me through. For the entirety of my stay here at this facility, I had questioned my faith on more than one occasion. I was always filled with questions of

Why would God allow this to happen? and *How could He let people like us suffer?* I was taught that our souls were immortal and would transcend our earthly bodies, then we'd be resurrected at the end of time. I was raised under the eyes of the Vatican, my whole life had been planned out since my mother discovered she was with child. I was baptised as my first sacrament and raised a Roman Catholic. Anytime I rebelled at home my father threatened to send me to a nunnery, but once I proclaimed my intention to become a doctor, those threats faded.

As I stared at myself in the mirror I wondered, would my soul ever ascend to heaven or was I too far gone from God? Would I be damned to hell? As the pills continued to corrupt my mind it felt like I was condemning my soul. But I wouldn't stop, I couldn't, there was too much at stake. If I was found with too little in my system they would force me to take a double dose, and who would I be then?

I had already committed murder, which was a mortal sin – but where could I repent? I couldn't go to confession; I was under oath not to speak a word of any operations on penalty of death. If I told anyone what happened, then the Academy would know about it. I saw what they'd done to that poor friend of Quinn's, I wasn't going to let the same befall an innocent priest.

Was God even real? How would He let this happen? Was there some sort of lesson to be learned?

I didn't have any crosses in my room but the rest of the girls knew about my faith; they'd even asked me to pray for them in the past. I knew they thought it was a load of nonsense but I didn't. My religion made sense and it brought me comfort, but after the incident at the theatre, all I felt was guilt. The man I shot had killed another so Jess tried to make me feel better by saying he deserved to die, but it brought me little consolation. I had taken another life. That power should have remained with God, but I'd done it anyway. I had committed a mortal sin. What would become of me? Purgatory or hell?

As I placed the brush back in the drawer I paused – what was that? At the back there was a small white piece of paper, tucked under that stupid handheld mirror my Aunt Sophia gave me. When did that get there? I always wrote on my laptop or tablet, never carried stationery. I reached in, pulling it back to reveal a long strip of lined paper that looked like it had been ripped out. It was crumpled but the words on it made the air catch in the back of my throat. They were in Willow's handwriting.

Don't trust Jessica, her mother works for the Pyramid Delegates.

She's a monster, a murderer.

What the fuck?

Now Willow went on rants, and she and Jess didn't have the best of relationships, but I would never go as far to say she was a monster. I would have taken her ramblings lightly, except Willow was dead and this paper hadn't faded so it was new – she must have put it in here before she died.

If this was her last confession then there would be no reason to lie. What did she know? Enough that she was too scared to say it to my face.

There was a knock at the door before it started to open, and I crushed the note in my hand. Oh God give me strength, it was Jessica. That must be a sign.

'Hey,' Jessica said, leaning on her good leg. 'I just wanted to see if you were OK.'

'Me? Course.'

'My head is like scrambled egg,' she said with a laugh, 'speaking of which, do you want some for breakfast?'

'No,' I answered, 'I'll sort myself out, thanks.'

'OK.' She nodded, then a thought came to her. 'Would you be able to check Lily over, says she has chest pain.'

I smiled. 'Yeah, I'll book her an appointment on the ward.'

'Great.' Jessica paused like she was going to say something else but decided against it. Then she closed the door.

I listened for her footsteps moving away before I opened the paper ball to reread the words.

Don't trust Jessica, her mother works for the Pyramid Delegates.

She's a monster, a murderer.

As I sat there, I knew. A dead girl wouldn't lie.

EMERY HALE

CHAPTER 21

Kalon

Moral beauty.

NAOMI JADE

Punch, punch, dodge.

Punch, punch, dodge.

Punch, punch, dodge.

Punch, punch – Ow!

'Oh my!' Quinn cried. 'I'm so sorry, are you OK?'

Did Quinn have pointy knuckles? Geez, I didn't think she'd hit that hard. My back lay on the cool carpet as my cheek throbbed. It was official, I couldn't do this for a living because someone would break my face.

'I told you to dodge.' Quinn grabbed my hand and pulled me back to my feet.

To say that this was the first time Quinn had punched me

would be a lie, she'd done it at least four times now because I'd forgotten the simple pattern. How was I ever gonna get this straight? It was nearly one o'clock and I'd made little to no progress, apart from learning you shouldn't tuck your thumb in your palm when you punched, apparently that was common knowledge.

This morning I was gently woken by Jessica banging a pot and wooden spoon over my head, who then proceeded to drag me from bed (by the ankles) before throwing workout clothes my way. When I came down the stairs the curtains were still shut but all of the lights were on and the furniture dumped in the hallway. At first I thought it was a weird time to be decorating, but soon figured out what it was for. Lily told me that because I was here in secret we'd have to train in the living room. Jess came down the stairs soon after, but left, saying something about a dress fitting and James offered to take her as he had to get some work done at the office. I couldn't understand Jess sometimes, the girl could barely walk and yet she was off to the theatre. The limp she sported was significant, maybe there was some physio on offer.

Not two seconds later Grace shot off like a bullet, claiming there was an emergency at work, but there was something off. Lily left about thirty minutes later saying she had a follow-up appointment at the hospital, so I was left learning hand to hand combat with Quinn. Although now that I thought about it, there was something off with her too – she came in all worried and frantic and said she'd speak about it with everyone later. What was she hiding?

'Why don't you sit down?' Quinn offered, moving to take my arm, but I brushed her away. I had to get to grips with this if I was going on a mission next week. 'Naomi, you don't need to act all tough, it's gonna take a while to learn everything. Come on, take a seat and we'll go over some of the plans that James emailed me.'

Then, appearing like magic, a dark voice chuckled from the door. Kayson stood there in jeans and a t-shirt – the bruise on his face was fading, but he still wore that condescending smirk with pride.

'You can't be serious,' he deadpanned.

'Shut up, Kayson.' Quinn said, her smile turning to a frown as she took my hand.

'All I'm saying is the new first years are doing better than her.' He raised his arms in surrender. 'Just stating the facts.'

Was Kayson determined to bring me down? Ever since I sorta blackmailed him he's been nothing but an ass.

'I'm getting there,' I said to him, crossing my arms defensively.

'Naomi, it looks adorable but I don't think you're getting anywhere.'

Great, he'd stood and watched while I got my butt handed to me and I hadn't even noticed. How the hell did anyone deal with this guy? Had no one smacked him around the mouth yet? Well, I think Jess did the other day.

Quinn rolled her eyes. 'What do you want?'

'I'm here to train Naomi.'

Piss off, nope not happening.

'Lily's not going to be long,' Quinn said, looking as confused as I felt, 'she'll be back soon.'

'She can't train Naomi, not in her condition. Besides, I've trained a couple of Runners.'

'Well, you've not trained a Carrier.' Quinn snapped back.

Woah, she seemed to hate Kayson more than me – even with the other girls she'd never been this snappy. Wonder what happened between them.

'No, that's what you're for,' Kayson said, like he was speaking to a five-year-old. 'I'll deal with the self-defence and then you can do whatever it is you do.'

'Did Jess agree to this?' she asked.

He didn't respond – was this a deal between him and Lily? Cause I had a feeling Jessica wouldn't have agreed to this. As the silence drew on Quinn pulled a sour look, while I stood there like an idiot, unsure what to do. Did I want to be trained by him? If he's trained others then maybe he had some merit.

'Jess isn't going to like this,' Quinn said warningly.

'Well Jess isn't here,' he mocked.

Then Kayson walked over, grabbed me by the hips and spun me around so my back was to his chest. That was a bit forward. He grabbed my arms roughly, moving them so my fists hovered in front of my lips.

'You're not gonna stop any punches if your hands aren't protecting your face first,' he told me. 'Now, your dominant hand can dictate your stance –'

'That's it, I'm calling Jessica!' Quinn announced, marching through to the kitchen.

No Quinn, don't leave! Oh poop.

Kayson was considerably taller than me so I felt his thighs press against mine while his hips controlled my movements. That was when he leaned down, resting his chin on my shoulder and whispered into my ear, 'You're tense, relax a little.'

I didn't even realise I'd been holding my breath until I let out a small pant. Kayson's biceps caressed my shoulders as he moved my body gently to the left, his touch warm but not clammy or sweaty. I could smell his cologne but it was different, like cool fresh water. The material of his shirt felt soft on my skin but his hands were dry and rough.

'Now, your enemy is coming straight at you, what do you do?'

'Run?' I offered.

'Yes, you can, but if you can't, then what?'

Was I supposed to come up with a battle plan?

'Well I have Quinn so she could direct me and tell me

what to do.'

'Never rely on the Tech so heavily,' he told me. 'You need to be independent, Quinn could be busy. What do you do next?'

'Kayson, I don't know,' I said, exasperated.

He sighed, pulling away, the warmth disappearing but I wanted it back, there was something about his hold. It wasn't just the heat, it was the security and safety of it, of him. Like Kayson's body was impermeable to bullets or pain.

He strolled to the other side of the room, rolling up his cotton sleeves and curling his hands into fists. His muscles seemed to grow in size as the shirt tugged just that little bit tighter.

'OK, maybe you need a visual. I'm going to try and take you down, you have to try and stop me.'

Not sure if I want to in all honesty – Naomi get it together! Stop it!

'Uh, OK,' I said, unsure. Was I supposed to rugby-tackle him?

'Raise your hands like you were a couple of seconds ago,' he told me and I nodded, lifting them to my lips. 'Not so close – if I manage to tackle you, you'll end up hitting yourself in the face.'

Oh right, right, OK then. I inched my hands away from my face until Kayson nodded, then he readied himself to run.

'You ready?' he asked.

'No.'

Then he bolted towards me. My first instinct was to run out the door but it was like my feet were stuck to the floor with superglue. I could tell why Kayson was a Runner, he was fast as hell. Definitely faster than me. Within a blink of an eye he had reached me, so the only thing left to do was turn away. His arms wrapped around my chest and I felt his soft shirt slide across my skin and his strong grip clench my hands.

'Now, that was a bit pathetic.'

'Hey!' I exclaimed. 'I don't know what to do.'

'You're right, sorry – utterly pathetic,' he corrected himself. 'Now, I have my arms around your body, what do you do?'

Well, from all the talk with Katie the next move was usually a lot of kissing and then sex, but that was never happening!

'Uh . . . '

'Think, what could hurt me in this position?' he asked.

What do I have? Christ what were the different parts of the human body? My mind had drawn a complete blank. I knew I wasn't as knowledgeable as Grace, but even so. What had this guy done to me? It was like the doorstep all over again.

'Naomi, you'd be more than dead at this point. Come on, think.'

Elbows!

As the thought came to my head I pushed my right hand against his and then with force drove my elbow into his side, before thrusting my hips back, pushing him further. Kayson actually let go of me as he stumbled back winded. Had I hurt him? Had I actually – no way!

'Well, glad to see you have more common sense than I anticipated, but you need to be quicker.'

Not even a well done?

Suddenly he grabbed my wrists from behind and out of instinct I thrust my hips back trying to twist out, but he kept a firm grip.

'Naomi –' Kayson started, but then I stepped on the toe of

his shoe and twisted again. I didn't get too far with that idea because I'd forgotten we were holding hands, so when I turned I sent us both tumbling to the ground.

We landed with a thump, my head hitting the carpet, but I took it as my opportunity to escape. I wiggled and shimmied, but before I knew it I'd been flipped over, arms pinned above my head. Oh yup, this was – well, this was happening.

Kayson was straddling me, his jeans rubbing against my bare legs, oh Jess why didn't you give me leggings instead of shorts? As he gripped my wrists a little tighter his muscles bulged and to be honest, if he was trying to conceal anything it wouldn't be worth it, he may as well just throw away the shirt. Oh no! No, seriously Kayson, don't do that.

I hadn't realised how close we were until I caught his eyes and lips inches from mine.

'Figure your way out.'

Seriously, I really didn't want to.

This time his voice was soft, not a hint of ego or malice. From here he could actually pass for a genuine guy, but I knew better. Kayson was just pretending with me – it was what he did for a living – but still, there was that sliver of doubt that lingered.

He was that close I felt his warm breath on my face and was trapped in his gaze for what felt like the first time. He wasn't staring at my lips or chest, just me.

Now that we were close I saw all the little things I hadn't before, like the details of the small thin scars near his hairline, there were three of them. Now I knew they'd be from Academy punishments, no doubt someone had carved those into him. He had even more faint bruising on his neck and some that went below the neckline of his shirt. Kayson must have contoured his jaw and cheekbones because those edges were sharp enough to cut paper.

His grip loosened around my wrists like he was making things easier but I stayed completely still, mesmerised by his gentleness.

Then I found my eyes slowly trailing to his lips, oh this was bad.

I quickly threw them back up to his, but of course being so close he'd seen, so in return Kayson laughed, a mischievous grin on his face.

If he wasn't a complete asshole I would have kissed him. Maybe.

'Perfect way to win a girl over, pin her to floor,' a new voice said, and my eyes widened.

I threw my head back to see a random man standing there! Kayson let go of my wrists and I quickly pushed myself up, pulling my knees to my chest. I couldn't believe I'd thought about kissing him.

Kayson pulled away, but held the man's gaze firmly.

'I was teaching her some hand to hand combat.'

The man's eyebrows raised as he looked between us both.

'Training? That was – well, I see you've made great progress.'

He was older, and by the way Kayson looked at him, had way more experience – maybe even superiority. He wore a brown leather jacket, blue shirt, black jeans and loose combat boots along with a thin silver chain that dangled down his . . . exposed chest. Wow OK, did men have a thing about shirts here or was there something in the water?

'What do you want, Barnes?' Kayson asked crossing his

arms over his chest.

Oh my god, Kayson was intimidated – actually physically intimidated. The man was a little taller than Kayson, a little broader in size and had fuller jet-black hair, but I doubted that had anything to do with it. I felt like I was in the middle of a turf war.

'Nothing to do with you,' the man replied. 'Didn't think you lived here, unless you've joined the girls' team.'

'Get out.'

'Oh, still touchy after I handed you your ass?' the man asked, his American accent a littler thicker. 'It's alright, you're still in training. Plenty of time to build up the courage, *again*.'

What was I witnessing right now? This guy couldn't have been at the Academy – was he an actual agent or did he work for Harkness? Whoever he was, I prayed he didn't know I wasn't supposed to be here.

Just then Quinn appeared at the door, phone in hand. She turned to the man, surprised, then her attention snapped to Kayson, then me. She slammed the phone into the man's chest before pointing a menacing finger at Kayson.

'What did you do to her?' she asked.

Quinn seemed to have found that fire from earlier because it looked like she was going to kick Kayson in the no touch zone.

'I didn't do anything!' he exclaimed.

'He was straddling her,' the man added. I screwed my eyes shut and buried my head in my knees. 'She didn't seem to mind, though.'

Oh God! This wasn't happening. Make it stop! This could not get any worse.

'Who was straddling who?' I heard Jessica ask, a laugh in her voice as she limped through the door.

WORLD IMPLODE WORLD IMPLODE

She stopped short seeing the scene in the living room, her brother James lingering behind, and Jessica seemed the most horrified of all as she walked in a little further. She locked eyes with Kayson and they had a nonverbal conversation, but neither budged.

'Ashford, go find Lily in the medical wing, she has the plans for next week,' Jessica said, her voice void of any emotion.

Kayson hesitated. 'Jess I'm fine here, Lily asked me to train Naomi.'

'You're the second Runner who is now on my team, this so-called training wasn't authorised, so get out,' she ordered.

I wanted to shrink back like a fly on the wall, anything would be better than this. I thought they would be all for it, considering they were more than happy that Jess got a hoo-ha every now and again. Not that it was ever going to happen between me and Kayson, but still.

What I would give to blend in right now, chameleons were lucky.

'Jess,' Kayson started, but she held up a hand, shaking her head.

'Go,' she said, motioning out the door, this time her voice cold and harsh.

Kayson hesitated but quickly gave in to the order and left the room, barging through the mystery man as he left. The guy laughed in pity, but Jess threw her head round giving him a look and he held a hand up in apology, falling quiet.

Then he spoke to me.

'You must be Naomi,' he said, with a charming smile. 'Word of advice, stay away from Ashford. He's not good for anyone, not even himself.'

'Chris,' James stepped forward, 'Let's leave the kids alone, we have things to discuss.' He nodded to the kitchen and the pair left.

That was Chris? Him? Well, I got what Jess saw in him.

'I thought he'd be taller,' I said, but Jess only glared.

'You, go upstairs.'

I laughed. 'Jess you're not my mother.'

'If you're wondering why I'm treating you like a child, it's because you're acting like one.'

'We were training, he fell on top of me.'

Jessica shook her head – why the hell was she so uptight about this? She was the one fucking Chris, she couldn't talk. I thought Grace was meant to be the party pooper.

'You're here to train, not stare into a man's eyes all day. You're here for a job. Start acting like it,' she snapped.

Oh, screw you! I stood up and shoved past her as I ran out of the room and up the stairs. I didn't care if I knocked her off her feet, she deserved it. We both fell, it's not like anything was going to happen! It was an accident, for crying out loud.

SLATE RETRIBUTION

Quinn being protective was one thing, but Jessica treating me like a child was another – how could she speak to me like that? I don't work for her! I thought we were equals, but apparently not.

I threw open the door to Quinn's room, slammed it shut behind me and went to the window. Through the sheer curtains I saw Kayson's back at the other side of the complex. He was just standing there, but he must have felt someone watching him because he turned and then saw me. He nodded, giving a mock salute, before he headed down the small path out of sight.

Nothing would have happened – it couldn't have, right?

EMERY HALE

CHAPTER 22

Apocalyptic

Imminent disaster.

JESSICA-GRACE WINTERS

Of all the things I wanted to do with my morning, a dress fitting was not one of them – apparently the designer had lost my measurements. Now, I have no hate because stuff like this happens all the time, but did it have to happen today? I wanted to have a long lie for once in my life, pretend that mum was downstairs cooking breakfast and dad was coming home from the nightshift. Yeah, like that would ever happen.

'Stop it,' I heard my brother groan.

I shifted in bed, my eyebrows furrowing. 'What?'

'You're doing your thing,' he said groggily.

'What thing?'

'Your audible brooding. Stop it.'

With a huff I threw off the covers and pushed the hair out of my face, it always got frizzy during the night.

'Don't,' James warned.

Oh, what now? I rolled my eyes and stood up, but then a sharp pain cut through my knee and just like that, I was on the floor.

'Told you so.'

Fuck, I'd forgotten about my stupid knee.

'Yeah, yeah whatever,' I muttered.

Apart from my knee occasionally giving out I was able to get dressed without too much bother – James, however, was a different story. He went on one of his ramblings about how the world sucks, and even though I was inclined to agree with him, my phone pinged and after reading the text, the world seemed a little brighter.

Chris *I have some time off and heard you have a dress fitting. I'll see you there in thirty.*

I threw the phone into my hoodie pocket, grabbed my

shoes and then threw one of my spare water bottles at James's head.

'Oi!' he cried.

'We have to go, I have a dress fitting!' I shouted back.

'Being injured makes you so demanding.'

After I'd beaten a pot and spoon together, dragged Naomi out of bed, thrown clothes at her, then spoken to a weirdly-behaving Grace, I was out the door. There was part of me that wanted to question why all of the furniture was in the hallway, but it was too early to care. I was in my brother's car and out the Academy gates before a single fuck crossed my mind, oh wait no, that one flew away too.

As James drove I rested my head against the window; it was still early so the roads were quiet. It was nice this, just us two.

Having Naomi involved in the op next week was a complete shambles. I didn't want her on my team because then she became my responsibility. The poor girl couldn't throw a punch. Naomi was fast but there was a difference between sprinting round a track and dodging bullets.

Was her life worth risking? James barely knew her and yet

threw her into my team like nothing. Naomi doesn't know how to put in an HDMI cable! How the hell was she supposed to do any of this?

How could I have let her?

The car pulled to a stop as the lights flashed red and I sighed – this was just one big ball of shit. As we sat there I heard the echoes of cars as they whizzed by. If I set a foot outside, the sheer force of a car would throw me to the ground and my head would hit the tarmac with a sickening crack.

I could end it, right here and now. Everything would stop.

Then the lights turned green and we were off again.

Death wasn't something I ever feared. Shouldn't I care about it more, or at least have a small emotional response? When I thought about throwing myself in front of a car there was nothing – there had to be something wrong with me. Even with Willow, I hadn't cried once – hell, I'd barely thought about her. Was that sick? You're supposed to honour the dead and here I was forgetting it even happened. Had Willow been buried? I didn't even know when the funeral was or even if there was going to be one. I hadn't thought about planning it, everything just seemed to be piling on and I had to prioritise. Sure, Willow and I weren't the closest of friends but I thought I would have felt at least something after she died. All I felt right now was an empty pool of nothing.

What's wrong with me?

Thirty minutes later we pulled up outside the theatre and I unbuckled the seatbelt before throwing the door open. I jumped out on my good leg then tested the bad. It was throbbing with a couple of sharp spikes, but once I started walking it eased.

'Do you want any help?' James asked.

'No.'

'Why do I even bother?' he muttered.

Then with a wave and a smile he pulled away from the kerb.

James had to convince his boss to go through with the plan so decided he should at least tell Nicola about it first, then assess the damage and the amount of sucking-up he'd have to do later.

Suddenly my phone pinged again with a new message.

Chris *I'm here baby, show me that beautiful face of yours.*

Despite the chill that whipped through the air and the stink of yesterday's rubbish, I couldn't help the giddy smile running up my face – I'd have to go find him after the dress fitting.

I shoved the phone in my pocket and headed inside. I had to stop and rest a couple of times, but once I got to the costume department I found walking a little easier. It always smelled of hairspray and sugary sweets.

The costume room was filled to the brim with racks of dresses and suits, all labelled and steamed for tonight's show. I wished I could get back on the stage, I craved the ecstasy of losing myself, but Harkness had caught us with the stupid wire so I got a scalpel to the knee. I hardly remembered anything about it. Maybe next week I could get in a show before the op – a matinee perhaps?

'Hello!' I shouted, since I didn't see anyone around, it was unusually quiet. There was always music playing or one of the wardrobe team pottering about.

I leaned against the table as I made my way through the racks of clothes but there was no sign of anyone. I could have sworn they said a morning fitting on the email. As I went to check, a smooth and sexy baritone voice called to me.

'Jess, it's been too long.'

I spun around to see Christopher closing the door, a smug grin on his face. His blue shirt hugged his torso in all the right places, but what caught my attention the most was the measuring tape dangling around his neck.

He grabbed one of the dresses from the side and I noticed it had my name on it.

'Nice dress.'

Seeing him made something flutter in my chest. As he took my hand, I tried to hide it by feigning confusion, but even then all I could do was stutter a few words.

'Chris, you're – what are you doing back here – you shouldn't –'

Then he cupped my cheek and brought me closer, before his lips caressed mine.

'Just wanted to give you that,' he answered softly, then his eyes moved down my body. 'What happened?'

In hindsight, I probably should have told him the truth but that would have taken too long. I wanted to spend as much time with him as possible, since it would be the last. I had to end things, the Academy was getting out of control and now I had Naomi to look out for. There was no time for a relationship in my life – I barely had time to see my brother, never mind a lover. Was that what we were? I didn't think I was capable of such a thing.

'Training exercise gone south, nothing to worry about,' I shrugged.

Chris looked like he was contemplating my answer, then he let out a sigh, slowly turned me so I faced the mirror, grabbed the measuring tape and drew it across my collarbone.

'Now, the ladies are having the morning off and besides, they already have your measurements.'

What? Then why the fuck did I get up this early?

'I got an email that they lost them.' I told him.

Chris scrunched his face a little with a playful grin.

'I may have sent that email.'

I laughed, shaking my head, this guy was something else – No, this had to stop. It wasn't fair on me and it certainly wasn't fair on him. Chris was a great guy, he was amazing to spar with, gave unbelievable shoulder rubs and made the best hot chocolate. He deserved someone better than me.

'Chris,' I tried, taking his hand, but he continued speaking like I hadn't said anything.

'Now, I said I would meet you after your fitting and take you to this little coffee shop across the street while we wait for James to get the OK from his boss. That gives us two hours?'

'Chris,' I said forcefully, trying to get my thoughts together, but all I could think about was his lips on mine, his rich cologne. 'Chris, seriously, we need to talk about this.'

He took off the measuring tape and squeezed my hand, then led me to sit on one of the nearby chairs. Chris had that look, like he knew what I was going to say. He knelt down, his palm caressing my thigh, soothing.

'I know we were never officially an item,' he said, 'but I want you to know that just because you go to the Academy doesn't mean we can't see each other. I know it doesn't have the most pristine reputation with the other services, but I don't care, baby.'

Oh if he only knew. Quinn had her mother as leverage, Lily had her sister and Grace had her parents. The Academy would exploit them all if it meant getting one more soldier, but I wasn't going to let them touch Chris. He was too good, ya know? There's only a couple of hundred in the world, but he was too nice and too smart and too loyal and, well, just an amazing fucking guy. I didn't deserve him, not after everything.

'It is the Academy,' I said. 'You know why no one has any kind of relations with us. It's dangerous.'

'I don't know if you've noticed, but I do dangerous for a living.'

'Chris, we can't keep doing this anymore.'

'It's Harkness isn't it?' Chris asked. 'I heard you need to cut all ties when you go to that place. It sounds like a cult.' May as well be, I wanted to say. 'Jess, I'll speak to him, he can't stop you from seeing people.'

'No,' I shot out, shaking my head. 'Please, you can't.'

Then he cupped my cheeks with his warm hands, his next words soft and caring.

'Baby please, tell me the truth.' And I did.

I told Chris everything, from the first year at the Academy until the present. I rolled up my legging, rubbed off the makeup and told him about the drugs. Before I knew it I was condemning him. I kept checking the door every few seconds in case anyone was listening, paranoia cracking like a whip. The whole thing lasted about twenty minutes – hell, it could have been an hour – all I knew was that tears streamed down my face as relief lifted from my shoulders. The more I talked about what was happening the easier it got, but guilt sat in the pit of my stomach like a dagger.

Chris didn't want to carry all my baggage, who would? I was a walking time bomb and there was no way to diffuse me. The Academy was powerful, it could make Chris disappear. If I broke this off, at least I would know he was safe; if I didn't I'd live in constant fear that he'd be sat by that tree, dried blood soaking his shirt and flies swarming in his eyes.

How could I let that happen to someone that I – no, I couldn't.

'No one's here,' was the first thing he said to me. 'It's just you and me.'

He took my hands again, kissing the left and then the right – why wasn't he running out the door? James had a reason to stay, but Chris didn't owe me anything. I couldn't be worth all this. My mother barely acknowledged I existed and my father left – why would anyone want me this bad?

'I'm sorry Jess,' he said, 'I'm sorry.'

'What for?' I asked. 'You couldn't have done anything.'

'See, that's where you're wrong, I could have done so much more. It should never have gotten this far – baby, look at what they've done to you.'

Please make this torture end. I had to let him go, but every fibre of my being told me not to. I yearned to be beside him, now more than ever, but if anyone found out then his death would be on my hands. How much blood was I willing to spill for my own selfish acts?

'We have to stop this. Us,' I said, standing up shakily. 'I'll never forgive myself if something happened to you Chris.'

He hesitated for a moment.

'Your brother asked me to help out on the op next week; he was going to tell me everything over that coffee.' A small, sad smile graced his face as he rose to stand with me, tucking strands of hair behind my ear. 'I didn't know what it was about. I thought that ... it doesn't matter. You're wanting to go back to professional then?'

Pain plucked my tight heart strings – if Chris left, my heart would freeze over for good. I cared for him and I never want to see him hurt because of me, I couldn't bear it. How was he OK with all of this? Why was he not yelling?

'I just – if something happened to you, Chris.'

'No, I get it. Until you go to trial we can't be seen together outside of work,' he said, shaking his head.

He didn't seem upset, but something told me there was a lot more going on behind the scenes. Chris, unlike me, felt proper emotions – but once again here I was, an empty pool of nothing. How could I be like this? I wanted to give up on our relationship to save his life, and save myself the endless torment, and I was *fine* with it? How did I not want to fight for our love? Love, it was a joke. How could someone like me be capable of such a vast thing?

Suddenly Chris wrapped his arms around my body, pulling me into a tight hug. I hid my face in the crook of his neck taking in a deep breath, trying to stop the tears. Wait, had I been crying? I'd forgotten – how could I – fuck! Even though the drugs were out of my system they'd done their work. I couldn't forget this, I couldn't forget Chris.

'I want you to promise me.' His voice just above a whisper. 'Promise me that whatever happens, if you need me, you'll call. I don't care what time of night. I won't leave you, Jessica.'

I pulled back. 'Chris, I can't lose you.'

He kept a firm grip.

'Promise me.'

How could I? 'Promise,' I lied.

Chris let out a sigh, his head falling forward as he held me. I wanted more, so much more, but I couldn't. I had a duty to perform and a relationship would only make things more complicated. This had to be the last time we saw each other privately.

We held each other for quite a while. I'm not sure how much time passed, but at some point my eyes closed as I breathed in his scent, winter berries. My hand fiddled with the back of his thick, jet-black hair, wanting to savour the moment for a little longer. I wanted to appreciate Chris, I wanted to give him so much more, but how could I? I was empty.

That was when he pulled back and tenderly kissed my neck. A breathy gasp escaped my lips, but Chris just laughed.

'Every time.' His voice soft and raspy. 'Every single time.'

Then his hands ran through my hair, tugging ever so slightly as he pulled my head to the side, slowly working his way down. I felt every tingling sensation as his lips dug deeper. Chris's hand grabbed the bottom of my hoodie, his fingertips scratching gently at my skin.

'Chris,' I tried, but suddenly I couldn't speak.

The flutter of his hand running up and down my torso rendered me speechless, while his other hand gripped my neck as he kissed my jaw.

All I wanted was him; I craved his touch. Every moment I'd ever spent with Chris came rushing back, the late nights and early mornings, the sweet nothings in my ear and the promises that he'd never leave me. I didn't want to let him go.

Chris pulled away slowly, his eyes trailing to mine. I shivered as his hand dropped to my hip and his fingers fiddled with my hair. I wanted this moment to last forever.

His tanned skin had never been touched by a bullet or a knife; his face was unblemished by scars. His coal-dark eyes sucked me in, but when his thick lips pressed mine I was lost in an endless state of ecstasy. Sometimes we went for so long that I forgot where I was.

In my daily life I felt nothing, but when I was with Chris, I felt everything.

Gripping the back of his T-shirt I kissed him, then just like that I became lost, my eyes closed and every movement forged through instinct. My hands fell, clenching the belt of his jeans, but then I stopped. I breathed.

What the fuck was I doing? This wasn't how it was supposed to happen.

I rested my head against his, a small sob rising in my throat. This would be the last time I would see him, ever. The real him. Of course we'd get enough to go to trial, but then what? We'd just be put in another institution with more corrupt agents. Anyway, he'd find someone better.

'We can't keep doing this,' I said, not even looking him in the eye, I couldn't bear it.

'I know, baby.' Chris's fingers gently tipped the bottom of my chin, holding me there, his thumb rubbing my cheek. 'I know.'

I knew I should stop, but my body was in control. I wanted Chris; I needed him.

'This has to be the last time.' As I spoke his thumb rubbed smooth circles into my cheek. I cupped his hand, trying to remember every touch, because I knew that soon I'd be forced to forget him. 'If I lost you –'

'Shh, don't talk like that,' he said. 'I'm gonna be fine, you need to worry about yourself.'

'After the mission, promise me you'll leave – promise you'll be far away before any of this goes down.'

'Hey, come on now, give me some credit,' He said, that playful grin of his sneaking back out. 'Focus on surviving, then when this whole thing goes to trial, we can be together. Alright? Just, stay alive for me.'

'Stay alive for me,' I repeated.

They weren't questions, they were promises.

'If this is our last time, what do you want me to do?' He asked, his lips inching closer to mine, the roughness of his fingertips leaving tingles on my skin. 'What do you want me to do to you?'

'Make me miss it.'

Chris threw me roughly against the wall, grabbing my ass and biting my neck, his teeth pinching at the skin as his lips mercilessly sucked. His hands gripped the bottom of my hoodie, hoisting it off and throwing it across the room, then he went to work on my top. His lips travelled down, focusing on my collarbone. His hand cupped my breasts with a force that hovered between pain and pleasure as he sprung open the buttons of my vest, revealing my black lace bra.

'You're teasing me.' Chris looked up, lustfully pulling at the bra material, slowly at first, then forcing it down to my chest. His hands reached round the back, unhooking the clasp with a snap, throwing the thing to the ground.

'It's a good thing I'm not wearing any underwear, then,' I replied.

He smirked, his thumbs hooking into the sides of my leggings, pulling each side down. The cool air conditioning sent goosebumps over my skin, but Chris's warm breath spread like wildfire as he moved further down. His tongue licked across my clit, already spiking that pulse of excitement, my back arching and head falling. I wanted to reach for his hair, to hold him there longer but I was pleasurably paralysed.

As he rose I found movement, released from the elation, and grabbed for his belt, ripping it off and busting open the button of his jeans. I grasped his cock in my hand, now breathless as the sweat and heat began to rise.

A small moan escaped as he went inside me. My nails clenched at his back as he went harder and deeper, any sound now stolen, our hips grinding together in one solid movement.

It was then I knew I could never leave him.

* * *

As soon as we pulled up outside the dorms I was more than prepared to tell James to turn around and drive like a bat out of hell. I could run and what made it worse, I wanted to. Jamie would happily drive out of here and Chris would back me all the way.

Of course I couldn't leave. I'd never leave my team behind.

James, an officer of MI6 had been given the go-ahead to

delegate this terrorist op to the Academy, specifically the Omega team, my girls. There wasn't a thing Harkness could do about it – and what made it even better was that if anyone were to ask about Naomi, she was officially instated as an outside source, so she'd be given full immunity. Harkness couldn't touch a single hair on her head; none of the staff could. To say I was relieved would be an understatement.

Chris jumped out first and offered to hold the door, but I nodded my head in James's direction. He understood quickly and closed the door, heading inside.

My brother, on the other hand, noticed I was lingering.

'What happened?' he asked, taking his seatbelt off. 'I keep telling you that if Quinn does illegal shit in her bedroom I don't wanna know about it.'

'No,' I said, with a small laugh. 'I wanted to tell you something in case the op goes sideways next week.'

'If you're gonna start saying goodbyes, don't even think about it. It won't happen, not to us.'

'Oh god no, I'm rubbish with those.'

That was when the nerves set in and I grabbed the car door

handle and hopped outside, using my good leg as a stabiliser. James jumped out from the driver's seat, immediately taking my arm as I sucked in a dry breath, pins and needles spiking through my knee.

'Jess, if it's not goodbye and it's not about Quinn then what is it you wanted to tell me?' James asked, grabbing his briefcase from the car.

When we made it to the front door I paused, took in a breath and turned to my brother with the most confident look I could muster, knowing that the next phrase could make or break our relationship. Well not ours, the one he had with his best friend.

'I slept with Chris.'

James stopped, his mouth dropping open and eyes darting from me to the wooden door. If I didn't know any better I'd say he wished he had lasers in his eyes to burn through his best friend's skull, but I did know better, shit.

'More than once,' I added.

My brother remained speechless as rage simmered on his face. I didn't want to stick around for much longer, so without another thought I opened the door and hobbled inside. I really hoped he didn't hurl that new briefcase at Chris's head.

'He was straddling her. She didn't seem to mind, though,' I heard Chris say, and I burst out laughing. What show did I miss?

'Who was straddling who?' I asked, walking into the living room.

When I saw the scene in front of me nausea rose in my throat – what the fuck? Kayson was straddling Naomi, who had all the stability of a melted snowman right now. Shocked didn't even begin to cover it – I'd asked Kayson to protect Naomi, not fuck her!

I glared, ready to beat the shit out of him. Being a dick was one thing, manipulating Naomi when she was vulnerable was another. Oh, and also she was my best friend. When the hell was your ex about to shag your best friend OK? Naomi didn't even know the guy!

We dated for a year, did that not mean anything? Did he not have enough respect for me not to do this? Apparently not. I knew Kayson was shitting himself as he locked eyes with me, like a deer caught in the headlights.

'Ashford, go find Lily in the medical wing, she has the plans for next week,' I said, trying to suck my anger out, because if I didn't I would have started screaming.

Kayson's face immediately filled with regret. 'Jess, I'm fine here, Lily asked me to train Naomi.'

Oh, did she now? Well that wasn't sanctioned by me so you can tell Lily while you're there that whatever deal you had was off! I wanted to scream – how the hell could he do this? Kayson had the pick of anyone in the school but he chose her?

Then for the hell of it, I pulled rank.

'You're the second Runner who is now on my team, this so-called training wasn't authorised, so get out,' I demanded, pointing to the door.

I may have been injured but that didn't mean I was any less likely to kick him in the dick. I couldn't even look at Naomi right now, all I could see was him. I told Kayson to protect her and now he does this? Unbelievable. You know, I'd actually been starting to trust him again.

'Jess,' Kayson begged. He knew exactly what I was thinking but I wasn't in the mood to listen.

'Go.' I motioned to the door before casting my gaze to Quinn.

She looked angry herself. She hated guys like him; her step-father was one of them.

Kayson marched out of the room, barging into Chris. I rolled my eyes, pressing my tongue to the back of my teeth, clenching the anger. He could be so arrogant at times, thinking he could just take whatever he wanted, just because he's good looking. It was his only redeeming quality.

Chris started laughing but I shot him a glare, so he shut up pretty quickly. There was no time for this. We needed to plan.

'You must be Naomi,' Chris said, with a smile that could unhook any bra. 'Word of advice, stay away from Ashford. He's not good for anyone, not even himself.'

Oh here we bloody go, did dick-measuring go down while I was outside?

'Chris. Let's leave the kids alone, we have things to discuss.' James said but it came out like an order from a superior. Oh fuck, not this.

The whole reason I told him about it outside was so that

fists didn't start flying; I did not need any more blood on the kitchen walls.

Chris naively left with James, closing the kitchen door behind them.

'I thought he'd be taller,' Naomi said, speaking up for the first time. Jesus.

'You,' I said, pointing to the girl's chest, 'Go upstairs.'

Then, she had the audacity to laugh in my face. 'Jess, you're not my mother.'

'If you're wondering why I'm treating you like a child it's because you're acting like one.' I may be a hypocrite, but Naomi wanted to be here so badly, then the moment she got the chance to train, she decides to do that? Of course if Kayson had done anything without her consent he'd be on the floor, but by the look on her face and what Chris had said, she didn't have any problem with it.

'We were training, he fell on top of me.' Oh yeah, totally.

'You're here to train, not stare into a man's eyes all day,' I snapped. 'You're here for a job. Start acting like it.'

Then, like a child who didn't get her own way, Naomi

stormed out of the room and ran up the stairs. That went well.

Quinn crossed her arms, plopping down on the couch.

'This whole thing is so messed up,' she said.

Well, she wasn't wrong.

SLATE RETRIBUTION

CHAPTER 23

Cinders

Rubble: ashes.

JESSICA-GRACE WINTERS

One week later

I wanted to scream.

The jeep shook and jolted as it drove down the back roads of Brora, a small town up north, and even though I'd never struggled with motion sickness, I couldn't help but feel the pit of my stomach burrow deeper. The mere image of Naomi sitting in the back only brought the sickness to my throat. James said that whatever plan Trojan were following it would be worth the documentation – at this rate she's going to be filming me kicking his head.

James drove down to Thames House in London yesterday

so that he and his boss (girlfriend) could control and monitor the situation from there. When he left, it was clear something was troubling him. He didn't divulge anything but I got the feeling he no longer trusted the people he worked for.

I pushed the thought from my mind, focusing on the task ahead. My team was separated into two jeeps: the first consisted of Lily, Grace and Kayson, who'd taken the lead. Runners and Medics always travelled together. The second was made up of myself, Christopher, Quinn and Naomi. The two girls chattered away in the back seat, going over the plan for the eighth time, Carrier to Techie. I thought it might have stuck in her head by now but Naomi was determined to keep the noise up. I would kill for some silence.

Like we'd agreed, Chris and I had kept it professional. It had to be, otherwise I was going to chuck a bunch of red pills down my throat. Forgetting had become more appealing after the week I'd had.

Quinn had told us about the new floor of the Academy and their plans to create holding cells. Seriously, how did they come up with this shit? Then there was the whole situation with

Harkness. We told him repeatedly that we forgot to take them off after a practice op, which he apparently believed. After that, I'd walked in on Kayson and Naomi sparring – it was a sight I wished I'd never seen.

I hated to admit it, but she progressed well. Naomi had learned all the basics of hand to hand combat and a few defensive moves. It took her a while though, since she didn't want to punch anyone in the face – if she was sticking around for longer I'd tell her that comes naturally with time.

My opinion on the matter of Naomi didn't seem to matter anymore, now James was in charge, and I hated him for it.

There was a crackling in my ear and Lily's voice rang through.

'Blackbird, comm check.'

'Received. ETA two minutes everyone,' Quinn piped up, her eyes darting to her laptop before Lily went silent and Grace spoke up.

'Nightingale, comm check.'

'Loud and clear.'

'Ronan,' Kayson said.

SLATE RETRIBUTION

'I have you.'

I heard Quinn typing away from the back of the car but I didn't look. She was in her element, best not to disturb her. Even though Quinn was running through comm checks I could guarantee there was more going on behind the laptop: traffic cams, news reports and agency intel. The Technical Support needed to be up to date with everything happening in the area that might affect the mission. Of course I had my own job to do, but right now, I was enjoying watching the world go by. The one I grew up in. Ever since I found out Brora was our destination, there was something that just didn't sit right. Before my mother moved us all around the country I'd spent most of my childhood in this coastal town, a lot of my childhood memories were made here – and now, there was this gut feeling of certainty that something would go horribly wrong.

'Carrier One,' Naomi said shakily, fiddling with her earpiece.

Of course we weren't giving her a codename, they were sacred and since this was a one-time thing, a simple one was appropriate.

'Got you,' Quinn said.

Through the rear-view mirror I noticed she took Naomi's hand, squeezing it for reassurance before going back to the laptop. Jealously lashed like a whip; I should be the one to protect Naomi.

She looked ridiculous – sure, it was everyday clothes but even so, she was going undercover as a tourist. They were Lily's clothes so they didn't even fit her, and the earpiece stood out like a sore thumb – to me, anyway. She didn't belong in this world.

'Kane,' Chris said.

'Lilith.' I pulled the wire round the back and tucked it behind my hair.

'Thanks guys. All good, vital signs are strong. Green light from me.'

When the jeep in front stopped so did we, but I didn't move, I needed more time to think. Of course we had a backup plan but what about the backup to the backup plan? This was one of the most dangerous zones I'd ever been in, and getting out of the seat behind me was a civilian. She'd only had a week of training and that was nowhere near the kind of Carrier we needed.

I watched as Lily and Kayson got out of the jeep, both

arming themselves as Grace slung on her medical backpack. The Runners were our first line of defence, so to say they were handy with a gun was an understatement. Quinn was going to hike to a building west of here, which was far enough to give her a secure location. If anything were to go wrong Kayson was to head back immediately. Of course the girl could defend herself, but after last time I wasn't taking any chances.

Naomi had been told to stick by Lily at all times, but if something went wrong Chris would swoop in and get her to the exit route so Lily could help me. Either way, she was protected.

Chris's job was Senior Team Lead, but his orders didn't overrule mine – well they did, but he could never pull rank on me, even if he wanted to.

I took in a breath before getting out the car and heading to the boot. It was filled with guns and ammunition which were to be guarded by the team James would be sending in later. Precautions were something I no longer took as a joke. I grabbed two nine millimetres, four magazines and two silver knives which were small enough to slip inside my thin jacket. Even as I was arming myself, I found it difficult to breathe. Naomi was here, of all fucking places!

She couldn't even work a firearm, not that I would give her one.

There was so much that could go wrong, way too many variables, there were only so many eventualities I could deduce. There was a high chance that if things went wrong I wouldn't see Naomi until after it was over, if I made it that far.

'Jess, she'll be fine,' Grace said as she walked over to me, grabbing a gun for herself.

'I know that.'

'Tell that to your face.' I only rolled my eyes.

'Kayson's guarding her with his life and so is Lily. They may dislike each other but they'll do the job. I don't like having her here either; once she's done filming, she'll be escorted out.'

I just had to keep thinking about that: once Naomi had filmed any evidence of Trojan then she was out. Then at least she'd be back behind closed doors – although it was more like enemy lines.

'You did the right thing though, with Christopher.' I nearly dropped my gun, did the Holy Spirit make this girl psychic? 'Too complicated, you know. Don't look at me like that Jess, ever since you two got back he's gone into work mode. You'll be better for it.' Grace patted me on the shoulder before she jogged ahead and out of sight.

Had I done the right thing? Of course I had.

'Lilith, Pilot is on the move to rendezvous one,' I heard Naomi say in my ear. That sounded wrong coming from her.

'Received,' I said quickly, closing the boot of the car and heading up the beaten path.

The two jeeps were parked at the side of the road. One of the paths headed towards Dunrobin Castle (rendezvous one) while the other lead into town. We'd come a couple of days earlier than Trojan was scheduled to arrive: our job was to find any sign of their agents or activity, document it for later use in court and then get out. It seemed simple, but the pressure was on because we had no intel on our enemy. We were completely in the dark. The only thing we did know was that they planned to burn this place to the ground.

If we found they had weapons of their own already set up, this would become a much bigger operation.

As my team made their way through the field we kept quiet apart from the occasional comm check or question. Naomi was near the back with Lily, while Kayson, Grace and Chris walked behind me. As we waded our way through the tall grass I wanted to turn to Chris and ask him if he remembered one of our first secret dates was in this field, he'd brought the wine, but I silenced the notion. Now wasn't the time for this. I needed to keep a sharp mind, evaluate where we stood on this chessboard. Too many moves with too little time.

For a town on the coast this place wasn't exactly all sand and sea breeze – the stench of cow manure shrivelled my nose. The smell unlocking many a memory of what were meant to be romantic spring walks, to Chris and I turning around and going back the way we came – Stop it! Focus on the job.

After ten minutes we'd made it into the small familiar town, deciding to spread out to cover more ground. Grace was posing as a tourist while I posed as a jogger. Luckily my leggings and hoodie were thick enough to hide the gun holstered at my back. I had pushed a single magazine into my legging pockets and placed the other two at my torso.

SLATE RETRIBUTION

As I picked up the pace there was no sign of Trojan or any enemy agents – in fact, there was no sign of anyone. The place was deathly quiet; the only sound was the smack of my feet on the cobblestones. I thought this place would be busier given it was a Friday afternoon.

'Report,' I said.

All I got back from the team were negatives; they hadn't seen anything either. Where was everyone? It was like a ghost town – they even had a creaky pub sign blowing in the wind. From my time here as a child it had always been busy, surely it hadn't changed that much?

'Blackbird to Lilith, I can see smoke but it's probably just some kids having a bonfire,' Lily said.

Wouldn't surprise me, considering there weren't any parents around. As I passed shop and café windows, there weren't any people inside, not even a waitress. Which was weird since the little bakery to my right was always bustling, when I was younger anyway. I remember this older woman who ran it, she always gave me a free cupcake on the sly. Surely she still had to be around here somewhere? Anyone?

'Pilot, is there some sort of event or festival we don't know about?'

'Negative,' Quinn replied. 'There's nothing.'

'Then where the hell is everyone?' Kayson asked.

'Get inside the buildings,' I ordered, 'see if there are any clues. Carrier One, start the camera.'

'OK . . . uh – there, that should be it.'

I stopped at a newer-looking shop, my hands pressed against the glass, peering inside. It was a clothing shop, mannequins and dress racks as far as the eye could see – but then I saw smashed glass all over the floor, blood smeared and spattered everywhere. I assumed that wasn't over a misplaced receipt.

I headed cautiously for the door, opening it slowly, but as I did, glass crunched underneath my foot. I slowly turned, four distinct bullet holes, all marked with blood, were lodged into a mirror next to my head. Shit.

'Report. There's been a shooting,' I started, but a loud screeching noise ripped through my ear, nearly sending me to my knees.

When I tore the thing out my eardrum rang, almost

vibrating —what the hell was that?

Trojan weren't meant to be here for a few more days; this couldn't be them. But how could it be anyone else?

Just as I was about to run out the door I stopped – something silver was glinting in the sunlight. It was an engagement ring. Why take that off if you're being shot at? Certainly wouldn't be on my list of priorities. When I looked up, however, the sight ahead nearly sent me flying back into the clothing rails.

A woman, mid-twenties, nailed to the wall by her hands and feet, all her fingers missing. Nails hammered into her skull like a crown, while the bullet-holes in her body covered nearly every inch of skin. The dark blood oozing down looked like a dress, the flesh peeling from the weight, white foam dripping from her mouth – but what I focused on were her eyes. They were off to the left.

There was a message written there, in thick blood that dribbled down the wall.

TIME TO PAY FOR YOUR SINS DON'T YOU THINK?

What the fuck? Was this some kind of ritualistic sacrifice?

It couldn't be, because then I saw the curved symbol written in the woman's blood above her head. Trojan's mark. No.

I bolted out of the shop, not looking back.

My earpiece wasn't working – I had no way to contact the rest of my team and presumably neither did they. My one thought was that they'd found Quinn, but then again, I understood Trojan. They wouldn't have gone to the trouble of finding the Techie, they'd have just blocked the channel. Quinn had to be working with James to fix the problem and Kayson would be on his way back to guard her.

I, on the other hand, couldn't stand about waiting for good news, not when this was evidently a set-up. We had to get out of there.

I pulled out my gun, loaded it and held it by my side as I quickly made my way to Exit Point One. Everyone would soon be heading in the same direction. Suddenly a pair of thundering footsteps barrelled towards me – I whipped around and pointed my gun straight ahead but then lowered it, as Grace stood there.

'There was a man, he was hung by the neck.' Her face was grave, her hands curled into fists, eyes as wide as saucers.

'Woman in the clothes shop, she was nailed to the wall. Then someone had written –'

'Time to pay for your sins?' she asked and I nodded.

Grace let out a shaky breath, running a hand through her hair, eyes now fixed on the sky.

'Hey. This isn't God, OK?' I said, and thankfully it caught her attention.

'This isn't because you killed that man. This is Trojan. We just need to find them before they decimate the place.'

I knew she felt guilt for what she did and I respected her beliefs, but this wasn't God. Just someone who thought they were. Grace grabbed her gun, took the safety off and held it at her side.

'If the comms are down we need to find the others. We're walking around blind here.'

'If they're down, Laurent will be sending in his team and ours will be heading to the exit point.' Even though communications were down I wasn't risking my brother's identity.

'Jess . . .'

I looked up to see the smoke cloud Lily must have been talking about. It looked awfully big for a bonfire, but then the smell hit me. I gagged – the stench of burnt hair and boiled skin rendering me motionless, the smell of rotting flesh lingering in my throat. *If there's a God up there I beg you, let me be wrong.*

It only took five minutes to walk up the hill but with every step the smell became more unbearable. Flies swarmed through the thick trees, blood lining the way like an aisle, but it wasn't just a dribble – the dirt squelched with the stuff. My grey trainers were now soaked in blood, every movement we made caused a sea of red to rise from the ground, like some biblical event. Probably shouldn't say that to Grace.

There was no sign of the others, but silence usually meant good news.

'I don't like this.' Grace said, as we waded our way through the dirt.

Just as I was about to respond, I heard it.

SNAP

I spun around, my hand thrown out – a man in dark

clothing was pointing a gun at my head. Grabbing the barrel I yanked it towards me before I raised my own and pulled the trigger.

BANG

The man flailed as he fell, blood spurting from the ground – and, funnily enough, his head.

As I checked over his gun I felt Grace's eyes bearing down on me. I glanced up but she didn't look away, sweat brimming on her brow, hands clenched and figure tense. She did remember we've done this before?

'Willow was right.' she said.

'What are you talking about?'

Grace didn't get a chance to respond as a bullet shot through her shoulder, sending her back. I grabbed her by the hips and tackled her to the ground, pressing her back against a nearby tree. Shit, there was a sniper. This wasn't an op, this was a trap.

From our position I couldn't see anyone, but I needed to prioritise Grace.

I went to grab for her bag, but she pulled away.

'Grace?' Confusion burned across my eyes. 'Tell me what

to do, you must have bandages in there.' She kept moving, her lips almost disappearing as she grimaced in pain. 'Grace?'

CRACK

Wood splintered just above my head as a round of bullets sprayed the tree, splinters ransacked my skin and hair. Thankfully it remained standing. OK, that was it! The angle was downward so he had to be on the hilltop ahead of us.

I turned back to Grace.

'I'm going to draw their fire, you need to get back to base. The team will be there soon.'

I didn't look back as I bolted out – the field was vast but there was a clear hillside. Despite the harsh wind the smoke was getting thicker, but I kept running. Bullets clipped at my heels and my knee throbbed, but I had to keep going. I pushed myself to the bottom of the hill, slamming my body into the banking, my nails clenching the crumbling dirt and grass. The sniper would have to reposition to get a shot at me.

Then from above, rustling. The sniper was moving to – left!

I pushed myself forward and aimed, seeing a man

scarpering to get cover – but before he could dive down, I plugged two bullets in his throat. That should keep him occupied indefinitely. Then I fell against the grass, the raw thick blades gnawing at my skin, and I waited. There wasn't any more noise, just silence and, fortunately, no more bullets.

I looked over to the lone tree but there was no sign of Grace – she had to survive long enough to make it back to the jeep. James's team was only fifteen minutes out, tops – she'd get the help she needed.

Without another glance in her direction I stuck to the grass and headed around the corner towards the smoke. Once again the smell of rotting flesh curled my tongue; I had to pull up my top over my mouth to make it somewhat bearable. After walking for a couple minutes I saw the heart of the blaze; searing red, yellow and burning orange.

As I inched closer I knew it wasn't just a pile of bodies, it was a wall. People of every age, gender and race were piled high, flesh melting from their corpses. Should I be thankful it was no one I recognised? The heat was immense, unlike anything I'd ever felt. If I got any closer, I was certain my skin would burn. The flames were the height of a skyscraper, almost touching the heavens.

And the devil shall walk the earth with fire and brimstone.

Then, through the flames, I saw them. Naomi was kneeling in front of the wall; Kayson and Lily both had at least three thugs on top of them, all with guns – but a hand flew over my mouth when I saw Chris lying on the ground, because he wasn't moving. *Please no, I beg you, please.*

'No!' Naomi cried.

'You bastard!' Kayson roared. 'How could you?'

Kayson must have been intercepted before he got to Quinn, I knew she could handle herself but given the situation it didn't calm my mind.

A screeching droned from my pocket and I yanked out the comm, ready to smash the thing when I heard a playful voice scratch through.

'They're both dead son, get used to it.' A man's voice replied.

The comm unit was back online.

The voice was familiar but I couldn't place it, the name on

the tip of my tongue. Was he the one responsible for all of this?

As I placed the comm unit back in my ear I heard Naomi's shaky voice.

'I don't believe you. They can't be.'

I crouched down low, crawling along the ground and keeping my nose and mouth covered as trying to get a better look at the situation. The man in question was in a cream suit, had bleached blonde hair and walked like he had a spoon up his ass. I knew him. Where did I know him from?

'Little one,' the man said. Kneeling down in front of Naomi, he grabbed her chin, forcing her to look at him. 'Jessica and Grace are long dead by now. I took care of that, but not to worry. They aren't in pain, I've released them from their mortal shells.'

Through the wall of burning skin and bone I saw that the man had a large birthmark on his neck. A key identifier – but to what? I'd never seen him at the Academy.

When I tried to get a better view my eyes locked with another's, those of a small child, the remains of her dress now ash that fell like rain. Rage corrupted my vision as I stood tall; the flames reached out to me but I didn't feel their touch. I was all for sacrificing myself for the greater good but not her, not an innocent, not a child.

'I hate to disappoint, but I think it's the other way round, mate.' I snapped.

Everyone's head lifted, looking for me, then suddenly, the birthmark and face of the man clicked. It was Gabriel Hale. The man we tried to reach out to, the man we trusted to help us, the man who ignored our cry for help. I'd only seen him a few times growing up, when mum had to take me into work – wasn't he supposed to be on our side?

Why had he turned? What could Trojan offer that we couldn't? I'd heard from my mother he liked to travel – he must have neglected to mention that he spent his time with terrorists, not landmarks. Could my mother have known? No that was ridiculous, just because she was a neglectful cunt didn't mean she sided with terrorists.

Gabriel stood up, glancing around the area, but I planted myself low on the ground: if he didn't know where I was then I had the advantage.

'Miss Winters, lovely to hear your voice,' Gabriel said. 'Care to join us?'

'You're meant to work for us,' I said.

The man laughed. 'You are ignorant aren't you? Trojan showed me a better way.'

'There are children in this wall, innocent people.'

'Oh, no one is truly innocent. Especially you.'

'Let my team go.'

Silence.

Shit, had someone spotted me? I lifted my head a couple of inches but couldn't see anyone on the hilltop. Then, through the comms, Grace cried out.

I crawled closer towards the wall, lifting a hand over my face to block the heat. I needed a better look at Grace's condition. The right side of her shirt was soaked and red blotches dotted her face. They'd caught her; someone had followed us. This entire thing had been a trap. Where was the team James was sending in?

'I want to see you, little one, get out here,' he demanded, but I stayed firmly put. He grabbed a gun from one of the thugs and pointed it at Grace's head – she started to blubber and sob, her entire figure quaking. 'Now, preferably, or I'll just have to shoot Grace. She is the Medical Response isn't she? Be a shame to waste such talent.'

I wasn't going to comply.

'There's another team arriving now, leave while you can.'

'Oh, I don't think they'll be bothering us any time soon,' Gabriel said snidely. 'No really, they won't. You see, I had access to this so-called mission – in fact I was the one who assigned it to your dear brother. After your little incident, I knew he'd give it to you.'

'You bastard!' Kayson yelled.

'I thought your mother would have taught you to think before you speak,' Gabriel said. 'Besides, this was the perfect opportunity to see you, as Trojan will take their rightful place at the top of society very, very soon.'

'That will never happen!' Lily thrashed. 'You aren't powerful enough!'

'Jess, little one, get out here.' I didn't move. 'One.'

CLICK

'Two.'

SLATE RETRIBUTION

CLICK

Grace's cries turned to shrieks and wails as the gun pressed to her forehead.

Without thinking I grabbed the small silver knife from my sleeve pocket, put one foot in front of the other and, with every ounce out strength I had, threw it towards Gabriel. The blade spun as it hurtled through the air.

However without missing a beat the man whipped round and grabbed the blade, the slice of his skin tore through the field but all he did, was smile.

A sadistic grin slithering up his long face like a snake. He dropped the knife before twirling the gun in his fingers, arms open for an embrace, but I didn't move any closer. My eyes flickered to Chris, his body splayed out on the ground, *blood* seeping from a wound I couldn't see. I needed to stop the bleeding, was he conscious at all? I couldn't lose him, I promised myself I wouldn't lose him, how could I – No, focus. Breathe.

'You got what you wanted – now, why are you here? I thought you were meant to burn this place to the ground?' I asked, my hand firmly resting on the holstered gun.

Who was quicker, him or me?

'Oh that?' he said. 'No, that was just to grab your attention. I would say this spectacle would tug the public's heartstrings more than simply blowing a crater in the ground.'

'Step away or I will shoot you,' I said, but it was an empty threat. I was outnumbered by a long shot, but better to go out swinging.

'The Academy,' he said, 'they train and train you children, but you never see the bigger picture. Trojan is not the enemy.'

'You put a bomb in a bank and then tried to blow up a the theatre of innocent people.'

'Answer me this then. Willow's death, was it *just* an accident?'

What? Of course it was, how could he even question that? We were sent on an op, got split up and then she died, end of. Did he know something we didn't? Then the thought hit me like a brick wall. Trojan murdered to make a point. So did the Academy.

'Of course it was.'

'Who shot her?' Gabriel asked. 'It certainly wasn't us.'

'It had to be.' I told him, but the man cackled.

SLATE RETRIBUTION

'As far as I know, Willow's father needed her out of the way, but of course I don't imagine the request was perceived as literal. He's high up in the Academy, you see. Didn't need daughter dearest causing a fuss or exposing him for who he really was. Shame really, I heard she had a bright future.'

The entire field fell silent, the only sound to be heard was the crackling of the fire and crisp wind cutting through the air.

'Oh, I'm sorry, you didn't know?' the man mocked.

If I closed my eyes I could pretend I was in the mountains beside a fireplace, wrapped up all cosy and warm. But I couldn't. My eyes were open, more so than they'd ever been.

Willow's father was high up in the Academy – how could I never have realised before? She always lied about her parents' whereabouts. We've probably met him, who knows how many times. Could it be Duke? Harkness? Thompson? Ames?

I knew one thing for certain, we were never the heroes of this story.

EMERY HALE

CHAPTER 24

Dichotomy

Incompatible or opposite principles.

NAOMI JADE

Half an hour into the mission we were ambushed. Men with guns had us surrounded, then bullets rained from the sky. I dived to the nearest building, Lily covering me from behind. Each shot she took rang in my ears, thudding in my chest. The world was on the highest exposure and volume, even the leaves scattering along the ground sounded like nails on a chalkboard.

I covered my head – all the training I'd gotten never covered this. I knew some hand to hand combat but I had no idea how to fight against people I couldn't see. I was way out of my depth here.

I didn't realise until a couple of seconds later that my eyes had screwed shut, fear forcing them to stay closed, my legs trembling. I wanted to get out of here.

Wasn't this how Willow died?

We split up in the beginning – I knew Kayson was close by, as was Chris, but I had no idea about Grace or Jess, they'd gone off on their own.

'Move!' Lily shouted, grabbing my wrists.

Then we ran.

Pounding footsteps bounded behind us, bullets clanging as they hit the ground – why were they aiming at our feet? I didn't get time to think as Lily sped up the pace and, in turn, so did I. From my days on the running team I knew to focus on my pacing, pushing myself through every step. I kept up with Lily, and soon the footsteps from behind echoed more distantly – we were outrunning them.

Lily yanked me around another corner and shoved me into a nearby shop. Without having to be told I darted behind one of the tables, trying to even my breathing. That was really close. What the hell was I doing here? They made it look so much cooler in the movies – easier, even. Lily hid behind the till, switching out the ammo, but her head was poised, ready for anything. I, on the other hand, was ready to call it a day. How the hell were we supposed to get out of here?

From where I was hidden I could see the shadows of what looked like eight people running past – they must have lost sight of us. It was only then I realised we were in a small café, but the place was completely abandoned; chairs thrown over and tables flipped.

'Report. There's been a shooting.' Suddenly a high pitched wail screeched in my ear and I threw the earpiece on the ground. When the sound stopped I put it back in, but there was only static.

Had something happened to Quinn?

As I glanced over to Lily I saw that she'd done the same, nursing her ear, the gun clattering to the ground. What the hell was happening? Trojan weren't meant to be here for another couple of days – it wasn't supposed to go down like this. Had they gotten to Quinn? Could they have taken her hostage?

Exit Point One, I knew that's where we'd have to get to, Quinn could be there, but the path we had to take could be swarming with Trojan agents.

'Fuck. This whole thing is a trap,' Lily muttered, picking up her gun.

'A trap?'

'All of us split up, and now they've cut our comms. People are shooting at us. You do the maths.' She shook her head. 'Trojan wanted us to come. James was the one who gave us this op.'

'James isn't working for Trojan,' I said – the idea was mad.

'Naomi, you may want to take Jess's family down from that pedestal of yours,' Lily said. 'Her family has notorious relations with Russia – I don't even know if I trust Jess anymore.'

What? Could that be true? Would James send us into a trap?

'Lily, you can't know that,' I said.

'What do you actually know about them? Jess, for a start?' she asked.

What was I supposed to say, her favourite colour? I went to speak, but Lily beat me to it.

'Her family, her past – yes, you went to school with her,

Naomi, but you don't know the first thing about her.'

'That's not true, I know my best friend.'

'Then you'll know she had a kill count of thirty-seven by the age of seventeen?' I felt ice growing in my veins. 'You'll know her mother trained her with the Pyramid Delegates, which have been infiltrated by Trojan for years. Naomi, she murdered her older brother Charlie.'

With every word I felt myself shrink – of course I didn't know any of this. Murder? That couldn't be right. She told me she hadn't killed anyone.

'You don't know her, OK,' Lily said, her voice a little softer. 'Don't be so quick to defend her.'

This couldn't be possible – the Jess I knew would never have done that. There must have been circumstances – Charlie was her brother. She wouldn't do it just because she was bored.

Did I really know her though? Everything that I'd learned over the past two weeks told me otherwise. Jess had a whole other life that she'd hidden from me; the idea that she could be so cruel wasn't out of the question. Could she be a murderer? A monster?

Was everything I knew about her a lie? We went to school

for years and she told me so many stories about her past and family – were they all fake? The days she ran off to last-minute rehearsals – were those the times she spent training with her mother? Jess told me she hated her, was that just another lie? If the team she was supposed to lead barely trusted her, then how could I?

I didn't get the chance to speak as something grabbed Lily's attention. She checked the coast was clear before standing up and walking behind the glass cabinet, her gun raised. I gripped the small knife she'd given me earlier and held it out in front. Not that anyone knew I had it but Lily trusted me enough to carry it.

But she lowered the gun, and I saw her face contort.

'Let's get out of here,' she said holstering her gun.

When she tried to usher me to the door I pushed away, skirting around the counter, but came to a sudden halt. It was a body: an older woman, probably in her late seventies. Water sat in her mouth like a pool, her clothes soaked.

'They drowned her.' Lily spoke from behind. 'Fuckers.'

I'd never seen a dead body before. I'd attended a couple of funerals, but never of anyone I knew. I didn't know this woman, yet I felt responsible for her. We were meant to save people.

Abruptly, gunfire sounded from outside. Lily and I both dropped to the ground, slowly peering through the glass cabinet. The door was also made of glass, so I had the perfect view of what was going on. Three thug-looking men stood guard outside while a tall man in a suit paced up and down the street. He looked like a James Bond villain, fanatically waving a long rifle in the air, letting out a couple of rounds. Each one jolting through me; ringing like it was right in front of me, inside me.

My mouth withered to a desert as I saw who the gun finally came to a stop at: Kayson and Chris. Both men were forced onto their knees and shouting things I couldn't quite make out.

BANG

Chris jostled back, his body slamming to the ground, his head bouncing off the concrete. Had they killed him? A dryness spread through the back of my throat, the spice of bile following suit. I didn't even register my knees leaving the ground as my eyes fixed solely on Kayson. I couldn't let him die. I wouldn't.

I felt a sharp tug from Lily, pulling me back down. I tried to explain myself but she only held a finger over her lips and shook her head. Maybe running head first into a gun-fight with a single knife wasn't the best idea.

I heard Kayson's yells and then quiet; the man in the white suit knelt in front of him grabbing his chin. They shared a conversation which only lasted a couple of seconds, before Kayson spat in the man's face.

Then Lily and I were forced to watch as Kayson and Chris were dragged away; the only evidence they were ever there, a small pool of blood.

I thought we were in the clear, I thought that the thugs and their leader had left, but the next few moments happened so fast that I only recall flashes. The door burst open, uncountable figures all dressed in black flooded the place with guns. I heard the snap of Lily's gun as she stood up to fight but soon lost her amongst the crowd. My eyes focused on the one man dressed in white, stalking towards me like prey.

'All this violence. So disconcerting, so unnecessary.' His accent was Scottish, but it was clear and precise. He wore a kind smile but there was something in his voice that made me reel back. 'Tell me, little one, where's your Team Lead? The boys were very uncivilised but I have a feeling you'll be most useful to me.'

Well, I didn't actually know where she was. I stayed quiet, lowering my head a little but then he grabbed my chin, forcing me to look at him. He didn't let up – and for a second I thought he might kill me.

'I don't tolerate insolence. Tell me, where is she?'

'I don't know,' I shot out, and even though it was the truth it sounded like a lie.

My whole body was shaking, adrenaline pumping through my veins at a colossal rate. Every second I spotted something new – the symbols on the thugs' uniforms, Lily's hand, different sizes of guns, and then Lily's unconscious figure, blood dripping from her head. My eyes widened and without thinking I stepped forward. No, they couldn't take her! Lily!

The man let go of my chin but grabbed my shoulders, throwing me into the arms of two men dressed in black. The material on their gloves was rough and their grip was unchallengeable. Even though I tried to squirm, the burning grip of their fingers clamped around my arms.

'Let's keep this quick, we're on a schedule.' The man motioned to the men restraining me.

I tried to wiggle my way out, even tried to unbalance one so I could run, but the thugs were as solid as statues.

'Sorry if we're interfering with it,' I snapped.

It wasn't the best move but I was pissed off and past showing fear – not to the likes of him. I was more concerned about my so-called best friend. Jess was lying through her teeth, no one trusted her. and now we were stuck in the middle of a terrorist trap.

'Oh, little one.' He walked closer, taking a strand of my hair and pushing it behind my ear. I yanked my head away but he only laughed. 'Don't worry that pretty head of yours. What is your name?'

I had my alias name that I used in the Academy which was Ellie Smyth, but if this man had access to the system, he would know it was a lie. I was too old to be a first year and looked nothing like my photo.

'Are you going to keep me waiting? The longer you do the more blood your friends lose,' he sang, mockingly.

'Katie Danvers,' I blurted.

Oh poop, why did I use her name? She's a real person!

'Well, Katie, I hope you enjoy the show,' he said.

I stared at him in confusion before a veil of darkness was thrown over my head, grainy shoots of sunlight spotting through, and two burly arms hurled me back at immense speed. The scratchy material grated my skin but I didn't put up a fight. If I went willingly they'd be less likely to hurt me – and hopefully, I'd find Jessica too.

* * *

Well this was a great way to spend the evening, being dragged through what I presumed was some kind of field with a bag over my head. It must have been raining earlier because my heels sunk into the mushy ground, but what made my pause was the metallic taste coating my tongue. That wasn't rain.

The two men's grip on my arms disappeared and I lurched forward, about to run, but stopped, hearing the crack of knuckles on bone. Throwing the bag off my head I saw Kayson had managed to take one down, then, with a final punch underneath the jaw, the second one fell. His movements were sharp, like he'd already calculated their movements and knew exactly what to do next. The cogs in his head that I'd seen turning before were still; now it was like his body was on auto-pilot. Like the weapon he'd been forced to become had taken over. Any ounce of emotion had been thrown aside, all his focus pinned on the men in front. From what I could see the two men weren't even men, they were our age, in dark uniforms with a serial number branded on the material.

Kayson stared long and hard at the men, both now on the ground but then he grabbed my hand hard, snapping out of it.

'We need to get you out of here,' he said.

His face was marked with dirt and dried blood, his lips cracked. Kayson's warm arms embraced me as we ran for cover through the trees. I didn't even know where I was, the Exit Point could be anywhere, but I trusted Kayson to get me there. I didn't look at the fire behind me because the smell was more than enough – what the hell were they burning?

'Let's not get too hasty!' a voice shouted. 'You wouldn't want my finger to slip now, would you?'

Kayson pushed me behind him but it did no good, I heard

footsteps approaching from . . . well, everywhere. A hand rose to my mouth as I saw the man from before holding a gun to Lily's head, three men pinning her down. Strands of her hair slowly drifted through the wind but her chest was manic and eyes wild. She screamed but it wasn't high pitched, it was low, like a feral growl. Her arms were branded red by her captors, while the blood trickling down her face didn't appear to have an end.

'Come back, it's no fun if you just keep running.'

'Gabriel for fuck's sake, let her go,' Kayson snarled. Wait, he knew this person?

Kayson stood in front of me like a shield – even when I tried to move his hand wrapped around my arm, forcing me to stop. This had to have been planned, or someone must have leaked our plans.

Suddenly, echoes and whispers surrounded us like ghosts, the dead rising from the ground.

'I know you could take down my men. Might take a while, but you could. They're all like trained monkeys, you see.' Gabriel stood a little taller as he grabbed Lily by the roots of her hair, tearing her head back, then placed the gun under her chin. 'Now if you would come back, this is a new suit.'

I tried to run to her but Kayson grabbed me by the arms hauling me back around – what was he playing at? We had to go back, I wasn't going to let her die. Lily squirmed as much as she could but Gabriel only seemed to enjoy it more. The sick bastard.

'Do it!' Lily snarled. 'Go on then, do it!'

I couldn't believe what I was hearing, why would she even say that? I turned to Kayson but his mind appeared wild, looking like he was trying to come up with a plan, but I would have no part in it. I wasn't leaving Lily behind, not now, not ever.

'Oh, Katie must be your Carrier,' Gabriel mused. Hopefully Kayson picked up on the memo. 'I guess they had to replace the old one at some point, didn't they.'

Abruptly, Kayson yanked me close, holding me tightly, his hand caressing the base of my neck, his thumb rubbing soothing circles. It was only then I realised two men stood behind us, both armed. Then he leaned down, whispering into my ear.

'Run to the left, I'll deal with the others. Just run,' he said.

'I can't do that,' I whispered back. 'I won't leave Lily.'

'You don't have a choice.'

'Oh, lovers' quarrel,' Gabriel mocked. 'It tickles me, now come back over or I will shoot her. If either of you run she dies. If that wasn't made clear. Don't try to plan around a trap, it doesn't work that way, little one.'

Lily's death wasn't going to be on my hands.

I threw my hands up and twisted, jostling to get out of Kayson's grip and landing a solid hit to his ribs, then marched towards Gabriel and didn't stop until I looked the sorry excuse of a man in the eye.

'Let her go,' I demanded, but even then my voice sounded weak.

If I was shaking before, now I was trembling because Gabriel moved the gun from Lily's chin to my forehead. My feet were frozen to the ground, the only thing I could see was the black barrel of the gun, unmoving and deadly. Would he shoot me? If I died here would anyone ever know the truth, or would it be covered up like Willow? Would I become a faceless girl in the newspapers?

I heard Kayson charge forward but Gabriel pulled the gun away with a laugh. 'Like a deer in the headlights,' he muttered under his breath.

There was a spark in Gabriel's eyes, a secret. The way he walked and talked was all too cocky, like he knew something we didn't. Had Gabriel figured me out? Was there a team already assembling the bomb? If this whole thing had been a trap, why not blow the place already? What was he waiting for?

The three men holding Lily hauled her up, snatching the comm unit from her ear and handing it to Gabriel. Before I could say anything, hands clamped over my chest, jerking me back. They weren't Kayson's. They were calloused and sweaty, and that was when I screamed and thrashed, all of my training gone. Adrenaline taking over. I needed to get out of here.

What if he shot me?

'Oh, she's screaming! Do it again!' Gabriel exclaimed.

I heard Kayson's grunts and Lily's cries as men in black emerged from the trees, like an endless army. Were they all Trojan agents? Where were they all coming from?

The man threw me to the ground and I knew I had to stay still; if I moved they would shoot me. There wasn't any sound or movement at my back but I was certain there was someone there waiting, just begging for an excuse to pull the trigger.

THUD

Chris's lifeless body was thrown next to me, his eyes fluttering open and shut as thick blood pooled beneath him. Fear enveloped my body but my hand didn't move to see if he was OK, it remained shaking at my side. Wasn't he meant to be older, wiser? If he had been taken down then what were the chances I'd make it out of here alive? I had to stay still, I couldn't end up like that. My mouth clamped shut, my lips pressed tightly together.

That was when I saw it, felt it, the insidious inferno. When I took a closer look I realised the searing wall was made of people. No . . . holy fuck, please don't tell me.

'Do you like it?' Gabriel asked. 'I made it myself.'

People, children, teenagers – 'No!' I screamed, tears flooding my eyes. I felt as if someone had put a boulder on my chest, the weight crushing my ribs, nearly sending me to the ground. My soft t-shirt like lead as it pummelled me down.

That was when Gabriel stepped forward. 'Then you probably won't like the news about your two friends. My sniper took care of them.'

'You bastard!' Kayson yelled. 'How could you?'

Jessica was dead? No, this couldn't be happening, she couldn't be. I would feel it. I knew for a fact she couldn't be, right? He had to be wrong, she couldn't be dead, they couldn't be gone.

All I felt was the breath of the fire worming its way through my body, pain stabbing through the rocks in my chest. It was almost as if she was up there on that wall, staring back at me, her cold blue eyes now empty. Even Grace's face haunted my vision, her arm hanging out from the wall, her disapproving glare. This was my fault.

I shook my head, this wasn't real. 'I don't believe you.'

I couldn't look at the wall any longer. This was Trojan's doing – they had murdered an entire town and for what? James had sent us here and now I questioned why. Was it to witness their power? Was James working for Trojan? I barely remembered that the lapel camera on my jacket was still recording, would anyone even watch this? Would anyone even care?

'Little one,' Gabriel cooed, grabbing my chin. 'Jessica and Grace are long dead by now. I took care of that, but not to worry.

They aren't in pain, I've released them from their mortal shells.'

She was dead, Jessica was dead. Grace was dead.

That was when a small crackling popped in my ear – had Quinn gotten control of the comms? That must mean she's alright. At least one of us will make it out of this. Gabriel looked at the comm unit in his ear, a look of confusion sweeping across his face before he placed it in his ear.

'I hate to disappoint, but I think it's the other way round, mate.' Jessica's voice snapped.

I couldn't help the sigh of relief that burst from my mouth – of course she wasn't dead. Took more than a bullet to kill her. I whipped my head around trying to find her, but couldn't see a thing. If she was close by she must have been masked by the fire. I didn't pay attention to what was spoken about next, I just relaxed knowing that Jess was safe, because that meant so was Grace.

Maybe this guy wasn't so powerful after all; maybe he was nothing against Reign students. I saw in his eyes that the playfulness had disappeared, replaced by impatience.

Grace's shrieks of pain cut through the field, her blood-soaked shirt falling to my right as a woman forced her to her knees. The sniper had got her, she looked ready to pass out, her eyes drooping and skin grey.

'Grace?' I asked, trying to go to her aid, but then I felt the cold barrel of the gun press against my head.

I froze, turned back slowly, my eyes returning to the burning wall. What was better to look at? A wall of corpses or two people bleeding out either side of me? Would Grace die? Was Chris already dead?

That was when my mind came back to the conversation at hand.

'Now, preferably, or I'll just have to shoot Grace. She is the Medical Response isn't she? Be a shame to waste such talent.'

I didn't move a muscle, I couldn't risk it. I had to stay alive.

As my chest moved in and out more slowly, I focused on my breathing. I wasn't any use to the team if I was freaking out.

'Oh, I don't think they'll be bothering us anytime soon,' Gabriel said snidely. 'No really, they won't. You see I had access to this so-called mission, in fact I was the one who assigned it to your dear brother. After your little incident, I knew he'd give it to you.'

So it was true – Jessica's brother worked for Trojan? Lily was right? No, I couldn't believe it, not until I saw proof. That would mean Jessica had to have known about it, they were close after all. She would have told me if her brother consorted with terrorists, right?

As Jessica talked in my ear and Gabriel responded it all became background noise. Was everything I knew about her family a lie? Did she have connections with Russia? Had Jessica been working for Trojan this whole time? Lily said she was already trained when she got to the Academy: why go someplace to train if you've already covered most of it? Everything seemed to be clicking into place – Jessica, what have you done?

'Answer me this then. Willow's death, was it *just* an accident?'

'Of course it was.' Jessica's ominous figure slowly crept into my line of vision but it wasn't like a phoenix rising from the ashes, it was a like a demon who walked amongst the flames.

'Who shot her?' Gabriel asked. 'It certainly wasn't us.'

'It had to be.'

'As far as I know, Willow's father needed her out of the way but I imagine the request wasn't perceived as literal. He's high up within the Academy, you see. Didn't need daughter dearest causing a fuss or exposing him for what he really was. Shame, I heard she had a bright future.'

So Willow's death was the Academy's doing? What had she known that warranted her death? They killed if someone spoke out, they killed if someone knew too much. What secrets did she take to her grave?

'Oh I'm sorry, you didn't know?' Gabriel mocked, turning to the wall. 'That, however, was my idea.'

Tears burned down my face, evaporating instantly from the heat. How could I trust Jessica? All this time I'd been building her up as a hero, when it was clear she was anything but.

'Better than some bomb, I quite like this town,' he muttered.

I wanted to cry, I needed my mum.

'Now I need you to send a little message, Katie, you're the Carrier after all.' Gabriel said to me. I shook my head, a small sob slipping out, but he didn't care. 'I need you to tell Harkness that

Operation Black Scorpion is to be left alone, or no one will survive.'

Black Scorpion, I'd heard that before, hadn't Helen mentioned that? How big was this mission?

'Please,' I begged him.

'Katie,' he said, 'be my little bird, deliver the message.'

Suddenly helicopter blades thundered from above my head, was that the rescue team?

'Ah that'll be the press – I look forward to whatever spin Thompson runs about this,' Gabriel muttered.

Then with a snap of his fingers, the cold barrel of the gun left my head and the endless army disappeared from sight. I wanted to fall forward, curl into a ball, but I remained solid. The fear of the gun still rang in my mind, my nails digging into my palms, my body completely numb, weightless.

'Have fun,' Gabriel called as he walked away, 'while you can.'

Warm hands took mine but I didn't look, it was her.

'Naomi, we need to get out of here before anyone sees us,' Jessica said as she pulled me up, but my eyes only gazed at the wall.

This was who Trojan were: murderers, psychopaths, who only wrecked people's lives because they wanted to, and Jessica was one of them.

'Look at me.' I tried to pull away, but Jessica's hands cupped my face, forcing me to look at her. 'We need to go – you know the exit route, it's near here. You lead the way with Lily, I'll get Grace.'

Then like a saint, she ran over to Grace, slowly helping her up. I watched as she carefully threw Grace's body onto her shoulder in a fireman's lift. I then realised Kayson was doing the same with Chris.

Two wounded, possibly on the edge of death.

I turned and took the lead with Lily who rubbed at her wrists. Soon we picked up the pace to a slow jog as the sound of helicopters and cars became louder, slicing through the silence of the trees we clung to. The jog became a sprint as we headed into a dense forest, the exit path covered well enough that we could get back to the vehicles unnoticed. But if that was so secure, why did I feel like what just happened meant the whole world would be

SLATE RETRIBUTION

watching?

EMERY HALE

CHAPTER 25

Nighted

Overtaken by night or darkness.

NAOMI JADE

The kitchen, equipped with a dining table, chairs, two pastry cookbooks and a knife with remnants of butter and toast crumbs. The dorm house was meant to be a sanctuary but instead it felt like a prison block. Grace and Chris were in the hospital ward while Jessica, Lily and Kayson were going over what happened with Quinn. I could hear them yelling from the next room but I didn't care to listen. I'd done my job, not much I could do now.

Blood stained my shoes and ankles, sinking into the cracks and lines of my shaking hands – how could anyone do this? What I'd seen was horrific, disgusting and cruel, and by evening it would be plastered all over the news.

If Thompson had control of the press and sway over the public, what story would he spin to cover this? In my mind there was no doubt, terrorists walked amongst us. If Gabriel was just the messenger then he must have superiors. We just had to figure out who.

When my mum got the footage from the lapel camera she could go to print – an inside video of the man himself. It was proof that terrorists existed and wanted to wreak havoc. No, not wanted – they needed to. Today showed how far they were willing to go; human life didn't come into it. On the ride back I was filled in by Jess on what she and Grace had found. Inhumane didn't begin cover it.

The door to the kitchen opened and I found that I pulled myself straighter as Jessica walked in – however, she wore a soft, honest smile. I didn't know what to make of her: there was part of me that didn't trust her but the other part, my heart, told me I should. Jess sat across from me at the table but she was cautious, as though approaching a scared animal.

'So, Katie,' she joked pushing hair behind her ear. 'I'm glad you didn't use your own name. If someone were to go after her, I don't think I'd be too bothered.'

'Jess!' I said, horrified. I knew Katie wasn't the best person but that was no reason to wish death on the girl.

'Oh, relax,' Jess said. 'It was a joke, miss serious.' How could she be so happy after what happened? We were at the same place right? You know, with the wall of burning people. 'Now I know this was a one-time thing but given the situation, I think you did quite well.'

'What do I get, a report card?' I snarked, my eyes falling to the table. I couldn't look at her.

I wanted to ask her about Trojan, I needed to know if what Lily told me was true.

'No, what's up with you?'

'Oh, I don't know Jess, probably the hundreds of deaths we just witnessed, maybe it was Grace and your so-called boyfriend bleeding out either side of me, or you know what? It could have been the gun Gabriel put to my head.'

Jessica sighed, reaching for my hand but I snatched it back. 'No, you don't get to do that.'

Jessica pulled back herself.

'Naomi, it's me.'

'Is it though?' I asked. 'Is it really? How do you know Gabriel?'

She stuttered. 'He works in the Government.'

'So you know all the MPs?'

'No, he uh – he worked with my mum for a couple years but I've never personally spoken to him.'

I scoffed – of course she would deny it. Like she would tell me anything. I'd need the whole team in here to get the truth out of her.

'Stop lying to me,' I said. The lie was clear and I knew she was holding something back.

'I'm not lying,' Jess said adamantly, but I only shook my head and leaned back in the chair.

'Your brother sent us there, he was the one at Thames House meant to be in control. Next thing we know our comms are knocked out and I get a stupid message to tell Harkness!' Now it was coming out, I couldn't hold it back anymore. 'So, I beg you, tell me everything.'

'What are you talking about?' she asked, like I was the

insane one.

'You – what the hell are you really doing at the Academy?'

'My mother enrolled me.'

'Really? See, I find that odd, cause if you trained with the so-called Pyramid Delegates all your life, I don't see why you had to come here, unless there was another reason.'

Jessica let out a righteous laugh. 'I'm sorry, you think I'm a double agent?'

'Well you're not making sense!' I exclaimed. 'You tell me one thing but Lily another!'

'Lily doesn't know what she's talking about,' Jessica told me. 'She thinks that everyone's a double agent.'

'Jess, seriously.

'There's nothing to tell.'

'Stop lying to me!' I slammed my hands on the table. 'For once in your life tell me the truth!'

Jessica looked utterly stunned, her mouth gaping like a fish out of water, but no answers came, not one fucking syllable. There we had it, ladies and gentlemen, Jessica-Grace Winters, blessed with many miraculous skills but incapable of telling the truth.

Then something changed: her body language, then her face, and finally her eyes, became softer. Jessica's eyes flitted down to the table and she picked at her nails.

She bit her lip and took in a breath, and as she spoke, she didn't look at me once.

'I was trained with the Pyramid Delegates from a young age,' she said. 'My mother wanted me there, my older brothers didn't.'

'Why are you at the Academy?' I asked.

'My mother did enrol me, there isn't another reason. Just somewhere to put me while she got on with her life.'

Was this the truth? Or could it just be one lie after another? I felt sorry for her, no mother should act the way Charlotte did, but there was something about the whole story that didn't make sense.

'Who are the Pyramid Delegates?' I asked.

Everyone was talking about them, how they'd been infiltrated for years, but I hadn't a clue who they were or what they did. Jessica hesitated, like she was trying to think of a way to worm out of the question.

Surprisingly though, she answered me.

'They are a separate agency within the Scottish Parliament, they provide training for agents with vulnerable children. My mother put me there when I was five, all the way through to when I met you. Then she enrolled me here and I left. No one knows about the Pyramid Delegates, not unless you have background in the services.'

I held up a hand.

'Wait, so let me get this straight, the Pyramid Delegates train children and then palm them off here when they're old enough?'

Jessica nodded. 'If you want to look at like that, then yeah. I don't know who runs it, before you ask – I had a teacher but she gave a fake name and I can't remember what she looked like.'

What was this country creating? Jessica was nearly nineteen now, whatever they'd done would be cemented into her bones. Had Lily been through the same thing? What about Quinn or Grace? I know we needed people to stop Trojan, but kids? How was that fair?

I went to Jessica's house once – even as I think back everything about it was fake. The house was big but not grand, the style inside minimalistic, although now I saw it as practically empty. It must have been a safe house like in the movies. Wouldn't taking me there have been a breach of security? Did she trust me that much?

'I'm not the bad guy here.' Jessica sat a little straighter in her seat. 'I'm not a double agent. Everyone around here just loves to jump to conclusions.'

'You say that like it's our fault for assuming,' I countered, my eyebrows furrowed.

'Well . . .' she trailed off, blowing out a breath.

That was it, if she was going to get cocky then I was finished with her stupid Team Lead persona.

'Did you kill your brother Charlie? Sorry not kill, murder.'

'You taking the piss?' Jessica asked, bolting up from her seat.

I nearly shrunk back – the glare on her face was the one that could challenge Harkness – but I stayed still. She wasn't the one in power here, not anymore. I stood up firmly from the table, arms crossed and face blank.

'Did you murder Charlie?'

'Fuck off Naomi, I can't believe you'd even ask me that!'

'Tell me the truth.'

'You're a bitch.' she said, but the name didn't hurt me. 'My own brother and you think I killed him?'

'You might have had your reasons, I never met him. I just want you tell me the truth.'

'Get out,' she demanded, but I didn't stop.

'Tell me the truth, that's all I want.'

'You have no idea what you're talking about!' she screamed.

'Then tell me!'

Jessica stayed quiet after that. She couldn't push me away anymore, there was no going back. The entire house sounded like it had come to a complete standstill, the voices from the other room turning to whispers.

'I want you in a car and out of here before seven o'clock tomorrow,' Jessica said, her voice low, almost like a growl.

'You've got to be kidding me,' I said, exasperated.

'Jessica, I'm not going anywhere.'

I felt like I was on an endless merry-go-round, we kept going over the same issues time and time again.

'Yes you are. Like you said, you had a gun to your head, you don't have the stomach for this. You're not made for this world, understandably.'

'Don't make this about me, you're the one with the issues here.'

'Me?' she asked. 'I didn't stand about like Katie's pet for years, I didn't become an inferior human being with no social life. The only reason Kayson met you was because I told him to.'

Jessica didn't look at me, but I knew what lay behind that stone cold façade of hers: anger. She was angry at me for pushing one too many of her buttons, but it only made me want to dig deeper.

'I'm sorry, you take drugs even though you don't know what they do to you, you're repressing your emotions and basically live oppressed. Don't talk to me like you have some higher power.'

'I don't run at the first sign of trouble,' she snapped.

'Quinn told me what you said to her, you were ready to run out that door.'

'But I didn't.'

'You wanted to, though.' Jessica turned around to face me, trying to calculate my next move. 'All you want is security – well I apologise, but not all of us have that life. Some of us actually have to fight for it. I fought for you that night in the theatre, you wouldn't be here without me.'

'You pranced around a stage!' I shouted. 'You didn't do anything!'

Jessica scoffed but she didn't reply, she just turned away and stared into the sink.

She was impossible to talk to, how did anyone get a straight answer out of her? Oh wait, that's right, they didn't. In high school she wasn't like this, she was confident, always smiled and had that air of sophistication, but now I knew better. She was a murderer.

'I want you out by seven o'clock tomorrow,' Jessica repeated.

Oh, if she thought I was going down without a fight, she

had another think coming.

'You know what?' I said, 'I'm gonna take James's laptop with me.'

I headed for the door but within the blink of an eye Jessica was in front of me, blocking the path. I smirked.

'Evidence.' I tried to move around her but she just followed me. 'What?'

'You're not taking the laptop.'

'Why?' I asked. 'Cause it has your dead brother's name on it? I'm sure that'll make for a great read on the train home.'

'You're not taking it,' she told me.

'Yes I am.' I took in a breath before standing toe to toe with her. I was the one in control here, not her. 'You scared, Winters?'

If she wanted to play at this game so could I.

'Of what?' she asked. 'You?'

'Of what I'll find on that laptop. There's always three sides to a story, and in this case it's mine, yours and the truth. Get out of my way.'

I tried to barge past her but that was when she grabbed my

wrist with an iron force that made me halt. I slowly turned my head but she didn't show any sign of letting go.

'Kayson will escort you to get your things from Quinn's room. Then, you're gone.'

'I'm not leaving.'

'I will drag you,' she threatened.

Then I laughed.

'Do it.' I challenged without thinking.

When I tried to take my wrist back she used the momentum against me, spinning my body around and pinning me to the wall. I sucked in a breath as my head smacked against the cold concrete and a sharp pain shot through my arm, but I didn't give her the satisfaction of a cry.

Lily was right, she was too far gone.

'You will leave. All the videos are stored here, the camera phone is in Quinn's drawer, and I will decide what we do with them. Not you. I don't ever want to see you again. Quinn can mail your things back to you,' she growled in my ear. 'Now get out.'

'See, this is what they do to you, they make you into something you're not. Three years ago you would never have done this,' I tried, fear gripping my throat.

'I would have. I just pitied you too much.'

I stayed flat against the wall trying to swallow the tears brimming in my eyes. I wouldn't let her see me like this; wouldn't give her the pleasure of my tears. She'd pitied me for all these years. That was probably the only reason she hung around with me; pity. Everything I'd feared for years had finally come to light.

'Jess, you need to come quick – Harkness is on the hospital ward, he's got a gun,' Quinn said, but came to a halt at the sight of us.

Geez, I thought I could be left with some dignity.

Jessica didn't respond, but as the clammy palm vanished from my neck, her footsteps retreated out of the door, followed by others. I didn't move.

'What happened?' Quinn asked.

I pushed away from the wall, swallowing the sob and rubbing my eyes, trying to stop my tears crashing down like a wave.

'Nothing. Uh, come on, we should get to the ward.'

Jessica was past saving, the others weren't.

SLATE RETRIBUTION

* * *

As Quinn and I ran through the Academy doors I felt nothing but exposed. The last time I was here I'd been hidden behind a disguise but now my true face was bare. Even though I was under the protection of James's boss, it no longer gave me security. What was worse? Trojan or the wrath of Harkness? Right now they could be the same thing.

We ran up the stairs to the fourth floor, cause we didn't want to make it obvious if a teacher was swinging a gun about. As we entered the stairwell I heard the smacking of feet a couple flights above – I saw a flash of Kayson's jacket and knew they had the same idea as us.

With each step I took the paranoia and fear dug deeper and deeper into my brittle bones – what awaited us on this ward? I assumed it was Grace who raised the alarm; I feared what she considered an emergency.

Kayson and Jessica were nowhere in sight so Quinn cautiously stepped towards the door, opening it slowly at first but then darting through. I followed suit. The ward looked like a real hospital, even the stink of disinfectant was strong, stinging my nose. The sun had begun to set, casting an eerie glow, shadows dancing along the floor.

Quinn crouched low as she tip-toed behind a medical cart. I looked around and quietly ran to the nearest pillar, pressing my back against it.

The only sound was the steady heartbeat from the monitors: no breaths or clicking shoes. I pressed my lips together trying to peer around the corner but Quinn waved her hand, shaking her head. From her position she could see straight ahead, and by the look in her eyes, what was about to happen wasn't good.

'Explain to me why your test results are faked,' I heard the voice of Harkness demand. 'Williams, answer me.'

'They're not faked,' a voice replied.

'We just took Aspin's blood, there are no traces of the drug.'

'She was shot, we had to pump her with fluids, it would have flushed it out of her system.'

No . . . Harkness was onto us.

'Dr Williams, if you want to keep your head, I suggest you

start telling the truth.'

Doctor – he was talking to a doctor like that?

I slowly crouched down onto my hands and knees, shifting myself round so I could get a better look. I needed to see how bad this situation was. The camera was still pinned to my jacket, so at least it would record this.

In front of me were more beds, most of them filled. Grace sat upright in one of them, but that was when I saw Harkness, his blue shirt covered in blood as he pointed a gun at a man in scrubs – presumably the doctor. He had his hands against his head but his face remained stoic.

Then I saw the reason Harkness was covered in blood: two nurses lay next to doctor, dead.

He was shooting the staff.

I wanted to run out, draw his fire, but what good would it do? The idea of a gun pointed in my direction terrified me. Everyone really was replaceable.

'We had to give Grace fluids,' Dr Williams said, his voice wavering. 'They would have flushed the drugs out of her system. Ask Dr McKay, he'll tell you the same.'

Harkness knelt down behind the doctor, placing a hand on his shoulder, the gun now pressed intently on the man's temple. Not a tremor or flinch in sight.

'I'm not asking him, he's busy with surgery. Now do you want to end up like your nursing staff or do you want to tell me the truth?'

Dr Williams shook his head. 'I'm telling you the truth.'

He was covering for us; he didn't go back on the lie. Did the doctor believe he was doing the right thing? He'd gone along with our plan in the hope that no one would notice – how did Harkness even know to check?

When I looked over to Quinn she was gone – she must have moved somewhere else, but as I lifted my gaze I saw Kayson hiding behind a medical partition, gun in hand. Would he do it? Would he shoot Harkness? Then to my left, Jessica was hiding behind another pillar, gun raised, pointed right at Harkness. It wasn't a question of *if* with her, it was when.

Lily was nowhere in sight – she must have been at the other side of the ward, but I knew this team would put a stop to this madman, he couldn't –

SLATE RETRIBUTION

BANG

Kayson yelled out and fell to the floor, clutching his side, his gun clattering on the hard laminate. His eyes screwed shut, his fingers pressing intently to the wound, his teeth audibly grinding together.

BANG

Jessica spun around, dodging the bullet. Now holding the gun to her chest, she went to spin back round but stopped as more bullets clipped the concrete.

I wanted to run to Kayson but Harkness had seen him, and he would annihilate me.

If I ran, I would die.

I slammed my hand over my mouth to silence my breathing, crushing my back against the wall, my knees to my chest and eyes screwed shut. I couldn't move – everything was happening at double the speed, bullets falling all around like broken glass.

As I forced my eyes open, Kayson caught them. He grimaced, starting to mouth something to me but I couldn't make it out. Dust from the concrete was flying everywhere and he was too far away.

What could I do? I wasn't a doctor – but then I remembered, there was a medical cart next to me. It must have packing material inside.

'Jess!' I called over the gunfire.

She quickly whipped round and saw my motion to the cart and then Kayson. She nodded before pushing away off the pillar and firing multiple shots.

BANG

BANG

BANG

BANG

BANG.

I darted to the medical cart, rifling through the drawers, trying to find anything, then I came across some medical gauze: there weren't any sutures or needles so this would have to do.

I peeked up but saw no one, there were patients at the other side of the ward ducking for cover. I was no longer in the line of fire – time to get to work. I took that as my chance and dived over to Kayson's side.

'You need to get out of here,' he said through gritted teeth.

'Well, you need to stop bleeding.'

'Oh yeah, right, let me just turn the tap off,' he groaned.

I didn't know what the hell I was doing but I packed the wound, hoping it would stop. All bleeding had to stop eventually, right?

'Naomi, go,' Kayson said, taking my hand.

'What, and leave you to die a hero? No chance.'

I kept adding packing and pressure to the wound but the bleeding didn't stop. He needed a real doctor, not me who's watched a couple of *Holby City*'s with my mum. I had to go in deeper. When I pulled up the bottom of his shirt I was greeted with a shallow bullet wound and a set of abs – well, nothing new there.

'How we looking doc?' Kayson asked.

'Well, unfortunately you're not going to die. I don't think.'

'I wanna see your diploma.' He cracked a smile.

The white net of the gauze seemed to be soaking up the blood fairly quickly so I kept adding more, while Kayson kept a hold of everything. That was when a bullet shot past my head, the metal shooting through the thick strands of my hair – a squeal leapt from my lips and I ducked – Kayson's arm shot up, his hand cupping the back of my neck as he held me down.

My head lay on his warm vibrating chest, and I could hear his strong heartbeat.

THUMP

THUMP

THUMP.

Despite the yells and bullets whizzing through the air my eyes slowly trailed up to meet Kayson's. he gave me a soft smile and placed something in my hand.

'Run,' he said. 'Go out the way you came, keep low. Go home.'

'Kayson, you're bleeding.'

'I'm well aware, you beautifully stubborn woman. Now get out of here.'

'Kayson –'

'Get out, while you have the chance.'

Would I be trapped here if I stayed?

I shared a moment with Kayson in the midst of the

carnage; a simple glance and firm nod. I'd see him again. I pushed up off the floor, keeping low and ran for the cover of the medical cart. Bullets flew into the walls behind me – I bit back a scream and ran from the cart to the pillar.

Now I just had to get to the door.

Just as I lifted my foot, I saw Grace scrounging for cover through the crossfire, sliding under one of the beds. Jessica and Lily stood in front of Harkness, guns raised, but none of that seemed to matter as the man in question pulled the trigger, killing Dr Williams.

The entire scene played out in slow motion, his whole body jolting like it had been struck by lightning, before plunging to the ground. Blood spattered in droplets to the floor and sprayed from his head to the curtains behind. His eyes were lifeless and dull, but for some reason they pierced mine as his head battered against the cold floor. I couldn't pull myself away, even when I heard Kayson's yells, there was just something deep inside that forced me to stay.

'Go!' Kayson yelled, the low growl in his voice now booming.

My feet remained firmly planted on the floor, even when Duke and other faculty members ran in from the other side of the room. Even when Jessica was restrained and another person in scrubs injected something into Lily's neck.

'You continue to disobey me, Winters,' Harkness said. 'Now you've forced my hand.'

Suddenly I could move my feet and I felt the concrete pillar underneath my hands. I sidestepped slowly, eyes focused on the door. This wasn't the life I wanted; this was my way out. Then I noticed what Kayson had slipped into my hand: a gun. The weapon rattled in my fingers but I kept it close. Now I had a choice. Shoot or run?

'Don't touch her!' Jessica screamed.

'I've wanted to try the new batch of drugs for some weeks now.'

The new drugs? The untested ones? Weren't they meant to go through the water first?

Lily's whole body suddenly dropped, going limp – she could barely keep her head up. What did they do to her? What was running through her head?

Duke marched over, grabbing Grace from the floor, holding her out to another man in scrubs. I couldn't help the tears that fell as I watched the injection spike into her neck. I should do something, what could I do?

I couldn't just leave, but if I didn't, would I ever get out? Would I end up just like them? I tried to find Quinn but she was nowhere in sight, so without another thought I ran towards the door, slipped through before it shut and barrelled down the stairs. My heart leaping into my mouth as I heard the ward door open from above but I was already one flight down.

All I knew was, I had to keep running.

EMERY HALE

CHAPTER 26
Sanguineous

Accompanied by bloodshed.

NAOMI JADE

30 April 2016, 18:00

Scotland, The Jade Household

Halloween, Guy Fawkes Night, Christmas, Boxing Day, Hogmanay, Burns Night, Valentine's Day and Easter Sunday – all those holidays had passed, and not a peep from the Academy. Absolutely nothing.

How I managed to get out of there I'll never forget: after bolting through the school, past reception and out the front door I managed to stop one of the cars, claiming I was Marsha Evans of Thames House and needed to be taken into town immediately. The driver didn't even question it, I think he was just thankful he didn't run me over. An hour later I was in the heart of Glasgow and taking every back alley and quiet street I could think of – if Quinn taught me one thing, it was that cameras saw everything. I needed to disappear. Well, that was a little dramatic, I just needed to get a bus back home, they were quieter than trains and had fewer cameras. Whatever I did worked because I got home without so much as a glance from anyone.

My mum was glad to have me back while my dad was more than confused to learn that I hadn't been on an internship course in Edinburgh. Apparently my mum was serious about keeping this story from him. It took a lot of explaining, over three and a half hours in fact (especially with my mother interrupting with more questions). All of the footage I'd collected was stored on Quinn's computer, and the videos and backups had disappeared from Mum's as well. We had no case – now it was up to Jessica.

I'd hidden the gun Kayson gave me under my mattress just in case – there was no way I was throwing it out. Even though owning a gun without a license was illegal, I thought that given the situation, we were probably all past that point now.

I wondered if Jessica ever release the videos: maybe one day I'd turn on the TV and the Academy would be breaking news.

SLATE RETRIBUTION

I've hoped that for over seven months now. With each passing day I waded my way through the internet to see if Quinn had uploaded them, frequently refreshing news outlets, but there was nothing. It was like they'd given up on the entire thing. Harkness had disappeared the day after I left, mum had been looking – she even asked her boss but it was like he'd dropped off the face of the Earth. A new Head of Scotland Yard took his place a few days later.

My life when I was with the Academy was exciting – there was always something to do, something to plan for. But now, as I lay on my parents' couch, the experience seemed terribly short-lived. I should never have run that day, but deep down I knew I'd had to – what would I have become if I stayed?

My mum told me I'd done the right thing and so did my dad, but it didn't feel right. Sure, it was what I needed to do, but it wasn't what I wanted. I knew one of the Government's best-kept secrets and I couldn't do anything about it. We had no proof, my mum's life was on the line if Thompson ever figured it out, and if I ever tried to contact anyone myself, it would raise the red flag. After the incident on the ward I had a strong feeling security was more of a priority than ever. I just hoped they didn't come for my family.

I instructed my mum to keep her head down at work and my dad to do the same, we didn't need to attract attention. That and I'd bought them all burner phones, paid for in cash... being around the Academy had made me paranoid. The phones were for emergencies only, but it made me feel more secure.

I worried for Quinn, though – would she ever see her mother again? I worried for Kayson – did he survive that bullet? I was fraught with fear for the entire team – the new drugs would have been injected into all of them, who were they now? Did they even know?

'Move over would you?' my dad muttered, sitting down as his stupid war movie started.

I pushed up from my lying position, grabbed a cushion and sat back. One of the new traditions was to watch a movie every Saturday, apparently it was a bonding experience, to try and forget about the Academy. How could I, though?

Even though I was only there for a short time I saw so much, but did so little. I still felt responsible, I knew the torture and abuse they suffered. I was sure it would be near-impossible to get back inside. Besides, would anyone want me there in the first place? Jessica was going to throw me out and Grace, the second in command, was indisposed at the time, so as far as I was concerned, no one would want me. I wasn't needed, and in Jessica's eyes that meant there was no point in being there. She was like a machine, probably more so than ever now. I wondered if she even remembered her own name?

'Naomi, are you watching the movie or doing that lovely Judy Dench stare out the window?' Even though I only heard half of what he said, the sentence confused me enough that I turned to him.

'What?'

'You're thinking about the Academy again. Let me tell you something, you're better off now you're rid of the lot of them.'

'Dad.'

'No. Don't defend them. You know what's going on in there, and one day it'll come out. Except you will have nothing to do with it.'

'Someone has to do something. I can't just sit here watching movies with you every week and hope.'

'What's the alternative?' Dad asked. 'Your mother and I attending your funeral.'

'I'm going to be attending at least five if I just sit here.'

'Of people you barely know.' Those words struck hard in my chest.

Sure, I didn't know everyone's entire backstory but I knew them well enough. Quinn, she was kind, caring, sensitive and smelled like flowers wrapped in caramel. Grace didn't like me much but if she was studying medicine and the second in command she was smart. I'd also noticed the chain around her neck – Grace was religious, Roman Catholic at that. Lily was a Runner, her room was bright red and she had a tongue like fire. Kayson was a complete asshole but for some reason he had a caring side and Jessica was . . . my friend. Did you need to know someone's full life to trust them? I didn't think so. Trust takes years to build but that entire team trusted me to do a job, even though they'd only known me a couple of days.

'You're better for it, it would have broken your mother's

heart if something happened to you.'

'I think it would break Quinn's mum's heart too,' I answered plainly.

'Naomi, you're not going back, end of story,' my dad snapped.

My brows furrowed as he spoke to me in that tone – he didn't know the first thing about the situation, but he happily ordered me about. What if I went back? Would it break my mother's heart? Would she rather I did what's easy or what's right?

Eighteen, that's how old I was – an adult in society's eyes. Shouldn't I be able to make my own decisions? It was my life after all. I knew it was a stupid idea, to want to go back, but it was the right thing to do. Even if I just snuck in for half an hour, downloaded the footage, and then got out of there.

Now in uncomfortable silence we both turned back to the movie; my dad liked to have the final word on matters.

Abruptly my phone pinged and I grabbed it from my pocket ready to dismiss it. But it was a random number and the following message:

Have a surprise for you, front door. It's quite handsome.

A grin broke out on my face because I knew it could only be from one person.

'You know what?' I said, sitting forward. 'You can watch your film, I'm gonna go for a walk.'

'Naomi, we're meant to watch this together,' my dad said pointedly.

'Yeah, I hate these kind of films though, so you have fun.'

I grabbed my jacket on the way out, tucking my phone into the pocket before running out the door.

As soon as I did I saw Kayson Ashford, dressed in jeans, a tight t-shirt and a leather jacket, leaning against the streetlamp that was just beginning to glow. I bit my lip, shaking my head – he goes seven months without a word and he just thinks it's alright to turn up out of the blue? Well of course it was, but I wasn't going to let him know that.

'Where have you been?' I asked, tucking my hands into my jeans pockets.

He didn't look ill, not even malnourished. He didn't favour the side where he got shot – in fact, he looked fine. I thought he would have been on the new drugs for some time now, but the cheekiness and smug look on his face told me otherwise. Part of me worried it was just a false pretence, but there were certain things you couldn't fake. Like when Kayson grinned that way, the rise of his lips revealing the smallest little dimples.

'Oh, around,' he answered taking a couple steps towards me.

I crossed my arms over my chest; he wasn't getting away with such a vague answer. We stared at each other for what seemed like five minutes, before he grudgingly gave in to my silent demand.

'The Academy, Washington and Italy, although that last one was more a favour than a job.'

What – so even after the incident they trusted Kayson to go on missions in different countries? Weren't they worried he would run? Then it made me think, what have they got on him to make him stay?

'What about the team?' I asked.

He seemed surprised. 'Well, Luca's fine, being a bit of an ass if I'm honest.'

I rolled my eyes. 'No, Jessica's team.'

'Oh, that's actually the reason I'm here,' he said, the grin and dimples vanishing. 'They're – Harkness has had them in with the seniors ever since you left. The only person I've seen recently is Lily but that was two weeks ago.'

'Two weeks?' My mouth dropped open. 'Why has he put them with the seniors?'

'He wants them ready for this new operation, Black Scorpion.'

'But that was the one that –'

'Gabriel warned us about, yeah I know.'

If Harkness was taking Jessica's team and shoving them in with the seniors then something must have happened – perhaps Harkness knew about Gabriel's plan? What the hell was he preparing for?

'Why Jessica's team?'

'The new drugs made them compliant,' Kayson answered. 'Lily wouldn't even look at me, she's thinner and her fighting style – she's fighting to kill.'

'To kill?'

Kayson nodded.

'I tried to get through to her but she didn't even recognise me.'

Compliance, that's what the Academy wanted.

I shuddered. Whatever Black Scorpion involved, I feared it was something not even Quinn could come back from. These drugs must knock out free will completely, cause last time I checked both Lily and Jessica were shooting at Harkness.

'I managed to sneak Chris in a month ago, to try and break through to Jess. She didn't even remember his name.'

I didn't know the ins and outs of their relationship, although from what I'd heard it was intimate – surely you'd remember someone like that? How long before they forgot their own names?

'Why aren't you a mindless zombie?' I asked, inching a little closer.

Kayson blew out a breath, shrugging.

'I don't know, Harkness has completely avoided my team. My guess is he wants to see if they'll work in the field under pressure first. Apparently the new drugs take longer to kick in.'

'There must be an easier way to deal with this. There has to be.'

'I did some research on Black Scorpion, it's in Estonia. The rest is classified.'

'Oh Kayson, you've got to be kidding me,' I groaned. 'I've been in the Academy – I think classified is a little out of the question.'

'No, classified to me. I tried to get to it through Duke's computer but I needed a password. I don't have any techies on my team.'

Black Scorpion, the one Gabriel warned us against. What could Trojan be planning that was so deadly it warranted all of this? I couldn't decide how I felt when I asked the next question, honoured or utterly terrified.

'Why are you here?'

Even Kayson hesitated before he answered, unsure of himself. Then, he started to lift his shirt, exposing the beautifully carved sex lines at the bottom of his torso. I tried to look away but the streetlight was direly bleak compared to the sight in front of me. Christ, I was such a virgin.

'Try and keep your mouth shut,' Kayson said.

I hurtled my gaze to next available spot on the pavement, I could feel the grin crawling back out. 'I didn't see anything,' I muttered.

That was when a brown envelope was thrust under my nose. I took it curiously, flipping it over, the thing was blank but it wasn't sealed. Kayson leaned back against the lamppost, saying nothing.

I stuck my hand inside, practically waiting for a rubber spider to slide out, but the prank never came. Inside was a cheap-looking necklace, a tube of lipstick and pack of chewing gum.

'You shouldn't have . . .' I trailed off.

Kayson laughed. 'There's a second part.' Then he leaned down and pulled a black duffle bag out, dumping it at my side.

'That better not be your gym clothes,' I said, before unzipping it.

Surprisingly, it was anything but stinky socks – it was the Reign Academy uniform. Complete with a brown wig in a net bag, a small bag of make-up, coloured contacts and an ID card.

'The necklace is a camera, the lipstick has a memory stick

inside for you to download the videos from the computer and the pack of chewing gum is – well, I don't actually know how that got in there. I can get you into the school, all you need to do is download the files.'

There were already so many things that could go wrong with this plan.

'Kayson,' I tried. 'Quinn is a technical genius, I've seen her set-up. This isn't like James's laptop. I can't just guess the password. Then there's the disguise – Quinn was the one who put it together, did all the makeup.'

'The disguise is just so you can get in through the gates,' he said. 'I really need your help.'

'Why do you need me to do this?' Surely you could do it.'

'I can't just walk in. It has to be a two-person job, I can keep them away from you.'

'You might have forgotten, but I'm not a technical whiz. We still have the problem of the computer.'

He shook his head.

'I've got a solution to that. Right now, I need you to get changed and get in the car.' Hold up, now? Like right now?

SLATE RETRIBUTION

'You need to hold back on the romance there, I'm drowning in it,' I said sarcastically.

Kayson scoffed, letting out a laugh. 'Come on, you can't tell me you didn't enjoy our little date. I pulled out all the stops.'

'Sure, whatever,' I laughed in return. I tucked the envelope into the duffle bag, zipped it shut and slung it over my shoulder.

Of course I was hopping back into this, Kayson of all people came to me and asked for help! He must have thrown his pride out of the car window on the drive over.

This was the right thing to do. If I could get the information downloaded and bring it back, we could publish it. We'd have to do it discreetly, probably from a computer in an internet café or something. I'd work out the technicalities later.

But that was when a familiar blue Vauxhall pulled into the driveway. Seriously, how did my mother time these things? As soon as her heels smacked the ground she was out the car and bounding towards us. Santa, if you're up there, please stop my crazy mother from shouting at Kayson.

'The day I've had, then when I come home, pretty boy's decided to rock up.'

'Mum, don't start,' I tried, but it was no use.

'See, Naomi, told you she'd like me,' Kayson said, whacking on the charm but I only rolled my eyes.

'You, zip it,' Mum said, pointing to him. He opened his mouth to say something but she glared and he decided against it. Wise move, Kayson, wise move. 'Now, at work today the whole incident in Brora nearly broke headlines again.'

'It did?' I asked.

'In the office, we all wanted to go to print – a new source had come in, someone called Jacqueline Buchanan. She'd found footage of the entire thing.'

She what? Jackie? The same one that I'd met? The one whose parents had bought their way in with seven figures? Kayson turned to me as a look of recognition crossed my face. How the hell had a first year got into Quinn's computer? I asked him silently, but he shook his head. That told me one thing: whatever footage she had, it couldn't have been from Quinn's computer. Could it have been stored somewhere else? Quinn was smart, maybe she'd anticipated what would happen and put the footage elsewhere. She knew Jackie was with me that day on the orientation.

'But there's bad news,' Mum said. 'We've tried contacting Jacqueline all day. At first it went straight to voicemail but now it's saying the phone has been disconnected.'

A hand flew over my mouth, my eyes almost reeling back into my skull. Jacqueline had been found out. I didn't even need to look at Kayson for confirmation, the sombre expression was audible. A moment later my mother gasped – she'd caught on.

'They wouldn't,' she said, horrified, but that didn't stop my quivering lip.

How old did she say she was? Sixteen? I couldn't remember. Had they killed her? Was she left out in the middle of the accommodation for everyone to see? Jackie was still a kid, how could they do that to her?

'My boss wanted us to drop the story. Wouldn't let any of us publish it, said if we did he'd fire us. Make sure we don't get a job anywhere else.'

'Yeah, Thompson can be a bit of a dick,' Kayson said.

My mother was less than impressed. 'We have enough issues without your language, young man.'

Oh, here we bleedin go.

'Mum, we can talk about swearing another time alright, just. . .' I trailed off, looking down to the duffle bag by my side.

I bit my lip, took in a breath and nodded in confirmation to myself, before pulling mum into a tight hug, practically knocking the wind out of her. This could be the last time I ever saw her, if something went wrong in there, and I didn't want to leave on bad terms (I'm referring to the dishes that still weren't done from this morning).

'I'm gonna do something with my life,' I whispered into her ear. 'My life is going to mean something because I can help people. I can save my friends, mum.'

'You can't go back there,' Mum said, but her wavering tone betrayed her.

'It's the right thing to do and you know it,' I said, pulling back. She ran a hand over my face kissing my forehead.

'Of course I do.'

Kayson came forward, pulling a crumpled piece of white paper from his pocket, slowly opening it and holding it out for my mum to take, which she did. As my eyes scanned up and down the page it looked like it belonged in a chemistry lab. There were words and numbers there that sounded completely made up.

'Dr McKay gave me this, it's the formula used for the new drug,' he told us. 'I know you're not a pharmacist but you're a journalist, you must have connections.'

'Do you have any connections?' I asked.

'Oh, of course I do.' she said, tucking the paper into her blazer pocket.

'Naomi, if we're to get to the car on time we need to get moving,' Kayson said, pointing to the top of the street.

'You're going now?'

'Sooner we get in, the sooner we get out,' he said.

Mum appeared startled at my leaving, but nevertheless she pulled me into one final hug, this time knocking the wind out of me. I smiled softly, taking in the smell of her sweet perfume before begrudgingly pulling away. I wanted to stay in her arms for a few minutes more, the security that I clung to so longingly now out of arm's reach.

'Love you,' I said. 'You and Dad.'

'Love you too.' She squeezed my hand.

With that I let her hand go and took off, running with Kayson up the street. I was sprinting towards purpose, reason and morality – I just hoped it wouldn't be my doom.

SLATE RETRIBUTION

CHAPTER 27

Alexithymia

The inability to express your feelings.

JESSICA-GRACE WINTERS

One. Two. Three. Four. Five. Six. Seven. Eight. Nine. Ten.

One. Two. Three. Four. Five. Six. Seven. Eight. Nine. Ten.

One. Two. Three. Four. Five. Six. Seven. Eight. Nine. Ten.

Thirty steps, that's how many it took to walk down to the new sub-level.

The aisle between the cells was a dark green, while the reinforced titanium doors were black. On the ceiling a few naked bulbs swung freely. It was smaller than I had first thought, there were sixteen cells and then down the grey metal stairs were a further fourteen. They could put a whole year group in here if they

SLATE RETRIBUTION

wanted to. I couldn't peek inside the cells, sadly – only staff were allowed to speak to the students in isolation.

Why was I down here?

'Move it,' Duke ordered.

Get it together, I told myself, *you're here for a reason. Duke knows why, you don't need to*, I thought.

Duke would never lead me astray or make me do anything without reason. I wasn't here to be thrown into isolation, no, that wouldn't make sense. It happens without warning, the guards from upstairs come and drag you away. Shameful; the humiliation was enough to deter me.

I was a soldier. The staff wouldn't tell you to do something if there was no meaning behind it. They knew best, so who was I to question it?

We passed the guard on the door – well, it wasn't really a door, more like prison bars. As we marched down the stairs, there was a stillness in the air – some might think it tranquil. Then I heard it, scratching. Had a mouse gotten in?

Duke charged ahead to the end of the corridor, his boots

slapping on the concrete floor, then suddenly he stopped, third cell from the bottom. He took a key from his belt, fussing with it, then unlocked the door.

Inside sat a girl, around sixteen, dressed in the designated school uniform, hair untidy, shirt wrinkled. She sat at the back corner of the dark cell, hands clinging to her knees. Must have left her dignity upstairs.

'Agent 784T, do you know why you're here?' The girl snivelled and nodded, snot dripping from her nose. 'Good.' Then Duke turned and handed me his gun.

That was strange, I wasn't supposed to have any firearms. Why wasn't I supposed to have one? Did something happen? Must have.

'Deal with her,' Duke ordered, then left.

When I closed the door, the cell fell into darkness and I think Agent 784T started to scream. I didn't care, it told me her location as she scampered around the cramped cell. Emotion was pointless, I had a job to do.

This was my role in the world, receiving orders, carrying them out and then cleaning up afterwards. How hard would it be to get blood off these walls? Did they stain easily?

'Please,' the agent sobbed, 'please don't do this.'

I didn't believe anyone bothered to clean down here anyhow, it reeked of shit and piss.

You got used to it after a while, I'd been in here myself, after all. Can't remember much about it but who would? Who could recall anything about the dark? Except the bone chilling wind and the sun which never rose. To stay in the light, this consecrated sanctuary, I had to follow orders. If I didn't I'd be condemned to the darkness.

The agent scuttled to the right, I lifted my hand and shot once, the muzzle flash providing me with a burst of light. I only saw her for a split second but she was on her hands and knees like a wild animal, her eyes consumed with anticipation.

BANG

This time I wasn't afraid of the dark, in fact I welcomed it, as only a second passed before the door opened and I was brought back into the light. The job was done, onto the next one. That was how I proved my loyalty.

Duke held out a hand and I passed him the gun, he

holstered it at his side before walking into the cell. He sneered at the agent before meeting my gaze.

'I want your Medical Response down here to deal with the body.'

'Yes sir.' I nodded, then took off at a run back up the stairs.

I ran a lot of places now, it got things done quicker and kept my mind from wandering. I focused on my breathing; *in, out, in, out, in, out*. One foot after the other, *smack, smack, smack*. The fourth floor, that's where Aspin was. She'd been there since five this morning. She'd have to deal with the body of course, along with Doctor McKay. Then I'd have to go to Thompson, he'd make some story up about how it was a hit and run, then deny Agent 784T was ever a part of this school. Better to appease the public, can't have anything destroying the image Harkness had worked so hard to build.

The Academy was quieter than usual, a lot of people preferred to train in the evenings, but I could still smell the remains of Helen's takeout from reception.

When I made it to the fourth floor and stepped out of the

lift, I heard the rantings and ravings of some man at the nurses' desk. As I walked through the ward I caught sight of the lunatic, but didn't pay him any attention because I spotted Grace looking at some X-rays.

'Aspin, clean up in isolation,' I ordered.

'Did you at least leave me a face this time?' she asked.

'Got her in the heart, it's the only bullet you'll need to take out.'

'Great, last time the embalmer had a nightmare of a job.'

'Just get it done,' I snapped, heading back to the lift.

Thompson was the next man on my list, I needed to tell him about Agent 784T. The sooner the story got out the sooner we could be rid of the body. Didn't need her cluttering up the place.

Suddenly as I got to the lift a force threw me forward, slamming me into the back wall. I spun around throwing my arms out, but the man caught them. I swung my leg out, then threw my fist forward, landing a solid hit to his chest. The man let out various grunts, his shoulders slamming into the lift wall as the doors closed. The light above us flickered from the impact of his head banging against the metal as I delivered a swift punch to his

Adam's apple. I thought the man had learned his lesson but he came back for more, grabbing me by the shoulders. Easy.

I spun around, kicking one of my legs in the air before propelling the other one up, twisting my body like a corkscrew and quickly slithering out of his grip before punching him in the face. But he still didn't give up – he tried to grab my arms but I threw one to the side, blocking it with a half step. I turned, about to deliver a swift elbow to the face but he stopped it, grabbing my arm and twisting it behind my back.

I let out a grunt as he hurled me against the wall.

'Jessica, let me explain, you need to listen.' I heard his fist pound the wall and saw out of the corner of my eye the yellow glow of the emergency stop.

'You want a bullet in your head?'

'Don't say that, Jessica, don't say that to me.'

'Let go.'

'Not until you listen to me.'

'I don't want to hear it.'

I jolted my heel into his toes, hoping to cripple him, but the man remained solid as a pillar. I tried to wrestle my way out but he only moved closer, his breath making the hairs on the back of my neck stand up and a shiver tingle through my spine.

'Jess, baby, please.'

'Don't call me that.'

'You're stronger than this, you have to fight it.'

'Let go, or the next thing that will go through your head is my fist.'

'Charlie.' What? Who was he talking about? My brother? He died years ago, why was he of any relevance? 'You told me what happened, do you remember?'

I-I don't know, what happened? It was in a hotel room, the window was open, there was a gun in my hand.

'It doesn't matter.'

'You do remember don't you?' he asked. 'What's my name?'

'I don't care.'

The man fell deathly quiet, his warm clammy breath easing away as he let go of my arms. When I turned around to face him I knew there was something familiar, but nothing sprang to mind. He had dark hair, mid-twenties, tanned skin, black eyes with a brown leather jacket and a green shirt.

The expression on his face wasn't one of defeat, it was one I had seen countless times in all the romance films Quinn forced me to watch: heartbreak.

'You don't remember my name?' His voice was soft, weak.

The man in front of me sparked something in my mind, was it his thick lips or the way his eyes sucked me in? What was his name? My eyes trailed down his body until they came to his hands. He wore a gold plated ring on his thumb, a crest embellished on it.

'Chris, your family would hate me.'

'No they wouldn't, if anything my sister would become your annoying best friend and force you to play dolls with her.'

Images flashed before my eyes, the man and I were someplace familiar, not the Academy. Somewhere warm, fresh cinnamon in the air.

Abruptly I was back in the lift. Chris, that was his name. Christopher Barnes.

'You're . . .'

SCREECH

The lift doors opened, pried apart by clawing hands belonging to Dr McKay whose eyes bulged at the pair of us, frantically looking to Chris.

'You have to get out of here,' McKay said to him. 'If Harkness knows you're here – come on now, quickly.' Dr McKay held out a hand but Chris didn't take it.

Why wasn't he leaving? This broke protocol, no visitors unless express permission was given. He couldn't be here, shouldn't even be in this lift.

Chris's eyes focused on mine – why did he care so much about me? He tackled me into a lift and forced me to listen to him. Must be a madman, no one should care about an agent that much, if they did they'd grow attached. Soldiers were easily replaceable. Had to be in this line of work.

In one swift motion Chris cupped my face, caressing my forehead with a gentle kiss, his lips soft and warm. It unlocked something, something familiar, something that felt like home.

'I'll come back for you, I promise,' he told me before he took the doctor's hand and left.

But his scent lingered, fresh spice.

I knew his name, and even though my mind told me I didn't know him at all, my heart screamed otherwise. The way he touched my face, the way he kissed me. His hands were rough but his touch was tender, and I needed more.

That was when Dr McKay came back and pressed the button for the ground floor.

'You are to repeat what just happened to no one, do you understand?' he asked.

His voice wasn't commanding at all but there was meaning behind his words. I nodded, of course I wouldn't tell anyone what happened. It was a breach of protocol and I didn't want to go back to isolation, not when I'd just earned my place back.

The lift doors closed and I was on my way down, shouldn't there be music? I remember there being music in this lift – or was that at the hotel, with Charlie. Stop. Not important, not relevant and certainly not helpful.

Then the lift doors pinged and opened.

Today the world seemed determined to stop me from my tasks as the clatter of heels strode down the corridor towards me.

It was strange, considering no one walked like that here. I didn't need to see the person to know the walk was one of authority.

As I left the lift I saw it was a woman, early thirties, rich mocha skin with textured curly hair, defined cheekbones and full lips. She wore a black power suit and had a long-strapped bag resting on her shoulder.

As soon as she spotted me she curled her finger beckoningly.

'Winters, I need you.'

'I'm busy,' I stated.

The next words out of her mouth practically commanded me to follow.

'Command Room 2, now.'

I spotted a white badge clipped to her trousers as I walked closer, a gold chip in the middle. Her name was Nicola Ramos. Once again it sounded familiar, and yet recognition slipped from my grasp. If I didn't know her straightaway then she wasn't important to my missions. Why had she taken an interest in me?

A couple of rogue students stared as I followed Nicola through the corridors towards the command rooms, her heels soon becoming the only sound I could focus on. *Click, click, click.* What had Chris unlocked? I hadn't thought about the hotel in months. All I felt now was pain setting deep in my bones, like they were breaking one by one. Fracture by fracture. The Academy promised to take away all of my pain and guilt, why was it flooding back?

Nicola stepped into one of the command rooms and waited until I was inside before closing the door. Then she slung her bag on a nearby desk, but didn't move to turn the lights on. As I went to do so, she held up a hand.

'Leave them off.' She pulled up a chair and sat herself down. 'Now, Jessica. You're a hard girl to pin down. I've visited numerous times and yet you're never here. Isn't that strange for someone who hasn't left the compound in seven months?' she asked. 'You're never available and yet, here you are.'

Had it been that long? I must have missed my birthday, Christmas – what happened at Christmas? Did I meet up with anyone? James must have come to collect me, we always spent the holidays together. James? The name appeared but then eluded me like a ghost.

SLATE RETRIBUTION

'Is there something I can help you with? I have other duties that need attending to.'

The woman clasped her hands. 'My name is Nicola Ramos. I'm the director of your brother's section at MI6.' What the hell was MI6 doing here? They never visited, they hated us. 'I've come here to apologise for what happened on the last operation we ran. The comm units should not have been hijacked so easily. Measures have been put in place to prevent that in the future.'

What was she talking about? I hadn't worked with MI6 ever. I'd never seen this woman before in my life. I mean the town up north we went to ... Brora. Why was that name familiar? Wasn't that where I grew up? It's a coastal town up north, had fields that stank of cow manure and dirt that squelched of blood. A raging fire with burning flesh. I could almost taste the smoke filtering down my throat. How had I forgotten about that?

'Jessica?' Nicola asked.

'Is there anything else?' My fingers fiddled behind my back.

She nodded. 'You'll be transferred from the Academy

tomorrow morning and brought to work in my section.'

What? No! I didn't want to work for anyone else, this place was my home, my sanctuary. I didn't want to leave. I'd just gained their trust and now they'd give me more missions. I needed to prove that I was worthy of their time.

'I have a team, I can't abandon them.'

'Your safety has been compromised,' Nicola said pointedly. 'You've been pulled out of the programme.'

'Since when?' I demanded.

'Ten minutes ago. I suggest you pack a bag.'

'You don't have the authority to do this,' I nearly yelled.

'In fact, I do,' she snapped. 'Your brother brought the matter to me and I made the decision. You're a great agent, we could use you in our department.'

My brother? Right, his name was James. He was tall, well-built and taught me how to read. I'd forgotten about him.

'I don't want to go.'

'You don't have a choice.' Nicola stood up, grabbed her bag and headed for the door. 'You're going to be free, Jessica, take the opportunity. We can worry about your friends later.'

SLATE RETRIBUTION

Then, just like that, the door swung shut behind her.

I wasn't going anywhere. I was loyal to the Academy, not to anyone else, and certainly not any of the other services. My brother wanted me out, but why? Didn't he know all the good we'd done? The great achievements of this institution within society? We had control over the entire country, agents within parliament, the high street, the doctors, the pharmacists and even the theatre.

Sure, she was the head of a department, but she had no right to come in here, the Academy was above the other services. Were they, though? I'd never really thought of rankings. I just knew we were separate, so really, there was no competition.

Maybe I was being released – a job in espionage was what I wanted.

Would Harkness allow this? I knew every decision came down to him – he ran the Academy, after all. I was his solider to do with as he pleased – would he send me away? Perhaps if I left it would be best for the team. All I caused was trouble and my last Carrier died on the job.

The videos that were stored on Quinn's computer had

remained there for a while; I decided not to release them. Over the last several months Trojan attacks had gone from weekly to none at all; the seniors and my team had prevented countless tragedies. There was no need to tear down the facility that was saving innocent lives.

Before all of this I worried that something was wrong with me, that I lacked empathy. Now I didn't have to worry anymore because emotion never came into it, not in this line of work. Now, I was free.

SLATE RETRIBUTION

CHAPTER 28

Ubuntu

The belief that we are defined by passion and kindness towards others.

NAOMI JADE

You know, getting changed in the back of a car was definitely harder than I expected. Trying to put on a uniform without flashing my bra or knickers at Kayson was my first obstacle but with some shimmying, my grannie panties weren't exposed. The next problem was the wig. I threw it on and pinned it but the driver (who was blocked from view by the partition) had a thing for sharp corners, slamming me into the door even though I was wearing a seatbelt. Thankfully Kayson pulled out his phone so I could use it as a mirror because, and I quote, 'your wig's a bit skew-whiff.'

For once he was helping me, holding the different bits and

bobs while I tried to recreate the disguise on my face. Kayson told me he'd stolen everything from one of the first year teams, bet they would have swooned at the sight of him. A handsome older guy just strolling in unannounced – *Naomi! You have a job to do, stop daydreaming.*

As we got onto the motorway, butterflies fluttered in my stomach. The disguise wasn't too far off what Quinn had created, yet I was terrified. The thought of going back there made my heart thunder against my ribcage.

Fight or flight response – come on, Naomi, this time you have to fight.

After fixing my make-up I slipped on the black heels which were considerably taller than I was used to. Quinn had let me wear lower ones.

'Kayson, how the hell am I meant to walk in these?' I asked quietly.

'They're heels and you're a girl, I just thought you always wore heels.'

Oh Kayson, you idiot. 'I'm gonna let that one slide,' I told him.

'All the girls wear them when they're on outside duty, which is your cover.'

'Not all girls have ankles of steel and bones of titanium.'

'I've seen girls run in these heels.'

'Well, you should fear them.'

The heels were at least four inches which, for someone who rarely wears anything over three, was a challenge. I'd have to hold onto Kayson until I got the hang of this. Great, up close and personal with Mr Kayson Ashford.

He chuckled after my last comment, leaning back in the seat, and throwing everything I'd used into his duffle bag. Then we fell into comfortable silence as I focused on folding my clothes neatly. I made sure to do it as slowly as possible because it stopped me daydreaming about Kayson.

He asked me for help – me. Kayson could have chosen anyone, but he turned up on my street with hope and a plan. I wondered how long he'd thought about this, and how he'd come up with the idea in the first place. How desperate had he gotten? There must have been other plans before this one. I couldn't have been his first option.

As I zipped the bag closed, I fiddled with the white plastic ID card Quinn had whipped up for our unsanctioned break-in. Did she even remember that? Me?

'How many fake identities do you have?' I asked, trying to make conversation.

The silence was nice, but I needed some form of background noise – a distraction from what I was about to walk back into.

He seemed surprised at the question. 'One.'

What, seriously? He'd been to different countries all over the world, didn't he get a new name for each one?

'What happened to protecting your identity?' I asked.

Kayson shook his head.

'Naomi, it's not like the movies,' he told me. 'There aren't boxes stashed away in lockers all around the world with fake passports, money and guns.'

What? So that was all made up? Oh . . . disappointing.

'Your alias identities are specific to you and to whatever agency you work for. Can't be running around with eight different names – if you ran into trouble you'd have no idea what cover to play.'

I guess that made sense. I had two so far, although Marsha Evans didn't really count. I presumed they used that pass any time they had to sneak someone in for emergencies. Did Marsha exist? Was she just a name in a file? Was that where everyone at the Academy would end up? Tucked away in some filing cabinet. Willow was.

'You can never just be yourself in this industry can you?' I asked and then motioned to myself – but to my amazement, he shook his head.

'You can always be yourself around your team. You train together, fight together, and more importantly, you're constantly surprised by them, every single day. No matter how scared someone is, with the right words they're able to do anything.' Kayson chuckled, his eyes falling to the ground as he reminisced. 'You know your team inside out. Their weaknesses, their strengths, their fatal flaws. You see them on the roughest days of their lives, the ones you think they'll never crawl out of.' He paused. 'But they do. Your team isn't just a bunch of friends, there's trust and loyalty, like a family.'

I had to clench my jaw to stop my mouth falling open – where was all of this at the beginning? Kayson was ranting like he'd had no one else to talk to for years.

'Since when were you so sentimental?' I asked.

'Since I lost my family. I don't think I'm ever going to see them again.' Tears brimmed in Kayson's eyes – they were small, but nevertheless, they were there. 'I treated you like shit, Naomi, even when I didn't know you. A couple of minutes after you left I was made to sit and watch as the spark of humanity drained from every one of those girls' eyes. I took them all for granted, took you for granted.'

I certainly wasn't prepared for that speech.

He'd witnessed something that day. He'd been forced to watch them drug his friends, friends who were so close he considered them family. I've never seen life become void, never seen the flame extinguished, but I can imagine it puts things into perspective.

Kayson ran a hand through his hair, tugging at the ends, his fingers trembling and then his entire hand.

'I've lost them, Naomi, I've lost them and there's nothing I can do.'

I sighed, trying to think how best to word my reply.

'Kayson, you've done something, you've planned this entire thing.'

'Naomi, I have sat and watched them for seven months. I watched as they trained, I watched as Harkness made Lily shoot a student for sport.'

Sport? What other horrors had Harkness inflicted?

'Because you were scared,' I said, putting an end to his list which to him I imaged was endless. 'It's alright to feel like that.'

He laughed. 'Soldiers don't get scared.'

'I think they do. Of course they might not show it, but I believe fear comes into it. There's something about the human mind, Kayson, no matter how much you want to stand up and fight there is always fear. After I saw what happened to Lily I nearly walked out the door, left them to fend for themselves.'

'That's what I've done.'

'But look at what you're doing now. You have a plan, focus on that.'

The tremor in his hand turned violent, but as soon as he

noticed my gaze he quickly hid it, tucking it under his jacket.

With everything these people have been through, it was no wonder they acted the way they did. Outbursts were met with torture, while others ended with a bullet between the eyes.

It wasn't guilt that lurked within Kayson. From what I could see, it was shame.

* * *

After flashing my ID at the guard on the gate, having a nervous breakdown while he had a good old stare at it, then mentally facepalming myself as I clearly needed to calm down, I was back into the Academy.

The night was cold and damp, the chill in the air only making my body shift closer to Kayson as I clung to his arm for dear life. These heels weren't doing me any favours and neither was the stupid blazer, which wasn't thermal in the slightest. It was freezing out here!

I couldn't tell if it was the cold glow of the lamps or the moon but I'd seen Kayson in a different light this evening. He was a man who needed help and wasn't afraid to admit it. He cared about his friends and wouldn't let them suffer any longer, and to me, that was everything.

'You good?' he asked, but I had a feeling he was talking about the heels rather than the arctic temperature.

'Fine, can't feel my toes but we'll manage.'

'Who needs toes anyway?' he joked.

You know what? Next time he could wear the stupid heels, see how he liked it.

Just as I was getting the hang of it, the sound of clicking began to echo, and then it started to lag. Now I wasn't a major in physics or an expert in sound waves, but I didn't think heel clicking lagged. Kayson stopped suddenly, but instead of that hard expression I'd come to know, it was soft.

I teetered around slowly to see a woman walking towards us – oh, so that's where the sound came from. She was dressed in an expensive looking power suit, with jet black curly hair, mocha skin and sporting a classic red lip. Note to self: invest in world-dominating fashion choices.

'Mr Ashford,' her voice rich like chocolate. 'You're lucky, I was just passing through.'

'Miss Ramos.' Kayson let go of my arm to shake the

woman's hand. 'Naomi, this is Nicola Ramos, the head of James's division at MI6.'

This was the girlfriend? James was punching! She was a goddess – even in the harsh light her skin glowed. I blinked quickly, holding out my hand for her to shake, which she did.

'Naomi Jade, nice to meet you,' I blurted.

Wow she was gorgeous, I wondered what skincare she used.

'Pleasure,' she replied, her London accent a little more prominent than I'd expected.

'Miss Ramos is the one who is going to solve all of our computer problems, she's a Techie at heart.'

A Technical Support leading an entire division, that was insane! I assumed all the secret services didn't work in the same way, but whatever she'd trained in must be the equivalent.

'I'm a little rusty but I'll see what I can do,' she said, and there was a knowing look on her face, bordering on disappointment. 'I've seen first-hand what these drugs do to the students. Let's start the operation to fix that, shall we?'

The playful grin returned to Kayson's face as he motioned

to the dorm house behind us. Nicola nodded, crossing her arms, and with that Kayson shot off. He knocked the door a couple times before barging right in, leaving it open – so that was our entrance plan.

Literally, walk through the front door.

When I took a couple of steps forward a sharp spasm shot through my ankle, jerking me to the left. I threw my hands out to get my balance, but it was like trying to walk a tightrope.

As I teetered to Nicola, I was met with a teasing smirk rather than a judgemental glower.

'Why on earth are you wearing those heels?' she asked, 'you can't even walk in them.'

'Kayson chose them.'

She rolled her eyes with a tut. 'Men.'

Nicola took off towards the house, slipping her heels from her feet and clutching them to her chest as she approached the front door. Welp, here we go again.

The heels were off my feet faster than my mother at the Boxing Day sales. Then, just for good measure, I chucked them in the bin. No one should have to wear those torture devices.

When I got to the door Nicola was already halfway up the stairs, the cold light from the hallway pouring onto the front steps. Before, it was inviting, but now the place was so cold and stale that it made my skin crawl. The once-luxurious wallpaper now dull and the gold accents aged. It was like I was stepping into a different building, the sweet floral scent that usually filled the hall replaced with sterile bleach. I wondered if the floor would light up if I shone a UV light.

Suddenly, Kayson's voice sounded from behind the closed kitchen door. 'What are you talking about?' he asked. 'That doesn't make any sense.'

Even though I wanted to know more, there was a job to do. Kayson could fill me in later.

I quietly tiptoed up the stairs, following Nicola to the next floor. The whole house was absent of laughter, of Lily's fiery comments.

As we reached the next floor I took the lead towards Quinn's room then stopped, leaning against the door. I listened for any movement or clacking of a keyboard, but there was nothing. Good, that meant she was downstairs. I opened the door gently, letting Nicola inside before closing it, pressing my back against it in relief.

That went smoother than I'd expected, but wasn't any less stress-inducing than before.

'I wouldn't celebrate yet,' Nicola told me. 'Getting in is the easy bit, it's getting out that's the challenge.'

OK Nicola, don't know if you know the script here but I'm a civilian! I would take all the small victories I could get.

She made her way over to the computer and loaded it up, sitting down at the desk. Anyone could tell she was an expert by the way she immediately went to work on the keyboard and analysed the monitor. Then there was me, armed with a USB hidden in a lipstick tube.

Nicola's fingers flew across the keys as she hacked into the computer, while I kept guard at the door. Kayson said he'd start yelling to warn us if anyone headed this way. Though we had Nicola, and I presumed she could pull rank.

'So tell me, how did a civilian like you end up in a place like this?' Nicola asked, snapping me from my thoughts.

'I knew the Team Lead in high school, she was acting

SLATE RETRIBUTION

strange and I wanted to know more,' I told her.

'Jessica-Grace, she's a difficult one.'

'You can say that again,' I muttered.

Jessica could be a double agent – she never told anyone the truth, and even if she did it was vague. Her brother wasn't here anymore so I presumed as soon as the op went sideways he was thrown out. If Lily had joined the dots, the superiors at MI6 probably did the same.

'She cares about her friends a lot.'

I almost snorted. 'Yeah . . . '

Nicola stopped typing and turned to face me. 'What was that for?'

I sighed. 'It's just with Jess there are a lot of rumours about her family. Lily, the Runner of the team, told me they have connections with Russia.'

'Do you believe them?' she asked. 'The rumours, or what she tells you?'

'Jess never told me anything, I practically had to force it out of her.'

'Don't you think there might be a reason for that?' she

asked, but then turned her attention to the monitor, beckoning me forward. 'I need you to check the footage, make sure it's all there.'

Could there be a reason? If it was about protecting me then that was just stupid. Was she afraid to admit something? There was always the possibility that she could have murdered her brother, but something told me there had to be more to the story. Where was the motive?

I slowly inched towards the screen, barely looking at it as Nicola flicked through the different clips. I just nodded every time I saw something familiar.

'Everyone's family has secrets, Jessica's especially, but they aren't for a malicious reason.' Nicola told me, her eyes drawing mine down. 'I know James, he didn't send you on that mission to die. You should have seen him pacing the room at Thames House. We sent helicopters in and a rescue team as soon as the comms went down, but for some reason we couldn't get a response until you'd fled the scene. He didn't conjure this up.'

'Why would you think we're blaming him for this?' I asked. How could she have known about our theories?

'I know people,' she said. 'James's family have been under scrutiny their whole lives. Personally, I don't think people should blamed for their parents' sins.'

What, so Jessica's parents were involved in this? Did Nicola know how this looked? It was her job to manage people, after all.

Just as I was about to rethink my theory, my fingers ran over a drawer handle and it slid right open. I jerked back, startled. Seriously! Inside was filled with stationery, organised meticulously. That's why the crumpled bit of paper that sat at an angle to everything else stood out like a sore thumb.

I wasn't paying attention to what Nicola was scrolling through on the monitor as I unravelled the thing.

Don't trust Jessica, her mother works for the Pyramid Delegates.

She's a monster, a murderer.

What the hell?

'You were saying?' I asked, holding up the paper for

Nicola.

Quinn had showed me some of her ex-lover's stuff and let me tell you, it was Willow's handwriting alright.

'These are the words of a dead girl,' I stated.

'Are you saying the dead don't lie?' she asked, plucking the USB from my hands and slotting it into the side of the computer. 'Because they do. Why do you trust Willow?'

'She hasn't given me a reason not to.'

'Have you ever actually met her?'

'No.'

'So, you're trusting the word of a dead girl you've never met over someone you're obviously close to?'

Was that what I was doing? Why would Willow write this if she didn't mean it? What reason did she have to lie?

'It's not just that, Lily doesn't trust her.'

'There's a little wobble in the ranks so you decide to cave?' she asked.

'Why are you making me out to be the bad guy here?'

'I'm just saying, you're not looking at all the facts.'

What facts?

SLATE RETRIBUTION

I crossed my arms over my chest trying to look anywhere but Nicola's face. Maybe she did have a point. Jessica lied about her family who had prominent connections with Russia, apparently, and she trained with the Pyramid Delegates before coming here, while her brother was a possible Trojan agent.

Nicola was dating James but I had a feeling she'd leave him if she found out he was with Trojan. It was clear she wasn't one to tolerate lies. It gave me hope, because if James truly didn't know what was going on, then perhaps Jessica didn't either.

There were too many variables with little to no evidence behind them, and the theories were endless, as if I was spinning around in the same circle: who was Jessica-Grace Winters?

I almost jumped out of my skin when a bleeping noise blared next to me – even Nicola seemed startled. She pulled out a black box from her pocket, springing up from the chair, and it was then I noticed the engagement ring on her finger . . . oh.

'You're gonna have to deal with this,' she said, pointing to the USB, her mind abruptly elsewhere.

Suddenly the thunder of feet outside the window and smacking of shoes bounced around the complex. I looked out the window to see the backs of Lily and Quinn, both sprinting towards the Academy.

'Me?' I asked, backing away. Every time I took out a USB it told me it wasn't ejected safely. 'What's happened?'

She shook her head, not even looking me in the eye.

'Deal with this and get out as fast as you can, find Kayson.' Nicola ordered before she took off out the room.

What the hell was all that about? Why were Quinn and Lily leaving in such a hurry? Had they gotten the same message as Nicola? She was the manager of a high division in MI6 so whatever had happened must have been an emergency.

Footsteps bounded down the corridor but they were heavy enough that I knew they belonged to Kayson, who stopped short at the door.

The look of sheer dread didn't leave his face, not for a second.

'There's been an accident.'

SLATE RETRIBUTION

CHAPTER 29

Fuilech

Valiant in battle.

JESSICA-GRACE WINTERS

I couldn't leave my team – if they wanted me that bad they'd have to drag me. I didn't care about MI6 orders, I was where I belonged. James didn't understand the good work we were doing here.

Of course I was grateful for the food he brought my team but he shouldn't have, the Academy cut supplies for a reason and we weren't in a position to question them.

Then, from the quiet, came a stampede.

Ames, Thompson and Dr McKay barrelled down the corridor ahead of me, shoving their way into one of the command rooms. I'd never seen anything like it before.

Heels lightly clicked from behind, it was Lennox, in her usual pristine attire, but then she grabbed my hand.

'You and me dear, we need to have a little chat in my office,' she said, trying to pull me in the opposite direction to the command room.

'I don't need a psychiatrist.' I said, pulling my hand from hers.

Faint shouts sounded from behind the closed doors – what was going on?

'You're to follow me,' Lennox demanded.

Something pricked in my stomach, a gut feeling, a notion that something was going terribly wrong. What was this? I had to follow orders, Lennox was a member of staff – but what was happening in the command room?

'I need to see what's going on in the command room.'

'What you need to do is come with me.' Her voice harsher this time.

I was meant to follow orders without question but this was too random. I've barely ever visited Lennox and now she just shows up out of the blue?

A wave of nausea ran up my throat, the warmth and sting of sick rising. Lennox started muttering under her breath as she grabbed my arms but I only pushed away. What time was it? Was I late taking my meds?

'Come on dear, let's get you back to my office. You're not well.'

I wasn't? I thought I was in perfect health.

Lennox grabbed for me again, but that was when the bubble of sick popped in my throat – I was gonna throw up. With a swift elbow into Lennox's side I fell against the wall, trying to breathe through the nausea, but it didn't stop there. It felt like someone was drilling an ice-pick into my eye and lights flared in my vision, everything becoming fuzzy.

What was happening?

Lennox's cold hands wrapped around my shoulders as she tried to guide me away, but then I heard it.

'Laurent, report!'

James? What was he doing out in the field? Why hadn't he told me? Why hadn't I seen him?

'Jessica dear, let's go to my office.' Lennox's voice, sickly sweet.

There was reassurance on her face but I knew something else grew in her heart. Wasn't she the one who'd introduced the new drugs?

'No.'

I pushed her away as hard as I could, stumbling towards the command room. Her nails scratched at my skin but I was too far away for her to grab me.

'Jessica!' she called after me, but I didn't look back.

I had to run.

Questions flooded my head, with possibilities I would never dream of. Then at the end of the corridor I saw the woman who was practically my sister.

'Nicola!' I shouted.

Something clicked in her and she broke into a smile, pulling me into an embrace. I hadn't seen her in months – hadn't I seen her today?

'You're you, right?' she asked.

'I think so.' I shrugged, pain spiking behind my eyes, but I screwed them shut trying to remember why I was so frantic in the first place, then it hit me. 'Why is James in the field?'

If anyone knew the answer it would be her – she was his boss after all.

I stared at the solid doors, knowing I needed a glimpse inside. If Harkness was in there and I stormed through he'd have me removed, but I needed to know why. Why was everyone running? Why was Nicola?

'He and a small team undertook the Black Scorpion operation.' Her voice was quiet but that didn't make the words any less powerful.

'Black Scorpion was meant for us,' I told her, trying to remember Duke's briefing from yesterday. 'It was given to the Academy.'

'James insisted,' Nicola told me. 'He thought he could get his team in without being caught.'

Without being caught, that meant – no.

I didn't think before throwing the doors open, my eyes going straight to the large monitor ahead. Brown rubble and broken bricks, dust falling like snow.

'What's going on?' I asked, turning to the faculty in front of me.

Harkness stood at one of the desks, Duke at his side while Ames and Dr McKay were busy on the phones. My eyes flitted upstairs to see Thompson behind the glass wall, frantically typing away at his computer.

'Winters, get out.' Harkness demanded.

'No.' I stood my ground, but didn't move any closer.

All the staff stopped when I refused, all slowly turning to me and then briefly to Harkness – even he looked surprised.

Ames didn't wait for orders, solely focusing on me.

'Trojan knew they were coming,' he said. 'The information was retrieved and sent back through the server but MI6 re-routed the feed here in the hope that we'd know how to deal with it.'

'Ames!' Duke roared.

'No one else has to die!' he yelled in return.

Die? James couldn't, he – he couldn't.

'Who authorised this?' I heard Nicola asked from behind.

'Your superiors. This was supposed to be our mission but

you thought you knew better,' Duke said condescendingly. 'Sending in a small team like that, what were you thinking?'

'I didn't sign off on this, someone above me did. James left before I could stop him.'

Someone above Nicola? I didn't even know who that was, no one did.

Why did they go out with a small team for something that required specific training and planning?

The video on the monitor shifted, rubble tumbling down, coughing spluttering through the speakers. It looked like an abandoned warehouse: huge plates of concrete had fallen, like the ceiling had collapsed in. The camera the feed was coming from was at a slant but it didn't obscure anything, especially what came next.

I wanted to run towards the screen as James crawled across the floor, his hair matted with blood and hands clawing at the ground. If he wasn't wearing white I wouldn't have seen the bright red stains that covered him from the neck down.

'James . . .' the word slipped out.

No, this couldn't be happening. He told me it wouldn't, not

to us. Why did he take this job in the first place?

'Laurent, report,' Harkness repeated.

I darted forward, grabbing one of the comm units that lay on the desk and shoving it in my ear. I needed to talk to him. We were going to figure a way out of this, together. Growing up he always told me there was a solution.

'Realistically, daily, we don't deal with ideal situations. That's what separates the circumstantial from the adaptable.'

That was all I needed to do, adapt.

'Laurent,' I said, trying to keep my voice even. 'We have you, are you in a safe position?'

'Get her out of there, she doesn't need to see this,' my brother warned.

Oh don't you dare, don't you – no, he wasn't saying that.

Nicola's trembling hands fell on my shoulder but I didn't move. James was going to be alright, I'd make sure of it.

I looked over to Dr McKay as he spoke. 'Medical team is thirty minutes out.' His shaking voice didn't fill me with confidence.

'Half an hour?' Ames asked. 'Can't they get there any

quicker?'

'Trojan are still firing bombs off in the lower town, they need more time to get through.'

I knew what they were saying, but that didn't mean I believed it. James had survived worse than this. It'd be fine, we'd get him out of there.

'Laurent, the medical team is on its way. You need to hang on,' I told him.

'Get out. I mean it, sweetheart.' His voice faltered.

I watched as he slumped, the grimace on his face deathly, his eyes screwing shut.

'I'm not leaving.' I'd stay by his side.

'Is she there, that amazing boss of mine?' he asked. 'Think I'll be fired after this.'

'Laurent, hang on, the medical team is coming. Is there somewhere safe for you to hide?'

'It's an imploded building and I've been shot twice, I think safe is a little out of the question. Besides, where else am I going to get a view of the stars?' James fell onto his back, arms thrown out.

Loud booms catapulted from the speakers but James didn't even flinch, he just stared at the sky.

'Why did you do this?' I asked. 'You're such an idiot, this isn't even your division.'

'Oh don't, you sound like Mum. She'd better not come to my funeral.'

'Shut up!' I yelled. 'We're going to get you out of there, you're coming back and when you do –'

'I'm dying, you can't yell at me.'

'No, you're not. You're not leaving, you can't.' I whipped my head to Harkness who only stared in disappointment – oh, fuck him. 'You need to send another team in there, to help the medics.'

'When will you learn you don't have the authority here?' His voice full of loathing.

'If we don't do something he will die!'

'Then he will bleed to death,' Harkness snapped.

I stumbled – how could he abandon him? Someone that I cared about, what about his loyalty to me? It goes both ways. I fought for the Academy, killed for them.

'Jess,' James's pained voice scratched in my ear, 'it's alright.'

'Why?' I asked. 'Black Scorpion, why?'

James hesitated.

'This op had a black stamp.' What? 'One of my team sent the recovered files from the stolen computers back to MI6.'

'Anything with that label is a suicide mission.' I practically slammed my hands on the desk, tears brimming in my eyes. 'Why?'

'Because at the end of the month it would have been you in this position. After last time, I couldn't let that happen again.'

Last time? The hotel, we were in Vienna with mum and I had a gun in my hand, my unconscious hand.

'Watching those men tear apart the room meant nothing, I thought you'd died and I prayed for a second chance. This was it, this was that chance.'

'You could have talked to me, we could have worked something out.'

A thick lump of metal dropped in the back of my throat as shivers wracked my body – this wasn't happening, it couldn't be. I felt the tired ache of tears springing to my eyes and a weighted migraine plunge deep inside; we couldn't be saying goodbye.

'We both know you've been gone. You didn't recognise me, sweetheart.'

When did James visit? I don't even remember him coming to the dorm house, did we meet in the Academy? Why couldn't I remember?

Thick arms wrapped around mine but I didn't give in. I twisted, jumping up with one leg and thrusting my hips back, sending Duke flying over my head. He crashed into the desk, his head smacking off of the table but I didn't care, no one was going to stop me this time.

'Don't make me call security,' Harkness threatened.

I marched right up to him without fear. I didn't try to hurt him, I just stood there. My brother was bleeding out and needed rescue, so whatever the consequences were, I would take them. The worst thing he could do was throw me in a cell and plug me full of drugs – I wouldn't remember my brother but at least he'd be alive.

'Do it,' I told him. He didn't scare me anymore, not when I

already knew what awaited me.

I tore down the command room to Dr McKay and Ames – now it was time to improvise.

'Give me a rundown, what's the situation?'

Without a single glance to Harkness, Ames pointed to the computer. 'The op is in Estonia. Long story short, Trojan started at the bottom and they've been working up through the country.'

'Doing what?'

'Bombs, shootings, mass murder,' Ames listed. 'The country is decimated but the medical team should get there soon, Trojan agents have left the scene.'

BOOM

'Rachel come in, Team Lead come in,' Dr McKay ordered down his phone. 'It's gone dead.'

I couldn't hide the horror anymore, we were supposed to be winning this war. My team had fought every single day and won every battle but now I understood, Trojan only had to win once.

BOOM

As the monitor began to shake, I asked, 'Can we get a

SWAT team?'

'Too far away.'

'Helicopter?'

'I can't just pluck one from thin air.'

'Use a phone, find me one!' I yelled. 'MI6 thought we could handle this so let's handle it!'

'Medic Team One have gone dark,' Dr McKay told me. 'There's no response.'

Fuck. Jessica, come on – take charge, you can do this, adapt to the situation. Damn the consequences. Think, think!

'Do we have any agents in the nearby area?' I asked.

Ames nodded. 'We have three.'

'We only need one. Get them on a helicopter and then reroute to the nearest hospital.'

Thompson scampered down the stairs shaking his head – what was that supposed to mean? Harkness made a move towards me, but Thompson grabbed his arm, whispering something into his ear which for once made him stop and listen.

Right, well fuck you, I'm busy.

My teeth clenched the inside of my mouth as I tried to

come up with a quicker exit strategy, a better plan. *Come on, think!*

'James Winters signing off, I'm gonna take my earpiece out. You all know how it ends.'

'Don't you dare!' I nearly screamed. 'James you can't, please.'

'It's gonna be OK, to hear your voice sweetheart, it gives me hope.'

'Hope?' I asked.

'That through it all, you're still there. You do this thing when you get upset, your voice cracks and you barely blink. I always thought it was like you were having an intense staring competition with yourself.'

That's when I clocked the ground beneath James, a sea of red. No, please no. How much blood was there? The limit of the human body was 40%, how was I supposed to tell if he'd lost that much?

'When you were younger and you couldn't figure out how to read, you'd get so frustrated. Throw the book across the room, but you got there in the end,' James said.

'Yeah, cause you taught me how,' I said, nodding, 'I remember.'

'Mum wasn't much help, someone had to.'

I couldn't tear my eyes away, it was like they were glued to the screen. James lay there shivering in a pool of his own blood and there was nothing I could do about it.

A clammy hand clasped mine.

'Jessica, you really don't want to see this.'

Fresh tears sprung to my eyes. I was supposed to be able to do this, we trusted each other, how could I let him die?

'I'm not leaving, we promised each other.'

'I'm sorry, sweetheart,' James tried, but I slammed my hand down.

'No!' I cried. 'You're all I have left, I can't lose you!'

I turned to Ames but he no longer had a phone in his hand, he just shook his head.

The medical team had gone dark, a rescue mission was out of the question and now James was bleeding out – this couldn't be happening.

I would be nothing without him – I had to do something!

'Tell my boss that I love her,' he said. 'But I need you to do something for me. Keep fighting.'

It was like an earthquake had ransacked my body, threatening to break every bone.

'I can't, not without you.'

'Promise me you won't stop fighting.'

I couldn't do this anymore.

A sob burst from my mouth, pain piercing through me like needles – he couldn't say goodbye. Everything we did together, everything we fought for would mean nothing. I remembered now he said he would help us.

'Promise me.'

'Promise,' I lied.

'No, promise me, Jess. Promise me you won't stop fighting.'

How could I? I'd be thrown in a cell, I'd forget about all of this.

The rough material of scrubs and jeans rubbed back and forth as Dr McKay and Ames left the room, Duke motionless on the desk – *No! Stop pretending it isn't real! James needs you!*

There must be something else, some helicopter or a SWAT team nearby, there had to be, I had to think of something.

'OK,' I told him with a firm nod. It wasn't a lie – I'd promised to keep fighting and that's what I'd do, until he came back.

'I love you, sweetheart.' His voice was soft, without grit or pain, and I wondered what that would feel like.

'I love . . . thank you, for everything.'

I couldn't think what to say, what to do or what to think, everything was blank.

My eyes returned to the pool beneath James and all of a sudden, it'd grown bigger.

'James don't go!'

I couldn't be strong, not like him, everything was crumbling.

BOOM

The camera shook this time, falling from its place and skidding down the rubble. All I could see was the sky that raged like a tsunami, but the stars glittered like sea glass, the moon a giant pearl among it all. The night sky was screaming, one cloud crashing over another, and I wanted to scream too.

'Look at the sky Jess, just look at the sky.'

BOOM

The monitor fell to black.

'James?' I asked, but all I got was static in return. 'James, answer me!'

In one swift motion I threw everything from the desk to the floor. This couldn't be happening, no, no, no, he couldn't be gone. This was just some plan, he'd faked his death before. He'd be alright, of course he would – no, he wouldn't. He'd been shot twice, lost a significant amount of blood and fell who knows how many storeys as a building collapsed. James was dead.

I screamed.

Everything that had been bubbling inside of me for so long let rip. I screamed so hard and for so long that my vocal chords felt ready to snap. Willow was dead, Dr Williams was dead, my brother was dead, my team were mindless and in a couple of hours I would be too.

'Grab her,' I heard Harkness say.

I didn't have time to move before two sets of hands

grabbed me by the shoulders. Everything I'd learned was thrown out the window as I thrashed and screamed. He had to be OK, he had to be!

Nicola's yells were barely audible as I was dragged from the command room, the cold air from the hallway hitting me like a brick wall. Ames and Dr McKay stood there, not two metres away from me, but they were looking the other way. Why weren't they doing anything? Why were they not stopping this?

'Let go of me!' I writhed, but the air caught in my throat.

Just as I lifted my head I saw them, Lily and Quinn, standing like statues at the end of the corridor, their faces completely blank.

'Move out of the way!' Harkness ordered and without a second's hesitation, they split to the sides, their backs to me.

'Quinn!' She didn't move. 'Lily!' Not even a flinch.

CRACK

My head rocked to the side as someone's knuckles cracked off my cheekbone, the sting reverberating through my entire body. Now there was nothing to lose, and I didn't give a fuck, they were going to hear me scream! It may be the last time anyone did.

Before I knew it we were down in the lower levels and then I was flying, the world spinning as pain bludgeoned through my skull – they'd thrown me down the stairs. Every curve and edge hit my ribs, every crack and step sending nothing but agony through me. I tumbled down each flight until my body rolled to a stop and I gasped for air.

'That's what it takes, emotion?' Harkness' voice echoed. 'That's what it takes to break the cycle. One burst of emotion. Well there will be no more of that now, will there.' His fingertips caressed my hair but then he grabbed it in a fist, yanking me to my knees. I cried out but, as always, he didn't care. 'Because now, Winters, you're alone.'

Everything started spinning again as my body lifted off the ground – all I could see was the green paint of the floor, but now it was spotted with something darker. The smell of piss and shit meeting my nose, catching in the back of my throat. I heard the creaking and clanking of a cell door as it opened.

The darkness sat waiting for me like an animal and then, it consumed me.

SLATE RETRIBUTION

CHAPTER 30

Carnifex

An executioner.

DANIEL HARKNESS

Lunacy, sheer insanity. Who did MI6 think we were, babysitters? Sending their agents into the field on an op they knew nothing about. Complete idiots.

James was right to be paranoid that Thames House had been infiltrated: according to the agents I had posted there, he rarely showed up.

The new strain of drugs have luckily had a lasting effect: Lily Chan shot someone, not for sport, because I told her to. Winters Jr. shot a first year this morning on Duke's orders, but now she's been reduced to a snivelling mess. Pathetic. Emotion was the key. If I could perfect the drug, with regular doses of course, this state of compliance could be permanent. Then I would have soldiers for the war.

Terrorists weren't the problem, someone had to do something about our current climate. If they stopped to think then maybe I wouldn't have to go through what I do every day.

The Omega team were tricky to handle at the best of times, but now they'd been subjected to the correct course of medication, any risk they posed dwindled. I'll never forget their former Carrier, Willow Mae, the hardest of them all to control. She'd discovered the money trail from my computer and followed it, to fifty megatons of explosives. Ultimately she found out Gabriel Hale was working for Trojan after she discovered I'd paid him to take care of the bomb. Although I hadn't deduced if she'd figured out my plan yet, it didn't matter now, she was dead. One of my agents shot her after all.

Nicola Ramos was my next problem: she hadn't seen anything but no doubt James had shown her compromising footage. She had to be dealt with, discreetly. Perhaps she could be useful here? Thompson caved after I shot his wife and threatened his son, everyone had a pressure point, I just had to find hers.

Now, Jessica-Grace Winters, throw her in the cells for a week, enforce daily doses of the drug and she'd be wiped clean. I'd have my agent back in no time. She was the perfect specimen and yet everything and everyone was getting in the way: her brother, her team and a particular agent, Christopher Barnes.

She thought she walked around this world unnoticed, but I owned her.

As I stared at the useless girl pining for the impossible, a thought lingered at the back of my mind. For this to work she had to believe she was utterly alone, though of course she wasn't. Charlotte told me herself, but best to keep her in the dark.

Then all of a sudden Jessica flipped, started commanding my staff. Look at her go, there was the Charlotte in her. My joy was interrupted when that weasel Thompson scurried over, whispering in my ear.

'Every one of us knows he didn't go into the field willingly.'

'I don't know what you're talking about. He chose to go.'

'It's not like you gave him much of a choice.'

SLATE RETRIBUTION

Ultimatums work exceptionally well under the right circumstances: James didn't want to see his poor little sister crushed by a building or plugged with bullets. I'd given James the Black Scorpion briefing last week and gave him a choice: Jessica could go with her team, or he could. Simple. Of course he chose to sacrifice himself, James was a man of honour. I admired his valour but not his stupidity. James was one of the best interrogators in this country but he gave it all up for one of my agents.

I know he helped raise the girl but as I proved, the pathetic love for his sister was his downfall. We were better off without him.

Everyone in the industry will know that James Winters hijacked this operation for his own purposes, and that the so-called information he retrieved was sent directly to Trojan. When this goes to court it will be made clear that Mr Winters conspired with known terrorists, planning to decimate countries and murder thousands of people.

At least, that's what I'll tell everyone.

EMERY HALE

CHAPTER 31

Dies Irae

Day of wrath.

NAOMI JADE

Our feet pounded the tarmac, the measly short path stretching on for eons, the wretched building always just out of reach. Kayson told me that James's team had taken the Black Scorpion mission without Nicola's consent.

The soft breeze turned arctic as the moon beamed down on us like a spotlight – would anyone see us? Report us?

I kept to Kayson's back as we sprinted down the small path and up the stairs to the main reception. A small hole burrowing open through the toe of my tights. As soon as we got inside he took off to the left and I was about to follow when I heard it – a scream of utter anguish tearing through the halls, but it wasn't Lily's, it was Jessica's. The sound pierced my heart, ripping through my body.

Had James died?

Kayson continued, charging ahead, the sound driving him forward while it brought me to a standstill. I know what I said about Jess, but that didn't mean I wished her harm.

The corridor was long and narrow, one I hadn't seen before, the shadows creeping towards me, the walls resembling catacombs rather than concrete. Doesn't the girl who walked down a dark corridor towards a scream usually die in the movies? Dammit.

Even though I wanted to screw my eyes shut I kept them wide open, taking off down the corridor. My imagination leapt to life, pictures and cabinets morphing into gruesome monsters, door handles reaching out to grab me. Reality hit me when I saw a flicker of red hair tossed down the corridor, stalked by a dark silhouette, Harkness. His posture was rigid but then something leapt out, like a primeval raptor chasing its prey.

Kayson hooked an arm around my waist, tugging me to the side, but I wasn't done. We couldn't leave Jessica to that savage!

'Kayson!' I whispered harshly.

'She's going to isolation, we're outnumbered, and if Harkness catches us, we're screwed.'

'Us?' I asked. 'Her brother could be dead.'

'Do you want to join him?'

The question bought my silence.

As the hallway cleared we scuttled down the corridor quiet as mice, making sure to stay close to the wall, as the shadows provided some cover. Ahead I saw two smaller figures, heads bowed and bodies still as water. When I turned to Kayson, the same look of shame I'd seen in the car had returned. I guessed the shorter figure was Quinn, so the other one had to be Lily, since she was considerably taller than any of the others, but they didn't look like themselves. Their clothes were grey and their dull faces almost blended in with the wall.

Kayson brought a finger to his lips with a mischievous grin before he threw me back into an alcove, my arms flailing to catch myself. What the hell was he playing at? Was he just going to leave me here?

He was blatantly loud as he walked – was he drawing their

attention for a specific reason? Was I meant to do something? Sneakily, I peeked around the wall.

'Orders from upstairs, you've both to go to the medical bay straight away.' Kayson was firm, but I had no idea what he was on about.

'Whose orders?' Lily asked, but her voice was dull, without an ounce of fire.

'Don't know, don't care.'

Why was he sending them to the medical bay? Was there another part of the plan Kayson hadn't told me about?

Silence lingered in the air then collective footsteps receded down the corridor. But then another, lighter set of footsteps made their way towards me. I couldn't tell who they belonged to; I was sure Kayson's were heavier. Could it be Lily?

I raised my hands just like I'd practiced then swung – and by the time the familiar leather jacket came into view, it was already too late.

SMACK

Kayson staggered back, a hand shooting up to his nose.

'What did you do that for?'

'I thought you were Lily,' I whispered.

'So you thought you'd punch your way out,' he muttered, pinching his nose.

'Sorry.' My hands danced in their air, unsure what to do. Kayson didn't seem to be in too much pain but I still felt terrible. He'd apologised for everything, so punching him the face didn't feel like payback anymore.

'Come on,' Kayson said, heading to the right. 'We'll take the stairs.'

'Why the medical ward?' I asked.

'Cause you punched me in the face.' Kayson looked back to me, and the playful smirk I'd grown to like sat there. 'Nah, Dr McKay is waiting up there, he's going to try one of his experimental treatments on Lily, Grace and Quinn. Hopefully we should have them back by morning. Sorry I didn't tell you, kind of a whirlwind that this plan is even working at all.'

Hold up, he'd gotten a doctor involved? He remembered what happened last time, right?

'Kayson, Harkness shot the last doctor that tried to do that,' I said.

'Believe me, I wasn't the one who came up with this part of the plan. Dr McKay was.'

'He – what?'

Kayson pushed open the door to the stairwell and as I pressed my hand against the cool wood the whistling wind hurtled through me. Now I didn't believe in bad omens but that felt like one of them.

'The faculty are starting to have doubts,' he said. 'Well, all the medical staff are, and there's rumours that Ames and Thompson are starting to question Harkness.'

'But wouldn't Harkness just get rid of them?'

'Can't kill everyone. Harkness must need them, he'll hurt their loved ones.'

Loved ones? Harkness must be the ringleader of it all, and if he had to threaten his staff's family, this really was a cult.

Unlike last time, we walked up the stairs at a steady pace. Kayson had this all planned out, siding with a superior of MI6 and an Academy doctor. This was a full-blown rebellion.

As Kayson pushed his way onto the ward, I stuck to his back. The entire floor was quiet, with only small murmurs floating in the air. The beds were emptier than before, only three were filled, and I knew all the occupants: Grace, Lily and Quinn.

Grace lay flat on the bed, a thin blanket tucked around her soundly-sleeping figure. Had they sedated her?

Lily seethed as Dr McKay struggled to pin her to the bed – Kayson ran from my side to take her legs as she thrashed. Was their great plan to sedate them all?

'Get the needle in!' Kayson demanded.

'Hold her still!'

As much as I wanted to help I knew that I couldn't, so I set my sights to Quinn. She didn't even flinch; fresh bruises marked her forearms. My teeth ground together: had Harkness done that to her? Thompson?

'Quinn?' I asked, but made sure to keep my distance.

Then she presented her arm to me, but her face remained blank. Did she think I was going to inject her with something?

Slowly, Lily's protests quietened, the laboured breathing of the men overpowering her voice. Dr McKay grabbed something from the nearest cart and hooked it up to an IV pole before injecting the receiving end into Lily's arm.

Kayson focused on straightening out her body, his hands gentle. I turned my attention back to Quinn and cautiously walked towards her.

'Quinn?' I asked again, but her eyes didn't falter.

Dr McKay's warm palm pressed against my shoulder.

'She won't respond. Lily fights every time no matter what she's up here for, Quinn just takes it.'

'She does?' I could scarcely believe it.

'The drug is cognitive – it wipes out anything that Harkness doesn't want in there. She cried the second time but after that, nothing.'

The Quinn I knew would fight; the girl in front of me was just an empty shell.

A tug on my sleeve pulled me to my feet, and Kayson led me away from the bed. The way he placed his hand on my back, it was like he didn't want me to see what Dr McKay was doing as he moved to her bedside.

'Kayson, I know he's desperate for soldiers or whatever, but there's no need for this,' I said.

'I hate to break it to you, but shouting morals at Harkness

SLATE RETRIBUTION

isn't going to do anything.'

'You had to sedate them, for the love of God.' The entire thing was horrific. Did Lily even know who she was fighting against? Fighting for? How many interrogations had she undergone while I was tucked up in bed at night?

My hand fell over my mouth as I began to pace: how could we be sure this plan would work? Was there any of the original flame left in Lily anymore? Did Quinn still have a spark of hope? If the drug was cognitive it would wipe the slate clean – would any remnants of who they were be tucked away, or had the Academy obliterated them?

'Hey, hey.' Kayson took my arms but I tried to push away. I didn't want to be near him right then, I needed to think. 'Naomi, look at me.'

With a firm shove I untangled myself from his grip and scampered to the other side of the ward, flinging a set of doors open. I needed to breathe.

The lipstick-tube memory stick rested in my pocket – I should have been high-tailing it out of there, but for some reason I couldn't bring myself to leave. The teams' faces haunted me, screams and cries echoing through my head. Now I'd seen the situation, how could I leave them? How could anyone?

Yes, I was terrified, but the thrashing body of Lily, the still figure of Grace, the empty expression of Quinn and the heart-wrenching scream from Jess made my feet stick to the ground like glue.

They protect us, but who protects them? Answer: I will.

I'd calmed down a little and was ready to walk back on the ward, when the television at the end of the corridor grabbed my attention:

BREAKING NEWS: ESTONIA DECIMATED IN TERRORIST ATTACK

There was no sound, but the headline read clear enough. This must have been why James was out in the field, to try and stop it. He couldn't be working for Trojan – he really was dead wasn't he?

'Naomi, listen, I know it's a lot.' Kayson threw open the doors, darting to my side, but stopped short when his eyes fell to the television. 'It's started.'

'Started?' I whipped around. 'What do you mean, started?'

'Trojan, they're taking control.'

The doors burst open again but this time Dr McKay marched through, his eyes fixed on the screen.

'I knew it,' he said. 'This whole thing has been a set-up from the beginning.'

'You knew about this?' Kayson asked directly, on the defensive.

But the doctor shook his head. 'James commandeered an op that was meant for us. The info was transferred back to base but the whole thing was a massacre. Black stamp.'

'Black stamp?' I asked.

'Suicide mission. They're always given to us and recently Harkness has been dishing them out to the seniors. All except this one.'

Suicide missions? Why would anyone hand those out in the first place?

'What information?' Kayson asked.

The doctor shrugged. 'Damned if I know, it's important

though.' He pointed to the screen. 'But that – that was supposed to happen. We thought we were winning but really, we were playing right into their hands.'

Harkness had to be working for Trojan, it was the only thing that made logical sense – he was the mole in one of the highest ranking jobs in the country. If the seniors were already drugged they wouldn't even know if they were working for the winning side; you could palm them off to Trojan and they'd never know the difference . . .

'How many black stamp ops have been issued?' I shot out.

Dr McKay shook his head. 'Don't know if you've noticed, kid, but I'm in scrubs, I don't assign ops.'

Kayson looked at me expectantly. 'Why do you want to know that?'

'I have a theory,' I said.

Kayson pointed down the corridor, his feet dancing like there were ants in his shoes. 'Come on, we'll be able to sneak into one of the tech suites.' Then, like a shot, he took off.

I did have a theory: it was a crazy one, but not impossible.

Jessica always talked about a war but I'd never heard of

such things – there were protocols in place to prevent them. But what if the terrorists wrote the protocols? What if the Reign Academy was training soldiers for Trojan?

* * *

The tech suites were huge, taking up the last section of the fourth floor. As I walked in Kayson was already sat down at a computer pulling up files. The room smelt of stale coffee and biscuits; brown stains and crumbs littered the white desks.

'OK, you want black stamp ops?' Kayson asked, fingers clicking on the keyboard.

'Yes.'

Another couple of clicks.

'OK, here we go.'

'I thought you said you weren't a computer genius? How'd you get access to these?'

'Well the Academy is run on a main server, it's really complicated, you wouldn't understand." I could tell he was lying through his teeth and my thoughts must have transmitted to my face because he sighed in defeat. 'Alright, before everything went tits up Quinn showed me how to get into Helen's account.'

I sat down, peering into the monitor. Countless files littered the screen, none of which had obvious labels, but as Kayson clicked on the first one I knew instantly what it was: crime scene photos. Blonde hair matted with blood and an ID card. Willow Mae's.

'Shit,' Kayson muttered, and clicked to the next document. As he scanned it over he let out a breath, inching closer to the screen. 'Codenames, these will be the people involved in the attack.'

'Are there seniors here?' I asked.

Kayson scanned over the list of names before singling one out, Artist.

'That one, I know him. Fuck.'

'Kayson, you aren't preparing to fight Trojan, you're soldiers for them.'

When the words slipped from my mouth it looked like he stopped breathing, his hand clenching the mouse. His usually unreadable face now snarled in anger – I honestly thought he was going to launch the computer through the window.

'I'm going to kill him,' Kayson said. 'I'm going to fucking

kill him.'

But he didn't throw the chair back or punch a hole through the wall, he continued looking through the files, each click of the mouse louder than the last.

There were files and pictures I didn't recognise, but then a small grainy picture at the bottom of the screen caught my eye: a boy sat in front of a tree, dead. Was that Quinn's friend?

The next file was filled with maps and aerial photos: Brora, the op I'd signed on as a Carrier for. It clearly stated the intention to ambush us from behind; they knew everything, right down to the exit plan. The folder after that was marked Black Scorpion and was laid out exactly the same. Estonia was planned out to the letter: where the team would go and how to. . . take out the backup medical team, listed as collateral damage underneath.

How far had the human race sunk? I felt sick, the spicy bile rising in my throat.

When Kayson clicked on another folder I tore my eyes away, but immediately turned back: it was a video and the sound blared. Clips were jammed together like a video package, footage from Brora and Estonia. I saw the clips they'd played on the TV, then some others from a theatre dressing room, two bodies lying motionless on the floor. The footage from Brora I soon realised was from my lapel camera: someone must have found it.

'They planned this from the beginning, the bastards. Even prepared that for the press. Sending us to Brora, the theatre, the bank, they were making propaganda,' Kayson spat.

'What for?' I asked.

'National panic.' His eyes ignited with a rough darkness, and I almost pulled away.

'What are you doing?' I asked as he closed everything down and clicked on the internet.

'National panic is just that, panic. It doesn't last for long.'

'I'm sure it does,' I said, as if it was obvious. If my mum saw this whole thing on the TV, she'd be running around the house like a loony, packing a bag.

News headlines popped up one after the other.

AIRPORTS CLOSING THEIR GATES

PRIME MINISTER UNACCOUNTED FOR

BUCKINGHAM PALACE REMAINS

SLATE RETRIBUTION

SILENT

TERRORISTS WALK AMONG US

ARE WE SAFE? WHO CAN WE TRUST?

'This isn't something they decided months ago, this has been years in the planning.' Kayson's voice shook as he stood up, but it wasn't fear, it was anger. 'The agents we fought in Brora, at the theatre, even Estonia – they weren't just Trojan agents, they were us.'

The Reign Academy wasn't training agents to fight against Trojan, they were conditioning assassins to join their ranks.

I imagined Kayson wanted Harkness dead, his head on a spike, but what does it take from you, killing someone? It must crumple and twist a part of your soul. I knew they were trained but there was a difference between a target and a human being.

'We're gonna fight back,' I said confidently. Every ounce of flight response had left my body; we were going to stop this.

Suddenly Kayson took off from his seat, legging it from the room and down the corridor, his leather boots smacking loudly against the floor.

'Where are you going?' I called after him.

'Armoury, we're bringing the war to them.'

SLATE RETRIBUTION

CHAPTER 32
Mettle

The courage to carry on in the face of adversity.

NAOMI JADE

1 May 2016, 21:00

Scotland, The Reign Academy, Omega Dorm House

Sleep crumbled in my eyes as I pulled the tangled sheets from my legs, the warm linen for once bringing me no comfort. As soon as we'd reached the armoury on the second floor, Kayson had grabbed multiple bags and started firing in everything from guns to hand grenades.

We'd decided it was best to set up a base so we headed back to Grace's room at the dorm house. We'd pushed her desk to the middle of the room, and laid out all of the weaponry: to see it sitting there made my blood run cold. The way Kayson had meticulously placed everything down on the table was quiet, but his body screamed of hate. The way his nostrils flared, his stiff

SLATE RETRIBUTION

upper lip and precision as he loaded a gun. With every slam and click I knew he didn't need a weapon: he was one.

Kayson slept in Jessica's room while I'd stayed in Quinn's. I even sprayed some of her perfume that was tucked away in a drawer. It brought me a little petal of happiness, and I thought that's all we can hope for in the end because sometimes, a little is enough.

I pushed straggles of hair from my face as I sat up in bed, and as I did the cool metal of the gun Kayson had given me slipped into my hand. He'd given it to me in case we were somehow found out during the night, even though I didn't know how to use the damn thing.

I got changed, slipping back into my clothes from the day before, tucking the gun into the waistband of my jeans (although I did still have a fear of blowing my ass off). Kayson had mentioned something about putting the safety lock on, which I sincerely hope he did before he handed it over.

The thought that the Academy was training soldiers for Trojan and making them chemically compliant still brought bile to my throat, it was barbaric. I'd never really seen the seniors – not even the team mentioned them. Did they know they were fighting for terrorists? Did they ever question who they worked for?

When I looked out of the window students were walking about as normal, like they didn't know the first thing about this place. I even saw a group of girls laughing hysterically, holding onto the person next to them so they didn't fall over. I feared I'd never able to go back to that, carefree and naive. None of us would be able to; we weren't those kids anymore.

A knocked sounded at the door as Kayson walked in, his eyes red with tiredness and hair greasy, but he'd put on a fresh shirt.

'Thought you should be kept in the loop with what's going on out there,' he started, shoving his hands into his pockets. 'Nicola ran, she's underground.'

'Ran?' I asked, crossing my arms.

'The Academy will go after her, she's a new target for Harkness. He can use people like her, but if he can't find her then at least she'll be safe.'

Did Harkness want everyone to join his ranks? Join or die.

'So, we really are on our own then,' I said, but this time it

SLATE RETRIBUTION

wasn't a question.

No one from the outside could help. James was dead, Nicola was on the run and Dr McKay could only do so much.

Suddenly the front door opened and my hand instantly went to the gun – what was I doing? I couldn't fire this thing! No one else was meant to be here, all of the team were stuck at the Academy. A look of steel solidified over Kayson's face as he grabbed his own gun and edged down the corridor towards the stairs.

We trickled out of the room, guns at our side as we made our way to the top of the stairs. There was a sound of multiple footsteps on the wooden floor and then the door slammed shut. Had Harkness sent a team to sweep the place?

Kayson slowly bent down, taking off his shoes before silently descending the stairs, what class did he learn that in? My hands clenched the gun as I held my breath, the weapon rattling. Kayson tiptoed down the first set of stairs pointing his gun straight ahead at the door, without even thinking I ran down the stairs after him doing the same – but at the sight ahead, I nearly dropped the thing.

'Woah fire thong!' Lily yelled throwing her hands up in the air.

'You gave her a gun? Is the safety on at least?' Grace asked, hands pressed to her hips.

'You're back!' Quinn exclaimed.

'Fuck me,' Kayson muttered. 'It worked?'

'Well of course it did.' Grace threw her hands up like it was obvious. 'Now, can you stop pointing a gun at me.'

Kayson apologised, tucking it back into his jeans, but I just let mine fall to the carpet as I threw myself down the stairs, flinging my arms around Quinn, her small hands curling around my waist as she hid her face in the crook of her neck.

I was so glad to have them back, I didn't know what I'd do without them.

Then I pulled away, grabbing Lily's hand and yanking her into a hug. She awkwardly patted me on the back before I turned to Grace.

'I'm really not –' but I didn't give her another moment to think before I threw my arms around her '– a hugger.'

'I don't care,' I said squeezing her tight, and after a couple seconds I smiled, because Grace returned the hug.

They were back, the team was back, now we just had to rescue its leader.

***

We led the three girls up the stairs – they still seemed a little woozy but didn't complain, and Kayson and I made sure we were available should anyone decided to pass out. No one had come back around from these drugs before, so we had no idea if they'd be totally fine or keel over at any moment. Dr McKay's little experiment actually worked wonders, hopefully it didn't run out.

When we reached Grace's room she wasn't pleased that we'd moved everything around, but we came to a mutual understanding, once Kayson explained why all of this was necessary. Lily went straight for the weapons table, picking up a couple to inspect, while we all filtered in the room. And that was when the other shoe dropped, and Kayson told them why they were training in the first place: for Trojan.

The reaction was sheer silence: not what I expected.

Lily placed the gun back on the table, Grace politely sat down on the chair and Quinn hovered towards the door, her eyes flitting to Willow's old room across the hall.

'All this time, we've been the enemy? The Trojan agents were us?' Lily asked.

'The bomber in the theatre,' Grace said. 'I knew I recognised him from somewhere, the one on the lighting rig. He must have been a senior, we barely ever see them so it's possible.'

'No,' Quinn shook her head 'The Academy can't be their only source of agents, there's too many.'

Lily bit her lip.

'I say we get Harkness, Duke and the rest of these fuck-ups in a room then blow them straight to hell.' With a slam she loaded ammo into a sniper rifle.

'We can't do that,' I said. 'We need to know what they're planning.'

'I might have a way to find out,' Quinn said softly.

What? How the hell did she know already? I thought her brain would have been scrambled from the drugs. Quinn left the room and crossed the hall, then after a bit of banging and clattering, returned with a black tablet in hand.

'This was Willow's, the idea came to me before we had

the second round of drugs. She'd always said she was onto something but would never tell me what.' Quinn tapped the device a couple times before the screen illuminated. 'I didn't have the resources to put the pieces together before.'

She handed the tablet to Grace who scrolled for a while but by the look on her face, she hadn't found anything.

'All I have is some place called Newhaven Harbour along with a fruit and veg delivery slip for the Academy.' she said, looking up.

'What really?' Quinn took another look at the tablet. 'If I encrypted it then there must be something.'

'Your brain was scrambled love, who knows what you thought you were doing.' Grace looked like she was about to dismiss the whole thing when she paused, peering a little closer at the screen. 'Wait . . . ' She stood up, showing the tablet to the rest of us. 'I don't know about anyone else but I've never heard of a fruit called Svenreud.'

'Must be a typo.'

Grace shook her head.

'I would have thought that too but there's nothing even

remotely similar to this.' She spun the tablet to portrait and started going through the same file again.

Lily laughed.

'A harbour and a delivery slip, not exactly damning evidence.'

When I took a closer look nothing seemed out of the ordinary – there was a reference number, the Academy's address and then the list of food. What was Grace getting at? Quinn popped her head over Grace's shoulder, eyes scanning the screen like a laser. If she'd encrypted it months ago then it must have meant something – it had to.

'The reference number,' Grace said, zooming in on it.

Kayson snatched the tablet before tossing it back down.

'All I see are the letters X, I and V.'

'Yeah, that's called roman numerals, try to keep up,' Grace snapped, taking the tablet back. 'There must be a code somewhere.'

Grace crouched down pulling one of the drawers in the table open, taking out a paper and pen, then in one swift motion swept all the weaponry to the floor. Kayson and Lily cried out in protest she but didn't pay them any mind as she scribbled down the translated numbers.

13, 1, 25, 19, 5, 3, 15, 14, 4.

'So now you've wrecked my guns and we have a bunch of random numbers. Great, thanks Grace, really glad to have you back,' Kayson said spitefully collecting the weapons from the floor.

But Quinn perked up like a cat. 'No . . . ' she trailed off. 'It can't be that simple.'

'Guys, start talking.' Lily said. Apart from the two enlightened ones, we were clueless.

Instead of talking, Grace started to scribble and I soon caught on that each number was a letter of the English alphabet. 'A' being number one. She played about with the numbers before spinning the paper around.

MAY SECOND

'May second, what like the date?' I asked.

Grace smirked. 'Whatever Harkness is planning goes down at Newhaven Harbour on the second of May, which is tomorrow.'

They had to be joking, that was it?

Suddenly Quinn grabbed the tablet and typed away frantically – seriously, the smart people in the room needed to explain this to us common folk.

'Quinn?' Lily asked. 'I know the drugs took away our memories and shit, but it didn't take away your voice.'

'Sorry,' Quinn fumbled as she turned the tablet to the rest of us. 'Newhaven Harbour is near here and there is a boat leaving there called the Verendus.'

'That's not the same name as the weird fruit,' Kayson said, like he was talking to a child.

'Yeah, it is.' As soon as she spoke I knew Quinn was about to hand Kayson's pride right back to him on a silver platter. 'It's an anagram.'

The only man in the room looked down at the table, fiddling with a magazine clip. 'Well yeah, that's obvious now, I didn't even get a good look at the thing.'

'Let's just say, Kayson, there's a reason you're the Runner,' Quinn muttered under her breath.

'Oi!' Lily called, 'I'm a Runner too.'

'Yeah but sweetheart,' Grace cut in, 'your cock isn't shoved up your ass.'

I didn't know where to look or stand – now the team was back I felt out of place. When it was Kayson things were easier, but Grace and Quinn had everything figured out in ten minutes. Did Willow ever feel like this? The Carrier was supposed to get info and then get out – strictly speaking she didn't have to be a part of this process.

'Look!' Quinn exclaimed suddenly, pointing to the slip. 'There's twenty-two fruits and forty-five vegetables.'

'Quinn, speak English!' Lily shouted right back.

'Twenty two, forty-five. It's a time – quarter to eleven at night. That's when the boat is going to be there.'

Grace laughed proudly.

'We have a date, time and location. Honestly, Kayson, what would you do without us?'

That was when Kayson said something I'd never expected. 'You should thank Naomi.'

'I'm sorry?'

'I put the plan together to get you guys back but Naomi

was the one who figured out the link in the black stamp files. She put the whole thing together.'

Three heads snapped my way and I immediately wanted to curl back, all the attention flustering me a little. I assured myself that it was my place to put things together, and that I'd done the right thing despite everything Jessica had said.

I was met with three very different faces. Grace's was masked in utter shock, Lily's was the cheeky smirk I missed so dearly, while Quinn's toothy grin was practically bouncing off the floor.

'It was, uh . . .' I trailed off, unable to think of the words. 'Maybe you just needed an outside perspective. You guys live here and see the same things and people every day. Just needed a fresh set of eyes is all.'

Quinn sucked in a breath before walking over to me. She reached up, scraping something from my forehead.

'Wig glue,' she chuckled. 'Listen, don't ever put yourself down. You figured this out.'

'You and Grace just figured out a code – you had a tablet hidden away that we wouldn't have found for ages.'

Quinn took my hand.

'That why we're a team. Kayson planned to set us free, you figured out the true purpose of the Academy, Grace and I figured out the code.'

'And what did I do?' Lily piped up.

'You're the view.'

'Oh Quinn, I love it when you talk sexy.'

Quinn blushed, tucking hair behind her ear and biting her lip, and I had one thought: *God she's adorable.*

The moment didn't last long. I took a look around the room: there were five people here and one missing. Jessica.

'Jessica was taken to the isolation cells.' I thought over my next words carefully before I spoke. 'Are we breaking her out?'

Quinn looked at me like I'd just asked the most ludicrous question. 'Of course we're going to.'

The rest of the group didn't reply, they just exchanged looks with one another. Quinn picked up on it pretty quickly. 'We have to break her out.'

Again, silence.

I shared their concerns. Jessica could be a double agent.

The note from Willow wasn't damning, but it didn't look good either. Her mother enrolled her trained daughter into this school for a reason I didn't want to even think about. If Charlotte knew the true reason for the Academy then she had to know about Trojan's involvement. As I scanned over everyone, I knew the same thought had crossed their minds: Jessica could be working for Trojan. Even though it was a possibility, it was like my mind didn't want to consider it. Would Trojan make her go through all of this? Build a story, create a life, make friends and even fall in love, were they that heartless?

Grace's hand shot up, her eyes flickering to the floor for a few of seconds before regaining their ice-like composure. 'We've all considered the possibility that Jessica could be a Trojan operative.'

'Are you mad?' Quinn exclaimed.

'Quinn, admit it, Jessica's life doesn't make sense. But then again, do any of ours, officially?' Grace said.

'What about the connection with Russia that you and I found?' asked Lily, biting her lip nervously.

'It doesn't look great,' Grace admitted. 'I found a note in

my room, in Willow's handwriting, telling us not to trust her because of her mother.'

'Charlotte has shares in this place,' I told them. 'Jessica said she wrote the rules or something like that.'

'Jess hates her mum, always has.' Kayson spoke up. 'She's never said one nice thing about the woman.'

'There's a chance she could be a double agent,' Lily said quietly.

'There's a chance she's just like us,' Grace retorted, but it wasn't in that know-it-all voice of hers, it was soft and hopeful. 'We've talked, the pair of us, and honestly I don't think she's the enemy.'

'What did you talk about?' Kayson asked.

'You won't believe me, but Christopher.'

Kayson sneered. 'The American.'

I exchanged a look with Lily, each of us as confused as the other.

'Boys. You two talked about relationships?' Lily asked.

Grace sighed. 'She didn't understand why Chris wanted to stick around. She was insecure – Jess's dad left and her mum doesn't want anything to do with her. She wanted to know what love was. Forgive me, but I don't think admitting you're terrified of love is something a cold-blooded killer would do.'

'What about Willow's note?' I asked.

Grace sighed. 'They never got on, and from the moment Willow found out that Charlotte worked with the Pyramid Delegates she never trusted her. When I found the note, I fell into the same rash thinking Willow lived by.'

'You knew?'

'I'm her second, of course I knew,' Grace told me.

'Why didn't you tell us?' Lily asked, stepping forward.

'Lily, you were paranoid enough ever since we uncovered the connections with Russia, I didn't want to add to that. Besides, thinking about it rationally, Jessica has always been loyal to us.'

Apparently, as well as theories, this team had been keeping secrets from each other – Quinn's obvious bewilderment told me she knew nothing about it. Lily and Grace were locked in a hard stare-off, while Kayson tiredly sat down on a chair, hands cradling his head.

'She could be working with Trojan,' Lily stated.

'Yeah? Then why save me from gunfire in Brora?' Grace asked. 'She pushed me out of the way. Willow's death, she carried Lily from the scene.' Then she looked to me. 'If she really was a double agent, then why keep in contact with you?'

'I – uh,' I fumbled trying to come up with an answer.

'Naomi, Trojan keeps ties for usefulness. You weren't useful when Jessica joined but she tried her best to keep in contact because she cared. I argued with her for months but Jess wouldn't let you go. Then when things looked tense she sent Kayson to watch out for you because she couldn't.'

As Grace laid the facts out, waves of guilt rolled over me. She was right. Speculation had impaired my judgment. When Jess was being interrogated by Harkness, she hadn't given me up. If she was a Trojan agent, she would have given me up easily.

Kayson lifted his head. 'Her brother just died and she was carried away screaming. Harkness didn't know we were there so it wasn't for show. Jessica isn't working with Trojan.'

'Then we're all agreed?' Grace asked.

Everyone nodded, but then they all slowly turned in my direction. Sure, I hadn't nodded along, but I agreed.

'Naomi?' Quinn asked.

'What?'

'Do you agree?'

'Yes, everything you said makes sense. I don't see why you have to ask me, though.'

Quinn gave a soft sad smile, her eyes glittering with her past before she came back to the present, taking my hand.

'You're the Carrier on this team, your opinion matters.'

Hold up, that was only meant to be a temporary thing. My mouth dropped but Grace spoke before I could muster a response.

'I'm Team Lead when Jessica isn't here so Naomi, will you be our Carrier?'

I didn't know what to say, wasn't I replacing Willow? How could I replace a girl that had such an impact on this team? I couldn't replace the one that Quinn loved.

'I don't know,' I said, shaking my head. 'I'm not trained and have no clue what I'm doing.'

'That's what I'm for,' Quinn said with a bright smile as she squeezed my hand. 'Willow would have wanted someone to take her place, someone we trusted. You came back for us Naomi,

SLATE RETRIBUTION

people who the world couldn't give a toss about. I want you on this team, if you'll have us.'

A civilian on a mission to tear apart a regime – well, there were worse things I could spend my nights doing. Would Jessica allow it? The last time we spoke she shot venom from her mouth like a viper, and rightly so – I'd accused her of murdering her brother. Jess told me she never wanted to see me again, had that opinion changed?

Last night was the first time I'd heard her scream. She may have been a murderer but now it was clear, she was anything but a monster.

'OK, I'll do it.'

'Great, now let's plan a jail break.'

The meeting itself went on for what felt like hours, Grace of course took the lead, Quinn pulled up blueprints of the school while Kayson and Lily planned out our entry and exit strategy. It involved pretending to still be stuck under Harkness' thumb.

As I took in everything in, memorising my role, I couldn't help but notice the falling dread on Lily's face. The usual spark was once again fading, overcome with tears. As the meeting drew to a close and the team went off on their own to prepare for tomorrow I made sure to linger behind. Lily had taken it upon herself to clean all of the guns, her fingers diligently going over every weapon.

Once the room was empty I cautiously headed her way, hoping she'd tell me what was so clearly wrong.

'Lily?'

'Fire thong, seriously don't,' she jumped down my throat. 'Not in the mood.'

'You can talk to me if you want.'

'I don't.' Lily's knuckles turned white as she rubbed the barrel of the gun. 'Go find Quinn, she'll have stuff for you to do.'

'We both have a hard enough time getting through to Jess, I thought it would be easier with you, come on.'

'Naomi, I am really not in the mood.'

'Don't make me get Grace,' I threatened, but there was a smirk on my face.

Lily laughed heartily but then the smoke returned, smothering her expression, drowning her flame as she put the gun back on the table. She fiddled with the lone black ring on her thumb, twisting it gently. Her dark hair fell in front of her face but she didn't bother to push it back into place as she plopped onto the floor.

I sat down beside her, but not too close. I wanted her to know that I was there for her.

'We were meant to be saving the world but I'm being trained to destroy it.'

Unconsciously my hand shot forward, taking hers. 'Lily you couldn't have known.' But the comfort was short-lived as Lily snatched her hand back.

'I think I murdered someone – not just one person, five, maybe six people,' she admitted, her voice like a ghost. 'I don't remember, there was screaming and blood, but I don't know.'

I spun onto my knees.

'Lily this isn't your fault. Harkness did this,' I told her firmly. 'Dr McKay said they were cognitive drugs, they wiped out anything Harkness didn't need. When I saw you last night, you barely spoke or moved. Harkness took your dignity but he can never take your pride, your soul.'

Tears fell from her bloodshot eyes, then a sob broke from

her lips.

'Hey, it's OK,' I said, pulling her into a hug, my hands wrapping around her torso. I wasn't going to leave. 'You're going to get through this, we need you, Lily. You've seen me fight, I'm like Bambi on ice.' A watery laugh burst from her lips. 'You're amazing at your job.'

'Oh God,' she muttered. 'Don't go all motivational.' She pulled back, wiping the tears away.

I gasped in mock horror.

'You're kidding, I have a whole speech planned.' She laughed again and I smiled gingerly.

It was like we were those first years I'd seen outside, just talking and laughing.

'Don't tell me you're going to be that motivational Carrier who gives pep talks before every op?' she asked.

'No but I'll leave you with this one, what doesn't kill you makes you stronger.'

She cringed a little, but then the spark ignited in her eyes, like it had never left.

'What doesn't kill me better run.'

SLATE RETRIBUTION

EMERY HALE

CHAPTER 33

Alethiology

The study of truth.

NAOMI JADE

2 May 2016, 14:42

Scotland, The Reign Academy, Lower Levels

I don't think I'd ever been this nervous in my life.

'Carrier One, are you in position?' Quinn's voice floated through the earpiece as I slowly crept down the stairs to the lower levels.

They were darker than I thought, the walls even dingier. If I wasn't wearing a school blazer I would have cringed at the dampness on the wall, the wretched smell making my stomach turn. Was there an open sewer down here? As I hit the last step and pressed my back against the wall, a thumping sounded from the floor above and the naked lightbulb began to swing. Above us were the interrogation rooms I'd passed on the way here – what poor student had Harkness thrown in this time?

I tapped my earpiece twice to let Quinn know I was in position. There was no way anyone could whisper down here without being heard – then again, that was the point.

'Cutting security team comms now.'

The thumping from the floor above grew louder, the ceiling shaking. The movement meant the lightbulb swung closer to me so I shimmied to the left, cramming myself against the wall to avoid casting a shadow. I knew those games of hide and seek would come in handy.

Just then I heard two sets of shoes smack in unison down the stairs ahead, and even though my mind told me it was Duke or Harkness, I knew it wasn't. Kayson and Lily walked down, blank looks on their faces, but thankfully this time it was all for show. Neither of them made eye contact with me as they passed, and a couple of seconds later, their hollow footsteps came to a stop.

'We've came to escort our Team Lead to medical. She's in isolation.' Lily spoke, her voice void of emotion.

'No one leaves unless authorised by a member of staff,' a

gruff voice said, sounding like he smoked twenty a day.

'We were sent by staff, they're unavailable for this collection,' Kayson said.

God, he made Jessica sound like an animal or a piece of meat. When we planned this last night, she was always referred to as the package – shouldn't we have just used her name? Or her code name, since she chose it?

'Who sent you?' the man asked.

'Ames,' Lily replied, without a second's hesitation.

Silence lingered in the air for a moment, my breath going cold in my lungs – did he believe them? I heard some clicking and then static, before the man spoke again.

'I need to get Ames down in isolation . . . repeat, I need Ames in isolation now . . . is anyone there?'

Quinn's work was at play and boy, I loved the sound of it.

A chair screeched back as the man continued to yell into his comms, but then frantic footsteps sprinted down the stairs in front of me, a slender, crooked hand curling around the entrance. If they walked any further would they see me? Would Lily and Kayson let me get thrown into a cell?

'Cameron, comms are down!' another man shouted raggedly. 'Alarms are going off on the top floor, there's been a break-in.'

Not even a second passed before the gruff man ran past me, not even looking in my direction as he followed his colleague. I was about to run from my hiding place when the man's voice yelled again.

'You two come with us, you can't be down here!'

This couldn't have gone better.

I tiptoed, keeping my back pressed against the wall before flipping to the wall behind, standing right next to the opening. From my new position I could see straight ahead: a long corridor with a green floor, a security desk to the left and a few cells lining the walls, and further ahead, another set of black grate stairs. Kayson and Lily followed the man's orders and ran after him – just as Lily reached the steps she slammed a bunch of lanky, heavy iron keys into my chest, before disappearing up the stairs.

Quinn had hacked into Thompson's files and found that the cells unlocked with a standard key, no need for a security pass. Once Quinn had knocked the comms out, Dr McKay called from the fourth floor (the furthest away from cells) claiming there was a break-in, and when the guards went running, Lily grabbed the keys.

'Carrier One, cameras are down. You have approximately eight minutes to get in and grab the package before the security comms go back up and the guard returns to his post. Nightingale will meet you at the lift doors on the ground floor.'

Showtime.

With a couple of shaky breaths I took off running, the black grate stairs in sight. I couldn't help but wonder if there were students in these cells – were they all occupied? At the top of the stairs my mouth opened wide – it really was a prison. To my left and right were walkways, cells on each side, then below another whole floor filled with even more. The whole thing was in the shape of a silo, but as I descended the stairs to the lower floor, the close ceiling suddenly resembled the heavens, bright floodlights bearing down on me.

'Carrier One, you need to keep moving.' Quinn's words made me jump, the keys jangling. 'Seven minutes.'

Right, on a deadline, need to keep moving.

From the records we found it looked like they'd put Jess in cell number 47, and thankfully, the numbers were on plaques next to each door. Then I spied it, four and seven, forty-seven.

I hurled over but before I let hope overwhelm me I remembered I was holding a whole ring of keys and they weren't numbered. There had to be at least thirty keys on this thing.

'Carrier One, you have six minutes.'

'OK, slight problem, there's a lot of keys,' I said, spreading them out along my hand.

'You're going to need to try all of them,' Quinn said. 'They aren't labelled are they?'

I didn't see anything at a quick glance, but then I took a look at the stem of the key and saw a very familiar sight: X, V, L and I.

'What's the roman numeral for forty-seven?' I blurted.

'X, L, V, I, I.' Grace's voice cut through without missing a beat.

Fiddling with the keys, spinning them round the circle, I came to the key with those exact letters. Guess they had a thing for roman numerals around here. Thrusting the key into the lock I twisted it, yanking the door open.

I'd expected to see Jess crying in the corner but it seemed the time for that had long since passed. She was sat at the back of the cell, knees bent and body rigid, her face stained with dry tears. Her clothes askew, shoulders marked in red, lip split and bleeding.

'They send you to shoot me?' she asked, but her voice was tired, gritty like sand. 'Thought they would at least have sent Lily.'

I felt like I couldn't move – she thought I was here to shoot her? Didn't she know this was a rescue? As I stepped further into the cell, the light cast on my face and Jessica's eyes snapped shut.

'You're not real, these hallucinations are getting worse.'

'You're not hallucinating,' I said softly. 'Jess, we're here to break you out.'

'Now my mind is really going at it,' Jessica laughed bitterly. 'Got the hair colour wrong though and your face is weird.'

'That's just the disguise,' I told her, rubbing at the foundation to expose my skin colour but she didn't even notice, her gaze in constant battle with the open door.

She didn't even try to run. Did she not think she was worthy of rescue?

I knelt down, taking her hands. She flinched, trying to pull away, but I kept a firm grip. Then her eyes fixed on mine, her long slender fingers reaching out to cup my cheek, grazing my skin. Jessica's lips parted as a weight visibly left her shoulders.

Without a second's hesitation I pulled her into a hug, her hands tightly gripping my body.

'You're here.' Her voice but a ghost. 'You're real.'

'I'm here.'

How many times she'd been thrown in here? How many times had she dreamed of escaping this cell? How many times had she dreamed of me? Gripping her shirt, I hugged her as tight as I could, as if she might disappear in a split second.

'Carrier One, report,' Grace's voice demanded.

'I have the package.' At my words Jessica pulled away, her eyes flitting to my ear, but then I grabbed her hand, squeezing it softly. 'We're all here.'

Shock was the only way I could think to describe her expression, before it crumbled to relief.

'Why?' she asked.

'Someone has a very persuasive group of friends,' I told her with a soft smile. 'I also made a promise, that I nearly broke, and because of that we nearly lost this entire team.'

'Guys we can all have a good catch-up later, you need to start moving,' Lily warned.

'Four minutes,' Quinn's voice ticked away in my ear.

I took Jessica's hand, pulling her up from the floor and leading her out into the light. Now came the tricky part. I took the lead, barrelling up the stairs as fast as I could, past the security desk to the main entrance stairs.

Then I stopped, pulling out the gun I'd hidden in my blazer pocket and handing it to Jess. A small smile graced her face as she took the safety off.

'We need to make it to the ground floor, but these stairs lead to the floor above.' Almost on cue a thundering bang echoed from upstairs, but Jessica knew exactly what I meant. 'Shoot to injure.'

She paused at my words but nodded, unsatisfied, climbing the stairs.

'Carrier One, package is being transported,' I reported.

'You sound so fucking weird saying that,' Jessica said, and even though I was in front of her I could feel the grin on her face.

'Just focus on shooting people, please.'

As we came closer to the top of the stairs I slowed until Jess passed me, taking the lead. The thundering bangs now sounded like smacking and cracking, like a boot on bone.

'How did you get down here last time?' Jessica whispered, looking back at me.

'There wasn't anyone there when I passed, I just brought the gun in case.'

'Of what?'

'Well, you know, someone trying to attack me,' I mumbled.

'Naomi, do you even know where to put the magazine on this thing?' she asked.

'Well, I don't know how *Hello* magazine is going to help here.' Jessica turned back, her face almost asking if I was serious, but then she turned back around, shaking her head. 'What's that face for?'

SLATE RETRIBUTION

'Nothing,' Jess said, sounding like she was holding back a laugh.

The pair of us peered around the corner and I held my breath. The corridor ahead seemed to stretch on forever. The entire floor was mapped out in an L-shape with all the classrooms on the right-hand side – the walls were pure glass so the brick I'd hidden behind last time was nowhere in sight, shit. I knew getting down here was too easy, why did Harkness have to throw a spanner into our amazing but apparently flawed plan?

Jessica tapped my wrist signalling she was moving forward, and I followed suit. She paused every time we came close to a door, slowly observing the room before moving forward again. The only sources of light were the little ones lining the floor and the classroom at the end, and the dim light gave me the heebie-jeebies. Deep rumbling screams reverberated along the corridor but I carried on.

Jessica's stance was poised, the gun by her side. How could she keep going? She'd lost her brother yesterday, and had been thrown into a cell for good measure.

Suddenly, Jess held up her hand in a fist and I stopped

dead, catching the sight ahead of us. Blood dripped down the glass wall like a waterfall, but what lodged in my mind was the hand slowly slipping down until it slapped onto the floor, limp. Jess turned, pressing her back against the wall, but by her face I knew we weren't going to get out of here as planned.

'Do you need more time?' Quinn asked, and I double-tapped my earpiece, before hearing a stressed sigh from her. 'OK, I can try to get McKay to stall.'

As I glanced over to my friend it looked like her mind was working at a hundred miles an hour. We didn't have a backup plan for this because the lifts were the only way out of the lower levels.

'Give me your earpiece,' Jess whispered, holding out a hand, but her eyes were solely fixed on the glass doors. Fumbling for a moment I gave it over. 'Pilot, cut the power . . . yes, I know that means the whole school and the lifts, we only need a second.'

Cut the power? I remembered what Quinn said after last time – this floor worked entirely on an electrical system and in the case of a shutdown all the doors locked. Which would give us more time, but a power cut would look suspicious. The whole team was dotted all around the school, would other doors close?

Would we leave someone behind?

'Jess,' I whispered, trying to get her attention, but she held up a hand as she listened to Quinn.

'Pilot, I'll give you thirty seconds to get out of your secured area, then you cut the lights,' she said.

Start the clock.

Jessica gave the earpiece back to me with a nod, then inched towards the end of the corridor. Once we got past there it would be a sprint to the lifts, then we'd meet Grace and she'd take us to the getaway car.

That was when I heard Harkness yell.

'What is operation Red Dawn?' Smack. 'Your daughter died, General, you saw her swing. You've got nothing left, tell me!'

Jessica's body began to shake, and as I came around, her eyes fluttered open and shut, fear washing through her, taking over.

'Hey,' I whispered softly, taking her hand, trying to bring her back. 'Jess, it's going to be OK. He's not going to hurt you.'

The weight of the world returned to her shoulders, every

emotion I'd demanded from her bubbling to the surface. Part of me was proud, but the other part needed her to keep it together – she was the one with gun.

'Come on,' I squeezed her hand. 'A little further.'

'Lights are going down in ten seconds,' Quinn said in my ear.

As she started the countdown I ushered Jess forward. Something clicked in her mind and so she raised the gun, inching towards the edge of the bloodied glass room.

Then everything around us plunged into darkness.

'Lights down, three seconds.'

Jessica's clammy hand grabbed mine and we ran.

We passed the room at the end unseen, but even as the lights flickered neither of us let up. I sprinted as fast as I could, overtaking Jess and frantically pressing the lift button. I thought we'd gotten away with it when a furious fist pounded the class door. Shit, he'd heard us.

I heard the lift come down with a groan, the gears groaning but the doors remained closed.

'Doors will open in five seconds.'

'What about the lift?'

'Ten,' Quinn said, her voice full of dread.

Jessica shoved the gun into her waistband, gripped the slit in between the doors with her fingers and started to pull. I darted to the other side, digging my nails into the cold metal and yanked it as hard as I could, the lift doors groaning and scraping as they started to move.

Then booming footsteps pounded towards us. I didn't dare to look because I knew who it was – Harkness. The muscles in my arm started to spasm, my fingers red from the pressure – we had to get these doors open. Suddenly they rolled back just enough and relief swept through me as we both squeezed through the small gap.

As the footsteps came closer Jessica whipped the gun out and pointed it high – head shot. I threw my hand out and just as Harkness came into view, the bullet rang out – but instead of flesh it hit the floor. Jessica's eyes widened, then Harkness' hands slammed on the metal doors trying to pry them open.

'Always a disappointment,' Harkness snarled, looking directly as Jessica. She pushed my hand away but this time aimed a little lower, his shoulder. 'You can't do it, I created you.'

There wasn't a single moment of hesitation.

BANG.

Harkness stumbled back, a hand clawing at his shoulder, blood seeping through his white shirt as, finally, the doors started to close. I pressed the button for the ground floor and watched as Harkness simply smiled at us. He didn't try to squeeze in, just stood there shaking his head, as the doors closed.

As the lift started to move, Jessica started to yell. 'What the fuck?' She turned to me. 'I could have killed him, we could have ended this.'

'He's better off alive, we need him.'

Jessica tucked the gun back into her jeans, looking at me like I was insane. 'What exactly have you been doing?' she asked.

'I'll explain later,' I said, too stressed to answer, but then another thought hit me. 'Pilot, you need to cut all communications in the Academy, Harkness saw us.'

'All of them?' Quinn asked. 'I've not switched over to the independent server. It'll cut ours.'

'Do it,' Grace said. 'Pilot, that's an order.'

SLATE RETRIBUTION

A split second passed and Quinn's voice disappeared. All I could hear was the growl of the lift as it ascended.

With a ping the doors opened and Jessica was immediately hauled out by Grace and Dr McKay – she let out a yelp, but fell quiet seeing who it was. Thankfully, no one stared – but they started to as soon as we reached the main reception.

Even though I pressed myself against Jessica's back, keeping guard from behind, I clearly saw Helen and the two armed guards at her side. Abruptly, Dr McKay threw himself forward, pulling out a gun, shooting the two guards within a single second, then pointing it at Helen.

'Move!' he ordered, looking to the three of us, who had all come to a stop.

I grabbed Jessica's other arm and took off, sprinting towards the main door, not looking back. Dr McKay had put his life on the line; I wasn't going to let it go to waste. The three of us pushed the doors open and practically flew down the stairs, and just as we did a long black car pulled up in front of us, the window rolled down. Kayson and Lily were both inside with their guns pointed at the driver's head.

'Get in!' Kayson yelled and Grace tore open the door throwing herself inside. I jumped in after but Jessica didn't ... Quinn.

'Where's Quinn?' she said, looking around – but then, from inside the Academy, came rapid gunfire.

Beside me, Grace's eyes widened, she looked ready to run back inside. Had they killed him? Was Dr McKay dead?

Then, light feet running on the gravel drive came from behind. I spun in my seat, looking out the back window to see Quinn, bag in hand.

'Quinn, come on!' Jessica screamed – but that was when the tall front doors opened and Duke ran out.

Grace grabbed the handle and slammed the door shut.

'What are you doing?' I asked, horrified. I was about to throw it open but Grace stopped me.

As I looked back up Jessica had taken off, running round the back of the car, Quinn at her side.

'The window!' Lily exclaimed.

Kayson reached for the button, starting to roll it up, just as the door at my side was flung open and Quinn jumped in. The ping of bullets hit the car, all aiming for the doors and windows. My hands flew over my head and I ducked as a lone bullet shot through the window, glass spraying in my hair.

'Drive!' Lily ordered.

The car started to move, but Jessica wasn't inside, I knelt down on the floor holding a hand out for her to take as bullets raked the other side of the car, now acting as a shield. As the car picked up speed so did Jessica, her breathing frantic as she reached out to take my hand. Then I grabbed it and yanked her inside, Quinn closing the door.

Lily pressed a black button and through the open partition I saw the big black iron gates open. It had worked.

'Floor it,' Lily said to the driver, and suddenly I was thrown back against the seat. We whizzed down the drive and before I knew it we'd made it onto the main road.

'We did it,' Quinn said, a small smile on her face. 'We're free.'

'Not yet,' Jessica shook her head as she sat up, 'we've got a long way to go.'

* * *

The hours that passed before we reached the harbour were filled with running through back alleys and half-explained plans. We'd bought new clothes in cash, changed, gone over our inventory, set up the independent comm system and finally had a small break. I'd taken off the wig and makeup using a random shard of glass on the ground, it was a challenge to say the least. Lily was beside me at all times but I couldn't help it, I kept looking back at Jess.

The once emotion-flooded face was now cold and stagnant. Once again the switch had been flipped, the professional Team Lead. How could she be coping through all of this? She hadn't said anything, but we'd all drawn conclusions about her brother, and now she'd found out the true purpose of the Academy. I expected some reaction but there was nothing, just a nod of her head.

And now, I was crouched down behind some fishing crates at the harbour, rubbing my hands together to keep warm as the harsh wind whipped through me. The night sky was black as ink, but sadly the clouds obscured the stars. I really should have bought that jacket but, being me, I claimed the cold didn't bother me. I could practically hear my mother's voice nagging in my ear.

SLATE RETRIBUTION

'Carrier One, it's approaching the agreed time and the boat is stationed to your left. You need to get on board and find whatever's on it.'

Why couldn't Lily go check it out? The boat was rusted and barely looked sailable – for all I knew there could be rats.

'Carrier One you need to move, if Harkness is there at the agreed time we need to get there before it. Whatever this is, it's big.'

I stood up from the crate, keeping low and running to the boat, making sure to watch my footing, didn't want to fall in the water. If that happened I'd probably be labelled as the worst Carrier ever.

'Lilith is in position at the entrance to the harbour,' Jessica said.

'Ronan is on the street across,' Kayson added.

'Blackbird standing by, at the back of the boat.'

'Nightingale at the café opposite.'

'OK everybody, this is in and out,' Jessica said. 'Naomi, we don't have any cameras so you're gonna have to speak as you see.'

Unfortunately, Quinn could only bring comms and her laptop given the emergency getaway – I wished we had some form of camera, even just one for me. I'd feel safer with one. Placing one foot in front of the other I clambered aboard, careful of the rickety wooden plank acting as stairs. The ship itself was rundown; if all of us had jumped on here it might have sunk. Small droplets of water fell through the patchy tin roof as the coastal wind flurried and whistled through my bones. Some floorboards were squishy and damp while others were hard and brittle; the metal walls were lined with rust and mould. However, the one thing that stood out was that the boat was empty. A few small crates had been pushed into corners, but from here they looked empty.

'Are you sure this is the right boat?' I asked, poking around to make sure nothing was hidden under a shelf.

'It has to be,' Quinn replied.

'There's nothing here, apart from multiple health and safety violations.'

As I ventured to the front of the boat, there was only a crate filled with wires and random metal parts.

'Check under the floorboards, there's a good chance something is hidden there.'

Pausing, I looked down to the floor, mouldy water gathering around my foot.

'I am not touching that.'

'Carrier One.' Jessica's irritated voice ran through my ear. 'We don't know what this is, you need to search that whole ship. Blackbird and Ronan, move in, give the Carrier more security.'

I slowly crouched down reaching for a floorboard that looked a little raised from the others – it was also the driest. Could I catch something from this? Was that possible? My knees scraped against the wood as my hands grasped the end of the floorboard and lifted it slowly at first, then jerked it.

SNAP

The wood broke in two, sending me flying back. Great, now my butt was wet.

'Lilith, someone's just entered the harbour.'

'Is it Harkness?'

'No.'

'I've got movement from my side,' Grace said quickly.

'Five of them, maybe six, they're grouped together.'

'Blackbird?' Jessica asked.

'Shit, there's eight of them coming towards me,' Lily whispered.

I flung myself forward, then on all fours crawled over to the wooden crate and hid behind it. There were holes in place of windows, so if I stood up I'd be seen. My heartbeat thumped in my ears: I knew this was how Willow died. We were outnumbered.

'Ronan, you need to get Carrier One out of there,' Jessica said, but I almost didn't hear her as shadows danced across the boat.

'Negative.'

'Blackbird?'

'Negative.'

Jessica cursed and I sucked in a breath, my eyes squeezing shut. How could my life have led to this? Right, yeah, cause I ran back into this life, yearned for it, even. I felt a heavy stone slide down my neck and sit in the pit of my stomach, a sob catching at the back of my throat. Had I made a mistake?

'Is there any way you can get Carrier One off the boat?'

'Negative.'

A hand flew over my mouth to stop my frantic breathing. This meeting-place wasn't just for Harkness; he'd brought a whole team. This was for Trojan.

'Carrier One, remember plan B, stay hidden until told otherwise,' Jessica instructed. 'We'll deal with this. Numbers, everyone give me numbers – how many hostiles are in the field?'

Everyone tallied off, adding up to thirty, which set a chill colder than death in my mind. Thirty agents, that's how many students are in a year group. They'd brought people from the Academy.

'Remember, they don't know we're here,' Jessica said. 'Stay hidden, this must be a meeting ground.'

Didn't have to tell me twice.

As I opened my eyes a beam of white light flashed above my head. More people? How many agents were attending this meeting, and why were they so early?

'Car approaching from the entrance, I've moved positions to the café,' Jessica said. I heard some shuffling and clinking of plates from her end but my eyes were firmly fixed ahead.

Multiple heads, all in a line, marched past the non-existent windows silently. If my eyes were still closed I wouldn't have known they were there. Was this a shootout?

'Carrier One, they're moving in front of you, can you get a visual?'

'Are you insane?' I whispered harshly.

'We need to know if Harkness or Gabriel is there.'

I bit my lip, holding back a groan, and grabbed onto the lid of a small wooden crate to pull myself up. Then I paused, looking inside. It was the crate I'd seen earlier, filled with wires and random metal parts, but now I took a closer look, it was anything but junk. A black box took up the majority of the space, the random wires connected into metal-rimmed ports, and as I moved some of them to the side a red glow of numbers shone through. Oh no.

Then I spotted a stamp on the outside.

HOLYROOD, SCOTTISH PARLIAMENT BUILDING

SLATE RETRIBUTION

This crate was going to the Parliament, Trojan were going to use it to blow up the Scottish government.

'I found the package,' I said quietly, taking the lid off fully and placing it on the floor. 'It's a bomb, addressed to Holyrood.'

'Their great plan is blow up the government?' Grace muttered under her breath.

'They have people on the inside, anyone working for the Pyramid Delegates could take it into the building,' Jessica said.

Did that mean that the Pyramid Delegates were based in Edinburgh too? They had to be if they were able to take this crate inside without any questions.

'Is it active?' Kayson asked.

'Well . . .' I trailed off. 'There is a red line going round in a circle on the screen.'

'Right, it's armed. Carrier One, don't touch it,' Kayson said, and my hands shot up.

OK, Naomi, you are sitting right next to an armed bomb, don't trip or whack the box and hopefully it shouldn't explode. *Holy crap, I was sitting next to a bomb!*

'Ronan, get on that ship and disarm it,' Jessica ordered.

'We can't have it going off.'

Seriously? Kayson could defuse bombs? Was that where he disappeared to at the theatre? Geez, and I thought he was going for a bathroom break.

Staying quiet and low I leaned back on my heels, making sure to keep clear of the crate – until Kayson got on board there was no way I was moving. There were only small shuffles and grunts over the comms, but when Harkness called out, everyone fell silent.

'Gabriel,' he started, 'long time coming, this.'

His voice came from the left but the crack of shoes came from the right.

'I would shake your hand, but these are more agents than we agreed. They're protection, aren't they?' The snake-like voice of Gabriel slithered across. 'Quite a rude gesture.'

'It's nothing personal; I just prefer to feel secure,' Harkness replied. 'Is it on the boat?'

'Of course. I actually hold up my end of the deals.'

Shit, were they going to come aboard to look at the bomb I was currently staring at? I bloody well hoped not.

'Carrier One, stay in place, no sudden movements.'

No sudden movements – Jess, I wasn't that bloody stupid.

I couldn't take my eyes off of the bomb just sitting in front of me. My mother wouldn't like this one bit – probably shouldn't mention it when I get home.

'Is it set for the right destination?'

'Daniel, you forget my diligence when it comes to matters such as this.'

'Well the bank was quite a spectacle, blew someone's tits off.'

Gabriel laughed deeply.

'We had to start causing some panic – the seed of doubt within the public over their own security was planted then. Everything's led up to this. Now give me the agents and you can take that ridiculous boat.'

This was a trade-off, the bomb in exchange for more agents. We had to stop this – if they'd destroyed Estonia and planned to blow up our parliament, there was no telling what they'd do next. Was it world domination? Did they crave a new world order? One of chaos?

'We can't let them make the exchange,' I whispered.

'Carrier One, stay in position,' Jessica ordered, but there was no way I was shutting up now.

'Don't you see? More agents means that tomorrow Edinburgh might be the next Estonia'

'Lilith, they're moving.'

That's when I heard it, the unified thudding on the concrete ground, all moving towards Gabriel.

There were moments throughout this past year when I'd wanted to run, hide, leave the world to its own problems. Spend the rest of my life doing something mundane, wasting away the time I had left. That's all humans were; fragments of time. Each second ticking by senselessly until the clock breaks.

That's why I was going to do what I'd been scared to do for a long time. It might be idiotic, but there was no way anyone else was becoming collateral in these terrorists' games. No one else was going to lose a brother, a sister, a daughter or son. It was time to stop all of this. It was time for action.

Sucking in a deep breath I hurled myself out of the boat, my feet flying across the ground.

'Stop! You can't do this!'

'What the fuck are you doing?' Jessica nearly screamed.

Just like I'd expected, everyone stopped; Harkness and Gabriel seeming more stunned than anything.

'Who's this?' Gabriel asked, surprisingly casual.

Harkness looked me up and down, then marched a couple of steps towards me, his breath coming out like a dragon's.

'You're that idiot from MI6.'

'No,' I corrected him, standing tall and raising my chin. 'I'm not. I never belonged to an agency, just pretended.'

'Naomi, stop talking,' Jessica said harshly.

Out of the corner of my eye I saw movement but there was no need to look, I knew Jessica and the team were already in motion.

That was when I heard the click of a gun from behind and my throat ran dry. It was like we were in Brora, my body too terrified to move.

Suddenly, a body slammed into me, strong arms hooking mine, the warmth I'd grown to miss now standing firmly at my back.

'Another move, Gabriel, and I'll blow your fucking head off,' Kayson spat.

Then Harkness did something I didn't expect – he started to laugh.

I wasn't armed with anything so as he sauntered towards me. My hand reached back for Kayson's, fear almost consuming me. I wanted to shut my eyes, wanted to make him disappear, but then the voice of my favourite bird spoke.

'Don't touch her,' Lily said coming from the side, a knife in one hand and gun in the other.

'What is this?' Gabriel yelled, nerves creeping into his voice.

'Put that down, girl,' Harkness warned, but Lily didn't waver.

Skittish footsteps rattled behind the boat and just as I turned, Grace and Jessica appeared behind Gabriel. Before anyone knew it, Grace had a fishing wire secured around his neck, strangling him. As he thrashed to get free, Jessica walked towards us, her eyes fixed solely on Harkness.

'You're a manipulative bastard who deserves to die,' she

said. 'You murdered one of our team because her own father told you to. She was seventeen.'

'Everyone bangs on about age,' Harkness snarked. 'Doesn't mean anything. She was a task. Just like yours was to kill that *sixteen year old*, what was her name? She had rich parents, first year.'

Could that be Jackie? I knew we'd gone over the possibility, but hearing him say it made my blood run cold. Jessica didn't even flinch.

'I was brainwashed, drugged. I didn't know what I was doing.'

'You know, I know, and your teammates know, you're nothing but an engineered killer.' Harkness' words were laced with poison as he ranted like a madman. 'Chan won't kill me, not without your orders, Ashford won't kill Gabriel. It all comes down to you.' He threw his arms out; his visibly bandaged shoulder didn't appear to hinder him. 'Prove it, to everyone. You don't need drugs, Winters, you'll follow orders like a dog. Admit it.'

'Admit what?'

'You *enjoyed* it.'

Jessica remained motionless, void and silent. The only sound was the crisp wind as it blew through her hair.

'No more killing!' I exclaimed, and Harkness turned to me, tilting his head.

'Where did you pick this stray up?' he asked. 'She's pretty.'

'Don't look at her.'

'What are you going to do about it?' Harkness grinned. 'A couple of months in I bet she'd crack, I can promise I'll make her beg, *I'll make her scream.*'

Jessica sprinted forward, grabbing Harkness by the neck, jutting her knee into his ribcage before throwing her elbow into his cheek. Not once did he fight back, falling to the ground laughing hysterically, even after Jessica broke his nose with a sickening crack.

'Stop!' I tried, but she didn't listen, throwing punch after punch. 'Jessica you don't have to kill him, don't prove him right!'

That was when Jessica stopped dead, her head held high as she slowly turned back to me.

'Prove?' Harkness asked harshly. 'There's nothing to prove.'

Jessica leaned down, grabbing him by the shirt, but I wouldn't let this happen, she wasn't a killer. I ran, grabbing her arm, pulling her away.

'We won't let you do this.'

'Take a look around,' Jessica said.

Grace had reduced the once-mighty Gabriel to an insect on his knees, face turning purple. Kayson's gun was pointed at Harkness, as was Lily's.

'Who's going to stop me?'

All this time I kept telling myself I knew the woman standing in front of me, but I didn't. The waters of time and memory used to flow through her but not anymore, now there was only ice – and ice never forgives.

Jessica didn't need a weapon, she was born and raised into one. I'd made up the truth, the one that I needed to believe, but I couldn't deny the evidence in front of me. Some people *were* past saving.

Harkness took advantage of our silence, standing tall

before looking over to the thirty students.

'Kill them,' he said motioning to us. 'Kill them all.'

What?

Kayson's arm hauled me around the front, pressing a gun into my hand, and then touched a shaky yet tender kiss to my forehead, warmth radiating from his lips. He – what?

'Run.' He shoved me towards Grace and turned towards the onslaught of assassins.

No...

I'd lost sight of Jessica and Harkness, then Lily and Kayson, all of them disappearing into the sea of black and faceless bodies. My feet stumbled back but I couldn't turn, my ears bursting with cascading shells on concrete. The gun rattled in my hand, I barely knew how to fire it, could I even use it?

Then a girl, maybe three years older, ran towards me, her face void and eyes empty. My breathing hitched as my mind started to catch up with the situation. Shit!

BANG

This time I was close enough to hear the bullet tear through her skin and see the shiny metal break through her forehead. Then she fell down, like a wooden doll, her head bouncing off the ground.

Lily stood behind her, gun raised. She barely had the chance to look my way before an agent grabbed her shoulder, throwing a punch through her cheek.

Then, I ran.

Spinning around I took off in the direction of Grace who had her hand outstretched to me. Reaching her within a matter of seconds I jumped over the unconscious body of Gabriel and grabbed it.

Grace pulled me forward and before I knew it we were running, the sound of carnage still deafening, a sound I knew would never leave me.

'Wait!' Quinn screamed, her voice deeper than I'd ever heard it. 'Call them off or I'll blow it!'

The pair of us stopped in our tracks, whipping round to see Quinn's small figure standing in the middle of the docks, holding something in her hand. It was only then that I saw three people on top of Kayson, Lily struggling to get off her knees as attacks came from all around, Jessica fighting as hard alongside her.

'Quinn . . .' Grace trailed off, seeming to know what her plan was.

The scuttling behind the boat earlier, that must have been Quinn, and now she was holding – a bomb detonator.

'She's right,' Quinn said. 'We can't keep fighting, there's only so much a person can take. Even you, Harkness.' Her thumb hovered over the device. 'Call your agents off or I blow us all to hell.'

Harkness sneered. 'What are you talking about, you pathetic girl?'

'Don't play dumb, we know that bomb is going to the Scottish Parliament, we're not going to let you destroy the country.'

The fighting continued but Harkness eyed the device, and his eyes flickered around the harbour. Then he let out a yell.

'Stop!'

I knew then that he was a man of self-preservation; he'd never be willing to die for the cause. As if someone had flipped a switch, every agent simply stopped, and stood to attention. Kayson, Jessica and Lily now like lone figures in the crowd, although the mad man wasn't finished.

'Look how they obey me. Your little team won't stop our plans, you're a child.'

'A child with her finger on the detonator.'

Suddenly, tyres screeched from the entrance of the harbour, a black car sitting there like a jaguar stalking its prey.

As everyone else turned, I saw Harkness raise his gun and aim it at Quinn.

'Quinn!' I ran forward as fast as I could, adrenaline pumping through my veins. Quinn herself saw the gun and started to run but it was too late; a bullet clipped her leg sending her to the ground, crying out as the detonator rolled away.

'Rendezvous Two!' Harkness ordered, before he and every other agent scattered.

'Don't let them get away!' Jessica snapped in another round of ammo and the gunfire raged on.

As the agents ran, one after another dropped down dead. Kayson took the left, Lily the right and Jessica the centre.

Grace and I ran over to Quinn skidding to a stop.

'It's just a flesh wound,' Grace said, taking out a torch

from her bag and shoving it in her mouth, pulling out bandages and packing material. 'You're gonna be OK. Naomi, press your hand against it.'

I didn't think, I just did as I was told, my shivering hands pressing against the warm squelch of blood seeping from Quinn's leg. Her whole body was shaking, hands curled into fists, but I grabbed one and squeezed it. She was going to make it through this.

'You're crazy,' I said trying to lighten the mood. 'I'd never have thought that was going to happen in a million years.'

'Had to get them somehow,' Quinn trembled.

'By threatening to blow us all to kingdom come?' I asked, laughing a little.

'Willow always said go big or go home,' her eyes glazed over as she stared up at the cloudy sky, wincing every few seconds.

Then I heard the click of a car door and saw Harkness standing there, watching us from above, his slimy tongue licking his lips, before he got in the back and the car sped away. Of course he was free: in fairy tales the bad guy always lost, but this wasn't a fairy tale.

I couldn't help but look over to Gabriel whose body hadn't risen, his face still a sickly purple – was it bad to wish he would get up? The man had to pay for his crimes, he had to stand trial, then he'd get the sentence he deserved. A long life in prison.

'We got a lot but a few of them managed to get away.' Lily reported, running over, holstering the gun at her side.

'Lily!' Quinn cried, holding a hand out to her.

She knelt down, tucking an arm under the girl's legs just as Grace pulled away, lifting her bridal-style.

'I've got you, darling,' Lily told her quietly.

Grace stood with me as Kayson and Jessica ran over.

'We've got to get out of here, police will be on their way,' Kayson said, pointing at the small alley to the left, our exit route.

But the sight ahead dampened the hope in my heart: at least eighteen people splayed out like dead animals on the concrete, small pools of blood beside their heads, chests and legs. This was what the Academy created: mindless soldiers. Any one of this team could be in their place right now. Those agents didn't know what they were doing – couldn't there have been another way?

Tonight when the news broke, what would happen? How would Thompson cover this one up? How could anyone? There were too many things wrong with this picture, one you couldn't wash away with pretty words.

'Come on,' Jessica said harshly, and it was then I realised we were the only two left on the harbour, everyone else scurrying to the back alley.

'Jess, you're not a killer,' I tried, the last shred of hope glimmering, it was the only thing I could think to say. 'You didn't take the shot, you –'

'– just killed twelve people,' she interrupted, firing my own logic back.

It was like a stab in the heart: even though she'd done this I knew there hadn't been another choice. Sometimes violence was necessary, I just wished it wasn't.

I let her lead, following behind through the different twists and turns of the alley, heading towards the train station. The cover we'd discussed earlier was in full swing with some minor changes: Quinn was a drunk girl and we were the group of friends

SLATE RETRIBUTION

carrying her home.

Where was home? The Academy, my parents' house, or were we truly on our own?

EMERY HALE

SLATE RETRIBUTION

CHAPTER 34

Apricity

The warmth of sun in winter.

NAOMI JADE

2 May 2016, 23:15

Scotland, The Reign Academy, Dorm House

Driving through the Academy's tall gates and walking into the dorm house without the worry of Harkness enforcing the law brought relief to everyone. Sure, Duke was still around, but apparently he was like a lapdog, lost without his master. I was against coming back here, but it seemed we'd be safe until we could figure out a better plan.

There was something almost soothing, like the stillness of waves after a storm. Lily was constantly checking out of the window, but to every other student this was a normal night. Presumably no one apart from our team knew what had gone down at the harbour or what was planned. Harkness seemed like the kind of man to keep things to himself.

Quinn was in the hospital wing which to me seemed like a safe haven, although whether or not Dr McKay was still there would remain a mystery. Was he dead? I hoped not, he was a good man to have on your side. On the way back from the harbour Grace assured me Quinn's injury wasn't serious, but said she'd stay by her side the whole night to give us some peace of mind.

I fiddled with my fingers as images of the night ran through my head: the truth that I'd been avoiding for so long now. Jessica was trained from a young age to kill people, her family drowning in government secrets – she wasn't the good guy, but she wasn't the bad guy either. That was something I'd have to get used to – even if I didn't approve, she was still my friend. The promise I'd made long ago still stood and now Harkness had run, it was a little closer to coming true.

The gun Kayson had given me sat on the coffee table. I'd completely forgotten I had it: even at the harbour I'd never felt the need to use it. Guns just weren't my thing.

The living room door opened with a creak, the fiery embers of hair trickling down Jess's shoulder like a waterfall as she made her way over, sitting opposite, hands clasped but head held high.

'Kayson managed to get in touch with Nicola. After hearing that Harkness fled she sent a team of people she trusts to dispose of the bomb.'

'Good,' I responded.

'I'm sorry.' Her remark caught me off guard. 'I'm sorry I'm not the person you want me to be.'

Something that I'd come to accept was that Jessica, despite every little detail I thought I knew, wasn't the same person I'd grown to appreciate and love all those years ago.

For so long I'd wondered why she kept contact with me. There was no need to – like Grace said, I wasn't of any use. There must have still been some remnant of the young girl she was. She'd fought to survive, to make it to tomorrow, been brainwashed, drugged, and then, after everything, she'd lost her brother. The smile I witnessed at the coffee shop last year was long gone.

'Your brother, is he dead?'

Jessica let out a shaky breath, nodding her head, but there

was hesitation – almost a determination that the answer would never escape her lips.

'Even though the drugs scrambled everything, I can still remember the look on his face, the blood, the second the building collapsed.'

Tears sprung in her eyes but she didn't let them fall. Instead she focused above my head, through the opening in the curtains where the newly emerging stars twinkled in the night sky.

I stood up, ran around the table and pulled her into the tightest hug I could manage, no longer caring about what Jessica should have done, or should be. Her whole body was rigid and cold like an iceberg but then, after a moment, her hold melted into mine. Small warm droplets landed on my skin as her fingers gripped my arms.

I couldn't see or hear her but I knew she trusted me enough to let her guard down. Everyone here had doubts about Jessica's credibility, even me. It must have felt as if James was the only person she could talk to, but now he was gone.

'I'm here,' I told her. 'I'm here.'

We sat there for a moment before she pulled away, wiping

tears away with her sleeve.

'I didn't kill Charlie,' she said, and my heart sunk.

'Jess, I jumped to conclusions.'

She shook her head. 'Don't,' she sniffled, 'you're not the first person to think it. Charlie was killed by Trojan; they made sure I would be found with the murder weapon in my hand. I'd just started training with the Pyramid Delegates and people assumed.'

'Jess, I'm so sorry.'

All of her life was one trauma after another, trauma that she couldn't have talked to the team about – because if they'd known, they would have supported her, not rallied against her.

'I lead a dangerous life, it's all I've ever known. I can't change who I am, it's in my *nature*.'

'It's in your nature to love.'

'No, it's not.' She shook her head. 'There's something wrong with me, I don't know what.'

I squeezed her hand.

'You love Chris, you're capable of it.'

'I don't even know what it is,' Jessica said with a bitter

laugh.

'Does anyone?' I asked. 'Call him.'

'Why?' she asked, almost confused.

'To say hello.'

'Then what?'

'I don't know, whatever you two talk about, the weather, TV shows, Taylor Swift.'

'. . . Taylor Swift.'

I smacked her on the arm and she let out a watery laugh, standing up with me and giving me one last hug, before she left the room.

With everything she'd done I wondered if I ever could love my friend the same way, which in hindsight was a stupid question. Jessica-Grace Winters was the same person – but now, I knew her story.

SLATE RETRIBUTION

CHAPTER 35

Habromania

Delusions of happiness.

NAOMI JADE

18 June 2016, 16:55

Scotland, The Reign Academy, Training Room

Punch, punch, dodge.

Punch, punch, dodge.

Punch, punch, dodge.

Punch, Punch, dodge.

Punch – BLOCK – Ow! Seriously?

'Now that was the most adorable block ever,' Kayson's voice drawled down.

I groaned, rolling onto my side, the cool mat my only

comfort as the harsh floodlights blinded my vision.

'Shut up.'

'You're getting better at combinations, you just need to work on the puppy face.'

'The puppy face?' I was afraid to ask, as Kayson grabbed my hand, hauling me up.

'Yeah, the one you make when my fist comes flying towards you.'

The only answer to that was a roll of the eyes, what was he on about? When the impending cracking of bone on face occurs, didn't everyone look a little scared?

Kayson decided he'd mocked me enough for the time being and grabbed his water bottle from the side, his grey hoodie tight against his form. He hadn't broken a sweat, whereas I felt as if I'd just crawled out of a swimming pool.

Now that things had changed I was able to train out in the open rather than being crammed in the living room, although the carpet there was softer than this stupid mat. We were on the first floor in a room that resembled an extremely posh gym hall, light beaming through the small slits for windows above while blue mats were dotted all around. Instead of sweat it smelled freshly clean and, thankfully, there wasn't any blood on the walls.

There were a couple other students in here, younger than us but they kept their distance – well, I hoped they did, no one needed to see how terrible I was at hand to hand combat.

It had been a little more than a month since Harkness fled. Duke had followed suit a couple days after, and now Thompson ran the joint, with Nicola's supervision of course. The Academy had undergone a complete facelift: the drugs distribution had stopped, Lennox and Helen had been fired, torture was prohibited and Thompson's influence over the media simply stopped. Quinn told us he'd resigned from the newspaper so he could focus on reshaping the school. That shocked us all, especially when other members of the faculty like Ames wanted to pitch in too. Within the space of a month they'd rewritten the whole curriculum, focusing on espionage and, more importantly, freedom of speech. Dr McKay, who'd only been slightly injured in the gun fight, was at the forefront of the whole thing, acting as Nicola's confidant.

There were rumours floating about that the Government was going to force everyone here to sign the Official Secrets Act,

SLATE RETRIBUTION

but that didn't seem likely – no one here would agree to it. I knew for a fact Nicola was on my side about getting the evidence out; all we had to do was wait for Lily's sister to come back from America to represent us. Even though they didn't talk much, apparently her sister was all for it. With her and Nicola at our side, there was no way this corruption could be buried. The news had reported the dead bodies from the harbour and they'd been classed as a Trojan attack. Every one of them given proper burials and compensation sent to their families. The world was now seeing it wasn't safe; new protocols and tracking numbers when in the city had been issued to everyone. The politicians were in it up to their ears.

Ever since that final night a constant thought ran through my head: money. If Trojan really was behind building the school and finding the teachers, where did they get the money from in the first place? There must be more to the story because this one had too many loose ends. But for now, it left my mind. If I'd thought of it, then someone else had to have done too. There were people more qualified than me to deal with this.

For once in this whole ordeal, things seemed to be looking

up. Jessica had been spending more time with Chris so she came down the stairs practically gleaming every morning, and seemed to have found some closure since the funeral of her brother. Grace was able to focus on her studies, and our relationship grew stronger because I brought her coffee whenever I visited. Quinn finally flew out to see her mother at the safe house, spending a couple of weeks there, and when she came back, was happier and more adorable than ever. Lily had found her passion for sport once again, and she spent more time at the gym and going on runs. Convinced me to go once, and I will never forget the pain in my legs the next day.

'Same again, come on, let's go.' Kayson's voice dragged me out of my thoughts.

I'd been coming and going from the Academy for the past couple of weeks now, and even though the biggest adventure of my life was over, I didn't plan to stop. There was part of me that needed to keep going, keep bettering myself. In the field my mind had gone blank and I'd relied on others to get me out of hostile situations. Not anymore, I was done being helpless.

'Why isn't Lily here?' I asked, rolling up my sleeves.

'Since, ya know, you're not on Jessica's team anymore.'

Kayson let out a long sigh.

'Well, you know Jessica's left to help MI6 with an op, so Grace has to cover her briefings and stuff. Which leaves Lily to pick up the rest, although I hope she's not working on the ward, wouldn't trust her with a scalpel.' I laughed at the thought. 'So you're stuck with me.'

'Won't your team miss you?' I asked. 'I mean, surely you have briefings and other spy stuff to do.'

'Well, Luca goes to those and then gives us the rundown when he gets back. I'm a free man until seven o'clock. Think they're going to shoot us down to London to try and finds leads on Harkness or Duke. Doubt we'll find any, though.'

The way Harkness looked at me before he left still sent shivers down my spine. I would see him again, men like that had a tendency to come back.

'Hey, listen,' Kayson started, and this time his voice was serious. 'About before, the whole thing with the doorstep and the date, then me being a grade A asshole . . .'

'Yes?' I asked, confused where he was going with this.

'Could we be friends?' Kayson slowly made his way over to me. 'For a civilian, and your complete faith in spy movies being realistic . . . you're not half bad.'

Not half bad? I'll take that as a compliment.

The evening in the hospital he called me beautiful, the night at the harbour he kissed my forehead.

'Friends.' I said with a firm nod.

Even though the man in front of me was utterly gorgeous, after everything, I'd decided there was only so much that I wanted to know about him. Like, his favourite colour, music tastes and if he had any pets. The boring questions. Also, if he was meant to be a mathematics whiz I wanted to see him solve some algebra or find the dot on an imaginary line. At the shootout on the ward he'd called me beautiful, at the night of the harbour he'd kissed my forehead. I wanted to hold onto him, there was no way I was letting this man go.

Then there was the emotional side that I'd only caught sight of once, and I craved to understand him. There was so much more to Kayson Ashford that was uncharted territory and being friends was a great way to uncover some of those hidden treasures.

'Good.' Kayson blew out a sigh of relief before smacking his hands together. 'Right, combinations. Let's go.'

'We've been doing this for hours.' I threw my head back, every muscle in my upper body aching as the pain in my cheek calmed to a dull throbbing.

'Then we'll do it for one more,' he sassed. 'Now come on, hands up.'

Just as I was about to raise my fists the door to the training room swung open, slamming against the wall, and Lily barged through, worry creasing her brow.

'Code three, it's Jess.'

The playful grin dropped from Kayson's face, his arms falling limp at his sides, then he sprinted from the room for dear life, leaving me alone on the mat.

Even the students around me looked over worriedly – what the fuck was code three?

EMERY HALE

CHAPTER 36

Solivagant

Wandering alone.

NAOMI JADE

18 June 2016, 17:01

Scotland, The Reign Academy, Control Room

I don't think I'd ever run so fast in my life, my feet on fire as I darted round corners and pushed my way through students, not bothering to apologise. I'd never seen such a look of dread on Kayson's face before and truthfully, I preferred his anger.

Through the different corridors I managed to follow the backs of Lily and Kayson as they ran into the main command room. Just as the door closed my hand grasped the handle and I ran inside. It took me a moment to realise what I was looking at on the monitor – all there was for as far as the eye could see was an overgrown forest – but there was a voice I recognised, a small whimper. Jessica's.

'What's going on?' I asked frantically.

'Jess has been separated from the team, there's a sniper.' Grace's voice floated from the back of the room, and as I locked eyes with hers I saw the blood dripping down her scrubs.

Whose blood was that?

That was when I spotted Nicola standing at the back talking in a hushed voice on the phone – someone must have said something because she slammed the phone back on the hook.

Kayson's brutal voice barked orders down a phone at the other end of the room, Nicola stood stoically in the corner biting her lip, Lily gripped one of the desks, her nails scratching into the wood, while Grace started to pace back and forth. However Quinn, who stood in the centre of the room, remained silent.

I knew Jessica was helping MI6 with a mission, but how did she end up in a situation like this? The sound of her feet pounding faster and her breath quickening made my lungs feel like iron.

'Is it Trojan?' I dared to ask.

'The team were following a lead on Harkness, the bastard, he must have known they were coming. Jess is isolated so the team won't go back for her. I ordered them to go back –'

'Nicola, what the fuck?' I asked, spinning around. 'She buried her brother not long ago and you're sending her on a mission like that?'

'She volunteered to go!'

'So did James and look where that got him!'

I didn't care that she was a superior, she was wrong. James had been her fiancé, she still wore the ring – did she not see how messed up this was? I got that Jessica was an agent, but there was no need to send her on a mission so close to home.

'I brought over the live feed from her camera pin but the comms have been sabotaged,' Nicola told me. 'She's on her own.'

That was when all the phones in the room started to ring, but no one made a move to answer: all of us were glued to the large monitor. We were mere spectators. For once, everyone in the room looked like they hadn't the faintest clue what to do next. This wasn't an Academy mission, we had no idea of the plans or routes, and no way to contact her.

'She needs an evac team now!' Kayson roared, some of his hair falling in front of his face, then he raised his head. 'They won't get there for another half hour, she's too deep in.'

'Is there any way we can contact her?' Grace asked.

'No, the comms have been wiped out,' Kayson replied.

'How did that happen?'

'Wait, give me a minute . . . oh that's right, I don't know because I'm not a fuckin mind reader!'

This couldn't be happening, it couldn't. We'd sent Harkness running, we'd changed the school and were only months from exposing the years of government corruption. She was going to see this through, Jessica would see justice for her suffering. She was going to stand by my side and watch as Harkness, Duke and all the other pathetic agents rotted in prison.

'You're really not helping!'

'Could you not tear each other's throats out for one minute?'

'She'll be OK, it's not like it hasn't happened before.'

'Shut up!' Grace yelled. 'She's trying to say something!'

'I need evac now.' Desperation screamed through Jessica's

voice. 'I can't shake this guy!'

If I didn't know what this room was I'd have guessed it was a cinema, and from where I stood, it gave me the perfect view.

BANG

Even though the camera jolted, even though Jessica screamed, even though I saw her fall, there was no way I could believe what was happening. Like the thick raw blades of grass slicing through the camera's vision, it felt as if glass were piercing mine, burrowing deep inside, trying to blur the sight in front of me. How could I watch this? Was this what had happened to James?

Through my distorted vision I saw Quinn sit bolt upright, mumbling under her breath, watching the screen in anticipation.

'God, no.' Nicola pleaded, her hands falling by her side as she walked closer. 'God, please no.'

I glanced back at Grace, ready to take orders, but there were none. Instead her hands were clasped by her lips, praying.

I marched over to her, hoping she had some sort of answer for me. If she was the second shouldn't she know what to do in a crisis? She was training to be a doctor for crying out loud!

'Grace, what do we do?' I asked but the girl's eyes were fixated ahead, damn her. I ripped her hands apart, getting right in her face. 'Talk to me, what do we do?'

She stuttered.

'I don't know, the team should have gone back for her.'

'Why didn't they?' I shot out, now looking to Nicola.

The woman hesitated, but before I could ask again she spoke.

'Because she's a Reign student, they don't trust her.'

Bollocks. If she was put in a team then they should work together. No matter their history. What happened to the motto of never leave a man behind?

'Lilith, come in,' Lily demanded, a finger pressed to the comm unit in her ear. 'Team Leader, come in.'

Then we waited.

'This happens, this always happens, it only ends one way in this kind of work.' Jessica had told me that after James' funeral – apparently it had been a running theme in the family. She'd worn blue that day instead of black, saying it was his favourite

SLATE RETRIBUTION

colour. There were countless people there, many in uniform. I'd made sure to stay by Jessica's side at all times, holding her hand if she needed, a tissue pushed up my sleeve just in case, even though I knew she'd never cry in public. Christopher was there in uniform but he kept a little distance, which must have been a prearranged thing. He spoke to me though.

'Stay with her, she needs you.'

Even as the coffin was laid in the ground, not once did I see Charlotte. Their own mother hadn't shown up to the funeral. Through it all however, Jessica kept coming back to me, holding my hand and pulling me into her cold embrace.

Then afterwards, when everyone had left, we talked and one thing stuck in my head.

'We are all incredibly mortal in a world that is determined to put a bullet between our eyes,' she said, sipping her drink. *'If you get a chance, take it.'*

'What?' I asked confused.

'Get out, don't come back to the Academy.'

'But we fixed it? We changed everything, Harkness is gone.'

'Naomi, I'm begging you, stay away from this.'

Even now I couldn't understand what she meant – would I get the chance to ask?

'Who is that?' Lily asked.

My eyes shot round to the screen, there was a figure in dark clothing – no! I couldn't watch this. Why had I let her go on that mission? She'd been worried about something and I'd just pushed it aside. She'd warned me to stay away. How could I be so stupid?

I hissed in a breath as my nails dug into my palm, warm blood pooling in the centre, running to my fingertips like a river.

BANG

Static, crackling, no movement and no background noise.

Not one of us uttered a syllable.

Then the monitor collapsed into darkness.

'Jess?' Lily asked, her head hung, voice wavering.

No, please.

'Jess can you hear me?'

She warned me! She volunteered to take the mission and now she was . . . no. I wouldn't believe it, not until I saw proof.

SLATE RETRIBUTION

She was Jessica-Grace Winters, descended from a long line of spies, she had to be OK, she'd figure her way out.

I should have gone with her, why wasn't I there to watch her back?

BANG

BANG

BANG.

Quinn's hands slammed against the desk, her face stretched in a scream unlike any other, tears streaming down. Kayson had retreated into silence, hands cradling the back of his head, eyes wide with disbelief.

Jess was going to be OK. She's Jessica!

Nicola scrambled for one of the ringing phones.

'Nicola Ramos, head of division Alpha Four, I need vital signs and position of agent Jessica-Grace Winters ... put me through to Oscar now.'

'Nicola?' Quinn asked turning in her chair, wanting the answer we all desperately needed. 'Nicola!'

She held a hand up in an ask for patience but Quinn threw herself from the chair, running to Nicola. Lily beat her to it, grabbing the girl by the arms.

'Look at me, Quinn darling, it's going to be OK.' Lily pulled her into a hug as the girl's body wracked with sobs, every single one reverberating in my chest.

'Not again,' she pleaded. 'Please, not again.'

Quinn's eyes pleaded with both of the women in front of her, Nicola's face filled with anticipation – but for a moment Lily's eyes met mine and a harrowed cry nearly left my lips as I witnessed her expression. *Acceptance.*

Even though other phones rang, everyone's attention was directed at their superior. Then she pressed a button, putting the phone to speaker.

'Oscar, I need the vitals and position of Jessica-Grace Winters.'

A clear voice rang through.

'She's located at the Queen Elizabeth Forest Park ma'am.'

'Vitals?'

'None, ma'am.'

Quinn's screams tore through the room as Grace collapsed to her knees. Kayson locked eyes with mine but I didn't hold the

SLATE RETRIBUTION

gaze as I pushed my way out of the room. I had to get out of here, had to focus on something else. Jess told me this would happen but I didn't believe her, I didn't think something like this could happen to someone like her – but now I think of it, of course it did.

My hand pressed against the door.

All the lies she told me, for what? She tried to warn me, protect me but it was all for nothing.

'Agent down,' the voice on the end of the phone said. 'Agent Jessica-Grace Winters inactive.'

Inactive. Down. Dead.

I didn't even know where I was going, Jessica's face consumed my mind. She'd never sing again, never hold my hand, never walk into my arms. Jessica wasn't going to grow old, she wasn't going to get married. I'd always imagined she'd walk down the aisle one day but I'd never realised it would be in a coffin.

People bumped into me, throwing my shoulders but I didn't care. My fingers tangled through my hair like a spiderweb, gnawing at the roots – how could this happen? Jessica was meant to be here! She couldn't leave me alone!

I wouldn't believe it, not until I saw her. There was no way, this couldn't be happening.

Not a single tear fell from my eye, not one. Quinn was crying, shouldn't I? Jessica was my best friend and yet, nothing.

Right now I was numb. My fingers gripped the flat walls and hands pressed against the rigid cabinets, but there were no sensations – it was as if I was floating. My feet no longer felt like they were on the ground and the many voices around were muffled, like I was underwater.

I wasn't floating, I was sinking.

Then, someone pulled me out.

'You have to see this!' They shouted, yanking my whole body forward, sending me stumbling after them.

I needed my mum.

Before I knew it I was in another command room, but this time it was different: smaller, cramped, Thompson directing from the back while hordes of students worked the computers and phones.

'Someone give me a visual.'

SLATE RETRIBUTION

On one monitor was the breaking news.

DOWNING STREET OBLITERATED

What?

A live feed sprung up on the screen and for the second time that day I couldn't believe what I was seeing. Number Ten Downing Street, the home of the Prime Minister, was nothing more than a crater.

'What?' Thompson asked horrified, his voice but a whisper.

'It's all over the news,' a student said. 'It was hit minutes ago.'

'Casualties?'

'Undetermined. The whole building sir, it's just gone.'

'Stop!' someone yelled.

A new video replaced the one on the screen, and this time I nearly threw up. The Prime Minister's head was on one of the spikes at the gates of Buckingham Palace. Suddenly the camera shook and a boom came through the speakers, almost like a shock wave.

'What the bloody hell was that?' Thompson ran forward and grabbed one of the computers, searching on his own.

'It's Parliament! The UK Parliament!' someone shouted. 'I was watching the security cameras just in case – fire blew out the windows, sir!'

Everyone hurried to huddle around the computer, but I remained still, knowing I'd see the thing soon enough. Cars strewn all over the roads, boats pushed against the river walls, glass littering the streets – but what caught my eye were all the bodies laid out on the road, they were all so close together.

'Sir, I think we need a helicopter view.'

'Then do it!'

My nails dug into my palm, pain seemingly now the only thing I had control over. Jessica was dead, she was dead, and there was nothing I could do about it. We'd been becoming close like before, we talked, laughed and cried together, but now all I felt was alone.

That was when the images on the monitor switched and we saw exactly what Trojan wanted us to. The bodies of politicians laid out to spell the word SIN. That's what they'd been planning all along, release the videos of all the terrorist acts to the public, then blow up the Prime Minister's residence and the UK Parliament all at once.

Utter chaos.

We thought we'd stopped it when really, we only stopped a fraction.

'Someone get Nicola Ramos in here now!' Thompson ordered.

A random student scurried past me but then, someone else spoke.

'Mr Thompson, the First Minister of Wales is missing.'

'Sir! Northern Ireland has gone into a complete lockdown. Their power grid is offline. I can't get into any security camera.'

Trojan was attacking the entirety of the United Kingdom – this must have all been planned for years. They'd set up a school to train the soldiers they needed, then fed them some bullshit story, brainwashed them and now put their new agents to work. Pumping out more every year like a factory line.

A large clammy hand rested on my shoulder. I didn't turn.

It was Kayson.

'We didn't stop it.'

Then, just like that I was floating again. Images of my mum and dad flashing before me like the currents of the sea, then Lily, Quinn, Grace, Kayson and Jessica, even Katie.

This was it. The war had begun.

SLATE RETRIBUTION

CHAPTER 37

Absquatulate

To leave without saying goodbye.

NAOMI JADE

18 June 2016, 17:24

Scotland, The Reign Academy, Corridor

Kayson had control of my body because right now, it felt as if I couldn't move myself. Nothing was processing, nothing made sense. That's when the yelling started outside and he gently pulled me away from the devastation of the monitors.

'No I'm not sending them!'

'They are the only qualified team we have available, we need to get some ground down there. This is what the Academy was designed to deal with!'

'No it was designed to train assassins for the terrorists that caused this exact scenario!'

Nicola and Thompson stood arguing with one another in the middle of the corridor but the only thing I could do was focus on the girls up ahead, Lily, Grace and Quinn, their eyes bloodshot and faces wrecked.

'Then let's amend it!' Thompson threw his hands out. 'We can be the specialised unit that deals with terrorists like this!'

'If you hadn't continued to support Harkness, this wouldn't have happened in the first place!'

'You know that's not how it worked!'

Suddenly Grace's head shot up and she marched towards the pair, arms crossed over her chest, her dark hair falling from its ponytail.

'What are you talking about?' she asked. 'Sending who, where?'

Nicola sighed.

'Thompson wants to send the Omega team, your team, to London.'

'Observe and report, nothing more,' Thompson said, trying to reason with her.

'Well, an observe and report just got someone killed!'

Nicola yelled.

'Nicola, hundreds of people are dead.'

'She's talking about Jessica,' I piped up. 'Jessica went on an op to follow a lead and she . . .'

Thompson froze and turned to Nicola for confirmation, who nodded.

Kayson tried to take my hand but I pushed him away. I didn't want to be touched, not when I couldn't feel anything except the stale dried blood in my hand. I needed my mum, I needed Jessica.

'We'll do it,' Grace said, with the composure of a queen. 'We'll take the op.'

'Grace, I can't allow you to do that,' Nicola said firmly, but Grace wasn't taking no for an answer.

'Nicola, you can go fuck yourself,' she spat, before turning to Thompson. 'We have access to a plane, I assume?'

'Y-Yes.' the man stuttered.

'Let's use it. Have it fuelled and ready to go in forty minutes.'

Thompson nodded, then grabbed a phone from his pocket

and briskly walked back into the command room. Nicola's mouth hung open, stunned by the remark, but Grace didn't take a second glance at her as she focused on us.

'Kayson, I need another Runner.'

'I'm there.'

'Naomi, I need a Carrier.'

There was no possible way I could continue, not after this, couldn't I just stop? For a moment I thought Kayson had grabbed my hand, but then realised it was Grace. She'd taken both my wrists, pulling me close, her eyes boring into mine.

'I can't do this,' I told her. 'I can't, we can't, not after what happened.'

Her next words hit me like a train.

'You are here, you are alive, you are a part of this world. Believe me Naomi, I know what you're feeling right now, I do, but if we don't at least try then God knows what will happen. Jessica's death will have meant nothing compared to how many Trojan will slaughter. If you don't keep moving you'll be as dead as her. You're alive, do something about it.'

***

After thirty minutes of packing and ten minutes of driving to the airport, I was sat in the plane, ready for take-off. Once again I didn't have much so Lily had given me some of her clothes; there was no way I could bring myself to wear Jessica's.

Quinn took the top of the plane, setting up her laptop and equipment as fast as she could, Kayson and Lily next to her while Grace talked with the pilot.

As I gazed out the window onto the tarmac, phone clutched in hand, I kept my voice as level as possible because my mum was on the other end.

'Mum stop, please just – I'm going away for a little while OK?'

'Naomi, what's going on?' she asked, worry crashing through the speakers. 'It's all over the news. Tell me you're not going to London?'

'Mum, please.'

'You can't go there! It's not safe.'

'It's what Jessica would have wanted.'

'Sweetheart, I'm begging you, don't go to London.'

'Tell Dad I love him.'

SLATE RETRIBUTION

'Naomi!'

'Love you.' With that I hung up and tossed the phone to the floor.

Gravity aided me as my head fell into my arms, the cool leather seats chilling me to the core. What I was about to do was unorthodox but Grace told me she didn't trust anyone else, and I couldn't let her down.

How many daughters were lost in the explosions at Parliament and Downing Street? How many sisters? How many sons or brothers?

I picked up my phone, turning it onto aeroplane mode. I was half tempted to turn it off, but the lock screen made me smile. When it was brought to me last year, I never truly appreciated the photo. It was me and Jessica at the Christmas dance before she left for Reign, her smile charming, eyes full and bright. We were fifteen back then. Now I imagined her eyes were dull, the spark of humanity long since put out.

Grace was right, I was alive. Time to do something about it.

EMERY HALE

Thanks for reading!

Please add a review on Amazon and let me know what you thought!

Don't forget to share your review on social media with the hashtag #slateretribution

Thank you for taking the time to support my work.

Acknowledgements

Firstly to my parents for constantly supporting me throughout my journey. Thank you for letting me use and exploit your hilarious conversations with one another for my writing, even though you weren't really consulted in it, cheers.

Thank you to Sam Boyce my editor. This has been a new adventure for me, and you've given me insight into the industry as well as fabulous advice. P.s. I'm really glad you didn't see the first or second drafts of this – the amount of 'however' and 'although' and '. . .' probably would have sent you into a frenzy, as well as editing these acknowledgements. Thank you so much for all the suggestions you made, I really think they make the story sparkle.

Thanks to Ziyanda, the amazing artist who designed the character graphics for this book. The amazing feeling to see a portrait land in my inbox can never be recreated. You're an amazing artist, as well as great friend to bounce and hash ideas off of, since not all of them were great ones.

Thank you to Justyna, the Annaliese to my Erica. Artists

stick together, you use paint and a pencil while I use words. This book would not be what it was without your help, and supplying me with other words for 'sad'.

The world of thanks to Keri Frew who taught me in high school, explaining the intricate nature of narrative and how to delve into the deepest parts of a character's mind. I sorely miss you.

EMERY HALE

SLATE RETRIBUTION

Emery Hale is a young Scotland based author, who has longed to put her stories onto the page. Ones filled with danger, love, betrayal and blood. When she's not writing she's an avid filmmaker while also enjoying everything from heavy metal to Beethoven and laughing hysterically with her inspirational roommate.

CONNECT WITH EMERY ON:

Instagram: official_slate

YouTube: www.youtube.com/emeryhale

Printed in Great Britain
by Amazon